SWEET CHAOS

EMERY ROSE

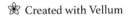 Created with Vellum

For my mom who always told me I could. Love you longtime. xoxo

PLAYLIST

"Circles" – Post Malone
"Venice Bitch" – Lana Del Rey
"Wicked Games" – Parra For Cava
"The Middle" – ZEDD
"Only" – NF, Sasha Sloan
"Be Someone" – CamelPhat, Jake Bugg
"If You Want Love" – NF
"Need You Now" – Dean Lewis
"Do I Wanna Know" – Arctic Monkeys
"Girls Like U" – Blackbear
"I Have Questions" – Camila Cabello
"when the party's over" – Lewis Capaldi cover
"Falling" – Trevor Daniel

1

SCARLETT

"Thou shalt not covet thy sister's secret boyfriend." – Scarlett Woods, 11

Ten Years Ago

A loud crash followed by a string of muttered curses drew my attention to the open window. Scrambling off my bed, I crept soundlessly across my plush white rug and stared down at the boy sprawled across my bedroom floor. He wasn't really a boy. Not a man yet either. A guy, I guess. My gaze flitted to the window, trying to figure out how he'd gotten in. Trees bordered the property at the side of our house, but he would have had to take a flying leap from one of the branches to get into my window. A thrill shot through me at his daring stunt. If he'd missed, he would have fallen two stories.

Crazy boy. My lips tugged into a smile I couldn't hide.

I knew he was here for Sienna, not for me. He cleaned our pool, and his name was Dylan St. Clair. He was Sienna's best friend Remy's twin brother and had a bad reputation. Although I didn't know exactly why or what he'd done to earn it. I'd overheard my mom talking about him with her friend, Amanda Hart while they were poolside, sipping chilled chardonnay and eating low-cal crackers that tasted like cardboard and birdseed. Ollie and I were cannonballing into the pool, but I'd paused to listen when I sensed they were talking about *him*.

"He's not the kind of boy you want hanging around your daughter. He looks like trouble. If he gets anywhere near Sienna, I would put a stop to it immediately."

"Simon would never allow it." My mom sighed loudly. *"We miss having Tristan around. I'm still hoping they'll get back together."*

"They were perfect for each other."

The boy on my floor got to his feet and my gaze drifted upward, over the black T-shirt molded to his lean muscles—I knew there were muscles under his T-shirt because I'd seen him shirtless, sweating in the hot SoCal sunshine, his body slick with sweat as he pulled Sienna into a kiss that had scorched my eyeballs and made me feel... I wasn't sure what to call how it made me feel.

My eyes raised to his. He blinked a few times, trying to bring me into focus. I was close enough to smell his sweat and his soap and the scent of sweet smoke that wasn't from cigarettes. A black and purple bruise mottled the skin stretched over his right cheekbone and there was a gash above his eye that split his eyebrow in two.

I looked down at the cuts and bruises on his knuckles then back up at his face. He was watching me with a mixture of amusement and something else I couldn't identify. His tongue swept across his cut lip and he narrowed his eyes, running a hand through his dark as midnight hair. Like him, his hair was a beautiful mess. It went every which way like he'd been running his fingers through it over and over.

I cleared my throat, wanting to break the silence. "Wrong window, Romeo."

One corner of his mouth tilted up. Not really a smile. A

half-smile, half-smirk kind of thing. "Hey Starlet," he said in that low, husky voice of his.

"It's Scarlett." Secretly, I preferred his nickname for me. It made me feel special.

He smirked. "I know. Did I scare you?" he asked, his voice softer, his eyes searching mine for signs of fear.

I raised my eyebrows, ignoring the butterflies swarming my belly and the warmth that spread through my whole body. "Do I look scared?"

The corner of his mouth tilted higher. "No. But you should. A strange guy just crashed into your bedroom."

His eyes roamed my room, taking in the décor. I had no say in it. My room was painted pale pink, stenciled ivy trailing up the walls, my canopy bed cocooned in pale pink gauze, all in keeping with the fairytale princess vibe Mom was going for. Or, rather, the interior designer she'd hired to transform my bedroom and every room in this house into some kind of fantasy world. His eyes settled on my face again.

"You gonna make me go back out the way I came?"

I grinned, liking the sound of that. "I should, really. Just for fun."

He chuckled. "You're gonna be a real ballbuster when you get older, aren't you?"

"If that means I won't take crap from anyone, then yes. Sign me up for the Ballbuster Academy. I'll be head of the class." I gave him a two-fingered mock salute.

He was laughing now. He was laughing so hard it split his lip again. He swiped the back of his hand over his mouth, catching the blood.

I sighed and handed him a box of tissues from my bedside table. They had pink flowers on them. He waved them off.

"I'm good."

"If you say so." I set the box back on my bedside table and crossed my arms over my chest, waiting for his next move.

He jerked his chin at me. "Why are you still awake?"

"Why are you crashing into our house at midnight?"

"Why didn't you scream? You should have."

He seemed upset that I hadn't acted the way I should have. That I hadn't freaked out when he'd crashed into my room. But I craved adventure, the thrill of the unknown, and loved to flirt with danger. And this boy standing in front of me, he was dangerous in a delicious, forbidden way. My whole body vibrated from his nearness. "I don't always do things I should. Answer my question," I said boldly.

He cocked his head and studied my face. "Can you keep a secret?"

I mentally rolled my eyes. My house was full of secrets and I kept them all. "Yeah, sure."

"Sienna doesn't want anyone to know about us."

"Why not?" I asked as if I didn't already know the answer. Sienna acted tough but when push came to shove, she always caved to my father's wishes and demands. Six years older than me, she was the chosen one, my dad's favorite, and with that came more responsibility. Like the heir and the spare.

I'd once overheard my parents arguing. My father had called me *an accident. "You can't patch up the gaping wounds of a marriage with a Band-Aid."* Those were his words. My mother hadn't even denied it. If she had, I couldn't hear her words because she'd been crying and begging him not to leave her. He hadn't left, although I'd often wished that he had. Why hang on so tightly to someone who doesn't love you anymore? It just seemed so stupid to me.

Dylan laughed but it wasn't a happy sound. "Do I look like the kind of guy you'd bring home to meet the parents?"

I studied his black combat boots. The leather was cracked and worn, the laces undone. His black jeans were ripped at the knees and there was a rip in the collar of his gray T-shirt. My eyes returned to his face. His cheekbones were sharp, and his dark eyelashes were so thick and long he could almost be called pretty if it weren't for the firm, square jaw that was so cut, the edge so clean he always gave the impression of being angry. Underneath the cuts and bruises, he was a thing of beauty. I knew because I'd been watching him for weeks without him knowing it. My best friend Ollie accused me of being obsessed, and I knew it annoyed him, but I couldn't seem to help myself. I found Dylan St. Clair fascinating. Like a wild animal, a big sleek cat, being held in captivity. Shivers of excitement ran up and down my spine. The same feeling I got whenever I did something that I knew would get me into trouble.

Dylan was watching me, waiting for an answer, his eyes narrowed as if daring me to contradict him.

"I would." I lifted my chin. "I would march you right through the front door and seat you next to me at the dining room table for our family dinners. And I would tell my parents that you're my boyfriend and if they didn't like it they could... they could go suck on a lemon."

Lame, Scarlett. Suck on a lemon? Really?

His eyes widened a little in surprise and I stood taller, feeling proud of myself for throwing him off his game. For giving him an answer he hadn't expected. "You would, huh?" He sounded amused. Mocking me, like he didn't believe me. It made me feel all prickly.

I held his gaze, my jaw clenched as I gritted out the word that for some reason felt important. "Yes."

I wanted him to know I'd meant what I said. "I would. I swear on my life I would." I crossed my heart, a solemn oath that I didn't take lightly.

His amusement faded, and his eyes turned serious. They were blue and gray swirled together and looked like the sea during a storm. "You're too young to make promises like that. Never make a promise you can't keep," he said harshly, the softness in his voice gone and his words coming out in an angry growl.

I bristled, his words cutting me to the core. I'd just told him the truth. Swore on my life and crossed my heart on it. And he'd dismissed my words like I was just a dumb kid who didn't know any better.

Screw. Him.

"Don't tell anyone I was here," he commanded.

"I'm not a snitch." I flopped down on my bed, returning to what I was doing before the boy with stormy eyes crashed into my bedroom and made my stomach all fluttery. I uncapped my Sharpie and concentrated on the design I was making on the back of my white denim jacket. Mom would have a fit, but I thought the skull wearing a wreath of tropical flowers was cool, a definite improvement on the boring white jacket.

"Sienna's room is across the hall." I pointed to the door without lifting my head to look at him. I wasn't even sure why I was being so nice or helping him out. I hated him for making me feel like a stupid kid. Sienna always did the same thing, kicking me out of her space and not letting me anywhere near her friends. Not that I wanted to hang out with her anyway.

His footsteps were soundless, and I lifted my head in time to see his hands gripping the windowsill from the outside. I didn't want to act like I cared but my feet carried me to the window just the same and I watched him drop from the second-floor to the grass below. He landed on his feet, in a crouched position, and then his shadowy form was swallowed up in the darkness as he retreated. I was still hanging out my open window, straining my eyes for a glimpse of him when I saw a flame flicker. Craning my neck, I followed the cherry glow of his cigarette along the side of the house until I lost sight of it.

Squeezing my eyes shut, I held my hand over my racing heart. Was this what love felt like? Did it make you feel all mixed up and confused? Angry and happy and sad all at once? Ollie didn't make me feel like this. None of the other boys at school did either. I opened my eyes and turned from the window, my gaze drawn to the drops of blood, dark red against my white carpet. He'd left his mark and then he'd stolen away like a thief in the night. Even then I had a feeling it wouldn't be the last time he destroyed something of mine.

Dylan St. Clair was chaos. And chaos always left a trail of destruction in its wake. I just never expected it to be my heart he destroyed.

2

SCARLETT

Now

"I don't understand why you have to make everything so unpleasant. If you would just do as your father asks, and stop being so contrary, life would be easier." My mother sounded tired. Weary from an age-old battle with her youngest daughter. The family rebel. The black sheep. By now this conversation had played out so many times it sounded like a broken record.

We were sitting in the 'great room' but not even the double-height ceilings prevented it from feeling claustrophobic. It was stuffy and pretentious, filled with Chinese antiques and chinoiserie. I stared at the angry red dragons painted on the ceramic lamp that sat on a black lacquer table next to the jade green silk sofa. No wonder my mom suffered from anxiety attacks.

"Why can't you be more like your sister?"

If I had a dollar for every time she asked me that, I would be a millionaire. Don't get me wrong. I didn't hate Sienna. She was my sister so, by default, I loved her. But Sienna and I were night and day, and I would never be like her.

My mother cast a disapproving eye over my outfit—leopard print leggings with rips in the knees, and an old band tee under a hand-painted denim jacket (my design) that said Kiss Kiss Bang Bang with a cartoon-style blonde bombshell in red boxing gloves delivering a right hook. *Boom!*

"You dress like a hobo and you're working at a surf shop. For an *ex-con*. With all the opportunities you've been given in your life, is that all you aspire to?"

First of all, I loved my job as a surfboard artist. Second of all, it was unfair to reduce Shane Wilder to the label of ex-con. He was a good guy. A loving husband. A soon-to-be-father. A cool boss. An ex-pro surfer. A million wonderful things. And the most wonderful of all was the way he and Remy loved each other. Couple goals right there. Nothing like this sham of a marriage my parents had. Furthermore, Tristan Hart's death had not been Shane's fault. Tristan had deserved to be punched for what he did to Remy. It was horrible luck and, yeah okay, tragic that Tristan had fallen and hit his head on the rock fountain by the Harts' swimming pool. But still, it was an accident.

And as for dressing like a hobo, well, you can't please everyone. I'd given up trying years ago.

"I love my job and I'm happy." I ripped off one of the silk tassels from the red velvet chair I was sitting on. Oops. I hid the evidence under my seat cushion. "Shouldn't that count for something?"

My mother sniffed. I wanted her to be happy too. But to do that, she would have to leave my father and she wouldn't. She was scared of being alone, of having to start over. She stayed for the money. She stayed because, for reasons I couldn't fathom, she still loved him.

At fifty-four, my mother was still beautiful. Thanks to her

plastic surgeon and Botox, she didn't look a day over forty. Except for her hands. Hands don't lie.

The diamond on her finger sparkled in the pool of light from the hideous dragon lamp as she took a sip of her chardonnay. Her nude nails matched the Louboutins on her feet and she wore winter white, not a strand of blonde hair out of place.

"I don't understand why you have to take everything to the extreme."

I really wish she'd find a new topic to discuss. My mother's world had shrunk to the size of these four walls. She needed a job or a hobby, something to occupy her time other than obsessing over her looks, her wardrobe, and my father.

"Guess that's how I roll."

She sighed and checked her phone for about the hundredth time since I'd arrived bearing gifts, a silk scarf she'd never wear and a bouquet of flowers that didn't match her new decor. My father had promised to take her for a birthday dinner tonight. The reservation was for seven. The clock on the mantel, guarded by two foo dogs, told me it was now seven-thirty. He was late, and I suspected he wouldn't show up at all.

"Let's order in," I said, clapping my hands together. "Just the two of us. We can watch a movie."

"He'll be here. He probably got caught in traffic." Always making excuses, not willing to acknowledge the real reason he wasn't here. After twenty-eight years of marriage, she still had to put up with his bullshit. It killed me that she cared so much when he cared so little. I wanted to spend time with my mom. I wanted to give her some of my strength to stand up to him. But she was unwilling or unable to change her situation and it made me angry and sad.

"Why do you stay? He treats you like crap."

She pursed her lips. "You know nothing about marriage or my relationship with your father. Marriage is about compromise."

Compromise, my ass. More like roll over and die. "I know it's killing you. I know that neither one of you is happy." *I know he's cheating on you. Kick his ass to the curb.* "What I don't understand is why you stay together."

No sooner were the words out of my mouth when I heard the door from the garage open and the sound of his footsteps crossing the kitchen tiles. My cue to leave.

"I need to go." I jumped up from my seat and grabbed my bag, slinging it over my shoulder. There was nowhere I needed to be tonight, but I wanted to get out of here before I ran into my father. We were like oil and water and it never ended well.

"Happy Birthday, Mom. I love you."

"I love you, too." Her words were punctuated with a long-suffering sigh.

I kissed the cheek she proffered and hightailed it out of the living room, catching my reflection in a gilt-framed mirror as I scurried away like a fugitive. If I didn't cause drama, my father barely acknowledged my existence. Better to be the invisible daughter than draw attention to myself.

As I crossed the Italian marble floor of the cavernous foyer, I heard him making a bullshit excuse for his tardiness.

My hand reached for the brass knob of the heavy oak door when his voice halted me in my tracks.

"Scarlett," he boomed without raising his voice. Quite a talent.

Without turning to look at him, I waved over my shoulder. "Hey Dad. Great seeing you. Gotta dash."

Freedom beckoned. I slipped out the door and followed the circular drive to my silver Audi, when he called my name again. Resigned to my fate, I turned to face the man himself. He wore a charcoal gray Brioni suit and the scent of another woman's perfume. It was so pungent I nearly choked on the betrayal. The bastard.

"I hope you haven't been upsetting your mother. You know how delicate her health is."

He was the reason she popped Xanax like it was candy and drank chardonnay to drown her sorrows. "I just stopped by to keep her company on her birthday." I didn't mention that I found her in the midst of a panic attack, on the floor of her walk-in closet, unable to function. "It's nice of you to show up. Was your mistress upset you deserted her for your wife?"

I just couldn't help myself, could I?

His eyes narrowed to slits. "Watch what you say in my house, young lady."

"I was just leaving *your* house." I climbed into the driver's seat and reached for the door handle, tugging on it. But he wrapped his hand around the door frame, preventing me from closing it.

"I expected more from you. You're a disappointment, Scarlett." He looked down his aquiline nose at me, his winter tan telling me that his recent 'business trip' had nothing to do with mergers and acquisitions.

You're a disappointment, Scarlett.

Why? Because I wasn't like him? Because I didn't want to chase the almighty dollar? Because I didn't aspire to live an empty life in a SoCal McMansion, trapped in a loveless marriage?

"Life is too short not to do something I'm passionate about."

He laughed hollowly. "Feel free to pursue your *passion,* as you call it, but you won't be doing it on my dime. If you insist on making poor life choices, you'll be forced to deal with the consequences of your actions."

What a joke. I hadn't been living on his dime since I graduated high school.

"Give me your keys, Scarlett."

I blinked, not sure I heard him right. "My keys?"

Of course. He wanted my car. It had been a high school

graduation present. Therefore, it belonged to him, not me. I slid the Audi key fob off the ring and placed it in the open palm of his hand then tossed the keychain into my bag on the passenger seat. The final string tying me to my father had been cut.

Without another word, he turned on his heel and strode away, leaving me sitting in the driver's seat of a car I couldn't drive. I closed my eyes and took a few deep breaths.

Inhale. Exhale.

Why did I have to take everything a step too far?

Perhaps I would have been a dutiful daughter, I would have tried harder to please him, if he had been a better father. A better human being. But I hated how he treated us, like we were his possessions and not people. All he truly cared about was money and power and he abused them both. Used them as a bartering chip to keep us in line.

After staring vacantly at the stone fountain on the front lawn for a few minutes, I cleaned out the car, tossing hair ties, zinc oxide, tubes of cherry Chapstick, and a pack of gum into my bag. I found a hoodie in the backseat and tied it around my waist. My dad could keep the empty Starbucks cups and the sand in the carpets from my surfing.

Slamming the door shut, I fished my cell phone out of my bag. The battery was at one percent. I mentally face-palmed myself as I called Nicola and chewed on my thumbnail, waiting for her to answer.

"Scarlett? I'm about to get my ass kicked by the head chef," she whisper-shouted over the noise of the restaurant kitchen. "I'll call you back."

"Nic. Hang on. I need you to—"

The line went dead, and I wasted precious seconds of my life staring at the dark screen, willing it to come back to life.

Perfect. Just perfect. Adulting at its finest. I groaned as I set off on my trek across town. It could be worse, I reasoned.

So what if I was living paycheck to paycheck and struggling to make ends meet? I was doing something I loved. Surrounded by cool people. Working on my designs that someday I'd be able to make a living at. *Hopefully.*

I dug around in my bag and came out with a maroon knitted beanie. It was Ollie's. Ollie could rock a beanie like nobody's business. I missed him and the way we used to laugh until our stomachs hurt. Why did we have to ruin everything?

I jammed the hat on my head and threaded my arms through the hoodie that was far too big for me, zipping it up to ward off the January chill. Tonight, the temperature had dipped down to fifty degrees. Too cold for my West Coast blood. The streets were dark and there were no sidewalks on this stretch of road that ran alongside the golf course, so I stayed close to the Bougainvillea. I'd listen to music, but my phone was dead, so I got lost in my own thoughts instead.

Tires screeched, and I threw myself back, my hand over my racing heart. Branches snagged my hoodie as I fought to untangle myself from the Bougainvillea bushes.

"The fuck are you doing?" he growled.

I knew that voice. Honey and gravel.

3

SCARLETT

C ast in shadows, his face peered from the driver's seat
through the open passenger side window of his black G-
Wagen.

"What does it look like I'm doing? I'm walking. What are
you doing?" His car was parked at an angle, blocking the road.
But I very much doubted that he cared.

"You were two seconds away from being roadkill. Were you
even looking where you were going?"

I planted my hands on my hips. "Well, thanks to your light-
ning-quick reflexes, I'm alive and in one piece." I threw my
hands up in the air. "I can't help it you drive like a maniac."

I couldn't see his face very well, but I was certain it wore a
scowl. Mr. Dark and Broody was always scowling or glaring. No,
that wasn't true. I'd seen his smile. It was rare. Fleeting. But it
was glorious. Back when I was just a stupid kid, I used to try to
coax it out of him, like it was a prize to be won.

Dylan leaned across the passenger seat and pushed the
door open. "Get in the car." He tossed his gym bag into the back
seat to make room for me.

"I'm okay to walk." I watched as a car was forced to go around him.

"You live miles from here."

"You don't even know where I live."

He exhaled loudly, losing patience with this conversation. "Stop being a pain in the ass. Get in the car, Starlet."

He still called me Starlet, and it was that stupid nickname that had me climbing into the passenger seat and fastening the seatbelt. Or maybe it was the thought of walking after another draining session with my parents that wore me down.

"Why were you walking?" he asked after he entered my address in his GPS and we were on our merry way.

I almost planted my Doc Martens on the dash like I used to in his truck but thought better of it. Unlike the rusty old pickup truck he used to drive, this car was spotlessly clean, scented with leather and new car. "I needed the exercise."

"Where's your car?"

"I returned it in exchange for my soul."

He side-eyed me but didn't comment. Then he turned up the volume on his stereo, probably to save himself from having to engage in conversation. Fine by me. I had nothing to say. I'd rather listen to Post Malone anyway. But I snuck a few glances in my peripheral. The years had been good to Dylan. He was all lean muscle and man now. His cheekbones were more prominent, his firm, square jaw more chiseled and he still had those ridiculously long lashes girls would envy.

I'd gotten over my schoolgirl crush on him years ago, but I could still appreciate his sheer male beauty. And his scent. God, he smelled good. Something warm and spicy and masculine. If pure sex could be bottled, it would be called Eau de Dylan St. Clair.

He wore sweatpants and a black hoodie, the sleeves pushed up to his elbows. Heavily inked tattoos trailed down both arms. I used to see him surfing, so I knew that his back and torso were inked. He had stars tattooed above his waistband, and I always wondered how low they went. Were there stars shooting from his dick? It cracked me up every time. Tonight was no exception.

"What's so funny?" he asked.

"You." I laughed again.

Dylan shook his head and pushed his tattooed fingers through his unruly raven hair. A lock fell over his forehead and I tucked my hands under my thighs to resist the urge to reach across the console and brush it away.

"You never told me why your dad cut you off."

He said this as if we hung out all the time and spoke daily. We didn't talk anymore. In fact, since I'd come back to Costa del Rey two months ago, we'd only seen each other a few times in passing.

"You never asked."

"I'm asking now. What happened?"

"Nothing too dramatic. It was my choice. His money comes with too many strings attached so I decided to do my own thing." My tone was breezy as if that had been an easy decision.

"And what exactly does that mean?"

"My dad expected me to follow in Sienna's footsteps. Go to one of the colleges he deemed acceptable. Study something useful like Finance or Marketing. Do my summer internships at his financial holdings company. I couldn't imagine anything worse. So I bailed on college and went up to San Francisco with my friend, Nicola. I took some art classes and worked odd jobs. Then we went up to Seattle for a while. Our friends are in a band. I worked in a coffee shop and had a market stall. Now here I am, back in Costa del Rey sans trust fund."

"So that's it? He cut you off because you didn't go to college?"

I cleared my throat. "Well, that and I donated my college fund to charity."

"Holy shit," Dylan said with a laugh. "I'm surprised you didn't give your old man a heart attack."

"Let's just say he wasn't too happy."

"Which charity?"

"A homeless shelter for women and children." My dad's view on the homeless: They're lazy. They're drug addicts. They would rather beg for money than get a job.

"What made you do that?"

"I just... it's stupid, I guess. But when I was a kid, I used to collect all those brochures that come in the mail, asking for donations, you know?" He nodded. "The pictures of those kids used to make me cry and I was always begging my dad to donate money because we had so much, and these kids had nothing. But he never would. He told me it was all a hoax to get money out of bleeding hearts like me and I needed to toughen up. He said it was survival of the fittest and if you wanted to stay at the top of the food chain, you couldn't let your heart rule your head."

Dylan glanced at me, and I thought he would comment on that, but he focused on the road again and said nothing.

"So that's the sorry tale of how Scarlett Woods became a poor little rich girl. It was liberating though. It freed me from his expectations. He can't hold the money over my head anymore. For better or worse, I can make my own choices in life. But in my father's eyes, I'm a failure and a disappointment."

"Fuck him. You're living your own life. Calling the shots. He doesn't get to play puppeteer pulling all the strings." I heard something that sounded like respect in his voice.

"You hungry?" he asked a few seconds later as we were cruising down El Camino Avenue, past the designer outlet mall, the hills and towering palm trees behind it.

"What?" I asked, not sure I'd heard him right.

"I'm hungry." Without waiting for my reply, he whipped the car around and did an illegal U-turn. I checked my side mirror, expecting to see a cop car with flashing red and blue lights chasing after us. Five minutes later, he got off the next exit and a few minutes after that, he pulled into the In-N-Out and got in line for the drive-thru.

"I love In-N-Out burgers."

"I know."

I wondered if that's why he brought me here. But then I dismissed the notion.

"Wouldn't it be easier and quicker to go inside?" I asked, noticing that the line inside was shorter even though I didn't really want to leave the comfort and intimacy of his car.

"Then I'd have to deal with all those people. This way I only have to deal with you and the person who takes my order."

"Sounds like you've given this a lot of thought. Guess it's not easy being a misanthrope."

"Takes work," he deadpanned.

I couldn't help but laugh as I settled back in my heated leather seat and focused on the red brake lights ahead of me. The line moved at sloth speed and I was practically salivating, thinking about the food Dylan had just ordered.

We ate in the back of his G-Wagen, sitting on the tailgate with a view of the hills and the canyon, dotted with lights from the houses. We were sitting close enough that I could feel the heat of his body and inhale his heady scent as I stuffed my face with a cheeseburger and fries that he'd refused to accept money for.

"Donate it to charity, Mother Teresa."

Dylan checked that I was done eating before he lit a cigarette. "You go to the gym and you obviously work hard for that body..." That was a fact, no use pretending I hadn't noticed. You didn't get a body like Dylan's by sitting around on your ass. "But you still smoke?"

"It's all about balance."

I laughed.

He took a drag of his cigarette, his eyes narrowed, the little lines around his eyes crinkling. He could even make smoking look sexy. But then, Dylan could make anything look sexy. Feeling bold, I plucked the cigarette out of his mouth and claimed it as my own.

He scowled. "You're not a smoker."

I took a drag and tipped back my head, blowing the smoke into the cold night air. "I know. But I know how to do it now without coughing up a lung."

"That's a shame," he said, extracting a cigarette for himself. Cupping his tattooed hand over the tip, he flicked his Zippo and took a drag. The cherry glow burned brighter as he inhaled and we sat side by side smoking our cigarettes.

The undercurrent of electricity I'd always felt was still there. I knew it was just a chemical reaction, a trick my body played on me whenever he was near, but I wished my brain would send a signal to make it stop.

"You don't talk as much as you used to," he observed after moments of silence ticked by.

"I thought you'd appreciate the peace and quiet."

"I never minded it when you talked."

I laughed. "Could have fooled me. You told me you didn't have time for my teen drama and shit."

He took another drag of his cigarette, blowing the smoke out of the side of his mouth and huffed out a laugh before he spoke. "You remember that."

"Why do you think I stopped texting and calling? You injured my pride." It had been more than my pride. Those words had hurt my foolish teenage heart far more than they should have. But he didn't need to know that I'd cried over him.

I opened the plastic lid of my shake and tossed the cigarette into the cup, the dregs of the milkshake dousing the fire and making it sizzle. I replaced the lid and tossed the cup in one of the takeout bags.

He gave me a sidelong glance. "Funny. I used to have a hoodie just like that." He smirked.

I stifled a groan. What were the chances I'd be wearing his UC San Diego hoodie tonight? The same hoodie he'd given me the night I snuck in to watch his underground fight. I took it off and handed it to him.

He waved it off. "Keep it. You ruined your sweater for me."

"You were bleeding. What else was I supposed to do?"

"Not ruin your sweater."

"You got in that fight because of me."

"I wanted to kill those assholes for messing with you."

He'd gotten into a fight over me, *after* beating his opponent in the underground fight. I remembered thinking that nobody had ever fought for me before. That was the night I'd fallen in love with Dylan, two months shy of my sixteenth birthday. It was also the night I realized that he would never be mine and I needed to forget him.

"You told that guy he'd be breathing out of a tube if he even looked at me again."

"Fuck. You shouldn't have been there."

It was true. I shouldn't have been, and Dylan was so angry when he found out I'd taken a bus and walked. The cops busted the fight that night. It was in an auto repair and collisions garage on the outskirts of San Diego—bareknuckle boxing, betting, drugs, underage drinking, it was a den of inequity and there I was, in a place I never should have ventured to. It was my first brush with the law and I'd been so nervous, but Dylan had gotten us out of there. Grabbed my hand and held on tight, dragging me down dark alleys and ducking into a park until we lost the cruiser on our tail. It was the last time I'd been alone with him. The last time I'd really spoken to him until tonight.

He eyed me as he crushed his cigarette under the sole of his high top. It felt like he was seeing me for the first time, his eyes hooded as his gaze lowered to my mouth. I licked my lower lip at the same time he did. Then he shook his head. "Let's go. I've got shit to do."

And just like that, I was fifteen again.

I jumped off the tailgate and gathered up our trash then jogged across the parking lot to the garbage can where he picked me up a few seconds later.

The ride to my apartment was quick and we rode in silence.

When Dylan turned onto my street, and my apartment came into view, I sat up straighter. A van was parked in front—a van I'd know anywhere. I painted it two summers ago.

Why hadn't he told me he was coming back?

I slunk lower in my seat and whipped off Ollie's beanie, tucking it in my bag. "Keep driving."

To my surprise, Dylan did as I asked. Minutes later, he pulled over and parked on the next street over from mine.

"The fuck is going on?"

"Nothing." I finger-combed my hair and searched my bag for a hairbrush. Ugh, what was I doing? I slumped in the seat and cleared my throat, feeling like an idiot. Dylan's gaze was focused on me, waiting for an explanation. "I overreacted. You can take me home now. Sorry about that."

Dylan, of course, wasn't buying it. "We're not going anywhere until you tell me what's going on."

"That was my ex-boyfriend..." I shook my head. "I mean, my friend... back there in the van." I jerked my thumb over my shoulder.

"Which is it? Ex-boyfriend or friend?"

"Both. I wasn't expecting him. I just needed a minute to pull myself together. It's all good now."

Dylan was quiet for a moment, his car still idling on the side of the street. We were parked on a hill in front of a two-story white stucco house decorated with red and green

Christmas lights even though Christmas was two weeks ago. "Are you scared of him?"

"No."

"Did he ever hurt you? Fuck with you?" His voice was low, and his grip on the steering wheel tightened, the muscles of his forearm flexing.

I knew he was talking about physical harm, not emotional. I shook my head. "It's nothing like that."

"But you don't want to see him," he concluded. "Why not?"

"How would you like it if you came home and found Sienna waiting for you?" It wasn't even close to the same thing, so I wasn't sure why I'd gone there.

"I wouldn't run scared," he scoffed.

"Do you still love her?"

He drummed his fingers on the steering wheel. "We're not talking about me."

"I know. But do you?"

"No."

No. Just one word. No hesitation. It had sounded convincing enough but still, I wondered how it could be true.

About a year ago, I had asked Sienna the same question. She said she didn't think she'd ever get over loving Dylan, but it was time to move on. And she had. She and Chase were living together in Los Feliz. They hooked up at our cousin Phoebe's wedding sixteen months ago. My parents loved Chase. He was Dylan's polar opposite—a Stanford graduate, born with a silver spoon in his mouth, with impeccable manners and preppy good looks, Chase said and did all the right things.

"So, just like that... you're over her? You loved her though. Or you wouldn't have kept getting back together."

He didn't like it when I turned the questions back on him. Without bothering to comment on my observations, Dylan turned the car around and drove back to my apartment. Ollie was still there, waiting for me. Dylan pulled up so his G-Wagen was nose to nose with the van and the headlights illuminated Ollie as he climbed out of the driver's seat and slid his hands into the pockets of his cargo pants. He looked good. The ends of his blond hair curled up a little, a gray beanie on his head.

"Why did you break up?"

"He cheated on me." It was true, but that felt like the wrong answer. "I mean, that's the easy answer but it's more complicated—"

He cut off the rest of my sentence. "Don't give him another chance to fuck you over," he said. "You hear me?"

"Yeah, I hear you. Maybe you should have taken your own advice."

I shoved my door open and hopped out, sparing one last look at Dylan before I shut the door. Jaw clenched, he was glaring at Ollie. Was he angry? I didn't have the energy to decipher Dylan's moods. Besides, to Dylan, I was just his ex-girlfriend's little sister. Nothing more.

I approached Ollie who was standing next to the van, watching my face like he was searching for a clue on how to handle this situation.

His smile was tentative, mine was genuine. Which was all the reassurance he needed. "Missed you, Smalls." He pulled me into his arms and I held on tight, remembering how good it used to be before sex ruined everything.

4

DYLAN

oney. The root of all evil. That's what made it so damn sexy.

There were three main players in Costa del Rey. Simon Woods, John Hart, and Cal Whitaker. But John Hart was being pushed out of the picture by Simon Woods. A few months ago, he sold his house. Last I heard, he and his wife were sailing their yacht somewhere in the Caribbean. Bon fucking voyage. Which left Simon Woods as my main competition for The Surf Lodge, an oceanfront hotel circa 1950s.

It had thirty-six rooms, a restaurant and a rooftop bar, all in need of refurbishment. I wanted to restore it and return it to its former glory. Give it a 1950s vintage surf vibe. It was prime SoCal real estate and I wanted it. Badly.

But first, I needed to get Cal Whitaker to sell it to me.

I pulled into the parking lot of the diner where I knew Whitaker ate his breakfast every morning and confirmed that his pickup truck was parked by the door. I beeped the locks as I strode to the door, reminding myself I wasn't that filthy poor kid anymore with holes in his shoes, sleeping on a shitty sofa.

My bank account was healthy, growing every day, and I had the money to buy a piece of the pie. I wanted it so badly I could taste it, but I wasn't stupid enough to let my hunger show.

I spotted Cal in a back booth, reading a newspaper while he ate his breakfast. Who even read actual newspapers anymore? He had a muddy tan, snow-white hair that brushed the collar of his plaid shirt and a handlebar mustache. He looked like a cowboy in a spaghetti western. I slid into the red vinyl seat across from him, uninvited. He glanced up from his newspaper, his shaggy brows raised in question.

Without preamble or an introduction, I stated the purpose of my visit. "I want to buy The Surf Lodge."

"Well, that's one way to cut to the chase. Not much for small talk, are you, kid?"

"Never saw the need."

"How about manners? Ever see the need for them?"

I shrugged. Proper etiquette had never been my strong suit. There wasn't anything proper about me.

"It's not for sale." Dismissing me, he returned his attention to his breakfast, mopping up the runny egg yolk with his toast.

Bullshit. Everyone knew it was for sale. A brunette waitress with a bright smile stopped at our booth and handed me a laminated menu. "Good morning. What can I get you today?"

"Just coffee," I said, handing back the menu without bothering to look at it. I'd already eaten and had a triple shot of espresso earlier. I wasn't here for breakfast.

"You sure you don't want a breakfast special?" she asked. "Or pancakes? The chocolate chip ones are to die for."

"Just coffee," I repeated.

"Do you take cream in your coffee?"

I shook my head no, losing patience with the twenty questions. As I drummed my fingers on the table, waiting for her to leave, her eyes roamed over the tattoos on my forearms visible below my cuffed sleeves. Why was she still standing there, staring at me like I was an animal in the zoo and she'd never seen this rare species before? I shot her a look, questioning why she hadn't left yet without saying a word.

Her smile slipped, and she took a step back. "Okay, I'll be right back with your coffee. And a refill for you, Cal," she said brightly.

"Thanks, darlin'."

"Anytime," she sing-songed, giving me another smile before she left.

Cal went back to eating and reading his newspaper so I leaned back in my seat, slung an arm over the back and waited. After he cleaned his plate, he pushed it away and eyed me over the rim of his coffee mug. "You still here?"

"Word on the street says you're looking to sell but only to the right buyer." That part I was making up. "I hear you want to spend more time in Nicaragua." That part was true. I'd done my research. Had kept my ear to the ground, gleaning information and storing it away for future reference.

He crossed his arms over his barrel chest and studied my face. I remained silent and I waited. I could sit here without talking until the sun went down and not break a sweat.

"Why don't you tell me why I should sell you that hotel."

"I'm not Simon Woods." I figured he wasn't a big fan of Woods. Otherwise, he would have already sold him the property.

His brows rose. "You got a beef with Simon Woods?"

"Nope." I hated Simon Woods, but my reasons were personal, and I wasn't interested in feeding into any gossip. If it had been up to him, I would have been run out of this town a long time ago. Which was my motive for moving back here after I graduated college. I wanted to make something of myself, and I wanted to do it in Costa del Rey. Not LA. Not New York. Not Silicon Valley. Right here, in the town where the people had treated me and my twin sister Remy like trailer trash.

"You're the kid from the wrong side of the tracks with a chip on his shoulder and something to prove," Cal guessed.

"Sounds like you've got me all figured out." Underneath the Tom Ford black button-down, I was still the guy who Simon Woods had called scum of the earth. White trash. The no-good punk who would never be good enough for his precious daughter no matter what I did or how much money I earned. I'd never be 'one of them.' Thank fuck for that. I didn't want to be anything like those rich pricks.

"You remind me of someone I used to know."

"Who's that?" I asked, humoring him.

"Myself. And that ain't necessarily a good thing."

"I've been compared to worse."

He chuckled. "I'll bet you have."

The chirpy server was back with my coffee and set it in front of me with a big smile then poured Cal's refill and cleared his plate. "If you change your mind or you need anything, just let me know."

I forced a tight smile and nodded.

"Why should I sell to you? I have two good offers on the table."

I hadn't heard about a second offer. Didn't matter though. I had no intention of entering a bidding war. "It's time to make some changes in this town. Shake things up."

"It ain't the Wild West, kid. Not anymore. And you sure as hell ain't Wyatt Earp."

"Dylan St. Clair." I extended my hand to him across the table. He stared at it for a beat before he shook it with a warm, firm grip. A proper handshake, thank fuck.

"I know who you are. You're the kid who built his empire app by app. Don't use 'em myself. Kids today can't do anything without consulting their damn cell phones. Not a fan of technology."

Funny how he kept calling me a kid. I'd be twenty-seven in June and hadn't felt like a kid in longer than I could remember. "Don't knock it until you try it."

He snorted with disgust. "If I want to go somewhere, I read a map. If I want food, I cook it. If I want the news, I read a goddamn newspaper."

I didn't mention that it was already old news by the time he read it. He was obviously set in his ways, and I wasn't here to educate him on the benefits of technology.

"How many apps have you got now?"

"A few." In the span of five years, I'd built and launched forty-three apps. Fitness apps, food delivery, airport transfers, interior design, medical cannabis, gaming apps, you name it, if there was a market or demand for it, I tapped into it. Building apps wasn't rocket science. I'd figured out how to reverse engineer a successful app and applied it to the ones I developed. Apps had made me a multi-millionaire.

"How's Rae?" he asked, doing a one-eighty on this conversation.

I shouldn't be surprised that he knew my mother. Cal frequented The Last Stand, a dive bar on the fringes of town that my mother used to hang out at when she lived here. I dragged her ass home from there plenty of times when she was too drunk to drive and hadn't managed to land a man to warm her bed that night. Maybe he had slept with her. Wonder how much she charged him.

"Last I heard, she was alive and well."

"So it's like that, is it?" He clucked his tongue and shook his head.

As if I hadn't done enough to help her. As if I was the heartless bastard who had kicked his poor mother to the curb and walked away without a backward glance.

The bell over the door chimed and I heard the sound of her laughter before I saw her. I glanced to my left as the waitress led her and the ex-boyfriend (obviously, she hadn't heeded my advice and dumped the asshole) to a booth across from us. A beanie covered her head, a tangled mess of blonde hair cascaded to the small of her back. It was ocean damp and water dripped from the ends, leaving a wet patch on the back of her oversized plaid flannel. My eyes roamed down her ripped jeans to the Vans on her feet, painted a riot of colors in a geometric design. Her handiwork, no doubt. She slid into the seat facing the door and I chuckled soundlessly at the words painted on her T-shirt: I'm A Little Fucking Ray Of Sunshine.

Damn right she was. The whole damn place lit up when she walked in the door. Her skin had a peachy glow like it did after a good surfing session. She looked downright edible.

Baby sister was all grown up. Small and ripe, curvy in all the right places, with pillow-soft lips so fuckable it should be illegal. She looked like the love child of Deborah Harry and Mick Jagger.

When Scarlett caught me watching, her baby blues widened, and she tugged her bottom lip between her teeth before she hid behind a laminated menu.

I spared a glance at the ex with his shaggy blond hair and droopy stoner eyes. Did she have sex with Shaggy Doo last night after I dropped her off? Why should I care?

I returned my attention to Cal, remembering the reason I was here. Which was not to get distracted by Scarlett Woods.

Cal took a sip of his coffee and didn't comment on my sudden interest in the booth across from us.

"You know, I grew up in this town. Back then, it was all cowboys, surfers, and Marines. I've been all three. A bunch of hell-raisers we were. This was back before everything got so built-up and expensive." He lowered his voice so as not to be overheard. "Back before guys like Simon Woods and John Hart

came along and turned this town into some kind of Disney-
land. Nicaragua, kid, that's where it's at now. Central America is
like the Wild West."

We pondered that for a minute although I had zero interest
in heading to Central America and conquering new territory.
Despite all the shit Remy and I had gone through in this town, I
loved Costa del Rey. Had loved it from the minute we rolled
into town when me and Remy were sixteen. Unlike any of the
places we'd lived in the past, it was a wealthy town. A surfer's
paradise with big fat waves, killer sunsets, and a laidback,
chilled-out vibe I envied in others but would never in a million
years achieve.

"Why do you want to get into real estate?"

"It's time to diversify my portfolio."

"Fancy words. Why do you want to buy this property
off me?"

"Because I can."

He nodded slowly like that made sense to him. "And I guess
there was a time not so long ago when nobody thought you'd
amount to anything. So you feel like you've got something to
prove."

"I like making money. That's all I ever wanted to do. Make a
shitload of money." That was mostly true, but my reasons went
deeper than that. Money didn't motivate me. What motivated
me was the way people treated you differently when you had
money. It was poor kid mentality, I was smart enough to recognize that, but nobody had expected a punk like me to make
good and that made the victory taste so much sweeter.

"For what? What do you want to do with all this money?
You can't take it with you. The fancy toys and the greenbacks
won't buy you a better seat up there." He pointed at the ceiling
as if heaven was right upstairs. As if there was a heaven and he
believed in it. "So what drives you to keep making more
money? Ain't you got enough?"

"It will never be enough."

"Let me tell you a story," Cal said. I sat back and listened like I had all the time in the world and was in no rush to close the deal. "After I got out of the Marines, I went to Texas with one of my Marine buddies. Got a job as a ranch hand. I met this girl. A real beauty.

Her daddy owned the cattle ranch. They were loaded. And I thought what's a girl like that doing with a guy like me? Her daddy wasn't happy about us, but she knew what she wanted, and she thought that was me. Her old man never did warm to me. Thought I was an upstart. A gold digger who was after the family money. He made her choose. Her family or me. She chose me and got cut off from the family and all that money. For a while, she was happy enough. But pretty soon she got tired of not being able to buy pretty dresses and shit. I wasn't around much because I was too busy busting my ass trying to get rich. But that day hadn't come yet, and she was getting tired of struggling to make ends meet. Just be patient, I told her. Trust me. This is all gonna work out. Well, what d'ya know, she ran out of patience and ran back to her daddy."

Cal's story sounded so similar to my story with Sienna. While he talked, I watched Scarlett in my periphery. She was laughing with Shaggy Doo, and I wondered what the hell could be so entertaining.

"So, she left you because you were poor," I summarized.

"No. She left me because she didn't believe in me. There's a difference. One you can overlook. Forgive. Move past. The other one you never get over."

Preaching to the choir. I'd lived it. Not once in my eight-year on-again, off-again relationship with Sienna had she ever believed in me or fought for me or stood up for me. "How'd you make your money?"

"Invested in oil. Texas gold. It wasn't long after she left that the money started rolling in."

"Did she want you back?" None of these questions were getting me any closer to my goal of buying that hotel but I was interested in hearing the answer.

"Maybe. Maybe not. Didn't matter. She'd already married someone else with a shitload of money and everyone lived happily ever after."

"How about you? Did you live happily ever after?" I didn't really believe in shit like that. Happily ever afters only happened in Disney movies.

"Time will tell. My story ain't over yet." He stroked his mustache, his eyes on me, and I could tell he was about to throw me a bone. "How about we go over and check out that hotel you're looking to buy?"

"You planning to sell it to me?"

"Haven't made up my mind yet."

I had a feeling he was going to sell it to me. But I kept my excitement contained, something I'd mastered at a young age.

I slid out of the booth and left a ten-dollar tip for a cup of coffee I'd left untouched. Scarlett was studiously avoiding me, attacking the food in front of her like it was her last meal. I swear I heard her moan. That's how she ate though. That's how she did everything. Her plate was piled high with a stack of pancakes, chocolate chip by the looks of it, and a side of bacon.

I stopped next to her booth, and she raised her eyes to mine. She still had a spray of freckles on her nose. So fucking adorable. And So. Fucking. Off. Limits.

The chocolate in the corner of her mouth beckoned me to lean in closer. Scarlett Woods... she was the sweetest temptation. I slowly dragged my thumb across her plump bottom lip and wiped off the chocolate. Her breath hitched, and her eyes followed my thumb to my mouth. Eyes locked on hers, I wrapped my lips around my thumb and sucked the chocolate off it. "So fucking sweet."

Her eyes flared. "What are you doing?" she hissed.

Moving my mouth close to the shell of her ear, I whispered, "You deserve better."

Without waiting for a response, I strode away. Even by my low standards, it was wrong to mess with my ex-girlfriend's little sister.

But when had I ever done the right thing?

5

SCARLETT

"You can't be fucking serious." Ollie stared at me like he couldn't believe what he'd just witnessed. That made two of us. Why had Dylan done that? My tongue traced my lower lip where Dylan's thumb had just been.

"Nothing is going on." I picked up a strip of crispy bacon and took a bite.

Ollie laughed harshly. "Oh right. You've only been in love with him for ten years."

"I'm not in love with him." I tossed the bacon onto my plate and took a sip of orange juice. I hadn't even mentioned Dylan to Ollie since junior high. "I've barely spoken to him in five years."

"He drove you home last night. Didn't he? That was him in the car?"

"Ollie," I said softly. "This... us..." I motioned between us with my hand. "It has nothing to do with him. I miss my best friend."

His eyes grew softer. "I know. Me too."

"We can't let what happened ruin fourteen years of friendship." More than anything, I wanted to go back to the way things were before sex ruined everything. But I knew life didn't work that way.

He exhaled loudly. "She didn't mean anything to me."

"I know that. I do. But you still did it. You were trying to hurt me." It was hurtful what he did, I wasn't going to pretend it wasn't, but finding out he had a one-night stand with another girl didn't devastate me the way it should have. The way it would have if I'd loved him the way he claimed to love me. God, why did love... why did *relationships*... have to be so complicated?

"What did you expect to achieve by cheating on me?"

His jaw clenched. "I don't know. Maybe I was doing you a favor. Giving you the excuse you needed to end things. I didn't have sex with her. I couldn't do it. Just like I couldn't leave you."

I shook my head and slumped in my seat. God, we were idiots. He hadn't even slept with that girl, but he'd let me believe that he had. "I don't want to play the blame game. I've had a couple months to think about this. To put it in perspective. And what I came up with was that we were never meant to be anything more than just friends, Ollie."

He looked out the window, his throat bobbing as he swallowed, trying to rein in his emotions. "What happens when someone falls in love with their best friend, but their best friend doesn't feel the same way?" He turned his head to look at me, his green eyes wounded. "What happens then, Scarlett?"

Oh God. His voice... the sorrow on his face as if he was mourning the loss of someone he once loved... it was killing me. I reached across the table for his hand and we interlaced our fingers. Holding hands with Ollie was like holding your best friend's hand. It was warm. It was nice. Comforting without setting my body on fire. It felt safe. And maybe that should have been enough, but it hadn't been. "I do love you. I love you so much. You know that."

He nodded and looked down at our linked hands. "Yeah, I know you love me. But you were never *in love* with me."

I opened my mouth to deny it, but I couldn't. It was true. And I hated that it was true. Why couldn't I have felt the same way he did? I hated that we'd hurt each other like this. I'd failed to love him the way I wished I could. But no matter how much you tried, you couldn't force yourself to fall in love. All along, Ollie had known the truth. He knew me the same way I knew him.

We'd been best friends since he moved into our gatehouse when I was seven and he was eight. His mother had been our housekeeper and when we were young, we never noticed the inequity. But as Ollie got older, he grew more resentful of the way my parents treated him and his mom. Like second-class citizens. They moved out of the gatehouse when Ollie was thirteen, but we remained friends. I was too stupid to notice that he'd been in love with me. All through high school, he hooked up with girls, and Nicola told me it was a ploy to make me jealous, but I'd always laughed it off and told her that was ridiculous.

"I'm sorry, Ollie."

He released my hand. "Don't. Don't do that. I don't want your pity."

"I don't pity you." I guess it would be in bad form to tell him there were a ton of girls out there and one day he'd find the right one. "Can we still be friends?"

He laughed a little. "From anyone else that would sound like a cheesy line."

I smiled. "The difference is that I really mean it."

"I know you do." He rubbed the back of his neck, his eyes not meeting mine. "I need some time. And I'm not sure how long we'll be here. Seattle has a better music scene. We just came home to regroup. Save some money before we hit the road again."

"Solid plan. And yeah, take some time... whatever you need."

Everything used to be so easy with us, but I didn't know if we'd ever get back to what we used to be before. We were a cautionary tale of why you should never cross the lines of friendship.

I was sitting cross-legged on the floor, painting an electric blue jellyfish on a board when Dylan walked in the front door of Firefly Surfboards. I didn't even have to look up, I knew it was him. It was his scent and the way the air changed whenever he was in my space. Like I'd touched a livewire and my whole body zinged from the current. My Posca paint marker kept moving, filling in one of the giant tentacles that extended to the bottom third of the rail, but I was hyperaware of his every footstep as he closed the distance between the front door and me.

Black combat boots stopped in front of me. They were a newer, nicer version of the boots he used to wear as a teen, the leather not cracked and worn, the laces tied, and the hems of his black jeans not frayed. His clothes were designer now, but his style hadn't changed much over the years. "Why are you sitting on the floor?"

"This is how I like to work. Why are you such an asshole?"

"Comes naturally."

He had known what he was doing that morning in the diner, but he'd done it anyway.

I side-eyed him as he moved to the side of the shop and stopped in front of the shelves stocked with the new T-shirts and hoodies that had arrived this morning. He took each one off the shelf, checked out the design, then stuffed it back on the shelf haphazardly. Creating chaos after Remy and I had so carefully folded them only a few hours ago. "Why are you messing up the T-shirt display?"

"These are your designs?" His back was to me, and I took a second to appreciate his broad shoulders and the way his biceps flexed under his black Henley as he reached for the T-shirts on the top shelf.

"Yes."

He moved on to the surfboards in the rack and studied the design on each one. "Did you design that denim jacket in the shop on Main Street?"

"Lillidiva? Yeah, why?" I capped my marker and looked over at him. It had been four days since I saw him at the diner. Four days since he wiped the chocolate off my lip. Four days since I told Ollie we were better as friends.

"Where else do you sell your designs?"

"Why are you suddenly so interested in fashion and design?"

"I don't give a shit about fashion or design. I'm asking you where else you sell your shit."

"My *shit* is only sold here.... the surfboards, T-shirts and hoodies. And I have a few pieces at Lillidiva."

"Starlet Woods." Heat crept up my neck and stained my cheeks. Yes, I'd used his nickname for me, but I'd never expected him to notice or seek out my designs.

I stood up and walked over to the shelves and I refolded the T-shirts and hoodies he'd rifled through.

"Is that what you want? To have your own shop?"

"Someday, I guess. Not a fancy clothing boutique though. More like a design studio. Surfboards, skateboards, denim jackets, T-shirts... home accessories..." I swept my hand in the air to indicate that I wanted all that and more.

"You don't want to limit yourself."

"Right."

"I could help you set up your own shop."

"I'm a long way off from that."

"I'm talking about an online shop."

"Why would you do that for me?"

"I'm all about helping to make dreams come true."

I snorted. "Since when?"

"Since today." I smoothed my palm over a coral T-shirt on top of the stack then turned around and smacked into Dylan's chest. His hands wrapped around my upper arms to steady me. It had the opposite effect. My heart was beating so hard I wouldn't be surprised if he could hear it.

I couldn't breathe. Couldn't think. Couldn't calm my racing thoughts.

The top of my head fit perfectly under his chin. What I wouldn't give to just lay my head on his chest and wrap my arms around him. I shook my head, trying to shake off those thoughts and side-stepped around him since he didn't seem inclined to move out of my way. Why was he all up in my space today?

"Where's Rem?" he asked.

"She went to get some food. She was craving fish tacos."

"That kid's gonna come out looking like a fish taco."

I returned to the surfboard I was painting and tried to concentrate on the design. "Could be worse. The baby could look like this jellyfish."

"That would be scary as fuck."

We both laughed.

He crouched in front of me and I lifted my head, my eyes locking onto his blue-grays. Up close, with only a surfboard between us, this felt far too intimate. My gaze lowered from his firm, square jaw to the veiny tattooed forearms resting on his black jean-clad thighs. The view did nothing to calm my racing pulse. "Did you dump the ex, Starlet?"

"He's my best friend. It's complicated. Why do you even care?"

"I've always cared," he said quietly.

What the hell? What game was he playing?

His gaze lowered to my mouth and he bit his bottom lip. The air was taut with tension, and it felt like I'd stopped breathing. No. *No.* I didn't want old feelings to resurface. I'd gotten over my infatuation with Dylan St. Clair years ago.

"Go away," I muttered. I shooed him away with my hand which only made him laugh.

Dylan stood up as Shane emerged from one of the shaping bays in the back. A dusty blue bandana worn pirate-style covered his longish dirty-blond hair.

I smiled at Shane then tuned them out and concentrated on my design and the good things in my life, instead of my mixed-up emotions. This shop was one of my happy places. Remy's surfing and ocean photography covered the driftwood walls and it smelled like surfboard wax and the sea salt-scented candles Remy always burned. Angus & Julia Stone piped from the speakers, the afternoon sunlight streamed through the windows, and Dylan wasn't allowed to cloud my thoughts.

I wasn't that same stupid infatuated girl who once believed she could fix the broken bad boy.

He was never yours to fix.

———

"What happened?" Sienna prompted.

"Nothing happened. He just asked for my car keys, so I gave them to him. It's no big deal." I put her on speakerphone and set my phone on the kitchen counter while I rummaged through the cupboards in search of something to cook for dinner. My roommate was a foodie and a culinary genius. Not always a good thing. Why would anyone need so many capers and anchovies? I grabbed the loaf of bread, butter, and a wax paper-wrapped block of cheddar from the fridge. Nic was like the food Nazi. She refused to allow the plastic-wrapped singles into our apartment.

"That doesn't make sense," Sienna said, still puzzling over our dad's actions as if she hadn't known him for the entire twenty-seven years of her life. "You didn't say or do anything to provoke him?"

"Well... I might have mentioned his mistress." I winced as I spread butter on two slices of artisan sourdough bread. I made a mental note to buy some plain sliced white.

"Oh my God, Scar." She burst out laughing. "You're such an idiot. You never learn, do you?"

"Guess not." Unlike me, Sienna was the perfect daughter. She graduated from USC with a 3.5 GPA and a degree in Finance and Marketing, did her summer internships at our father's financial holdings company, and was now working as a Business Development Manager at a consulting firm in LA. She was smart, rich, and successful. More importantly, she knew how to play the game.

"I'd rather live on my own terms than have every move dictated by him. His money comes with too many strings attached. If I have to bum rides everywhere until I save enough for a car, it's a small price to pay for my freedom."

Brave words. Truth was that it sucked not having a car, but I'd made my bed, so I wasn't going to whine about it.

My grilled cheese sandwich sizzled in the pan as I flattened it with my spatula.

"How does it feel?" Sienna asked.

"How does what feel?" I flipped my grilled cheese, my mouth watering at the golden cheesy goodness.

"Standing up to Dad like that. Telling him to go fuck himself."

"I never said those words."

"You didn't have to. The intention was clear."

"It's kind of scary," I admitted, "but it's liberating. You

should try it sometime." I hadn't meant for the words to sound like a dig, not really, but I guess that's how it came across.

"You're such a brat."

"So you've told me about a million times." Pulling up a stool at the island, I bit into my grilled cheese and cursed under my breath when I burned my tongue. Every. Single. Time. I reached for my bottle of water and guzzled it to soothe the burn.

"Because it's true. But I love you anyway."

I loved her too, and needed to remember that whenever Dylan showed up, looking fifty shades of hot and messing with my head.

Over the years, my relationship with Sienna had gone through a lot of ups and downs. When I was really young, I remember her being the best big sister ever. But by the time she was in junior high, she treated me like I was a pest and she didn't want me around. That carried through her high school years. It was only when I got into my late teens that we started getting close, but not so close that we confided our secrets or bared our souls.

"Are you okay for money? I can help you out."

"I'm good. But thanks. It wouldn't feel right taking money from you. It would feel like cheating."

"I'm your sister. And I'm loaded with money. Don't be so stubborn. If you need it, just ask, okay?"

"Yeah, sure," I said, although we both knew that I never would.

"How's Remy?"

"She's great. She—"

Banging on the front door stopped me mid-sentence.

I took my sister off speakerphone and held the phone to my ear, filling her in on Remy's life as I crossed the living room to the front door. Remy used to be Sienna's best friend. But after her break-up with Dylan, they'd drifted apart. "Anyway, she's really good and everyone is so excited about this baby."

"That baby is going to be gorgeous."

"Yep." I swung open the door and there was Ollie. He brushed past me and walked inside like he owned the place.

"I'll talk to you later," I told Sienna. "Ollie's here."

Since I'd never told Sienna that Ollie and I had ventured out of the friend zone, she didn't question it. I cut the call and followed Ollie into the kitchen. He was like a bloodhound, sniffing out food everywhere he went. By the time I reached him, he'd already helped himself to the other half of my sandwich. I smacked his arm and he held the sandwich hostage above his head. At five foot four, I had stopped growing whereas the scrawny boy I used to play with had become a hulking giant of six foot three.

"Back off, Smalls. I'm a starving artist."

"So am I." I flicked him on the arm and he flicked me back then finished the sandwich in two bites and washed it down with milk that he drank straight from the carton. Some things never changed, but I was happy that he was acting like my friend again, without all the weirdness.

"What are you doing here? Besides stealing my dinner?" I asked as we stood side by side making two more sandwiches.

"Look. I know this won't sound good coming from me," Ollie said, getting to the real reason he'd stopped by. "But be careful."

"Careful about what?" I had some idea what he was talking about, but I played dumb hoping he wouldn't go there.

"Dylan. He's trouble. And I'm saying this as your friend with only your best interests at heart. Your parents suck. Your dad's a prick. Your mom... I don't know what the hell she is except self-absorbed. Don't lose your sister because of a guy. He's not worth it."

He's not worth it. I'd heard those same words spoken about

Dylan—to Dylan's face—by my father ten years ago. I'd been getting a snack in the kitchen with the French doors wide open when my father laid into Dylan. I'd been privy to things I never should have known about.

"You're nothing but a no-good punk..."

"If you think for one minute I'd let my daughter bring your worthless bastard into this world..."

"You're not good enough for my daughter and you never will be..."

Dylan was worth it. But I knew that Ollie was just trying to look out for me. While I appreciated it, sort of, it was unnecessary. "I have no intention of getting involved with Dylan so don't worry about it."

Famous last words.

6

DYLAN

"We have a team meeting in twenty minutes," Cruz reminded me as I pulled into a parking spot outside Starbucks and cut the engine.

"When have I ever missed a meeting?"

"Never. But try to play nice. Whenever you're around, Melanie gets nervous. I've had to ease her fears on more than one occasion. She's hot though so it's not too much of a chore."

I hadn't even noticed. She was a people pleaser, she was efficient, and she got the job done. As far as Melanie was concerned, that's all that mattered to me. "She's our PA, for fuck's sake. We don't need a lawsuit because you can't keep your dick in your pants."

"I'm not boning her. Do you take me for stupid? Where are you anyway?"

"Starbucks." I beeped my locks and climbed the stairs to the side entrance. Two men in their mid-forties who looked like surf bums, were lounging at an outdoor table, their faces tipped up to the morning winter sun. One of them looked like Jimmy Wilder with his longish brown hair and suntanned skin. I felt a sharp pang of sadness that it wasn't him. Shane's dad, Jimmy was like the father I'd never had. I missed him every fucking day.

"Hang on," Cruz said. "I'll take orders."

"The fuck? I'm not the office errand boy," I said as I stepped inside Starbucks and got in line behind a few suits.

Cruz ignored me and came back on the line a few seconds later. "I'll text the order. It's a big one."

I shook my head and pocketed my phone.

"Hey Romeo."

I turned to look at Scarlett who gave me a dimpled smile, revealing her pearly whites. Today she was wearing an over-sized maroon knitted sweater, the hems unraveling, zebra print leggings and Doc Martens. Her blonde hair was pulled up into a messy topknot that tilted to the right and her face was makeup-free except for the smudged eyeliner under her bottom lashes. Yet somehow, this grunge angel was the sexiest thing I'd ever seen.

I wasn't sure when it had happened, but baby sister had become the stuff of my wet dreams. Literally. I'd woken up this morning hard as stone, and rubbed one out in the shower, envisioning her on all fours, my hand fisting her hair. In my head, we'd fucked on every available surface in my house and in every imaginable position.

"I thought you only did drive-thrus."

"If they had a drive-thru, I'd use it."

"Misanthropy 101."

"I aced that class."

We both laughed. When our humor faded, we just stood there and engaged in a silent staring contest. I had sex on the brain. More specifically, sex with Scarlett on the brain. But it was more than that. She was cool as shit and didn't care about anyone's opinion of her. She just did her own thing, had her own sense of style, and fuck what everyone said about it. She'd always had a rebellious streak, and it was one of the things I liked best about her. Unlike Sienna who loved her designer clothes and shoes and shiny toys, who used to tremble with fear at the thought of losing her trust fund, Scarlett had given her father the proverbial middle finger.

Fuck you, Daddy dearest.

That took guts.

"Hey. I'm Nicola." The brunette next to Scarlett gave me a little wave and it was only then that I noticed Scarlett wasn't alone. Because... sex on the brain.

"Oh. Sorry." Scarlett snapped out of it to make the belated introductions. "This is Dylan. Dylan, Nicola. Nicola's my roommate. She's a chef at Cinque Terre."

"I'm a line cook. But chef sounds better." She gave me a big white smile. She was hot, a brunette with big brown eyes and big tits. Exactly the kind of girl Cruz always went for. But she didn't do it for me.

My gaze returned to the blonde bombshell next to her.

Scarlett rocked back on her heels, her hands clasped in front of her. "Kind of weird that I never used to run into you and now everywhere I go, there you are."

"It's synchronicity," Nicola said. "You're in sync now so you'll probably see each other everywhere."

"Funny how that works." Because I did see her *everywhere.*

It was my turn to order, so I moved up to the counter and opened the text from Cruz. Son of a bitch. Eight drink orders.

"What can I get you?" the guy behind the counter asked.

"Can you give me everything on this text? But instead of the tall Americano make it a venti with a triple shot. And whatever they want," I said, ushering Scarlett and her friend up to the counter.

"Oh. You don't have to get ours. We'll go after him," Scarlett told the barista.

"Just tell the guy what you want," I huffed.

They put in their orders and tried to give me money which I

refused to take. Everyone knew that Starbucks was overpriced. When me and Remy were teenagers, we couldn't afford these little luxuries. Sienna used to bring Starbucks to school for Remy every morning. She'd been a good friend, I had to give her that, but it used to make Remy feel guilty that she couldn't afford to return the favor. Now we could afford it and ironically, Sienna's sister couldn't. Pay it forward and all that.

We moved down the counter to wait for my big-ass drink order and formed a cozy little circle of three. At this rate, I'd be late for the meeting.

"So Dylan, we're planning Scarlett's twenty-first birthday party," Nicola said with a smile. "Are you free on Thursday night?"

"You don't have to come," Scarlett hastened to add. "You probably don't even like parties."

"It's a beach party," Nicola said, ignoring Scarlett. "So you don't want to miss it."

"A beach party in January?" I cocked a questioning brow at Scarlett.

Scarlett shrugged. "There's no competition for the fire rings and the beers will stay cold. But like I said, you don't have to come."

"Are you saying you don't want me there?"

"Well…" She chewed on her lip and furrowed her brow as if I'd just asked her to solve a quadratic equation. Scarlett was always honest. I remembered that. "I do. But only if *you* want to be there."

Just then, my name was called, and ten drinks were set on the counter in front of us. We transferred them to cardboard trays, and Nicola and Scarlett insisted on helping me carry the drinks to my car. If any of this shit spilled on my interior, Cruz was dead. I'd only spent money on two things. This car and my house. And I was borderline OCD about both of them.

"Thanks for the coffee. Hope we see you at the party,"

Nicola said, pushing this whole party thing whereas Scarlett was more hesitant.

"Well, okay, so I guess I'll see you around," Scarlett said, giving me a little wave over her shoulder as she walked away.

Chances were, I wouldn't go anyway. There were plenty of girls who were willing and ready, girls who did not come with any strings attached. Get in, get out, don't stick around long enough to let anyone get too close or ask probing questions I wouldn't answer anyway.

I made it back to the office with two minutes to spare and set the drinks on the table. My good deed done for the day.

"Where's my tall Americano?" Cruz asked after he finished passing out the drinks like he was Santa Fucking Claus.

"It got an upgrade." I took a sip of my venti Americano as I walked past him and sat at the table which of course was round. Cruz claimed it made everyone feel like they were equals. The office was open plan and everyone else was thrilled with that concept and the overall relaxed atmosphere. Me? I had a door and glass walls around my office to give me privacy and block out all the noise. I didn't hate people. We had a good team—young, smart and driven—and for the most part, I got along with everyone I worked with. But I could only handle people in small doses. Anything more left me feeling drained.

"Cheers everyone." I lifted my cardboard cup in a toast. "Enjoy your Starbucks because that's the last time I'm doing a fucking coffee run."

Everyone around the table laughed as if I'd made a good joke. At least they saw the humor in my asshole tendencies.

Cruz muttered under his breath, *still an asshole*, and rubbed his eyebrow with his middle finger. The fact that he actually believed I'd bring him a morning beverage after he'd pulled that stunt made me chuckle.

Putting the Starbucks incident behind us, we got down to business. I fucking loved my job and even though I didn't need to be here half as much as I was and technically, I could work from home, I spent a lot of time in this office. I liked having structure. A place where I needed to be five days out of the week. Cruz and I were a lot alike that way. We'd both grown up with parents who were mostly MIA and had never enforced rules, structure or curfews. We were street kids from the hood made good, and neither of us had ever forgotten where we came from.

When we started this company five years ago, we were still in college and it was just me and Cruz, developing software and building websites from our kitchen table in San Diego. Now we had thirty employees, an office on the twelfth floor of a new high-rise near the marina, and an ocean view. Times had changed but I guess at the end of the day, I hadn't. Not really. I was still rough around the edges, still taciturn and somewhat detached, and I still had this fear that one day I'd wake up and everything good in my life that I worked my ass off for would be ripped away. That fear had been my constant companion since I was a kid. I didn't think it would ever go away.

7

SCARLETT

"I can't believe you invited Dylan." I took a sip of my caramel macchiato. I was so basic. "He probably won't come anyway."

"Then you'll have nothing to worry about," she said calmly.

"Exactly. It would be better if he didn't come."

"But you're still hoping he does." Nicola tilted her head and studied my face. She was a knockout—a tall, willowy brunette with huge dark eyes and full lips. Guys usually did a double-take when she walked by, but Dylan had barely glanced at her. Interesting.

"I don't know, Nic. I'm so... God, I'm a horrible person. Let's not even try to sugarcoat it."

"I won't. You're truly horrible. The worst. What a bitch." She rolled her eyes. "Get a grip. I don't see what the big deal is."

"Are you serious? He's my sister's ex-boyfriend," I whisper-shouted. Two businessmen at a table across from us looked over briefly before returning to their conversation.

Nic waved away my concerns. "Your sister moved on. She's living with another guy. She gets to be happy so why can't you guys be happy?"

I stared at her, completely missing the logic because her statement had none. "It goes against the sisterhood code. Everyone knows that."

"If you were going for him while your sister was still with him, yeah sure, I could see that. But it's over so he's fair game." She shrugged like this was something everyone knew. I wasn't too sure about that. "You can't help who you fall in love with."

"Nobody's in love." I took a few more sips of my drink. Love was a stretch. I used to have a crush on him but that was as far as it went. "And then there's Ollie. I really want to get back to being friends but if Dylan shows up—"

"Whoa." Nic held up her hand like a traffic cop. "Stop right there. Ollie cheated on you. He's lucky you're even talking to him, let alone wanting to be friends. Seriously. Explain that to me."

"He was drunk and..." My shoulders slumped. That had been such a bad time. I'd rather just forget about it. Erase it from history. I'd been pushing Ollie away but still trying to hang on because I didn't want to lose him. It hadn't been fair to him or to me and he'd goaded me, tried to force my hand so I would show him how much I cared. Obviously, it had backfired in an epic way and now we were left to pick up the pieces of a friendship we'd blown to smithereens. "I can't explain it, but he said he didn't sleep with her."

"That's no excuse. He was trying to get you jealous. Who plays those games besides junior high kids? He took it too far. I know you guys have been friends forever, but still. That really sucked and so does he for doing what he did."

"You know what sucks even more? I was relieved. Like, it gave me an excuse to call it quits. He'd given me the out I needed. That's pretty messed up, right?"

"Life is messed up. Take me, for example. Obsessing over my head chef. And all he ever does is yell at me. He's a total bully. A hot, hot, *scorching* hot bully. But still... a bully. Although he did compliment my julienne skills last night. My zucchini and carrots were on point." She gave me the universal hand signal for perfect then kissed her index finger and thumb. "He was kind of nice, actually. Oh Jesus." She smacked herself on the forehead. "I need to stop thinking about him. Besides, he's too old for me. Oh, and he has a kid. Let's not forget that."

"Wait, he's married?"

She shook her head. "No. He's single. A single dad. Kind of hot, right?"

"Where's the mom?"

"She took off."

"Oh. That's sad."

"Yeah." Her lips turned down at the corners. "Anyway, as far as Dylan goes, my advice—"

I jostled her arm to get her to put a lid on it as Remy walked in the door, her phone pressed to her ear. She gave us a dazzling smile when she saw us and held up one finger to say she'd just be a minute. God, she really was gorgeous. It was easy to see why she'd been such a successful supermodel. I'd never seen eyes like hers before. Blue-green, like aquamarine, and she had the same coloring as Dylan. Jet-black hair and tan skin that made her eyes look even more stunning.

Nicola and I were both watching her as she got her drink at the counter and then walked over to us. She was one of those people you couldn't help but stare at.

"I'll see you soon, lover," Remy said. She was obviously talking to Shane. Remy cut her call and slipped her phone in her bag. Even at eight months pregnant in yoga pants and a long sleeve T-shirt, her hair in a high ponytail and no makeup, she looked like she belonged on a catwalk.

"Hey Remy. Do you remember Nicola?"

"Of course. Shane and I keep talking about going to dinner at Cinque Terre but we've been so busy and I keep falling asleep at nine o'clock. I'm like an old granny these days." She laughed, and we invited her to sit with us which she did, explaining that the decaf Frappuccino with whipped cream was her reward for having survived another pregnant yoga class.

"I just met your brother," Nicola said after we'd discussed yoga and Nicola asked what Remy's due date was. February seventeenth.

"Did my brother actually talk to you?" Remy asked.

"He did," Nicola said with a smile. "I invited him to Scarlett's birthday party."

"Hmm. Interesting." Remy gave me a little smile. "He came over for dinner last night and your name came up."

"Oh? Um, what about?"

She took a sip of her drink and left me hanging for a moment. "He said you're really talented. Which I already knew. He sounded really impressed and it's not easy to impress my brother."

"Well, at least he has good taste," Nicola said. I side-eyed her, hoping she wouldn't say anything incriminating. "Scarlett has mad talent."

Remy agreed with her. "Speaking of which, I was wondering if you'd paint the nursery. We'd pay you, of course. But I was thinking it would be cool to do a beach theme. Or an underwater scene. Would you have time for that?"

I jumped at the chance. "Definitely. I'd love to do it. You don't have to pay me."

"Yes, I do. You should get paid for your work. Dylan thinks we should give you a space in the shop where you can sell your own designs. I think it's his competitive streak coming out. He doesn't like the idea of our surfboard designer selling her pieces at Lillidiva." Remy laughed. "Shane and I agree. We think it's a great idea."

All I could do was stare at her with my mouth gaping like a

fish. I was such a cool cucumber. "Really? He said that? And you and Shane would be okay with that? Are you sure?"

"If we weren't cool with it, I wouldn't have mentioned it. We're sure. Even though Dylan is a bonehead sometimes and isn't a big talker, he's really smart and has a good head for business." I could hear the pride in her voice. It was the same tone of voice Dylan used whenever he talked about Remy. They had such a strong bond and loved each other so much. It was one of Dylan's most redeeming qualities.

Remy checked her phone. "I need to get going." She stood up from the table and slung her bag over her shoulder. "But we'll talk about it some more later."

"Okay. Sounds good. Thanks." I checked my phone for the time. I still had an hour before I needed to be at the shop. "I'll see you later."

She told Nicola it was nice seeing her again and waved goodbye. I watched until she was out the door before I turned to my friend with a big smile on my face. She shook her head. "Sorry. I'm still a little star-struck. Where did Dylan and Remy come from? God, they're both hot." She fanned herself with her hand.

I had to agree with her. They were hot. Even in SoCal which had a higher than average number of beautiful people, the St. Clair twins stood out from the crowd.

If Dylan came to my party, I was screwed.

8

DYLAN

"Holy shit. You bought a fucking hotel." Cruz tossed a Nerf basketball into the hoop attached to my glass wall. "And look at that, ladies and gentlemen, he's smiling."

I was over the fucking moon. It had ended up being easier than I thought. The deal had gone off without a hitch, I'd gotten The Surf Lodge for a fair price, and I'd spent most of today on the phone, hiring service providers. A construction crew for the refurbishment, and an interior design firm for the remodel.

Cruz tossed me the ball and I took the shot one-handed. It banked off the backboard and swished through the net. He retrieved the ball and bounced it off the glass wall opposite him. Toss. Catch. Toss. Catch. Yeah, we were busy running a company. The blinds weren't drawn, and I caught Melanie watching us. She averted her head but not before I noticed the blush on her cheeks. I pressed the remote and the machine made a soft whirring sound, the blinds lowering so slowly it was painful to watch. The blinds were sandwiched between two sheets of glass. Saved the cleaning crew from having to dust them. Saved me from feeling like I was sitting in a fishbowl.

"How did we get here? Remember when we lived on Ramen and cheap beer and struggled to pay the rent?" Cruz asked. "And now you own a fucking hotel."

It wasn't big or grand, but it was still 'a fucking hotel' and I was feeling pretty damn good about that.

I leaned back in my leather swivel chair and folded my hands behind my head, watching the ocean from my office window. The hazy gray sky met the sea and you couldn't tell where one left off and the other began. I loved this view. Loved the ocean and the beach, especially on winter days when it was quiet and uncrowded.

"It's a risk though," Cruz said, ever the voice of reason. "Tying up your assets like that."

I wasn't tying up all my assets. That would be financial suicide. But every investment was a risk. "We wouldn't be sitting here if we'd played it safe."

"True." He scrubbed his hand over his dark buzz cut and squinted at the view behind me, his face troubled. Whenever he got that look on his face, it was usually family-related.

"How's Frankie?"

Cruz shook his head. He'd practically raised his little sister and had taken on adult responsibilities long before he should have had to.

"Got a new boyfriend. Guy's a tool. I told him if he messes with her, I'll beat the shit out of him." Cruz chuckled. "He was practically pissing his pants. Haven't seen him around since. Frankie hasn't talked to me in a week. Said I'm ruining her life. Fucking teenage girls and their drama. I keep getting doors slammed in my face."

I chuckled under my breath, picturing the scene over at Cruz's house. Frankie and Cruz were always fighting about something. After we graduated college, Cruz got a place in Chula Vista and moved Frankie in with him. She hadn't wanted to change schools and her friends were all there so Cruz made that sacrifice even though he would have preferred to move away.

"Once she graduates, I'm buying a place in Encinitas."

"Hang in there. It's only five more months."

"A life sentence, more like it. I was trying to talk to Frankie about her future, you know. She hasn't given it a thought. Doesn't want to go to college. Doesn't want to get a job. Thinks she can just sit around on her ass and the money will magically roll in."

"Cut off her allowance. If she doesn't have money, she'll have to figure it out."

Cruz leveled me with a look. "Just like you did with Rae, you mean?"

I had no defense for that, so I remained silent. I was still my mother's keeper. Always would be. "I'll give Frankie a job at The Surf Lodge this summer."

"You'd put up with that attitude? Somehow, I can't see that working out."

"I'm not going to manage it. I'll leave that up to the staff."

"Look at you. You've got fucking staff now. You planning to get a butler too?"

I snorted as my landline rang. It was my direct line and the caller ID told me it was Simon Woods. I looked over at Cruz who raised his brows and remained seated, not wanting to miss this. I answered the call on speakerphone and cut right through the pleasantries. "Did you need something?"

"How did you get Whitaker to sell you The Surf Lodge?"

"Turns out he'd rather sell it to a punk like me than let it fall into the wrong hands."

"I own that entire strip of beachfront."

Except The Surf Lodge. "Your point?"

"My point is that I could buy and sell you ten times over, you little shit. I still hold the power and you'd be smart to remember that. I've heard about your plans for it. The last

thing this town needs is to attract more beach bums and degen-
erates. If you think you've won this battle, you'll be sorely
disappointed."

"I didn't realize we were at war. Appreciate the heads up. I'll
be sure to stock up on ammunition. Nice chat." I cut the call
and looked over at Cruz.

"Is that why you bought The Surf Lodge? To piss him off?"

"No. But it's an added bonus."

Cruz's eyes narrowed. "What exactly are your plans for it?"

"I'm turning it into a surf hostel. I'm refurbishing, not bulldozing which was what Woods wanted to do. He was going to
build a boutique hotel."

"That would turn a higher profit. It's the savvier business
decision," he said, playing devil's advocate.

"It's not all about money. This is a surfing community. It's
one of the best parts about this town and that property is
within walking or cycling distance of fourteen breaks. One of
which is world-class. This town doesn't need another overpriced boutique hotel or fancy shop that sells their shit at ten
times what it's worth."

He held up his hands. "You don't have to sell it to me. You
know how I feel about this snooty town. But you have an
enemy now and he won't make things easy." He was right about
that. Simon Woods had never made anything easy on me, had
hated me from day one, and even now that Sienna and I weren't
together he'd still find reasons to hate me. Now, whether I liked
it or not, I'd started a turf war. Which was ridiculous. The Surf
Lodge was nothing to Simon Woods. A mere drop in the ocean
compared to all the property he owned in this town.

We were interrupted by a knock on the door. Three knocks,
to be precise. Melanie poked her head in. "There's a delivery for
you. Six boxes. Where do you want them?"

I stood up from my desk. "I'll take care of it."

Speaking of mistakes, I might have gone overboard on Starlet's birthday present. But if her dickhead father was too much of a pompous ass to recognize how talented she was, I felt it was almost my duty to help her out. Yeah, that was me. Mr. Do-Good. It had absolutely nothing to do with wanting to get into her pants.

Jesus. I really was an asshole.

9

SCARLETT

As far as winter beach parties went, this one was awesome. Bonfires blazed up and down the beach, protected from the wind by the bluffs. The red-orange flames danced across the dark sky and heated my skin. I felt all warm and fuzzy inside, the edges all blurred. Our mellow, chilled-out party of a dozen friends had grown bigger as word spread and friends of friends, half of whom I'd never met, turned up with six-packs and good vibes.

Nic and I were lost in the music blasting from portable speakers, our hair flying around us, bodies gyrating to the beat, arms akimbo.

"I love you," Nic shouted over the music and the sound of the waves crashing against the shore.

"I love you too." We launched ourselves into each other's arms and hugged each other tight, holding on to keep our balance.

"Woo hoo," I shouted.

We punched the sky and leaped into the air, body slamming into each other.

"Oh shit, that hurt."

We doubled over and laughed like loons before we recovered and went back to dancing like nobody was watching. We were twenty-one, young and free, buzzed on tequila shots and beer. It didn't get much better than this.

Ollie's laughter reached my ears and it put a smile on my face. He was sitting in a circle of friends farther down the beach, his arm slung around a blonde's shoulders, a beer in his hand. I felt no jealousy, I only wanted him to be happy. Beck, the lead singer, had a girl in his lap and his arm around another one. And Gavin, their bass player, was gesticulating with his hands, his face animated, most likely telling one of his outrageous stories that had the group howling with laughter.

Life was good, Ollie and I were finding our way back to normal, and tonight I didn't have a care in the world.

Nic's eyes widened then her lips curved into a mischievous grin. I didn't need to turn around to confirm who she was looking at. I swear, the air around me shifted and the particles rearranged themselves. I knew it was him, and only a moment later he made his presence known. Arms wrapped around me from behind, and he pulled my body flush against his as if we'd done this song and dance a million times and it was perfectly natural for him to greet me this way. His heat enveloped me, and I melted into him, my hips swaying to the beat of Parra For Cuva's "Wicked Games." The perfect song for the way I felt about him. Had *always* felt about him.

His lips found the sensitive spot on my neck—brushing, not kissing—and my heart galloped, my breath seized in my lungs. "Happy Birthday, Starlet."

I leaned my head against his shoulder and decided I could happily stay here forever. "I didn't think you'd come."

"Were you hoping I did?"

"Yes." I closed my eyes, realizing I'd just admitted something I probably shouldn't have, but I made no attempt to take it back.

His hands skimmed down my arms, gently, slowly, his touch igniting every cell of my body. I was surprised I didn't burst into flames and set the world on fire. He clasped my hands in his much larger, calloused ones, rough against my softer skin and looped my arms around the back of his neck. Our bodies moved in sync, slow and sensuous, his hands gripping the curves of my hips.

The flames from the fire painted my closed lids red as we swayed to the beat and I shouldn't have been surprised that he was a good dancer. Dancing was like sex, right? You either had rhythm or you didn't. I just went with it. I didn't want to break the spell we were under. Didn't want to think about the million reasons why this was so wrong. Not tonight when I wanted to lose myself in the moment.

"Are you drunk?" he asked, voice low and husky in my ear, raising the small hairs on the back of my neck. God, he was delicious. I wanted to lick every inch of his skin and see if it tasted like it smelled.

"I'm in that happy, hazy place when you're buzzed, and you know that if you have another drink it'll tip you over the edge. So I'll just stay here for a while."

"It's a good place to be."

"I like it here."

"I like you right here too."

But his actions belied his words. He spun me around, so I was facing him. He'd done it on purpose, forcing me to reconcile this heady, intoxicating feeling with the reality of who he was and the magnitude of what this could mean if we continued down this road.

His hooded gaze roamed my face and settled on my mouth where it often landed. My lips parted, a breath escaping them, and

I had a wild urge to throw myself into his arms and kiss him dizzy. He read it on my face and saved me the trouble of making the first move. Wrapping his hand around the back of my neck, he yanked me toward him, and my body slammed against his hard chest.

I'd always thought of Dylan as long and lean and cut, but this close, his body felt harder, bigger, more muscular. Just *more*. His hand fisted my hair and he tugged, forcing my chin up and my eyes to his. I bet he was rough in bed. Merciless. My core clenched, and I squeezed my thighs together, the ache between my legs throbbing, almost painful. I was so wet for him and he hadn't even kissed me yet.

This was dangerous. We were venturing into forbidden territory and even as a voice inside my head screamed no, my body said, *Yes, yes, yes.*

Oh God, I wanted him.

"Tell me no, Starlet. Tell me you don't want this, and I'll leave."

And I knew he would. He would walk away without looking back, and I'd never hear from him again. He was giving me the choice. He wanted me, I knew that. But I wasn't going to fool myself. This—whatever we were—had nothing to do with romance. Dylan St. Clair was about as emotionally available as a rock cliff. The one I was about to throw myself off, praying there would be a safety net to catch me. There wouldn't be. I already knew that too.

I *should* say no, such a simple word, but when I opened my mouth to speak, no words came out. Nada. Crickets. I licked my lips because they were dry, and God help me I wanted him to kiss me even though the voice in my head warned me this was wrong.

"Last chance," he warned as his hand glided through my hair and held the back of my head, guiding it to where he wanted it. I had a feeling that he'd never asked any girl for permission before. Decision made, I rose on my toes and wrapped my arms around his neck.

Dipping his head, he slanted his mouth over mine, and he patiently traced my lips with his. Softly. Slowly. Like the world wasn't on fire and there was no sense of urgency.

Desperate for more, I grew impatient and crushed my lips against his. They remained stubbornly sealed. I growled. Yes, I actually growled. Like a wild animal. What was wrong with me? He laughed, his chest rumbling against mine, and kissed the corner of my lips. My jaw. My neck, just below my ear before he returned to my mouth and kissed me so hard, so suddenly, it stole my breath. His tongue parted my lips and I let him in. He tasted like something dark and forbidden. Like every fantasy I'd ever had.

He changed the pace and kissed me slow and dirty. My hands fisted the thick cotton of his hoodie. I had zero chill. Zero self-restraint. Shivers raced up and down my spine and heat pooled in my belly as his tongue stroked the roof of my mouth. I moaned in pleasure, grinding against his erection, seeking the friction. I was two seconds away from climbing him like a tree and cinching my legs around his waist.

"Careful, Starlet," he growled. His fingers bit hard into my soft flesh. *A warning.* "Keep doing that, you'll be getting more than a kiss."

"Will you punish me?" My voice sounded breathy. After all, he'd stolen the air from my lungs.

"Mmm hmm." I felt him smile against my lips before he sunk his teeth into my bottom lip and then he sucked on it to ease the sting. I bet he gave good pain. I wanted it. All of it. All of him. My lips were kiss-bruised, raw and swollen and it still wasn't enough. I wanted more.

The sound of slow clapping jolted me back to reality. I was on a beach, surrounded by people, and I was kissing my sister's ex-boyfriend as if we were alone in the dark. Dylan's muscles tensed, and he pulled back, his arm around my waist a steel band locking me in place.

I looked over my shoulder.

"So much for not getting involved with him," Ollie said bitterly.

Shame heated my already flushed cheeks. I had no defense. I couldn't even say it was *just* a kiss. Not when it had felt like so much more. Dylan and I had crossed a line, and I'd done nothing to stop it. I turned around to face Ollie.

"Isn't this the guy who cheated on you?" Dylan asked.

Oh my God. I winced as the hurt flashed across Ollie's face. *Not cool, Dylan.* Even worse that I'd been disloyal to Ollie by sharing that information.

"You told him about that?" Ollie shook his head, disappointed in me.

I hung my head. "I'm sorry."

"Not like it isn't true." Nic rallied to my defense, firmly placing her in my camp. Ollie glared at her. She just shrugged and moved to my side, a loyal ally. I'd been stupid to think we could all go back to the way things used to be. The aftermath of my relationship with Ollie had divided our friend group. Gavin and Beck, of course, had chosen Ollie, and Nic had chosen me. Lines had been drawn, and even though we all *acted* friendly toward each other, it wasn't the same as it used to be, and it never would be.

"I didn't mean to say anything. It just slipped out."

Ollie snorted with disgust. Shoulders rigid, he turned and strode away. Torn between wanting to make this right and just letting him go lick his wounds in private, I hesitated a moment before I called out to him. "Ollie, wait."

As if he hadn't heard me, he kept right on walking.

Dylan wrapped his hand around my arm to hold me back. "Let him go."

"He's acting like a dick," Nic chimed in.

"I can't just let him go. I hurt him. I need to talk to him."

Dylan released me and crossed his arms over his chest, clearly not happy with my decision. I didn't look at his face. Didn't want to see what he was thinking. Instead, I chased after Ollie.

When I caught up to him, I grabbed his arm to stop him and moved so I was standing directly in front of him. He rubbed his jaw, his eyes narrowed on something in the distance. "I never stood a chance, did I, Scarlett? It was always him."

"What happened between us had nothing to do with Dylan. You know that."

He laughed harshly. "Sure it didn't. Why him? Of all the guys you could have gone for, why did it have to be him?"

Ollie made it sound like he and Dylan were mortal enemies, and I'd chosen the wrong side. When in fact, they didn't even know each other. My eyes sought out Dylan. He was too far away to hear us, and he was talking to Nic, but he was watching me.

I returned my gaze to Ollie and considered his question. *Why him?* I'd asked myself the same thing so many times. It wasn't something I could put into words. And even if I could, it wasn't something I wanted to share with Ollie. "I don't know."

"I can deal with us not being together. I get it. I do. We're better off as friends. I wouldn't even have a problem with you hooking up with someone else. I'd get over it. I wouldn't like it, but I'd be good with it because I want you to be happy. But I can tell you right now, he won't make you happy. He's fucked up, Smalls."

"You don't even know him. He's not the same boy he was at seventeen." But even if he was, it wouldn't matter to me. I had crushed hard on that seventeen-year-old boy and it seemed that time hadn't changed that.

"*Always* defending him." He shook his head and exhaled

loudly. "Just go back to him. But when he fucks you over, when everything falls apart, because it will... don't come crying to me."

His words, and the venom in them, stunned me into silence. Where was the boy who had once promised me that nothing, and nobody, would ever get in the way of our friendship? Our bond had been forged fourteen years ago when he taught me how to ride a bike because my parents were always too 'busy' and my sister told me to get lost and stop pestering her. He was there for me when Sienna used to kick me out of her room and slam the door in my face. When my father heaped praise on my sister and treated me like nothing I ever did was good enough.

And I was there for him when his dad stood him up on the weekends he was supposed to spend with him. I was the one who begged my dad to buy Ollie a drum kit for Christmas. It was all he had ever talked about. All he had ever wanted. But his mom couldn't afford it. My dad said no because he was a stingy bastard. So, I sold my brand-new bike, *my* Christmas present to buy Ollie a drum kit and I didn't care that I got grounded and lectured. It made Ollie happy, and that was all that mattered to me.

"Wow. Okay. Thanks for being a friend. Good to know you have my back."

"Just returning the favor."

"I always defended you, too," I whispered. But he didn't hear my words. He was already gone.

Tears coursed down my cheeks as I stood on the beach and watched him walk away. I wrapped my arms around myself, suddenly feeling the cold. He grabbed the blonde and pulled her into a kiss as if he wanted to show me how it felt to have it shoved in my face. It hurt, but not because he was kissing someone else.

Ollie and I weren't kids anymore. We weren't even on the same team.

Suddenly this party wasn't so fun.

I turned at the sound of Dylan's voice. His eyes searched my glossy ones and he brushed away the tears with his thumbs and tucked my wavy, windblown hair behind my ears, his touch so gentle, so unbearably soft and sweet that it made my chest ache. Dylan could be kind. But I also knew he could be cruel. Nobody was all good or all bad. Not Dylan. Not me. Not Ollie.

He wrapped me in his arms and it took me a few seconds to recover from my surprise and wrap my arms around his waist. I pressed my cheek against his beating heart and was reminded of the eleven-year-old girl who used to squeeze fresh lemons and limes and carry the ice-cold drinks to him when he was cleaning our pool. I didn't know why I was thinking about that now, on a starry beach on a winter night ten years later. Maybe because of Ollie's question. Why had I always seen something in Dylan that others didn't? Why had I always believed in him? I couldn't answer those questions. Half the time, he hadn't even been nice to me. He'd never once said please or thank you. And yet, I knew deep down he cared.

"You good?" he asked, releasing me to assess the damage.

I didn't know what I was. "I just want to go home."

"I'll give you a ride." I nodded and trudged across the sand, weary and defeated, while he strode ahead and left me trailing behind. As I passed Ollie, I looked over at him. He was still making out with the blonde, but his eyes were on me. I'd hurt him, and now he wanted to return the favor.

Nic joined me and we trailed Dylan to his car. "I've got you, babe. We'll go home and eat ice cream and watch 80s movies." She wrapped her arm around my shoulders and squeezed. I gave her a grateful smile as she sang the chorus of "Don't You (Forget About Me)", her fist raised like Judd Nelson from *The Breakfast Club*.

"Sounds perfect."

The ride to our apartment was silent. My happy bubble had

burst, the mood ruined by that kiss and the aftermath. I expected Dylan to just drop us off, but he cut the engine, got out of the car and opened the hatch. "Got something for you."

Nic and I exchanged a curious glance and met Dylan at the back of his G-Wagen. I stared at the brown boxes, trying to make sense of it. "What is all this?"

"Your birthday present." He carved a hand through his hair and looked like he regretted this grand gesture, but knew he was screwed. It was too late to take it back now.

"My birthday present?" I repeated. *He bought me a birthday present?*

All three of us carried the boxes upstairs to our second-floor apartment and Dylan had to go back for a second trip. The boxes were big, and heavy and crowded our living room. Our two-bedroom apartment was small, but still, this seemed excessive. I hadn't expected anything from him, and I'd even convinced myself that he wouldn't come to my party, much less come bearing gifts. Nic looked like she was bursting at the seams, desperate to rip into the boxes and see what was inside.

Dylan dropped the last two boxes to the floor and pushed them against the wall then straightened up and crooked his finger at me as he headed for the front door. Like I was his beck and call girl. Like a fool, I followed him outside and leaned against the brown stucco. He caged me in his arms, a hand planted on either side of my head, and I watched him from underneath my lashes. Those turbulent blue-grays were the only thing that gave away his emotions. Dylan had this intensity about him, like he was a ticking bomb only seconds away from detonating and he had to use all his restraint to keep it contained.

It should scare me, but it didn't.

"Are you in love with Shaggy Doo?"

"*Shaggy Doo?* His name is Ollie. And no, I'm not. But he's

my friend and I care about him," I admitted. "I hate it that I hurt him."

His fingers curved under my chin and he brushed his thumb over my jaw. "That's you, isn't it, Starlet? Why are you so good?" As if he truly believed I was good, even though I knew I wasn't the good girl he seemed to think I was. "You hate to hurt anyone, don't you?"

"And yet I do it all the time." I averted my gaze. I wanted some answers. "Why did you kiss me, Dylan?"

"Why did you let me kiss you?"

Perhaps that was the better question. "Because... I wasn't thinking straight." I swallowed as he wrapped a lock of my hair around his fingers and gently tugged on it. "What game are you playing?"

"I don't play games. I'm not a boy," he scoffed. He wanted to make it clear that he was nothing like Ollie. They didn't even know each other but the animosity was still there.

"Then what is this? What about Sienna?"

He lifted one shoulder in a shrug. "What about her? We've been over for a long time."

"It's still wrong."

"Then why does it feel so fucking right?"

I had no answer for that because it did feel right. Not right, exactly. It felt good though. But lust always felt good in the moment, didn't it?

"You belonged to her first."

"I've never belonged to anyone."

And he probably never would. "But you can't deny that you once loved her."

I wasn't expecting a response. Dylan had a habit of not answering questions he didn't like. So it surprised me when he did answer, and so honestly.

"There was love for a while. And other things. Mostly other things. Sienna and I were fundamentally wrong for each other in every way. We liked the idea of each other but I'm not sure we actually liked each other that much. By the time it ended, there was nothing good left to hang onto."

I searched his face to see if that made him sad, if she had left him heartbroken. But his expression was neutral, and I wasn't getting any sad vibes off him.

I wanted to ask him if he liked me. If he thought we were right for each other. But that would be pushing it. We barely knew each other, although in some ways I felt like I knew him and understood him better than he could ever know. Our backgrounds were vastly different. I grew up privileged, wanting for nothing. But I knew how it felt to be told you weren't good enough. And I knew how it felt to be betrayed by Sienna.

My sister was not a bad person, but she was weak, and she was selfish, and I had known from a young age that she would always choose herself, even if it meant throwing someone else under the bus.

Dylan dropped his forehead to mine, his soft breaths mingling with mine, and his fingers trailed down my arm. My eyes closed, and I flattened my palms against the rough wall behind me to stop myself from fisting my hands in his shirt to steady myself.

He made my knees weak. He made me tongue-tied and confused. He made me want things I shouldn't.

"I picked the wrong sister."

His voice was low. Quiet. But I heard the words as if he'd shouted them over the loud beating of my heart that thrashed against the walls of my chest. He wasn't allowed to say things like that. How dare he?

I picked the wrong sister.

There was nothing *right* about this. Except for the way he made me feel. But even that was riddled with contradictions. I felt so alive. So desperate. Anxious. Aroused. Scared. Excited. Restless.

And so, so screwed.

I was still trying to get a grip on my emotions, to formulate a response, when he pushed away from the wall and left me standing there alone. Without another word, not even a good-bye, he was gone. Moments later, my feet still glued to the same spot, I watched his taillights disappear into the darkness.

It felt like I'd just gotten off a roller coaster. Yet I had a feeling that the ride had only just begun.

10

DYLAN

On Sunday evening, after I put in a few hours at the gym
to compensate for the weed and the whiskey the night
before—it's all about balance—I went over to Shane and
Remy's coral-pink beach house, and nearly tripped over a box,
sitting right inside the front door.

"Rem," I called, and heard her footsteps coming down the
stairs.

"Hey Dyl." Remy smiled at me then frowned at the box. "I
forgot about that. I think it's the car seat. So much stuff got
delivered." She bent down, wrapped her arms around the box
and tried to lift it. I wrestled it out of her hands and glared
at her.

"You can't be carrying shit. Step away from the box."

She laughed and followed me into the living room. Their
house was cool, decorated in blues and grays with an open, airy
feeling to it. Remy's framed photography lined the walls—her
ocean shots, Shane surfing, one of me swimming the fly in my
pool but thankfully you couldn't see my face. I hated having my
picture taken. Remy always joked that she was stealing a piece

of my soul and that was how it felt. Like my privacy was being violated. I couldn't begin to imagine how she could have posed for the camera in her modeling years. I would have had to be drunk and stoned the entire time.

I shoved the car seat box against the living room wall next to the other boxes of baby furniture that needed to be put together and turned to look at her.

I had an unrealistic fear that something would go wrong. Not that I'd ever share my fears with Remy or Shane. They'd been through so much shit to get to this place, I didn't want my dark thoughts to dim their happiness. I'd had weird premonitions, bad dreams that had woken me in a cold sweat in the middle of the night. I used to get these premonitions a lot when I was a kid, and they'd usually been proven reliable.

"How are you feeling?"

"Like a double wide."

I snorted. Remy had always been rail-thin, too skinny during her modeling days, and from the back, you'd never know she was eight months pregnant. It looked like she had a basketball tucked under her tank top while the rest of her was all long-limbed, toned and thin.

My twin sister and I looked a lot alike. She was the female version of me with the same skin tone, dark hair, and high cheekbones. We looked like our mother but must have inherited our light eyes from our sperm donor, whoever the hell he was.

"You need me to put that crib together?"

"Shane will be home soon. You can help him." She went to the bottom of the stairs and called up, raising her voice to be heard over the music coming from above. "Hey Scarlett. Call me if you need my help."

"It's cool. I've got this," came her response.

I hadn't seen Scarlett since Thursday night. If she had been any other girl, I wouldn't have given that kiss a second thought.

If she had been any other girl, I would have fucked her and left. Or not. When it came to women, I was mostly ambivalent. Take it or it leave it. I'd never had to work hard to get a girl into my bed. *Ever.* But Scarlett wasn't just a random fuck. Which was part of the problem. I wasn't lying when I told her I had always cared about her. And I wasn't lying when I told her I'd picked the wrong sister. But I wasn't sure what had possessed me to be so honest.

"What's Scarlett doing here?" I asked Remy as I followed her into the kitchen.

"Painting the baby's room. Wait until you see it. It's so cool. I'm so glad you talked us into hiring her."

"You never mentioned it to her, did you?" Bad enough I'd bought her enough supplies to open a whole chain of shops, I didn't want her to know that I had a hand in getting her a job as well.

"Don't worry. Your secret's safe. God forbid anyone would think you actually cared." She rolled her eyes. "She's great, though. I never really knew her until she started working for us. Kind of weird, right? Sienna never let her hang out with us when we were in high school."

"She was just a kid." Sienna and Scarlett had never been that close. Their six-year age gap had always seemed so much wider when we were younger but now it seemed insignificant. As I was all too aware, Scarlett was twenty-one now, and no longer a kid.

"I guess." Remy handed me a bottle of water from the refrigerator and took one for herself. I swapped my water for a beer, almost certain that I was the only one who drank beer in this house, and my sister kept the fridge stocked especially for my visits.

"Did you know Scarlett? I mean, did you ever hang out with her when you were in college?"

"She used to text me and shit. I saw her around." I took a

long pull of my beer, not really wanting to get into the details of my history with Scarlett.

"You used to text?" Remy raised her dark brows, waiting for more.

"What did you want to talk about?" I asked, steering the conversation away from me and back to her.

She wrung her hands and chewed on her bottom lip, a clear sign that she was nervous about something.

"What's wrong?" I tried to keep the alarm out of my voice as my gaze dipped to the bump under her tank top. "Is the baby okay?"

"Yeah, it's nothing like that. The baby is fine."

My sister's gray cat, Pearl, weaved in and out of my legs, meowing to get my attention. I scooped her up and held her in my arm like a football, worry gnawing at my gut as I parked my hip against the kitchen counter and absently stroked Pearl's soft fur.

Remy gave me a soft smile. Before I could stop her, she snapped photos of me holding her cat. Her camera was always within easy reach and over the years, she'd taken far too many photos of me, knowing damn well I hated it.

I held up my hand as she zoomed in with her camera to get close-ups. "Stop with the fucking photos already."

Laughing, she set her camera on the butcher block island and pulled up a stool. "Wait until you're holding a baby. I'll take millions of photos. Get used to it, Uncle Dylan."

Uncle Dylan. Holy shit.

I set the cat down on the distressed wood floor and shooed her away. I didn't even like cats but that damn cat always came to me anyway. Crossing my arms over my chest, I jerked my chin at Remy, prompting her to tell me what was wrong.

"Do you know where Mom is?"

"Why?" I hedged, reaching for my beer.

"I've given this a lot of thought and I just... I don't want her to be part of our baby's life." Remy rearranged the fruit and avocados in a glazed blue bowl as she talked, needing to keep her hands busy even though it was a useless endeavor. "She never protected us or took care of us and I don't trust her. She left us at a truck stop, Dylan. What kind of mother does that?"

The bad kind of mother. That was the day Remy and I made our blood oath. We promised never to leave the other behind. No matter what, we'd always be there for each other. We were six years old, hiding out behind the dumpsters at a truck stop, already street smart enough to know that we couldn't risk anyone finding out we'd been left behind. It wasn't the first time it had happened and certainly wouldn't be the last, but that day stood out in our memories.

Remy had been scared shitless that I would bleed to death. Being me, I'd slashed my wrist with a shard of glass from a broken bottle to make our blood oath. Always the smarter one, and not as self-destructive, Remy had pricked her thumb to achieve the same goal.

"Don't worry about Mom. She won't bother you." That was a promise I could keep. Rae St. Clair knew where her bread was buttered, and part of our agreement was that she needed to stay away from Remy. She'd caused Remy enough trouble, flirting with Tristan Hart when she'd paid a rare visit to our high school. Because of that, Tristan Hart had treated Remy like a whore. Then she'd made a move on Shane, not giving a shit that her daughter was in love with him. A fucking clusterfuck, just like everything was when our mother got involved.

"How much did you pay her?" Remy asked, leveling me with a look.

Fifty grand. But that was over a year ago, and I suspected she'd burned through that money by now and would be calling for more any day soon. I didn't give a shit about the money though. If it kept her out of Remy's hair, I'd pay our mother whatever she asked. I still felt responsible for her, although God knows why. She'd been a shitty excuse for a mother. But sometimes she called me just to talk. And for reasons I couldn't explain and didn't care to analyze, I always answered her calls. I still paid her rent and her health insurance every month and I still worried about her even though she'd never done the same for us.

"Don't worry about it," I repeated.

"Does that make me a horrible person? That I don't even want her to meet her own grandchild?" She brushed away a tear. I'd noticed that pregnancy had made her more emotional.

"You have nothing to feel guilty about and you don't have to justify this to me or anyone else. I was there. I lived through it with you."

We had a shitty childhood. You couldn't even call it a childhood. I don't remember ever being treated like a child. We moved from place to place on our mother's whim, always with the promise that the next town would be better. Spoiler alert: A change of scenery had never changed a damn thing. She was still a drunk, still spread her legs for money, and we were the baggage she carted along until her load got too heavy and she left us curbside.

"I know," she said softly, brushing away another tear.

I hated seeing Remy cry. She'd always been so tough, more out of necessity than anything else so this felt... I don't know, strange. It gave me a tight feeling in my chest. I finished my beer and helped myself to another one, flipping the lid into the swing bin under the sink. My mother... my shitty childhood... the weight of my crushing guilt... they drove me to drink.

"I think... if it hadn't been for you, I wouldn't have survived," Remy told me. "You picked me up when I didn't want to go on anymore. You fought for me. You were my strength and you were always there. You had my back and you kicked me in the ass when I needed it."

I didn't deserve that kind of credit. I wasn't there for her when she needed me most. She lost Shane, and he lost everything—his reputation, his pro surfing career, the time he could have spent with his father who was dying of a brain tumor. Every-fucking-thing. All because I wasn't there for Remy like I'd promised. If I had taken care of Tristan Hart back in high school when he was bullying Remy, Shane never would have gone to prison for manslaughter, and Remy wouldn't have had to spend seven years being heartbroken. But like so many other things in my life, there wasn't a damn thing I could do about it now.

Bowing my head, I rubbed the back of my neck, so she couldn't see my face. I didn't want to talk about any of this.

"It wasn't your fault," Remy said. When we were kids, we had twin telepathy. Sometimes, like now, we still had it. She knew exactly what I was thinking about.

"What's done is done." I'd always carry that guilt, and there was nothing Remy could say to make it go away, but she didn't need to be saddled with my mistakes and regrets. Especially not when she was expecting a baby and she and Shane had found their way back to each other.

"You saved me from Russell."

Another thing I didn't want to talk about. Another shitty memory to add to the collection. Tripping down memory lane was not my idea of a good time. I'd become a pro at shoving all those memories deep down inside and not shedding any light on them and that's how I wanted them to stay. Buried. "Like I said, don't worry about Mom. I don't tell her shit about your life and she knows not to contact you."

"Love you."

"Ditto," I said gruffly as I heard the front door open.

Seconds later, Shane joined us in the kitchen. I tipped my beer at him in greeting before I took a long pull. My words were in short supply, and he was mostly used to it by now.

"Hello lover." Remy smiled at Shane like he put the moon and stars in the sky. Their love was like nothing I'd ever seen or experienced before. I doubted that anyone would ever love me the way they loved each other. But it made me happy that Remy had found a man who deserved her.

"Hello trouble." Shane wrapped his arms around her from behind and kissed the side of her neck then pinned his gaze on me. "When were you planning to tell us that you bought a hotel?"

"What?" Remy shouted. "Oh my god, you never tell me anything. You bought a hotel? What the hell, Dylan?"

I shrugged. "Are we putting that baby furniture together or what?" I was halfway out the door when Remy grabbed my arm and hauled me back.

"Pretty quick reflexes for a double-wide."

She wasn't amused. When I turned to face them, I was met with matching looks of accusation. Shane and Remy looked nothing alike. He had dirty blond hair and the quintessential surfer dude look. She was dark-haired and exotic-looking. But they were so in sync that even their facial expressions had become mirror images. *Synchronicity.* "It's not public knowledge yet. Just keep it to yourselves for now."

"Since I didn't even know about it, that shouldn't be hard," Remy fumed. She planted her hands on her hips. "Which hotel?"

"The Surf Lodge."

Remy's jaw dropped, and she tipped her head back to look up at Shane who was standing behind her, his hand splayed across her pregnant belly. "Isn't that where your parents were married?"

"Yeah, it is." He huffed out a laugh. "How did you get Whitaker to sell it to you?"

"No idea. I was just my charming self."

That made Shane laugh. Har har har. A little louder than necessary. "He sold it to me when I told him I was close with Jimmy," I admitted. "And when I told him I wanted to turn it into a surf hostel instead of bulldozing it and building an expensive boutique hotel, he was all in."

"Well, shit. You'd do that?" Shane looked amazed that I'd even consider it.

I shrugged. "I thought you might want to have some input. Since you stayed in a lot of surf hostels. I was thinking of doing team rooms. Get the Firefly Surfboards name out there."

Shane was silent a beat, processing the information. "Why didn't you tell us about this? Why did I have to find out from Cal Whitaker?"

I rubbed the back of my neck, not sure what to say, other than I would have told him eventually.

Shane shook his head. "You're a pain in the ass. Whether you like it or not, we're family. When are you going to start trusting me?"

I trusted him as much as I trusted Remy which was one hundred percent, but I'd spent the better part of my life not confiding in anyone. Shit like that didn't change overnight.

"I trust you."

"You have a funny way of showing it."

"It's nothing personal," Remy said. "He doesn't tell anyone anything."

"My dad always wanted to buy The Surf Lodge," Shane said.

I knew that.

"I told him when I won the world championship, we'd buy it."

Knew that too. Jimmy had told me that when Shane was in

prison. And *that* was why I'd bought the hotel. If I didn't already know that Shane would throw it back in my face and refuse to accept, I'd give him an equal share. But he'd never accept it, would look at it as charity, just as I would so I didn't even broach the subject.

"Shane," Remy said softly, her lower lip trembling, and I was worried she might burst into tears. "You could have been the world champion. You *should* have been."

I drained my beer and turned my back to them, tossing my empty bottle in the trash.

"Hey. Firefly. None of that. I'm happy. I have more than I could ever possibly have dreamed of." He held her gaze until she believed that he was telling the truth, and I suspected that he'd had to reassure her on numerous occasions but would continue doing so until he took his last breath if necessary. Satisfied that she believed him, his gaze moved from Remy to me. "My dad would be so fucking proud of you."

I hoped so. I'd done a lot of bad shit in my life, but Jimmy had never judged me. He'd supported me and made me dream bigger. Made me believe that I could be something better than a thug or a drug dealer. While Shane had been in prison and Remy had taken off to pursue her modeling career, Jimmy and I had gotten close. He was one of the best men I'd ever known. Shane had been blessed with two good parents and cursed when he lost them both. His mom had been killed by a hit and run driver when he was just a kid. Then his dad had died of a brain tumor a little over a year ago.

Life was so fucking unfair.

I left Remy and Shane in the kitchen and followed the music up the stairs to the second floor.

Stopping in the doorway of the baby's room, I leaned my

shoulder against the doorframe and watched Scarlett shaking her ass to "Truth Hurts" by Lizzo. I smothered a laugh as she sang along giving it a whole lot of attitude and gestures. She was going for it, oblivious to the fact that I was watching. Her back was to me, the paintbrush in her hand forgotten as she shimmied low, her ass nearly touching the floor before she shimmied back up, never losing her balance. It was like a soft porn show.

I was hard as stone. *Again.*

Which was fucking inconvenient, all things considered.

A minute or two later, Scarlett spun around and let out a yelp, her hand going to her heart. "Oh God, you scared me." I smirked as her gaze drifted down to the erection tenting my gray sweatpants then returned to my face. She blushed. It was cute.

"Nice twerking."

"Glad you enjoyed the show, perv." Her eyes lowered to my crotch again. Let's face it, it was hard to miss and impossible to hide and I was too shameless to care.

"Like what you see?"

"I've seen better."

I gave her a slow, lazy grin and advanced on her until her back was against the wall. "Doubt it."

"How would you know?"

"If Shaggy Doo is anything to go by, your taste is questionable. Let me guess. He has one position in his repertoire. Missionary."

"Stop calling him Shaggy Doo. And there's nothing wrong with missionary." She rolled her eyes. "Why are we talking about sex?"

"Why do you keep ogling my junk?"

Her eyes snapped to mine. "Because it's prodding me in the stomach. Get it away from me."

I laughed and stayed where I was, standing right in front of her, my dick prodding her stomach. She had paint in her blonde hair and a streak of blue on her cheek. That, and the fact that my dick was calling the shots, distracted me from giving more than a quick glance at the ocean scene she was painting. Dolphins? Starfish? Some type of sea creatures. I brushed my thumb over her cheekbone, smearing the paint across her face like war paint. Making it worse, not better. Her lips parted slightly, and her chest heaved. She wanted me as much as I wanted her.

There was no real moral dilemma for me here. I wanted her. Plain and simple. I wanted to fuck her. I wanted to hear the sounds she made when she was coming on my cock. I wanted to hear her scream my name and beg for more. Was she dirty? Did she like it rough? I wanted the answers to all those questions.

We were two consenting adults. My relationship with Sienna was over. We didn't stay friends because we'd never been friends, and our split had been messy and final. I rarely thought about Sienna, and whatever we'd once had felt like another lifetime ago.

Besides which, Scarlett was nothing like Sienna. She was stronger. More honest. Truer to herself. With an innocence that Sienna never had. It was sexy as hell.

Frankly, I was coming up empty on reasons why we *shouldn't* have sex. My mind was running wild with possibility and my throbbing dick was trying to worm its way out of my sweatpants and bury itself inside her sweet little pussy. It was all I could do not to shove her against the wall and fuck her senseless.

Until she dumped a bucket of ice-cold water on my fantasies.

"So, I've been thinking…" She gave me a sweet smile, nothing cunning or manipulative about it. "We should just be friends."

"Friends." Never had the word sounded less appealing than it did coming out of my mouth. That was a hell no from me. I'd never been friend-zoned in my life and sure as hell wasn't about to start now. But I'd let her entertain this little notion of hers until she realized it wasn't possible to be *just friends* with someone you wanted to fuck five ways from Sunday.

11

SCARLETT

When I told Dylan we should just be friends, I had meant it. Although, judging by the look on his face, it was safe to say that he'd never been friend-zoned in his life. I had even tried to return my birthday present, claiming that it was too expensive to keep but he refused to take it back.

It was the best gift he could have ever given me. Boxes of plain white T-shirts, Vans, tank tops and denim jackets, a treasure trove of blank canvases for my design-loving heart.

Nic and I had been speechless when we'd opened the boxes, and since then I'd spent all my free time working on my designs. Whenever I finished a piece, I sent Dylan a photo, surprised that he was interested and even more surprised when he commented.

He hadn't forgotten about his offer to set up a website for me so now here I was getting off the elevator on the twelfth floor and stepping through the glass doors of EZ Solutions on a Wednesday evening. The name of the company and the open-plan set-up went against everything I knew about Dylan.

"May I help you?" a woman with shoulder-length glossy brown hair and trendy horn-rimmed glasses asked me. She was wearing a pencil skirt and heels that showed off her mile-long legs. If I had to guess, she was in her mid to late twenties, attractive in that sexy librarian way. I hated that my first thought was, *Have you slept with Dylan?*

"Oh. Yes." I cleared my throat and wrapped my hand around the strap of my messenger bag. "I'm here to see Dylan. My name is Scarlett."

She checked her iPad for confirmation then nodded. "I'm Melanie, his PA."

Just how much personal assistance did she give him? I needed to stop thinking like that. Just friends, I reminded myself.

I followed Melanie to a corner office that I hadn't noticed, and she knocked on the door three times before opening it and ushering me inside.

I noticed the longing look she gave Dylan before she closed the door, and I'd be lying if I said it didn't thrill me that he seemed oblivious. But since we were just friends, it really shouldn't matter. That's what I had to keep telling myself as I took a seat on a black swivel chair across from his sleek black desk and let my eyes roam over his space. There was nothing personal in his office whatsoever. Just a laptop and a desktop computer. Folders stacked neatly on the corner of his desk. A black pen holder filled with, you guessed it, black pens. Dylan's office was in one of the new blue glass high rise buildings across from the beach and since he had a corner office, the views were amazing.

"Why does everyone else sit in an open plan area but you're locked up in the Bat Cave?"

"Because I'm me."

"So, what exactly do you guys do here? At EZ Solutions?" I choked on my laughter. Anyone who knew Dylan was aware that he was the antithesis of easy.

He leaned back in his chair and clasped his hands behind

his head and I tried really hard not to notice the way his shirt stretched taut against his muscles with that move. "You think that's funny, Miss Woods?"

"Um, yeah. It's hilarious. You're not easy."

"Are you easy, Scarlett?" His tone was playful but there was an undercurrent of something else in it. Yet another thing I desperately tried to ignore.

"Nope. I'm a lot of work. I require special care and attention." Oh my God, I was just feeding into this, wasn't I?

He bit his bottom lip and his eyes darkened as his heated gaze stripped me naked. That was how it felt. Was it suddenly hot in here? I swallowed and looked out the floor to ceiling windows behind him as the sun dipped into the ocean, the sky streaked with tangerine and violet. Nature at its most beautiful.

My gaze returned to him. Nature at its most violently beautiful. He was typing on his laptop, not even looking at me which made it easier to breathe. "So tell me what you do."

He peered at me over the screen then gestured with his hand for me to come and sit next to him, so I wheeled my chair around the desk and sat by his side, my messenger bag in my lap. "We're a software development and consulting firm."

"How many people do you have working for you?"

"Thirty."

"Wow. I'm impressed." I meant that sincerely. He was a self-made millionaire. Far more impressive than my dad who had inherited his wealth. "You did this all on your own."

He shrugged like it was no big deal. But it was huge, and he was being humble. Downplaying his achievements. "I have a partner. Cruz Vega. You met him once. Briefly. We didn't have time to chat." His mouth quirked in amusement.

Dylan was referring to the underground fight. I vaguely remembered meeting his friend who was collecting the money from his bets. "Oh. Right. We were too busy running from the cops. What a crazy night."

He shrugged one shoulder. "It was just another Friday night in my world."

And now look at him. King of the world. He didn't have to fight for money or deal drugs or clean swimming pools anymore. I'd always been curious about his life, what it was like when he was growing up, but whenever I'd asked questions, he had shut me down. I didn't even think Sienna knew much about it. She used to complain that he never told her anything.

"Are you sure you have time to set up this website for me?"

"Wouldn't have offered if I didn't."

I slid my laptop out my messenger bag, typed in my password and set it on the desk in front of us then folded my hands in my lap, all prim and proper. I thought meeting him at his office would make it feel less intimate than if we'd met at my apartment or his house. But we were in our own little bubble, the blinds drawn, the glass soundproofed to cancel out the noise outside these four walls. And with every breath I took, I inhaled his heady scent. So, it wasn't less intimate at all. But luckily, he was focused on the website design, all businesslike and brusque when he asked me questions about my brand, questions I was able to answer readily. My designs were one of the few things I didn't second-guess. Ever since I was a kid, it was the only thing I'd wanted to do with my life.

Dylan listened carefully to every word I said and let me talk without interrupting or injecting his own views, then implemented my ideas in the design. It was ridiculous how easy he made it look to set up a website. It was a side of Dylan I'd never seen before, and it was clear that he knew his stuff and was good at what he did, although I knew that the apps under his name were where his real money came from. Not from designing websites which he said he didn't do anymore. So I guess this was a special favor.

"How did you learn to do all this?" I asked as I scrolled through the site he'd created for me in just a couple short hours. I loved it. It was exactly my aesthetic. A midnight blue, jungle green, and metallic gold color scheme with a dash of dusty pink. Dylan had insisted that I needed photos of myself on the website, so I'd handed over my phone and let him scroll through my photos. I had nothing to hide. He'd chosen one of me on the floor of Firefly Surfboards painting a board. Another of me painting a jungle theme on Ollie's van. In the third one, I was at the beach and the camera had caught me mid-laugh. I was wearing oversized sunglasses, a plain white T-shirt and short white shorts that I'd painted giant palm leaves on.

"My senior year of high school I took classes at the community college. They taught me coding. Finally, a language I understood," he joked.

I laughed. Only the really smart kids in the Gifted Program had taken classes at the community college. I hadn't realized he'd been in that program.

I shut down my laptop and slid it into my bag. "Thanks for doing this for me."

"No problem." He stood and pocketed his keys and cell phone and was already halfway out the door when he said, "Let's go. I'll drive you home."

Like it was an afterthought.

Sighing, I shouldered my bag and took my sweet time walking to the elevators. If he was going to bolt ahead of me, the least he could do was wait for me. He punched the down button twice like that would make the elevator arrive more quickly. My ringing phone cut through our silence and I checked the screen as the elevator pinged and the doors slid open. Ollie. We hadn't spoken since my party.

"Planning to answer that?" Dylan asked as we stepped into the empty elevator. It sounded like an accusation, like I'd personally offend him by answering Ollie's call.

Truthfully, I had no intention of answering. I'd call him back later. It would be too awkward trying to talk to Ollie in front of Dylan so I'm not sure why I said what I did. "We're friends. Why wouldn't I answer?"

My back hit the silver wall and his arms caged me in. "*Just friends? Like us?*"

I didn't answer. I couldn't. His mouth hovered only inches from mine, those pouty lips—lips I'd kissed only six nights ago —taunting me. My heart hammered against my chest and I felt slightly dizzy. Oh God, I needed air. Or something.

His knee wedged between my legs and nudged them apart. I bit back a whimper as he skimmed a hand down the back of my thigh and lifted my leg, wrapping it around his waist. His hard length pressed against my groin and I resisted the urge to grind my body against it. *Just barely.* As he drugged me with kisses that left me breathless and desperate for more, my short fingernails dug into his shoulders. I'd barely had a taste of this forbidden fruit and already he'd turned me into an addict. The elevator doors opened, and he pulled away, looking down at me with a smirk on his stupidly handsome face.

"Do friends do that?"

"No," I croaked out.

"Hmm. Guess we'll have to change the rules then." With that, he waltzed out of the elevator and left me gritting my teeth and balling my hands into fists.

"Coming?" he called over his shoulder. For someone who claimed he didn't play games, this was definitely starting to feel like one.

"What are we doing here?" I asked when he parked in the lot by the marina nowhere near my apartment.

"I'm hungry."

"I'm not."

"That's why your stomach is growling? Because you're not hungry?"

My traitorous stomach growled again. When was the last time I'd eaten? It was hard to put up a good fight when you were starving. He circled the hood and opened the passenger door for me, holding out his hand for me to take in a show of chivalry. As if. "I don't bite. Unless you want me to."

I ignored his hand and his remark and breezed past him. Even though I had no idea which restaurant he was taking me to, this was my pathetic attempt to assert power that I clearly didn't have. He ushered me inside Sapporo, the Japanese teppanyaki restaurant, his hand on the small of my back like we were a real couple on a date. It was my favorite restaurant at the marina. I hadn't been here in years because, well, going out to dinner was a luxury I couldn't afford. We were seated side by side on high-backed stools with a view of the long silver grills and the chefs in white wielding their machete-like knives.

They were putting on a show, juggling eggs in the air and cracking them with their spatulas for the fried rice. It reminded me of the time I tried it. "For my twelfth birthday, I brought all my friends here, and I begged the chef to teach me the egg trick. No idea how I managed to crack an egg on my head, but it happened, and it was pretty hilarious. Nicola and Ollie laughed their asses off as the raw egg dripped down my face."

Dylan laughed so hard he was wheezing. "You're killing me."

"I'm pretty funny," I agreed, smiling a little that I'd gotten a laugh out of him, my annoyance at that elevator stunt temporarily forgotten. "This doesn't seem like your kind of place. I'm surprised you like a show with your dinner."

"I don't. But you do."

Just then our server, a small, wiry guy with spiky black hair, stopped by our seats and gave us his whole spiel, explaining the menu and how the food is prepared and the portion sizes. Or he would have done that if Dylan hadn't lost patience about two seconds into the poor guy's explanation and cut him off.

"We know how it works." Dylan nudged my arm. "What do you want?"

I always used to order the steak and shrimp combo, but this place was really expensive and way out of my budget so that wasn't happening tonight. "I'll just have dumplings." I pointed to the appetizer on the menu and handed it back to the server with a smile to compensate for Dylan's rudeness.

Dylan stared at me for a few long seconds, not even blinking, as if he was trying to read my mind. Satisfied with whatever he'd figured out, he turned to the server. "One steak. One steak and shrimp." My brows rose in surprise, and he gave me a smug smile, like he knew that he'd guessed right. "I'll have an Asahi beer." He jerked his thumb at me. "Bring her a soda."

A soda? He was treating me like a five-year-old. "Just the dumplings for me, please."

Dylan sighed in exasperation. "Bring us what I ordered and the dumplings." The poor guy. I continued to argue. Dylan looked like he wanted to gag me. The waiter's eyes ping-ponged from me to Dylan who gave him a look that said, *Are you seriously questioning me?*

Having concluded that Dylan was in charge, our waiter scurried away to get our drinks. When he was out of earshot I turned to Dylan. "What the hell? You're ordering for me now?"

"You're worried about money. Don't."

"I can't let you pay—"

"Stop being a pain in the ass. I'm not going to let you order fucking dumplings when you really want steak."

The waiter returned with our drinks, and I smiled at him, the *only* person who deserved my smile. After he was gone, I turned to Dylan again who was drinking his beer like the matter was settled because he'd said so. The last thing I needed in my life was a control freak. I'd been raised by one and had my fill of that, thank you very much.

"Why are we here? And don't tell me it's because you're hungry."

"I am hungry. I'm fucking starving." His hand found its way to my thigh where he rested it as if it belonged there and then, more boldly, his hand ventured between my thighs. No way. We weren't going there. I shoved his hand away. Undeterred, he whispered in my ear, "You could be my dessert."

It was all about sex, wasn't it? Every single thing he'd done was for one purpose only and the more I thought about it, the angrier I got. "Is that why you brought me to dinner? Is that why you're doing all of this? The website, the birthday present, talking Remy into letting me have my own space in the shop for my designs... was that all so you could get me into bed?" My voice rose on every syllable, and I didn't even care that we were in a restaurant or that people could overhear us. Dylan clenched his jaw and stared straight ahead, not even deigning to respond.

"God. How stupid am I?" I smacked myself on the forehead, trying to knock some sense into my thick skull. "It was, wasn't it? Everything you did was because of sex."

I grabbed my bag hanging on the back of the seat, and I hurried away, leaving him sitting there. I had enough problems without him further complicating my life. All because he wanted to get in my pants.

As I reached for the door, his hand clasped my wrist and he spun me around. "The fuck are you doing?"

"What does it look like I'm doing? I'm leaving. You said you weren't playing games, but this feels like one big game. Find someone else to use as your plaything." Fuming, I yanked my hand out of his grasp.

"Calm the fuck down." He moved me away from the door to let another couple out. It was only then that it dawned on me.

Anyone could see us together. This could easily get back to my parents or Sienna if someone recognized me and Dylan. The funny part was that it was the least of my worries right now.

I crossed my arms over my chest and glared at him. "What do you want from me, Dylan?"

He narrowed his eyes on me and clenched his jaw, the muscle in his cheek ticking. "I brought you to dinner because I'm hungry and you need to eat. The other shit... I did it because I want to help you out."

"Why do you want to help me out?" I pressed.

"Because I can."

I shook my head, not ready to let him off that easily. "That's not a good enough answer. What's the *real* reason?"

"The real reason, Scarlett? You want the truth?"

I nodded, my eyes darting to the door, ready to flee if he didn't give me something real. Something honest. A reason to stay. We were at an impasse, his posture mirroring mine, arms crossed over his broad chest.

I was about to give up on him, seconds from walking out the door and calling a taxi when he finally spoke. "Everyone needs someone who believes in them. I believe in you and this was my way of showing you. Just like you always did for me, even when I didn't deserve it. Even when I didn't acknowledge it, I saw you, Scarlett. I always saw you."

I hadn't expected that. My anger dissipated, and I deflated like a balloon.

"Now can we fucking sit down without you causing another scene?"

He didn't care about causing a scene. Things like that didn't bother him, but he did want me to sit down and eat dinner with him. Knowing he would never say please, that he'd already made himself more vulnerable than he was comfortable with, I simply nodded, and we returned to our seats.

Still trying to swallow past the lump in my throat that his

words had caused, I stared at his profile. His dark hair was cut longer on top, short around the sides and back, and tonight he wore it slicked back. It made him look more intimidating. The sharp angles of his cheekbones, the cut, clean jawline, and the perfect symmetry of his face more pronounced. He lifted his beer to his lips and took a swig, his throat bobbing on a swallow before he pointed the bottle at the spectacle in front of us.

"You're missing the show."

I wasn't. Dylan was the star attraction. But he didn't like me looking this closely, especially not after he'd shared a piece of his soul with me, so I turned my head to face the teppanyaki grill and watched the silver flash of knives, the scent of grilled steak and shrimp making my mouth water with hunger.

This was what Dylan did. He could make me angry one minute, and blink back tears the next. In a short span of time, I was wildly swinging from lust to love to heartache and a dozen other emotions in between. All because of him. The scary part was that deep down I had always known this wasn't just about sex. It was so much more, and even now, so early in the game, I didn't know how I would ever walk away. This thing with us, it couldn't last forever. All the odds were stacked against it. He was him, the guy who had never belonged to anyone, and I was me, the girl who desperately wanted him to be mine.

Later, when Dylan dropped me off at my apartment, my belly full and lulled into a food coma, he said, "Just to be clear, I *do* want to fuck you but that has nothing to do with me helping you."

Not sure how to respond, I shoved open my door and climbed out of his car.

"And Scarlett... stop fooling yourself. We are not *just friends*."

I slammed the door on that conversation. I hadn't fooled anyone. Not even myself.

12

SCARLETT

"We got a gig at Mavericks," Ollie said as we carried our boards down to the water, our bare feet leaving footprints on the cold sand. The sky was a crisp blue, with a few wispy clouds painted on the horizon, the sun directly overhead. We'd gotten a late start today, but the beauty of winter surfing was that it was only locals at the break and never got that crowded.

"That's great. I'm really happy for you."

He sighed. "Smalls, I'm sorry, okay?"

"I know. Me too." All we ever did was apologize these days.

"I'm just trying to look out for you."

It was more than that and we both knew it, but I wasn't in the mood to argue. "Let's just surf and put it behind us, okay?"

Lately, it felt like every time I was with Ollie we were trying to put something behind us. He looked like he wanted to say more on the subject but changed his mind and for that I was grateful.

"Waves are barreling."

They were amazing today. I grinned, excited to get out there. It was a perfect day for surfing, the air and ocean temper-

atures in the sixties and my full wetsuit kept my body temperature warm enough to last a few hours in the water.

As we paddled out, I spotted Dylan out at the back. He
was with Shane and Travis in the lineup, but I was too
focused on getting out there without getting thrashed by the
heavy waves to do more than glance in his direction. I duck-
dived, my head submerged under the chilly ocean water, the
wave breaking over my head as I battled against the undertow
trying to drag me back to shore. Emerging victorious, I
paddled hard to get past the breakers, my wet hair plastered
to my head and a smile on my face that had nothing to do
with Dylan.

Surfing made me feel so alive, so energized, it was impossible to feel anything but happy.

Ollie saw Dylan, I knew he did, but he didn't mention it,
thankfully. I mostly ignored Dylan. I was here to surf, not ogle
him in his wetsuit. Besides which, we'd put enough distance
between us that we wouldn't be hassling each other for waves.
Although, I did watch him ride a few.

Dylan was a goofy foot, surfed with his right foot forward
instead of his left. He was an aggressive surfer. Charged hard,
pumping the wave to try and pick up as much speed as possible. There was no Zen in Dylan's surfing whatsoever, and he
wasn't too bothered about technique or style. He just went for
it, balls to the wall, going full-throttle until he'd ridden the
wave for all it was worth. I guess he surfed the way he lived.

I watched Travis and Shane too. They were at a different
level than the rest of us. A different stratosphere. Travis,
Shane's best friend, was a pro surfer and a three-time world
champion so it would stand to reason that he'd be an awesome
surfer. But everyone in the surfing community knew that Shane
could have been world champion. Even though his career had
been cut short, he was still one of the best surfers around.
When you watched Shane surf, you could almost delude your-

self into believing that surfing was easy and effortless. Zen galore.

Whenever Shane rode a wave, Dylan straddled his board and watched him over his shoulder. I doubted that Shane even noticed that Dylan only watched him and not Travis, but I found it interesting. It was also interesting that Dylan barely glanced my way. Since our dinner three nights ago, I hadn't seen him or heard from him but his declaration about wanting to fuck me was still playing on repeat in my head. So were the other things he'd told me that night.

I saw you, Scarlett. I always saw you.

For a girl who had felt mostly invisible in her own family, overshadowed by an older sister, those words meant a lot to me. And somehow Dylan had known that.

Ollie paddled back out to me after riding a wave and straddled his board. I was staring at the horizon, soaking up the afternoon sun, peddling to stay on my board. There might have been a secret smile on my face.

"Are you planning to surf or just daydream?" Ollie teased, but there was an edge to his voice like he knew where my thoughts had taken me, and it didn't make him happy.

He was right though. I was here to surf. I surfed for fun. For the rush. And sometimes I showed off and made a total idiot of myself. I eyed a set of waves building that looked perfect for what I had in mind and grinned at Ollie. "That wave has my name on it. Just call me Superman."

Ollie groaned. "Oh no. Fuck no."

I was laughing as I paddled for the wave, paying no heed to his words. "Don't even think about it, Smalls. Waves are heavy today."

The adrenaline was pumping, and I was up on my board, false confidence riding high as I flew off the lip of the wave and caught air. I was Superman, flying high, my board sky-bound just the way I wanted it. Or I would have been Superman if it hadn't all fallen apart. Airbound and flailing, I windmilled my arms and legs, desperately trying to grip the rails of my board. Needless to say, that never happened. I plummeted back into the water, sans board, and got rag-dolled by the heavy waves. Tumbled and turned until I had no idea which direction was up, and which was down.

What felt like a lifetime later, battered by the surf and dragged across the sandy bottom, I washed up to shore and got on my knees, coughing up the water in my lungs. With all the grace I could muster which was none, I got to my feet on shaky legs, and retrieved my board. And got knocked flat on my ass in the shallows.

By the time I made it to the water's edge and sat on the sand to catch my breath, I felt like I'd just gone through a full cycle on the washing machine.

"Shit," Dylan said, appearing out of nowhere. He pushed his board in the sand, fins down to keep it from getting swept out to sea and crouched in front of me. "Are you okay?"

One might think he would be concerned but he was barely suppressing his laughter. Practically bursting to let it out. Couldn't blame him. Not one of my finer moments. Entertainment gold, no doubt. I sighed. "I'm fine. Except for my bruised ego."

"You almost had it." I shot him a dirty look. He couldn't hold it in anymore. He was laughing so hard he was doubled over. I rolled my eyes and waited for him to pull himself together.

"If you were trying to get my attention, you've got it," he said after he caught his breath from laughing. He pounded his chest with his fist. "Oh man, you're killing me." He plucked a handful of seaweed off the top of my head and tossed it over his shoulder. Well, that must have been a good look. Someone just shoot me. "You sure you're okay?"

I rolled my eyes again and stood up, slightly battered but not broken. "I'm fine."

He swiped his hand down his face to hide the laughter. "Holy shit. You made my day."

"I'll stop at nothing to make you laugh." He peeled down the top half of his wetsuit, complaining of being too hot, because yeah he was just too freaking hot, and my eyes roamed over the heavily inked tattoos on his chest. I'd been wrong. His entire chest *wasn't* covered in tattoos like I had thought. There was a blank space over his heart, about the length and width of my two hands. Blank. Empty. Like the artist had stopped midway through painting a masterpiece and left an unfinished canvas.

Who would do that?

He tugged on the end of one of my braids, drawing my attention away from the blank space over his heart. "These are cute." Then he leaned in close and brushed a lock of wet hair off my forehead. "I don't like it when you're with Shaggy Doo."

"You don't have to like it. Ollie is my friend. Get over it."

"A *friend* who's fucked you."

Ugh, we were back to that. I planted both hands on his bare chest and tried to shove him away. He wrapped his hands around my wrists and tugged me closer. "Come over to my house tonight. I'll pick you up."

"I'm busy tonight."

His eyes narrowed like he didn't believe me. Like I couldn't possibly have any plans that didn't include him. He took a step back and crossed his arms over his chest. "Busy doing what?"

"I promised Nic we'd do an 80s movie marathon. She's making pizza. Not that I owe you an explanation."

He snorted. Not sure what the meaning of that was but I didn't stick around long enough to find out.

"Catch you later, Dylan."

Without giving him a chance to respond, I jogged into the

water, my board under my arm as Shane was on his way in. His eyes darted toward where I'd left Dylan then back to me. "All good?"

"Yep." I gave him a big smile, and he didn't comment further. I got the feeling that he'd rather just stay out of it. Smart move.

"What did I tell you? It's synchronicity," Nic said as she followed the GPS to none other than Dylan St. Clair's house. A house I had never been to and hadn't even known the address of until Nic got it earlier.

"I can't believe you made this plan behind my back." What were the chances that she and Dylan would be pumping gas right next to each other? Slim to none. Yet it had happened.

"Oh come on. Tell me you're not dying to see his house and hang out with him tonight."

"You've undone all of my hard work."

"What hard work?"

"I chose a movie marathon with my friend over—"

"Hot sex with your other friend." Nic patted my arm. "Proud of you, babe. But this will be fun. We'll just be vibing."

"You've met him. He doesn't just vibe. He's all... moody and broody and he barely even talks." That wasn't always the case but for the purpose of this argument, it was accurate enough.

"Uh huh."

"You don't think this feels weird?" I asked as she turned down his street. This looked like a family neighborhood, so I was surprised Dylan had chosen it. In fact, I was pretty sure that one of my friends from junior high used to live here. I remember going to her pool party in seventh grade. The houses overlooked the hills and the canyon, with a view of the sea in the distance.

"No. What's weird about it? Obviously, he wanted to spend time with you. Besides, I've hung out with you and Ollie. And you've hung out with me and what's-his-face."

"Aaron."

"Ugh, Aaron. What did I ever see in him?"

"He had a big dick."

"He did. It was beautiful. Nice and straight. How's Dylan's dick?"

"I'm not talking to you about Dylan's dick." According to the GPS, we had arrived at our destination.

"You haven't seen it yet, have you?"

"No." But I've felt it.

"He looks like he'd have a big dick. Thick, you know? Hey, maybe he's pierced. He looks like the type—"

"Stop talking about dicks," I said, and we both had a giggling fit in Dylan's driveway.

I peered at his house through the windshield. It was nice. Really nice. Tucked away behind lush foliage and palm trees. A two-story Spanish style white stucco with a terracotta roof and black wrought iron trim—not what you'd picture a single guy Dylan's age to live in. Not at all the house I'd picture Dylan living in. Although what would I picture? Something sleek and minimalist. A penthouse apartment with a lot of glass and chrome?

"This is crazy. I can't believe we're doing this."

"I'll be like your personal chef. It's just pizza and a movie and afterward you two can—"

"I'm going home with you. Don't you dare pull a stunt and leave me at his house." We got out of the car and unloaded the bags from the backseat. All the ingredients to make homemade pizzas plus a pizza stone, pans and God knew what else she packed in these bags. Nic was extra but then, so was I. We got along great. "In fact, you should give me the car keys."

I held out my hand for her to turn over the keys to her

Nissan. Ignoring my outstretched hand, she rolled her eyes at me as we walked up to Dylan's front door carrying all our bags. With all these bags, we looked like we were planning to stay for two weeks.

I rang the bell and tried not to hyperventilate. I didn't care what Nic said. This was weird. Dylan was not a people person. I couldn't even imagine him striking up a friendly chat with Nic at the gas station and inviting us over tonight. She must have done all the talking. I bet she masterminded this whole thing. If she were a true friend, she'd be trying to keep me away from Dylan instead of pushing us together.

The door swung open and there he was, looking all chill in faded jeans with ripped knees and a black T-shirt. And then he smiled, a genuine smile that showed his straight white teeth, and I swooned.

Literally swooned.

There was no armor that could protect me from Dylan when he smiled. To make matters worse, he was charming. *Charming.* Almost boyish and all kinds of adorable, like he was happy we were there. I couldn't handle this. He took all the bags out of our hands and we followed him into the kitchen, sneaking a peek into the living room on the way. I loved his house. Not what I'd imagined, yet it was so him with clean white walls and dark hardwood floors covered with black and white Moroccan rugs. Black wrought iron chandeliers hung from the woodbeamed ceiling and his black overstuffed sofas looked so cozy and inviting. Like you'd just want to sink into them and not leave anytime soon.

"Oh my God, you have a chef's kitchen," Nic squealed, her smile mega-watt as she took in the expanse of stainless steel and black granite countertops. "This is amazing. A Viking stove." She lovingly ran her hand over the gleaming stainless steel while Dylan set all the bags on the island, amused by her excitement over a stove.

"Do you cook a lot?"

"Never," Dylan said with a laugh. Nic was in raptures again when her eyes settled on the bottles of red wine on the counter. "You bought the wine I suggested!"

Dylan lifted one shoulder in a shrug and carved his hand through his hair. Tonight, it was messy and disheveled. Secretly, I preferred it that way. Nic was going on and on about the wine and Dylan's awesome kitchen while he uncorked a bottle of wine and I just stood there trying to figure out what was going on.

Was he into threesomes? Oh crap. I hadn't even thought of that. Was he attracted to Nic? Did he want to fuck both of us?

He pressed a glass of wine in my hand, his fingers brushing mine as I accepted the glass and thanked him, my eyes focused on the ruby liquid in my glass. I didn't even want to look at him. It was always my undoing. "Don't be jealous, Starlet."

"Pfft. I'm not jealous. Why would I be jealous?" I took a big swig of liquid courage, using great restraint not to chug it and demand a refill. God, why did he make me feel this way? It was his scent. All those damn pheromones just floating around.

He gave me a slow, lazy grin. "I don't know. Why would you be?"

Thankfully, Nic chose that moment to ask for my help. Something to occupy my time and attention. Dylan, of course, did not help with the pizza making. He drank his beer and played on his phone while I assisted Nicola who acted like she was filming a cooking show. As a joke, Dylan changed the music and "Truth Hurts" blasted from his surround sound.

"In case you feel the urge to dance," he said. Nic and I obliged, dancing as she prepared the dough and I was put in charge of the toppings. I grated enough mozzarella to feed an entire village in Italy.

We were about to roll out the dough on the floured surface when the doorbell rang. A few seconds later, Dylan returned to the kitchen with another guy—Hispanic with cropped dark hair, built like a linebacker.

"Look at that. Baby sister is all grown up."

"Keep your eyes off baby sister," Dylan growled, handing his friend a beer.

The guy, who I assumed was Cruz, chuckled and then introduced himself.

"I remember. Good to see you again. This is my friend, Nicola."

"The chef," he said with a grin, his eyes doing a slow descent, taking her in from head to toe. "*Very* nice to meet you."

"*Very* nice to meet you as well." Nic was practically purring.

O-kay. Now they were just staring at each other across the kitchen island. Like they'd just found their soul mates after a lifetime of searching and couldn't imagine how they'd lived this long without each other. That's truly how it felt, watching them. I'd never seen Nic act like this with any guy, and it appeared to be reciprocal. Until finally, Nic shook her head, snapping out of it and gave him a dazzling smile. "Do you want to help us roll out the dough?"

"I'd love to." Cruz rubbed his hands together and rounded the island to stand by her side. She smiled, this little secret smile as they exchanged sidelong glances, and I felt like me and Dylan were intruding on their private moment. "Just show me what to do."

Dylan smirked. I suppressed a laugh. Who would have guessed that Dylan would play matchmaker? He was full of surprises, and with each layer of himself he revealed, I fell just a little bit harder.

13

DYLAN

They talked us into watching 80s flicks. Cruz took zero convincing. Dude was already pussy whipped. Within five minutes of meeting Nicola, he cracked like an egg and shared his entire life story. She'd done the same. Now I knew a whole hell of a lot more about Nicola Benedetti than I'd ever need to. Starlet and I watched from the sidelines as we ate our pizza, and she'd given me these sweet little smiles, almost shy like we were just getting to know one other and didn't already have a convoluted history.

I had no agenda tonight. I wasn't trying to get her into bed. Truth be told, I was content to hang out with her, watch movies, eat pizza, listen to her running commentary on the movie, whatever. Didn't matter what we did, I just liked being around her. Which was strange. I couldn't remember the last time I'd felt this way about a girl. Maybe never.

I had never done the whole dating thing. First time I had sex, I was fifteen. She was late twenties, early thirties. Shelby. I used to mow her lawn when we lived in Little Rock. She was rich, lived in a big house surrounded by a couple acres, and her husband golfed every weekend. It was just fucking. No kissing. No intimacy or sweet words required. Afterward, she'd tuck a wad of cash in my pocket, wink and say, "Thanks. Same time next Saturday?"

Fucked up? Maybe.

Would you sell your soul to pay the utilities, put food in the cupboards, and have a steady supply of booze and weed? Turns out I would, and I did. She didn't know I was only fifteen. Must have left out that little detail.

In high school, I had a reputation. I was the guy who could get you the best drugs, then screw your cheerleader girlfriend in the locker room and leave you bleeding all over the leather interior of your BMW after I fucked up your face. That was the guy Sienna had wanted. A taste of the forbidden. Her feeble attempt to give her daddy the middle finger. She knew what I was, and that's why she'd chosen me. I was the guy she fucked until someone suitable came along.

But Scarlett... she was different. She actually liked me for me, and I wasn't entirely sure what to do about that.

Turns out I didn't have to do anything. Scarlett was a lightweight, got drunk on two glasses of wine. Now, the credits were rolling on a movie about kids in detention, and she was passed out. Snuggled against me, her legs tucked underneath her like a lovable kitten. My arm around her shoulders was numb, but I didn't move it because I didn't want to disturb her. The fuck was I doing?

"You two look cozy," Nic observed from her spot on the other sofa.

"Like an old married couple," Cruz said with a snicker.

I gave him the middle finger and he chuckled. "We're gonna crash in one of the guest bedrooms."

"This isn't the Holiday Fucking Inn." But I didn't give a shit if they stayed. I had plenty of room and they'd had too much to drink to even think of driving home.

"It's nicer. And the walls aren't as thin," Nic said with a wink, no embarrassment whatsoever that she and Cruz were about to go upstairs and fuck like rabbits. She was pretty cool. A straight shooter. No games. I liked that. And obviously so did Cruz who had a little more swagger in his step than usual.

Meanwhile, I'd put a girl to sleep. That was a first.

I wasn't thinking with my dick when I carried her upstairs. I wasn't even thinking with my dick when I tucked her into my bed, leaving her in a skull T-shirt and leggings, her hair messy and disheveled. She smelled like vanilla and honey, the scent of red wine on her soft breath. It was a heady combination. Sweet, innocent, and forbidden. Like her.

She slept like the dead, this girl, and only stirred briefly, mumbling something incoherent before she dropped off to sleep again with a sigh of contentment. I pulled the covers up to her shoulders and sat on the edge of the bed, watching her sleep, her face so peaceful, a small smile turning up the corners of her lush lips like all her dreams were good ones.

A few minutes into creeping on Scarlett, my phone rang. I turned it to silent, checking to make sure my crazy mother hadn't woken her. One in the morning was her favorite time to call. Ducking outside onto the balcony, I closed the French doors to block out the sound of my voice and answered my mother's call.

"What'd you need?" I wedged the phone between my ear and shoulder and lit a cigarette.

"Is that any way to greet your mama, sugar?" In the background, I heard slot machines and glasses clinking. My mother bartended at a casino in Vegas. All her tips went back into the slot machines and the roulette wheel. A losing game if there ever was one. Every time she called, I waited for her to tell me she'd lost everything or that I needed to bail her out of jail. With her, anything was possible.

I exhaled a plume of smoke and squinted at the view from

my balcony. I swam in my Roman pool year-round and spent a small fortune to keep it heated to an optimal eighty-two degrees throughout the colder months. My lawn was manicured, the Moroccan tiles gleamed, and the glass fence around my property fucking sparkled, it was so clean and smudge-free. Not that I could see that from my vantage point, but I knew it, and that was good enough.

"I think Wayne's gonna ask me to marry him. I really do. It's different this time, baby. I think he really loves me. Wouldn't that be something?"

Sure as hell would.

It was always different, but only in her mind. She was talking a mile a minute, and I let her talk, not really listening to her words but rather, the way she was so amped up. Too high. Overexcited. Tripping over her words, her brain firing on all cylinders. I'd seen her like this so many times, had seen her highs and her lows, and her rock bottom about a year ago when she'd taken too many pills and washed them down with whiskey. A cry for help that landed her in the hospital and ensured I'd drop everything to be at her side. Exactly where she wanted me.

I'd never told Remy. She and Shane were traveling at the time. Koh Samui, I think. It was about a month before their wedding in Bali. They were happy, finding their way back to each other, and they didn't need to deal with my mother's shit. I'd checked her into a treatment facility. Five days later, she checked herself out. Then I'd taken her to see specialists, and a psychiatrist had diagnosed her. For a while, she was good. Even-keeled. But that hadn't lasted.

I interrupted whatever bullshit she was spewing. "You taking your meds?"

My head was pounding, those moments of peace watching Scarlett sleep derailed by my mother's phone call. She had a knack for fucking up everything that was good, but my conscience wouldn't allow me to ignore her phone calls anymore.

She sighed in exasperation. "I don't need them. They just make me feel like I'm... like I'm underwater or something. Sucks the joy and the color right out of the world. How could that be a good thing? Those doctors don't know what they're talking about."

My jaw clenched, and I pinched the bridge of my nose. This woman would be the death of me. "You need those fucking meds—"

"Oh, stop your worrying. I'm feeling great. Me and Wayne are going dancing. I wanna drive through the desert and dance under all those stars. I bought a new dress. It's red. And shoes to match. Wait until he sees me in that. You should come out and visit me soon. We'll hit the town. See a show. Go to dinner at that steak place you love."

I hated Vegas. Always had. Too loud. Too fake. Filled with too many bad memories.

"I was showing everyone your picture tonight and all the ladies said you belong on a billboard. Like those Calvin Klein underwear models."

The fuck? "Don't show anyone my photo."

"Just tryin' to fix you up. You'd get lucky in Vegas, I can promise you that. Well, I gotta run. I love you, baby."

She cut the call without waiting for my response, and I smoked another cigarette, praying to a God I didn't believe in that Remy's kid didn't inherit any of our mother's genes. Or mine for that matter.

Starlet was still fast asleep, Cruz and Nicola were down the hall doing God knows what, and I was wide awake, with so much restless energy I needed an outlet. Sex wasn't an option, so I went for a swim. Fifty laps later, I'd loosened up enough to sleep and levered myself out of the pool, grabbing the towel I'd left on the deck.

———

"Hey Romeo." I lifted my eyes to the Juliet balcony, the irony not lost on me. Starlet was leaning over the wrought-iron railing, my charcoal gray comforter wrapped around her shoulders like a cape, her wavy blonde hair glowing in the moonlight.

"What are you doing out here?" I asked, tying the towel around my waist and crossing the Moroccan tiles until I was standing right below her.

"I woke up and saw the pool lights," she said, peering down at me. "Why were you swimming in the middle of the night?"

"Couldn't sleep."

"You're not cold?"

"Nah." I ran my fingers through my towel-dried hair. Pool water dripped from the ends and goosebumps covered my skin, the night air thirty degrees chillier than the water temperature. But I could be standing butt naked in the Arctic and still deny being cold.

She pulled the comforter tighter around her body and shuddered as if it made her cold just looking at me. "Are you coming to bed now?"

Interesting turn of phrase. "Is that an invitation?"

"It's your bedroom."

Which begged the question, *Will you be in it?* In my bedroom. In my bed. With me inside you. It was on the tip of my tongue to ask her that. But I stopped myself. For the first time in my life, I wanted to be the good guy. I wanted to do the right thing. "Go back to bed. I'll sleep in the spare room."

Her lips turned down at the corners. Disappointment? Was she hoping I'd stick with the script? I wanted this to be her choice. I wanted her to make her intentions clear. I wanted her to choose me. But not like this. Not when I'd forced her hand by putting her in my bed without her consent.

"Oh. Okay. Yeah." She looked over her shoulder then back at me. "I can sleep in the other room. You should sleep in your own bed."

"I'm good. Just stay in my room." Go ahead, torture the shit out of me by leaving your scent on my sheets and pillows. "Night, Starlet."

"Goodnight." She smiled and waved goodbye over her shoulder, dragging my comforter back inside the bedroom. The French doors closed, and I stifled a groan as I walked into the house and turned off the pool lights.

I could have had her tonight. What had possessed me to play Mr. Nice Guy? Fucking idiot.

Chuckling to myself, I dropped my wet trunks in the laundry room and climbed the stairs to the second floor. My footsteps stopped outside my bedroom door. She was sleeping on the other side of it. I was standing in front of the door in nothing but a towel.

Keep walking, asshole. You're trying to be the good guy, remember? Not my strong suit.

In the midst of my internal debate, the door opened a crack and then it opened wider, spilling moonlight into the hallway. As if she had expected me. Had known all along that I'd be here.

Waiting. Wanting. Ready.

My gaze roamed down her body, her perky tits under the T-shirt, the curve of her hips, her bare legs. Somewhere along the way, she'd ditched the leggings. The hem of her shirt hit the top of her thighs. Modest enough to cover whatever she was wearing underneath but short enough to be distracting. Scarlett was tiny, but she was all legs.

"Hi," she whispered, biting the corner of her lip.

"Hi," I said and then we both laughed for no reason.

I planted a hand on the doorframe and leaned in. Close enough to smell her honey and vanilla scent. "What are you doing, Scarlett?"

"I don't know," she admitted.

She licked her lips, her eyes roaming down my bare torso to the towel tied around my hips. That's right. Just one flick of the wrist and it would be on the floor.

"Are those song lyrics?" Her gaze lowered to the inked words on my ribs: *I can't breathe but I fight while I can fight.* "I mean... your tattoo... I always wondered..."

"Eminem. 'Love The Way You Lie.' It was my first tattoo."

She traced the words with her fingertips, her touch featherlight yet it felt like she was branding me. Searing my skin and burrowing under the protective layers.

"Do you still feel like that?" she asked, her voice hushed, her eyes lifting to mine. Her lips parted, and a soft breath escaped them, and it was all I could do not to sink my teeth into that lush lip. "Like you can't breathe?"

Our eyes were locked, the house so quiet that I knew we must be the only two people awake. It felt like long moments passed before I finally answered. "Sometimes."

Right now, that was *exactly* how I felt. My breathing was shallow, and even though we'd barely touched, I was so hard for her it was starting to feel like a sick joke.

Last night, after the gym, Cruz and I had gone for a few beers. I'd run into Waverly who I'd hooked up with a few times in the past. With Waverly, it had always been sex with no strings attached. Which was fucking perfect. She was hot, liked to get dirty, and never overstayed her welcome. Yet what had I done when she offered a quick fuck? I'd said no.

Now I was standing in front of a girl who had given me nothing more than a kiss, who had the potential to complicate my life and fuck with my head, yet I wanted her more than I'd ever wanted anyone.

It was only minutes but felt like years that we stood there, staring at each other, locked in a silent battle of *will we, won't we*. Never in the history of foreplay had anything dragged out so long without a sound or a touch.

I didn't know who made the first move, but the next thing I knew my hand was tangled in her wild, unruly hair, her palms coasting up my chest, and my mouth collided with hers. I swept my tongue across the seam of her pillow-soft lips and they parted on a sigh to let me in, our tongues exploring the deepest recesses of each other's mouths like they held the key to unlocking the secrets of the universe.

Kissing Scarlett didn't feel like the prelude to sex, it felt like the main event. I wanted to kiss her until her lips were raw and swollen, and the only word on the tip of her tongue was my name.

Just one taste of her and what little resolve I had crumbled to dust.

She didn't protest when I gripped her hips and pushed her farther into the room. Kicking the door shut, I lifted her off the ground, her legs cinching around my waist, her mouth still fused to mine. Her back hit the tall dresser against the wall, our tongues dueling like this was a battle for possession.

I groaned, she moaned. Her fingernails raked down my back, scoring my skin, marking me.

It was nothing short of a fucking miracle that my towel was still firmly in place even though my erection threatened to rip right through the thick cotton and accidentally end up buried inside her. With the way she was grinding against me and the way I was acting like a teenager who had just discovered how to get off by dry humping a mattress, I wouldn't be surprised if I jizzed all over my fucking towel.

I spun us around and tossed her onto my bed, her back bouncing off the mattress, her T-shirt riding up to expose cotton boy shorts. Since when had cotton underwear become so sexy? When Scarlett Woods wore them, that's when.

"What are we doing?" she finally thought to ask, pushing herself onto her elbows as my hands wrapped around her ankles and dragged her to the edge of the mattress, her ass practically hanging off it.

"I can't... I'm not going to..."

"Fuck me?" I asked, sliding the cotton down her legs so her pussy was bare to me. Nudging her thighs apart, I planted her feet flat on the mattress and dropped to my knees in front of her.

I wanted to build a shrine to her pussy. Worship at the altar of Scarlett Woods.

"Do you want this, Starlet?"

"Yes. I mean... Dylan," she said breathlessly, a little whimper escaping when I dragged my fingers through her slick heat, wet with her arousal. She was every bit as delectable as I'd imagined. Ripe like a peach, her juices coating my fingers.

"We'll take it slow." Not sure I had a slow setting but there was a first for everything.

I guided my fingers to her lips.

"Taste yourself." She sucked on my fingers, her eyes at half-mast, cheeks hollowed, my cock swelling as she licked my fingers clean.

I draped her leg over my shoulder and used my thumbs to open the lips of her pussy, licking her from crack to clit.

Scarlett moaned, lacing her fingers through my hair and holding the back of my skull.

I pinched her clit between my fingers, my tongue diving inside her tight walls. I was in so deep I didn't think I'd ever get out.

Her moans intensified, and she was writhing in front of me, her eyes closed. "Oh, my God."

That's right. But instead of using God's name in vain, I want you screaming my name.

"You like this?" I asked, massaging her swollen clit and fucking her with tongue.

"Mmm hmm. I never... I mean... nobody..."

I lifted my head to look at her face. Even in the dim shadows of the room, I could see her blush a pretty pink. "Nobody's ever gone down on you?"

Her lashes lowered. "I don't give blow jobs." As if that was an explanation. But what the fuck?

"Why not?" My fingers bit into the flesh of her ass cheek, demanding an answer. Part of me was happy she'd never done this before. The other part of me didn't know what to make of it.

"Um... I mean, I tried but it made me..." She averted her head. "I just couldn't do it."

"Nobody's perfect," I said, making her laugh and then gasp when I slid two fingers inside her, stretching her tight walls, reaching and curling until I hit a spot that made her cry out and grind against my hand.

"I'm so close... I'm going to..."

"Come for me," I commanded, biting her clit. Sending her over the edge.

She came in a spectacular way, my name replacing God's, her entire body convulsing.

Boneless, her elbows gave out and her back collapsed against the mattress. With the flat of my tongue, I gave her long, slow licks until she rode out her orgasm.

Arms braced on either side of her head, my mouth moved up her body, and I pressed my lips against hers. She kissed me hard, reaching for the towel around my waist. With a tskk, I pushed her hand away and stood up.

"You don't get to touch me. Not until you're ready to fuck me or wrap your lips around my cock."

Her jaw dropped at my crude words.

"Night, Starlet." I strode out of my bedroom and left her lying on my bed.

Sweet dreams, baby girl.

I came, I saw, I conquered, and then I left. Correction. She came, I left, blue balls intact. And I wasn't even mad about it. I licked my lips. They still tasted like her.

14

SCARLETT

A thrill of pride shot through me when the petite brunette handed me her money for the denim jacket. It was from my Surf Voodoo collection—a medicine man in a top hat riding a killer wave. I rang up the sale and handed her the change and her purchase in a white bag with the blue Firefly logo. Before she left, we chatted for a few minutes and she promised to check out my website.

A few minutes later, I was refolding T-shirts when Ryan came out of one of the shaping bays in the back, an energy drink in his hand. He took off his Firefly ball cap, ran his fingers through his blond curls and replaced the cap on his head as he ambled over to the sales counter and picked up the most recent SURFER magazine.

"If you wanna take your break, I can cover the front of the shop," he said, not lifting his head from the pages of the magazine he was thumbing through.

It was quiet now, an afternoon lull so I took him up on his offer. "Thanks," I said, shooting him a smile on my way to Remy's office.

The door was open, and she was on the phone. It was the

landline, so I knew it was business-related. Remy handled all the orders for custom boards and was the spokesmodel for the brand. Careful not to disturb her, I grabbed my denim jacket and bag from her office, waved goodbye and left quietly.

Sunglasses on to ward off the sun's glare, I strolled down the tree-lined main street. It had all the charm of a Mediterranean seaside town with the chill factor of SoCal, the white stucco and blush pink facades housing trendy boutiques and surf shops and open-air restaurants perfect for people watching. While I'd been away, in San Francisco and Seattle, I had missed this town. Today it was a balmy seventy degrees and my skin was warmed by the sun on my face.

As I stepped up to the counter at Sweet Creamery, my phone rang. I was tempted not to answer but I did. "Hey Mom. Just a sec."

"Can I get Cookie Monster in a waffle cone please?" I asked the lady behind the counter. It was my favorite, a mix of Cookie Dough and Oreo.

"You got it," she said with a smile.

"Ice cream?" my mother said, sounding horrified. "Do you know how many calories is in one scoop of ice cream?"

"Nope. And I don't care."

"Your waistline does. You're not exactly skinny."

"I'm not fat either." Okay, so I had hips and a butt, but my body was toned from surfing and my stomach was flat. Ugh, why did I even let her mess with my head? I exchanged an eye-roll with the woman behind the counter.

"Mothers," she said under her breath with a shake of her head, her dark corkscrew curls bouncing. She set the cone of blue ice cream in a stand and I handed her a twenty. After pocketing my change, I mouthed 'thank you' and took my ice cream, continuing my stroll, with my mother's voice in my ear. I wended my way down the hilly street that funneled to the

beach and the pier while she talked about... I had no idea what
she was talking about.

"She just went into a boutique on Melrose."

"Who did?" I asked, taking a few licks of my ice cream.

"Cecily," my mother replied, exasperated.

That halted me in my tracks. "Um, how do you know this?"

"I've been tailing her. Do you think I should get a nose job?"

Oh Mom. "Your nose is perfect. You don't need a nose job."

"What does she have that I don't?" She sniffed, and I imagined her sitting in her car, parked outside a boutique in LA,
watching my father's mistress. Why did she torture herself like
this?

"Yes, I know. She's half my age. But you know what's
funny?"

I couldn't think of one single funny thing about any of this.
"What?"

"She looks so much like me when I was her age."

"Mom, you should stop following her. You can't keep doing
this to yourself. Ask him for a divorce," I pleaded, knowing that
my words would fall on deaf ears. But I still felt the need to say
them anyway. "There's someone out there who will love you for
you."

"I don't want anyone else," she whined.

I tossed the rest of my cone in a trash can and wiped my
sticky hand on my black leggings. "Are you going to be okay?
Do you want me to come over after work?"

"Your father and I are going to the club for dinner with
Hank and Trudy."

I rolled my eyes. Dinner with the mayor and his wife. Oh
joy. My mother must be a masochist. Now that she'd unloaded
on me, she felt better so we said goodbye and I tucked my
phone in my denim jacket pocket.

I needed to sit by the ocean. Dig my toes in the sand.

Breathe in the salty air. Clear my head and put everything in perspective. Which I sorely needed.

I was leading a double life. Surf shop employee by day with a side gig as a shameless hussy. It had been six days since the night I'd lured Dylan into the bedroom, like Eve tempting Adam with the poison apple. Come, take a bite, it's sweet and forbidden. I'd never let anyone go down on me, and I'd been too turned on to be embarrassed. But I couldn't believe I'd told him I didn't give blow jobs. One of these days, I'd put a filter on this mouth of mine.

Three days after that night, Dylan had stopped by Firefly Surfboards. I was holed up in the stockroom, going through the inventory, and he'd closed the door, planted my ass on a stack of boxes and proceeded to torture me with kisses and an orgasm, his hand covering my mouth to stop me from screaming and alerting the entire shop.

Since then, we'd been texting, and I'd been fantasizing.

Speaking of the devil.

I stopped and watched Dylan from across the street. He was gesticulating with his hands, arguing with a construction worker outside The Surf Lodge. Whatever the guy was saying clearly didn't make him happy. He planted his hands on his narrow hips and looked up at the sky as if his patience was being tested and he was about to lose it. The other man held up his hands and backed away.

I watched the guy climb into his truck—*AJW Construction* painted on the side—and drive away before my gaze returned to Dylan. His phone was pressed to his ear and he was pacing, jaw clenched and shoulders rigid. When he ended his call, he pocketed his phone and carved his hands through his hair, resting them on the back of his neck. Tentatively, I approached him and stopped next to him on the beach path.

"What happened?" I asked, looking at the three-story hotel in front of us. Weathered wood that had once been painted white trimmed in aqua blue. I'd always thought it was a cool hotel and liked to envision it the way it must have looked back in the fifties before time and the elements had worn it down.

Dylan shook a cigarette out of the pack, lit it and took a drag before he answered. "My construction crew quit."

Before I could respond, a middle-aged woman in Lycra and running shoes shot Dylan a dirty look and hollered, "Smoking kills. We don't need your secondhand smoke."

Dylan ignored her and took another drag of his cigarette. She fanned away the smoke with her hand and coughed a few times, power walking past us.

I dragged my attention back to Dylan. "Why did they quit?"

He laughed humorlessly. "Because someone is trying to fuck with me." I had a sinking suspicion that 'someone' was my father.

"Now what?"

"I'll hire another construction company."

If my hunch was right and he was going up against my father, it wouldn't be as simple as hiring another construction crew. My father would use any means to get what he wanted or, rather, prevent Dylan from getting what he wanted. And the one thing my father had that Dylan didn't was connections.

"Is this about my dad? Is he messing things up for you?"

"He's giving it his best shot."

I stared at the black and white checkered Vans on my feet, ashamed that my dad was such an asshole. After all these years, why was he still out to get Dylan? Why did he have to turn everything into a power struggle? "I'm sorry."

"Why? Did you tell my construction crew to fuck off?"

"No. But I know how he operates. If he wants something, he'll stop at nothing to get it."

"Fuck him." He looked at me more closely, the cigarette clamped between his lips bobbing on his words. "Why's your tongue blue?"

"Cookie Monster ice cream."

"Mmm." He took another drag of his cigarette then tossed it in the sand and crushed it under his foot. I thought he'd leave it there. But he picked it up and lobbed it into a trash can a few feet away from where we stood. "Don't mention this to Remy or Shane."

It took me a second to realize he was talking about the hotel, not us. "I won't."

He looked out at the ocean and squinted against the sun sparkling on the water, those sexy little lines around his eyes appearing. Seagulls circled over the gray weathered wood pier, and in the distance, a charter boat glided across the crystal blue water. It was a picture-perfect day.

"I learned to surf at this break," Dylan said.

I smiled. "Me too." A few guys were out there trying to surf, but it was a dumpy shore break, the waves breaking in the shallows and they were having a hard time catching a decent ride. "I broke my board surfing waves like that when I was sixteen."

His lip quirked in amusement. "Pulling that Superman maneuver."

I laughed. "I'll never live that one down."

"It's not the first thing that comes to mind when I think of you."

"No?"

"No." His mouth moved close to the shell of my ear and he pushed my hair to the side with his thumb. "I think about that sweet little pussy of yours." My pulse sped up as his teeth grazed my earlobe. "And the sounds that came out of your mouth when I was eating you out."

God, he was so dirty. My cheeks flushed with heat and I squeezed my thighs together to ease the ache. "We should—"

Stop before it's too late.

"Mmm. We should."

Catching me off guard, he grasped my chin, angling my face

up to him then kissed me hard, his tongue sliding into my mouth. It felt like my stomach was being invaded by a kaleidoscope of butterflies. I pressed up on my toes, sliding my hands up his chest.

What was I doing?

Coming to my senses, I pulled away, looking around to see if anyone was watching us.

We were getting so careless. "Someone could have seen us."

He gave me a slow, lazy grin. "Am I your dirty little secret, Scarlett?"

"Um, yes... no..." I let out a breath and closed my eyes, reminded of the time I'd bravely announced that I'd march him right through the front door and seat him next to me at a family dinner. Oh, how naïve I'd been. But that had been an entirely different situation.

"I don't know what we are," I admitted, searching his face for a clue. "What are we, Dylan?"

"We're two wrongs that make a right."

I laughed. "Not so sure it works that way."

"Fuck what anyone thinks." He clasped my hand in his and made lazy circles on my inner wrist with the pad of his thumb, sending delicious shivers up and down my spine. Today, his eyes looked bluer, the specks of gray shimmering silver in the sunlight. "You busy tonight?"

I nodded.

He quirked his dark brows. "Another movie marathon?"

"No. I'm going to Mavericks."

"Mavericks." His lip curled in disgust. "Looking to hook up with a jarhead?"

"What? No." I didn't even know Marines hung out there. I'd never been inside. "Ollie's band has a gig there."

"Huh. Nic going with you?"

"She has to work."

He stared at me like I had three heads. "You're going to Mavericks *alone*?"

"Yeah." I shrugged one shoulder. "It's no big deal. I'm sure I'll find people to talk to." That was obviously the wrong thing to say.

Dylan's eyes narrowed. "What time do they play?"

"Ten but—"

"I'll pick you up."

"No!" I said quickly, my eyes widened in horror. Now I was cursing myself for telling him the truth. Me and my big fat mouth. "You can't come tonight. You and Ollie don't get along. I don't want another repeat of my birthday."

He crossed his arms over his broad chest. "You're not going to that bar without me."

"I'll find someone else to go with me. I can ask Ryan or—"

"I'll see you tonight."

"No. You're not invited."

That was like waving a red flag at a bull. I could tell by the stubborn set of his jaw that he didn't care if he was invited or not. "Wasn't waiting for an invitation. See you later, Starlet," he said with a wink. *A wink.* So cocky.

As if the matter was settled, he strode away and climbed into his SUV, slipping on a pair of black Wayfarers to shield his eyes. He watched me through the windshield, a lazy grin on his perfect lips as he drove away.

My stomach plummeted. This was a terrible idea.

15

SCARLETT

"You're just coming as my friend. I don't want to mess up this gig for Ollie," I reminded Dylan as we crossed the street to the bar. "No touching or kissing or... just don't even look at me. In fact, you should stand on the other side of the room and pretend you're not even with me."

He stopped outside the bar and crossed his arms over his chest, an accusation in his voice. "Did he know you were planning to come alone?"

"Yes."

"And he was good with that?"

I lifted my chin, my hands on my hips. "Why wouldn't he be?"

"Last time I was at Mavericks, a fight broke out because some douche wouldn't take no for an answer."

"And who started that fight? Let me guess, it was you." I poked him in the chest.

"You're missing the fucking point." His gaze raked over me from head to toe, taking in the black tank painted with a skull in a wreath of thorns under a denim jacket, my snakeskin print mini, black fishnets, and Docs. His hand skimmed over my backside, cupping my butt cheek and pulling me flush against him. "Did you wear this for me?"

"No. I don't dress for men." It was true. I dressed for myself.

"So you were planning to wear this anyway to go to a bar *alone*?"

Sensing where he was headed with this line of questioning, I rallied to my own defense. "I should be able to wear whatever I want."

He scowled. "If you want a bunch of assholes hitting on you all night."

"Well, now I've got you to protect me from all the non-existent dangers." I rolled my eyes as he opened the door and ushered me inside, rock music blasting from the speakers. I handed the guy at the door a twenty for our cover charge, beating Dylan to it and we got our hands stamped.

Dylan led me through the throng of people crowding the bar, the walls decorated with Route 66 signs, Heineken mirrors, and dartboards. The crack of pool balls from the tables in the back cut through the music and clinking of glasses. It smelled like stale beer and sweat. A typical bar. Perfectly harmless.

I was happy to see there was a good crowd tonight, but I was paranoid about running into someone I knew. Or worse, someone who knew Sienna. On top of that, I'd texted Ollie to warn him that I was bringing Dylan and never got a reply. So yeah, this was a train wreck waiting to happen.

I was starting to sweat and I didn't think it had anything to do with the temperature inside this bar. I took off my jacket and draped it over one arm.

Dylan ordered two beers while I scanned the room in search of familiar faces. My gaze landed on the stage where Ollie was duct taping the cables, his back turned to the room. Beck and Gavin were farther down the bar, closer to the stage, drinking beers and chatting with a few girls, none of whom looked familiar. Normally I would go over and hang out with them but I couldn't do that tonight. Not with Dylan. Maybe if I just stayed here toward the back, nobody would even see me.

Dylan pressed a beer into my hand. I thanked him and chugged a quarter of it. He stared at me. "Planning to get shitfaced?"

"Will it help?" I wiped my sweaty palm on my skirt.

He chuckled. "Just chill. It's all good."

Easy for him to say. He leaned his hip against the bar and took a pull of his beer, his hand curving around my hip, his thumb brushing over the soft skin above the waistband of my skirt. Without thinking, I leaned into him, and slid my hand up his chest, over his lean, cut muscles, hard under the soft material of his black T-shirt. When I realized what I was doing, I removed my hand and took a step back, chugging more beer.

Dylan laughed, obviously finding this whole thing more amusing than I did. I really was a shameless hussy.

A few minutes later, the music from the speakers cut out and the lights dimmed. I relaxed a bit and looked up as Beck leaped onto the stage, his guitar slung over his back. He speared his hand through the bleached tips of his spiky hair and winked at a girl down in front, his hand curling around the mic and bringing it to his mouth. "Hey everyone. Thanks for coming out tonight. We're the Savage Nobles."

That earned appreciative applause from the crowd and a few cheers. Beck and Gavin were cousins and their last name was Noble, thus the name of the band which we'd come up with during a brainstorming session in the high school cafeteria.

Beck introduced Gavin who flicked his long, dark hair off his face then Ollie who tossed his sticks in the air and caught them one-handed, his biceps flexing under the sleeves of his white T-shirt painted with a black heartbeat and drums. I made that T-shirt for him. Over the years, I'd made a lot of T-shirts for him and the band guys.

"Well, alright," Beck said, shouldering his guitar. "Let's play some music."

Ollie set the beat, Gavin brought the rhythm, and Beck played the chords of "Halcyon Days," a song they wrote when they were on the road the summer after high school. It made me feel nostalgic to hear Beck's bluesy rock voice singing about the golden days of our youth as if we were ninety years old and looking back on better days.

"They're pretty good," Dylan said in my ear, his lips ghosting over my neck as I nodded. I'd spent countless hours listening to them, hanging out in Beck's garage while they jammed. Sitting on a threadbare sofa in a dingy warehouse in Seattle where they worked tirelessly on their sound, on the lyrics, their hopes and dreams pinned on someday getting their big break. More than anything, I wanted all their dreams to come true. Because they were good.

They were the real deal.

By the time the band wrapped up their set, I was on my third beer, sweaty from dancing, and high on the music. I'd forgotten all about being nervous, my inhibitions cast aside.

"We're gonna do a cover, if that's alright with you," Beck said into the mic.

The opening chords of "Do I Wanna Know" by The Arctic Monkeys filled the room and Dylan's hand came around me, his palm flattening against my stomach as his lips met my neck. We danced like we had on the beach that night, my free arm snaked around the back of his neck, his arm around my middle, our bodies moving in sync. The people around us faded away and it was just him and me and the music and my wildly beating heart.

I was so careless. So reckless. But nobody had ever made

me feel the way he did. I was love-drunk. Eyes closed. The beat of the music reverberating through my core, the heat of his body lighting an inferno inside me. I was powerless to resist him, his closeness so male, so intoxicating and delicious I got a natural high off it.

When the music stopped, the last note had been played, and the crowd started cheering, my eyes flew open, breaking me out of the trance. My gaze landed on Ollie whose scowl was directed at me. For a few seconds, our eyes locked across the crowded bar and I flinched as his expression grew hard and resentful.

He hates me. Ollie hates me.

My stomach dropped. I'd done it again.

Ollie jumped off the stage and stalked through the crowd, headed toward me. I tried to put some distance between me and Dylan, as if that would help when only minutes ago, I'd been grinding my ass against his groin. Ollie stopped in front of me.

"What is he doing here?" Ollie gritted out, skin slick with sweat, green eyes flashing with anger.

"I texted you that he was coming. You never replied." As if that was any excuse.

"You expected her to come to this bar alone?" Dylan said. "The fuck were you thinking?"

Be quiet, Dylan. He had a knack for making matters even worse than they already were.

Ollie glared at Dylan, hands clenched into fists, and for a minute I was worried he would punch him. But that wasn't Ollie's style. "This is between me and Scarlett." Ollie grabbed my arm and dragged me away from Dylan to a dark corner near the front door. His jaw clenched and the muscle in his cheek jumped. I had a sinking feeling that this time there would be no coming back. "So you're doing this. You're getting involved with him?"

"I…" I looked over at Dylan. I'd left him alone for two seconds and some blonde chick was already hitting on him. I wanted to scratch out her eyeballs. Scream that he's mine. *Back off, bitch.* He made me feel violent.

What the hell was wrong with me? My gaze swung back to Ollie.

"Forget it. I have my answer." He ran his hand through his sweaty hair and shook his head in disbelief. "You've made your choice. Hope you know what you're doing."

I grabbed his arm to stop him from walking away. "What do you mean?"

"You want me to spell it out for you?" He laughed harshly. "I can't be your friend, Scarlett. I tried but I just can't do it."

I stared blankly, not sure I'd heard him right. "But… what are you talking about? You can't mean that."

"It kills me to see you with him," he said, his voice strained.

"Ollie. Don't do this," I pleaded. "Please. We can… I can… we'll figure this out." I scrambled to find the words that would turn this around but there were none. "I don't want to lose you."

"I lost you a long time ago. You'll live," he spat out.

My heart squeezed in anguish at the realization that this was really it. Ollie and I were going to end fourteen years of friendship in a dark corner of a dive bar. "Ollie, please. Let's just—"

"Let's just what?" he seethed. "Let me put this in perspective for you. Give you something you can understand. I've been in love with you for as long as you've been in love with *him*. You broke my fucking heart, Scarlett. *Everyone* knew I was in love with you. Everyone except you."

"I'm sorry." My words came out in a broken whisper. Ollie was beautiful, he really was. Talented. Funny. With a big heart. He would do anything for a friend. Any girl would be so lucky to have him. Falling in love with him should have been so easy. "I'm so sorry. I never meant to hurt you."

"Yeah, well, from where I'm sitting, you'd never know it."

This time when he walked away, I didn't chase after him. There was nothing I could say or do to make this better. Blindly pushing through the crowd, my vision blurred by tears, I stumbled out of the front door and leaned against the brick wall for support. I took a shuddering breath, my heart in my throat.

How could I have been so cruel? So careless with my best friend's feelings?

Not once, but twice I'd thrown it in his face. If I were Ollie, I would hate me too.

I heard the door open and the music spilled out then it was muffled by the door closing. Dylan came to stand in front of me, his eyes flitting over my face, trying to read it. Shouldn't be hard. I swiped at the tears on my cheeks, angry at myself and angry at him.

"Happy now? Ollie's out of the picture."

Dylan leaned down so he was eye level with me. "You think it makes me happy to see you sad?"

My shoulders sagged, the weight of what I'd done pressing down on me. "How could I have done this to him? How could I be so horrible?"

"You're not horrible."

"Why did you insist on coming tonight?" The real question was, why had I let him? I should have put a stop to it. Should have told him no. Or at the very least, I should have kept my hands off him. That was the trouble with being with Dylan. Whenever I was around him, I couldn't think straight and made bad decisions.

I'd destroyed a friendship. What else would I destroy for Dylan?

Five minutes later, Dylan pulled into the 7-Eleven and cut the
engine.

"What are we doing here?"

"I'll leave the keys in the ignition, so you can listen to
music." He gave my thigh a gentle squeeze, trying to reassure
me that everything would be okay. "Be right back."

The door slammed behind him and I watched him walk
into the store and head down one of the aisles like a man on a
mission while The Neighbourhood's "Sweater Weather" played
from his Bluetooth speakers in the car.

I slumped in my seat and took out my phone to text Nic but
I wasn't ready to discuss what happened with Ollie yet and I
knew she'd pump me for details, so I tucked my phone back in
my pocket and closed my eyes. All I could see was Ollie's face.
Ollie had been my first, my only one. Even that was tied to
Dylan in a roundabout way, thanks to a conversation we had
when I was fifteen.

"Anyone ever fucks with you, you call me, understand?"

"Yeah, sure. But I've never been fucked with or fucked."

"Keep it that way."

"You think I should stay a virgin forever, Dylan?"

*"Wait until you find someone who treats you right. Someone
special. And don't say the word fuck. It sounds all wrong coming out
of your mouth."*

I'd taken Dylan's advice and I had waited for someone
special. Someone I trusted with my heart. I chose Ollie, and
he'd been so gentle, so sweet. But I'd broken his heart. My head
fell back against the headrest with a thud and I banged it a few
times.

I hated myself right now.

Dylan returned with two plastic carrier bags and stowed
them in the back. I didn't even ask what was in the bags. I didn't
say a word as he pulled out onto the road. Minutes later, he

parked in the public lot by the pier and tossed a hoodie at me from the backseat.

"Come on."

"Where are we going?"

"Something I want to show you."

"I just want to go home," I said, weary and defeated.

"And do what? Eat ice cream and watch 80s flicks? I've got a better idea. Come on," he coaxed. "The view's better where we're going."

With a sigh, I got out of the car and walked alongside him, the sea breeze cooling my flushed cheeks. I shivered, threading my arms through the hoodie and zipping it up, annoyed with myself when I burrowed my nose in the cotton fabric, inhaling his scent. I needed an intervention. We followed the curved sidewalk past the pink stone benches on a grassy hill over-looking the sea and passed a group of teens doing skateboard tricks off the low wall, their wheels grating against the concrete.

We stopped outside the front entrance of The Surf Lodge, and Dylan transferred both bags to his right hand and unlocked the door then ushered me inside and used his phone flashlight to guide the way.

"Careful," he said, giving me his hand so I didn't trip over the rolled-up carpeting and debris littering the uneven floor.

The construction crew had walked out halfway through the job and left walls partially knocked out and electrical wiring exposed.

We climbed the stairs, Dylan leading the way, and I stayed close behind him. The hotel smelled musty, the sawdust from the construction work lodging in my throat and making me cough. When we reached the top of the stairs, Dylan flung open a door and ushered me onto a flat roof. I took deep breaths of the fresh sea air and trained my phone flashlight on the space, arcing the light across the bar spanning the far wall, tarps covering what I guessed were tables and bar furniture.

Dylan dragged two Adirondack chairs over to the railing and set them up side by side. I took a seat next to him and looked down at the two bags at our feet.

"What's in the bags?"

"Trick or Treat."

Despite myself, I laughed a little and rooted through a bag of snack food. Doritos, Twizzlers, M&Ms, a bagful of sweet and salty junk food. I knew he hadn't bought them for himself. This was his attempt to try to make me feel better. I never would have dreamt that Dylan could be so sweet, but he was always surprising me.

He flipped the lid off a bottle of beer with his key and handed it to me before he opened one for himself. "Thank you."

He nodded once.

"It's beautiful up here." I leaned back in my seat that was sticky from the salty air, and took in the view of the ocean, a silver slipper of moon shimmering on the water, the sound of the waves crashing against the shore a soothing lullaby.

"Yeah. It is. The first time I saw the Pacific Ocean... any ocean... I was sixteen. It was the only time in my life that the reality lived up to the dream." Wanting to hear more, I waited, sensing that he was going to share a piece of himself with me.

"Me and Remy wanted to learn how to surf. We taught ourselves to skateboard, so we figured we could do the same with surfing. So, one day we rented boards from Jimmy... Shane's dad. He used to own a surf shop." I nodded, acknowledging that I knew who Jimmy was even though I'd never had a chance to meet him.

"He told us he'd teach us a few basics." Dylan chuckled under his breath. "He brought us out here and made us practice on the sand. I was so pissed. I just wanted to get out in the water. But, for some reason, I stayed, and I listened to everything he told us. I think it was because nobody had ever taken the time to teach me anything. And he was just this cool, chilled-out hippie dude. Big on finding his Zen and shit."

I smiled, envisioning a teenage Dylan and an older version of Shane bonding over surfing. "Like Shane?"

"Even more laidback than Shane. He always gave the best advice. Not that I always took it. But when I was in college, Remy was gone... Shane was gone... and I used to kick back with Jimmy, smoke weed, talk about life and shit."

"You miss him," I said softly.

"He was the best guy I've ever known. He got married on this roof. He told me that he wanted to buy The Surf Lodge someday and restore it. But he never got the chance."

I thought about his story. For Dylan, this wasn't just an old hotel and it wasn't about the money. He wanted to hang on to a piece of history, a piece of Jimmy, and one of the ways he could do that was by restoring The Surf Lodge. "This place means a lot to you."

He nodded. "But buying something for sentimental reasons is typically a bad business decision."

"I wish there was something I could do." I stared at the bottle in my hand, once again reminded of how little regard my father had for anything but the almighty dollar.

"Not your problem. I'll figure it out." He sounded so confident, but I got the feeling that he'd say those words no matter what the situation. "What happened with Ollie?"

"He said he can't be my friend anymore," I said, my stomach sinking as the finality of those words hit me all over again.

"He's still in love with you."

My spirits sank even lower, and I tried to swallow past the lump in my throat. Had I really been so blind, so stupid that I hadn't seen what was right in front of my eyes? A stab of guilt lay buried in my heart and I didn't think it would ever go away. "I don't know. Maybe."

"Come here." He patted his lap.

Tempting but dangerous. Whenever I got too close to him, it only made me want more. I shouldn't even be talking to him right now, not after what had happened tonight.

"Why did you insist on coming with me tonight?" I asked again, my voice tinged with bitterness.

"I told you," he said, sounding exasperated that I would question him. "I didn't want you to go to that bar alone." His tone softened. "I wasn't trying to fuck up your friendship."

I heard the sincerity in his voice but still. Maybe he hadn't intended to fuck up my friendship but it had happened anyway. In my heart, I knew I had nobody to blame except myself. I'd let Dylan come with me tonight. I'd done nothing to stop him when he'd wrapped his arms around me. He hadn't forced me to do anything, I'd encouraged it.

I sucked.

"I did a pretty good job of that all on my own."

He set down his beer, stood up and scooped me up in his arms like I was featherlight then sat down, holding me in his lap, my legs hanging over the arm of his chair, his arm around my back. I squirmed, trying to get away, my beer sloshing from the bottle and seeping into his hoodie. He held onto me and he didn't let me go.

"Stop fighting me. Just relax." He rubbed his nose against the side of mine and kissed the corner of my lips. "Look up, Starlet."

I tipped my head back and looked up at the stars reeling in the sky. When I was a kid, I used to think they were close enough to reach up and touch. Now they looked so impossibly far away.

"Do you still wish on stars?" he asked, bringing his beer to his lips.

"No." I searched for the brightest star and tried to remember when or why I'd stopped wishing on them. "Did you used to wish on stars?"

"Never."

My gaze settled on him. He was watching the stars, his head leaning against the back of the chair, his throat exposed. I wanted to lick it. Bury my face in it. Instead, I took a sip of my beer. "Why not?"

He shrugged one shoulder, eyes still on the sky. "Couldn't see the point."

"What about when you blew out your birthday candles? Did you make a wish then?"

"Nope."

"That's just... really sad."

Dylan laughed softly. "You think?" I nodded. He squeezed my thigh. "Did any of your wishes ever come true?"

"Yes." *You kissed me.*

"They say to be careful what you wish for."

"Maybe I should have listened to them."

His lips curved into a half-smile as if he knew what my wish had been. I didn't know if it was good or bad that I'd gotten my wish. It had felt inevitable.

In the moonlight, his edges looked sharper, his hair darker and skin paler. Like a black and white photo with all the color leached out of it. It was surreal to be here with him, sitting on his lap on the rooftop of a 1950s hotel on a starry February night. For so long, this had been my dream, my wish on a star, and now that it was happening, I wasn't sure what to do about it.

Be careful what you wish for.

Twisting my body around, I reached for the bag on the ground behind my back. Dylan reached over and grabbed it for me, setting it in my lap. I ripped open a bag of peanut M&Ms and tossed a few into my mouth, offering the bag to Dylan. He shook his head no so I kept them in my lap for easy access to a sugar high.

We lapsed into silence and drank our beers under the stars,

the waves crashing against the shore our soundtrack, my cheek resting on his collarbone.

It was my curse to fall in love with Dylan. Ollie was the first casualty, but I knew that if I continued, he wouldn't be the last. By pursuing whatever this was with Dylan, I stood to lose a lot. Whereas what did he have to lose, really?

My father would have gone after him anyway so that had nothing to do with our relationship. He and Sienna were over, so he'd already lost her. Remy, I knew, would always choose Dylan. She hadn't even stayed friends with Sienna. What if I lost my job because of this? If Sienna ever found out, she would disown me. Was it worth risking everything?

There were too many obstacles in our way, and there was no use pretending that Dylan could ever be mine. But whenever I was presented with a choice, to stay or walk away, I always did the wrong thing.

"You're thinking too hard." He smoothed his hand over my furrowed brow and brushed my hair off my cheek, his hand gliding to the back of my head, angling it toward him. Our mouths collided, suddenly and all at once, and our kiss was hungry, filled with need and want and the tantalizing promise of more.

We kissed until our lips were raw and swollen. The scruff on his jaw scraped my soft skin but I didn't care. I kissed him like a junkie who needed a fix.

Stars died and were reborn and my crazy heart changed its tempo, beating in time with his.

The line between right and wrong had blurred and shifted, and all I could think about was chasing this heady, intoxicating feeling where everything was so wrong yet felt so right.

Because of a kiss. Because of *him*.

16

DYLAN

"So... Woods wants to buy you out?" Cruz said, his voice low as the locker room door closed behind Raj, our software engineer. The trouble with using the gym in our office building was that everyone from our office used it too.

"Looks that way." I tossed my towel in my gym bag and pulled on a pair of black sweatpants and a T-shirt then sat on the bench to put on my high tops.

"And let me guess... you said no."

I'd had a few more choice words but 'no' was the gist of it. Woods hadn't called me personally, his lawyer had.

"Meanwhile, you're bumping uglies with his daughter. The *other* daughter. Is this a vendetta or something?"

"Scarlett has nothing to do with it."

Cruz gave me a skeptical look. "It just seems fucked up that of all the girls you could go for, you chose her. You know this can't end well, right? Look what happened with you and Sienna. And this is her *sister.*"

Like I needed a reminder. I slung my gym bag over my shoulder and we strode to the door. "They're nothing alike."

"She's not a bitch like Sienna was," he acknowledged. Not

sure if bitch was the right word for Sienna but I guess you could say I brought out the worst in her.

I was no Dr. Phil but even I knew that our relationship had been toxic. She'd fed me lies and empty promises and I'd kept the relationship alive by punching inanimate objects, breaking shit or just walking away and leaving her to deal with her own bullshit. It got to the point where we couldn't even be in the same room without her ending up in tears or screaming that I was an asshole.

Yet every single time I left her, she had begged me to come back, to give it another try because 'next time everything would be different.' Where had I heard that one before? Why had we kept going back for more torture? Fuck if I knew.

Here's the definition of stupidity: Keep doing the same stupid shit and expecting different results.

So yeah, I was over Sienna, but Scarlett was a different story. She was a challenge, and I'd never backed down from a challenge in my life. She was making me work for something I'd never had to work for before, and blue balls aside, it was not only refreshing, it was fun.

Scarlett made me happy but more than that, I wanted to make her happy. It hadn't been my intention to wreck her friendship with Shaggy Doo, but in all fairness, I hadn't realized that he was still in love with her. Should have picked up on that the night of her birthday I guess. But come on, the asshole had cheated on her. What did he expect? It was naïve of Scarlett to think that they could still be 'just friends.'

Let's face it, men were territorial, we staked our claim, and we didn't want any other asshole coming along and pissing on our territory. Scarlett was mine now. In the sense that I wasn't hooking up with anyone else.

Would it be better if I walked away? Hell yes. But was I going to? I *should*.

As it turned out, the universe had a sick sense of humor.

"Why do you want to talk to him?" Cruz asked, his eyes narrowing with suspicion, his phone pressed to his ear as we headed to our cars in the parking deck. He shook his head and huffed out a laugh. "They don't need you playing fairy godmother, babe."

Babe?

Cruz held out his phone to me. I raised my brows. "It's Nicola. Said she needs a favor."

I took the phone from him, wondering what the hell Nicola could want from me. "Yeah?"

"Hey Dylan. Listen, Scarlett's sick. She has a bad cold. I'm at work but I've made her some beef marrow broth."

"Beef marrow broth. The fuck is that?"

"It's really good for you. I've made enough for you too. Can you just pick it up from Cinque Terre and take it to her? Please. I would but I can't leave work. You're the only one I could call. She can't get Remy sick and if Shane gets sick—"

I cut off her long-winded explanation before she named every Tom, Dick, and Ollie in Scarlett's life and gave a reason why they couldn't help. "Yeah, I got it. See you in ten."

I ended the call even though she might have still been talking, and handed the phone back to Cruz.

Cruz scowled. "You were supposed to pass the phone back to me, dickwad."

"Call her back." I climbed into my car and slammed the door shut on his next words.

Armed with enough beef marrow broth to feed a small country, I rapped my knuckles against Scarlett's front door and waited. Nothing. I knocked again. Still no answer so I tried the door, never expecting it to open.

Fucking hell.

This might not be LA or New York City, but I didn't know of a single place safe enough to leave your door unlocked. Anyone could have walked in and robbed her blind. Or worse.

I flicked the switch on the wall, shedding some light on the living room and locked the door behind me.

"Scarlett?" I called as I crossed the small living area to the kitchen separated by a half-wall.

I'd only been to her apartment once, the night of her birthday. It looked like her. Vintage with a dash of modern. A midnight blue sofa, 1950s style wood coffee table, and two mismatched chairs. One was green, the other mustard yellow. A few pieces of framed artwork decorated the white walls and I knew they were her designs.

I set the containers of soup on the kitchen counter and called her name again as I strode down the hallway, poking my head into the rooms until I got to hers and stopped in the doorway. Fairy lights draped over her headboard lit up the darkness and her small form was huddled under a Hawaiian flower-print duvet. Hundreds of Polaroids hung from fishing wire on the wall above her bed.

Dragging my eyes away from smiling photos of her with Shaggy Doo and her friends—snapshots of happy memories from the past decade of her life—I crouched in front of her, so we were eye level. "Hey," I said quietly. "How are you feeling?"

Her eyelids fluttered open and she winced like the light hurt her eyes. They were glazed over, her cheeks rosy, and her lips chapped. Her wavy blonde hair was matted to the side of her head. She looked so young, like a child with a fever, but even sick, she was still so fucking pretty. The kind of pretty that was dangerous.

She made me hard, but she also made me weak. For her.

"What are you doing—" She started coughing and couldn't

finish the sentence. Her eyes closed again like they were too heavy to hold open.

I laid my hand on her forehead. She flinched at my touch, a groan escaping her lips.

"You're burning up."

"Your hands are so cold," she said, her voice hoarse. My hands were warm, just like they always were. She was shivering so hard I could hear her teeth chattering. "So cold. Can't warm up."

I debated for a minute before I kicked off my high tops and rounded the bed to the other side, pulling down the covers. A quick glimpse revealed that she was wearing my old hoodie with flannel pajama bottoms. I climbed into bed behind her in my T-shirt and sweats and pulled up the covers to trap the heat from our bodies. It was like a fucking oven under here, but she was still shivering so I pulled her close and tried to warm her up with my body heat.

Scarlett brought out all my protective instincts, always had. When she was in her teens, the thought of anyone messing with her used to make me feel nauseous. She was tough and strong in her own way, but she had this innocence about her, like the world was still a thing of joy and wonder. I loved that about her. I loved a lot of things about her.

I remember the night she turned up at my underground fight. Not the kind of place she should have ever ventured to. Especially not alone, at night, on a bus and on foot.

To make matters worse, she'd attracted attention. A tiny blonde bombshell with wide baby blues and those goddamn lips that just beckon you to sink your teeth into them. Or kiss them raw. Or have them wrapped around your... fuck, I couldn't think about that now. She was sick. Burning up with fever while I was sweating my balls off from the heat radiating off her body. But I stayed right where I was, her own personal space heater, trying to keep her warm.

"Better?" I asked a little while later when her teeth had stopped chattering.

"Mmm hmm."

So, it was the first time I slept with Scarlett Woods, we did not have sex or do anything even remotely sexual.

During the night, she drifted in and out of a semi-lucid state and confided things that I was sure she wouldn't have if she hadn't been out of her mind with a fever of 102. I knew it was 102 because I used the digital thermometer I found in the bathroom cabinet to check. Every hour. On the hour. Like a mother hen.

I plied her with water and some of that beef broth which tasted better than it sounded, and I listened to her ramblings. She was cute and funny and honest, and she made me wish for something I'd never wanted before. To be the hero in someone's fairy tale instead of the villain.

Because Scarlett Woods confessed that she'd been in love with me ever since she was eleven years old and I climbed into her bedroom window.

17

SCARLETT

There was a soft knock on my bedroom door and then it opened, light spilling into my dark room from the hallway. Nic gave me a big smile and flicked on my table lamp. I blinked a few times, trying to accustom my eyes to the light as she set a steaming mug of something on my bedside table.

"How are you feeling?" she asked, sitting on the edge of my bed. She smelled like grapefruit shower gel, her wet hair pulled back in a sleek ponytail, in terrycloth shorts and an oversized Lakers sweatshirt that used to be Aaron's.

I propped up the pillows against my headboard and sat up. Just that simple act made me dizzy and gave me a coughing fit.

Stupid cold. It had started with a sore throat and a cough on Sunday. When I woke up Monday morning, I was achy all over and even my eyeballs had hurt. "Like a limp noodle."

"I'm not surprised. Drink your broth."

"Broth?" I reached for the mug and wrapped my hands around it, bringing it up to my nose for a sniff. "What is this?" I asked, pulling a face.

"Just drink it. It's good for you. Trust me."

"Says the girl who loves anchovies." I took a sip. It wasn't too terrible, but I wouldn't exactly be clamoring for more.

"Well?" she asked, gesturing to my mug.

"Not bad." I took another sip to placate her. "Mmm. Yum."

She laughed, and crawled up the bed, sitting next to me with her back against the headboard, her enviably long legs crossed at the ankles.

"How long have I been asleep?" I glanced out the window. It was dark. Like middle-of-the-night dark.

"About twenty-four hours, give or take."

My eyes widened. "What?!" I scrunched my nose. "No wonder I smell like I just rolled out of a dumpster."

"Yeah." She pinched the end of her nose. "You smell, babe."

Couldn't be insulted when she was just speaking the truth. "What about work?"

"I called in sick for you. Shane said to take as long as you need. Remy called to make sure you were okay."

Knowing that Shane and Remy had been informed, I relaxed a little and drank my broth. We were quiet, but she had a big smile on her face. After eight years of friendship, I knew how to read her. She was bursting to tell me something big. I smacked her arm. "Oh my God. Did you and Cruz elope?"

She rolled her eyes. "It's only been one day, not ten years, Rip Van Winkle. But guess who nursed you back to health?" She looked smug. Therefore, untrustworthy.

"You?" I asked hopefully. Please let it be Nic.

Nic shook her head, her smile wide. *Don't say it, don't say it, don't say it.* "Dylan."

She said it. With a groan, I sagged back against my pillows. I vaguely remembered him being here, but I thought it had been a dream. Last night I'd had a lot of freaky weird dreams and at one point, a giant hot dog was chasing me down the street. I didn't even want to analyze that one. "Really? Dylan saw me like this?" I asked with dismay.

I lifted the covers to remind myself what I was wearing. Black and green plaid pajama bottoms and fuzzy Halloween socks with *his* hoodie. Ugh. Someone just shoot me. I looked like a bag lady.

Nic nodded, looking all proud of herself. "Yep. I called him yesterday and he rose to the challenge."

"Why would you call him?" Because, really, he was the very last person she should have considered calling. Nothing says romance like a cough and a fever. Ugh, we weren't romantically involved. Yes, were. No, we weren't. My internal debate sapped what little strength I had left in my body.

I was exhausted. Wrung out like a used dishrag.

"I had to work, and I didn't want you to be alone. If you had a different mother, I would have called her, but your mother would have been useless."

Sadly, it was true. When I was a kid, I was prone to fevers, and my mother had always let the nanny deal with my childhood illnesses. But still. *Dylan*?

"He stayed the night and left this morning."

I set the mug on my bedside table, buying time before I asked the question, dreading to hear the answer. "Um, where did he sleep?"

"In your bed."

"Oh my God. That's just..." I didn't know what it was. Mortifying? Crazy?

"He was really great," Nic said. "I thought he'd just drop off the soup or maybe, at a stretch, stay until I got home from work, but he went the extra mile."

"I don't think he does anything halfway." Which made me think of his words: *Not until you're ready to fuck me or wrap your lips around my cock.* Should I be thinking of that now? No, absolutely not. "But Nic, that whole thing at Mavericks..." It felt like a lifetime ago, but it still hurt like a fresh wound. "I lost Ollie."

"I know. That sucks."

I'd told her the whole story the following day, so she did know but I still felt the need to hash it out. "If Dylan hadn't been there, none of that would have happened."

"I've been thinking about this. If what Ollie said is true, that you broke his heart, he would have had the same problem seeing you with any guy. It just happened to be Dylan."

Someone was Team Dylan. She'd never once defended Ollie like she did Dylan. "Why are you trying to push us together?"

Before she could answer, her phone pinged, and she checked it, hiding the screen before I could read the text. It was probably from Cruz. They'd been texting non-stop since the night they met. Their relationship was so easy. Boy meets girl, boy falls for girl, girl wants to jump his bones. And it was perfectly acceptable for them to do that. There were no obstacles in their way. No sister. No Ollie. No conniving father.

"If you hurry up and finish that broth, you might have time for a shower."

No sooner were the words out of her mouth when someone pounded on the front door. It sounded aggressive. My mind immediately went to the most likely candidate. "Oh no. Tell me it's not—"

"What did I tell you about locking the front door?" Dylan growled.

My eyes widened when I heard the door close which meant that Dylan was inside our apartment. On the prowl.

"Nic," I hissed. "Tell him I'm not here."

"Hey Dylan. We're in Scarlett's bedroom," she yelled.

Traitor. I pulled the covers over my head.

Chase proposed to Sienna on Valentine's Day. He'd taken her to a trendy restaurant in West Hollywood and when the molten chocolate lava cake arrived, he'd gotten down on one knee in front of everyone and their mother and asked Sienna to marry him. There had been tears and champagne and she'd said yes.

I found this out from my mother who left it on a voicemail this morning while I was in the shower. There was another voicemail from Sienna telling me a similar story.

On my fifteen-minute walk to work, I called her back because it would be rude not to. Normally, I didn't mind the walk, but dark storm clouds had gathered, and I didn't have an umbrella. I was finally feeling human again and had kicked that cold to the curb so the last thing I needed was to get caught in a downpour.

"Congratulations," I told Sienna, forcing enthusiasm into my voice, and hoping it would override the guilt I was feeling. "I'm really happy for you."

"Thanks. Mom's already planning the wedding." I could practically hear the eye-roll on her end. It matched mine.

"Well, at least it will give her something new to obsess about."

I should tell her. Now was my chance. I kissed your exboyfriend. He gave me two orgasms. Okay, three. He nursed me back to health. He brought me spicy Pho and ice cream last night and we binge-watched *Stranger Things*.

How could I tell her any of this? What words could convey how deeply sorry I was that I'd fallen in love with the very last guy I should have? I was a skank. A ho. Candidate for worst sister ever.

"Um, so... you and Chase are happy, right? You really love him, don't you?"

Coward.

She hesitated a moment before answering, or I could have imagined that. "I wouldn't have said yes if I didn't love him. We're really good together. We're good for each other."

"In what way?" I darted over to Corbin who was huddled inside a sleeping bag in his usual spot behind the dry cleaners.

He was a war vet, one of the forgotten, and had lost his mind somewhere in a desert half a world away.

I set the plastic carrier bag next to his army green duffel bag and slipped away before he woke up. Sometimes he got angry. Sometimes he cried.

One of the cooks from the taco joint next door winked at me as I hurried past him in the alley, like we were conspirators.

"We come from similar backgrounds and you might not think that's important, but it is," Sienna said. "And we have the same core values."

Not exactly the answer you'd expect from someone who was madly in love. It sounded more like something a shrink would say. What were core values?

"Oh. Okay. That's good. Core values are good. I'm just glad you're happy and that you moved on and found someone... who's right for you," I finished lamely.

"It makes life a lot easier. I mean, with Dylan, everything was just so exhausting. He was hard work whereas Chase actually talks and acts like an adult."

Relief flooded my body. Dylan had been exhausting. She didn't want to go back for more of that. She was over him. "Well, I guess that's how it is when you find the right person. It's not supposed to be so hard, right?"

"I guess not." She was silent a beat. "Have you met anyone special?"

Yes, and sometimes he even talks to me. "Nope."

God was going to strike me down. I looked up at the sky. The clouds were getting darker.

"Maybe you'll meet a hot surfer dude at work. Hey, I have to run. I need to get to a meeting. Talk soon, brat," she said, using her old nickname for me but her tone was affectionate.

After we ended the call, I picked up my pace, trying to beat the rain. Seconds before I reached the front door, the skies opened up and the first lashings of rain hit my face.

Was this my punishment for lusting after Dylan St. Clair? How biblical.

Or it could be my punishment for justifying my behavior. Sienna had sounded happy. She was getting married to a man she loved. She had moved on. Why shouldn't Dylan be able to do the same? There was absolutely nothing wrong with what we were doing.

Keep telling yourself that. One of these days you'll actually start believing your own lies.

18

SCARLETT

This wasn't a date. It was just two friends eating a casual dinner together. At a little sushi place in Santa Ana. Thirty miles from Costa del Rey, where it was unlikely we'd run into anyone we knew.

Dylan had picked me up right after he finished work and was dressed in black jeans and a steel gray button-down shirt that brought out the gray in his eyes. They looked like summer lightning. Smolderingly hot. Like him.

When I'd climbed into the passenger seat, my fingers had itched to run through his thick, dark hair and make it messy and disheveled. But I'd refrained. *Just barely.*

On the drive to the restaurant, I told Dylan about Sienna's engagement and had watched his face closely to gauge his reaction. But as far as I could tell, he hadn't been distressed or surprised by the news. All he'd said was, "Sounds like she found the kind of guy she should have been with all along." Then he'd cranked up the music, and that had been the end of that conversation.

Now, I watched Dylan across the blond wood table as he slathered a piece of salmon sashimi with enough wasabi to clear his nasal passages for an entire decade. He guided the quivering raw fish to his mouth and I laughed when his eyes widened and started to water. "Whoa," he said, with a shake of his head that made me laugh harder.

The funny part? He loaded up the next piece of sashimi with even more wasabi than the last one. His eyes were streaming now. It was so ridiculous I couldn't stop laughing.

"You're ridiculous," I said, eying him over the rim of my teacup.

"I know," he said with a laugh.

Tonight I was getting to see a different side of Dylan. He was fun and playful, his posture relaxed and I was really beginning to believe that the news of Sienna's engagement hadn't rocked his world or crushed his heart.

"Are you a masochist?" I dipped a piece of shrimp tempura roll in my bowl of soy sauce and popped it into my mouth. Mmm, so good.

"I like the head rush."

"You're weird," I said around a mouthful of sushi, my chopsticks already reaching for a piece of salmon nigiri from the sushi platter we were sharing. That's how greedy I was.

"So are you."

"Thank you," I said, accepting it as the compliment it was intended to be. "Were you a glue sniffer when you were a kid?"

"Nah." He gave me a crooked grin with those pouty lips of his, the grin so boyish and adorable it was disarming. "Whip-its was where it was at."

"Never tried it."

He stabbed his chopsticks into the last piece of miso blackened cod, beating me to it. My jaw dropped, my chopsticks poised above the now-empty blue glazed dish, and he laughed at the look on my face when he popped it into his mouth. "You don't know what you're missing."

Ha. Well, he'd never be accused of being a gentleman. I

settled for the gyoza instead. Not like I was going to go hungry. Dylan had ordered enough food for six, not two. "When did your whip-it addiction start?" I asked, taking a sip of my tea while I surveyed the options in front of me. Seared tuna or another gyoza?

"When I was about eight or nine, we lived in this old lady's house in Savannah. Dot. She kept whipped cream in the fridge for her ice cream sundaes. I loved that shit. Best day ever when I figured out that if you suck on the nuzzle, it gives you a high. Poor Dot. Made her crazy thinking she ran out of it again or forgot to buy it. I used to steal it and hide it in my room as soon as she bought a new one."

I laughed. "A thief and a druggie at eight."

"Started young."

I decided that I'd eaten enough and if I had another bite, I'd explode so I poured myself another cup of tea from the ceramic pot on the table. "How many places have you lived?"

He set down his chopsticks and leaned back in his seat, taking a swig of his beer. "Too many to count."

"Why did you move so much?" I asked, curious to know more about his childhood. More about him and where he came from and what his life was like.

He shrugged one shoulder, his gaze roaming the small, minimalist sushi restaurant. We were in one of the wood booths across from a long sushi bar where the chefs served customers seated at the bar. "My mom was always looking for something better."

"What did she do for a living?" I asked, wondering if their frequent moves were work-related.

"She bartended. Among other things."

I waited to hear what 'other things' meant but he was done talking.

"You done?" he asked while simultaneously motioning for

the check. Our waiter was so efficient he was at our booth, check in hand, within seconds.

I still had a cup of tea to drink and food to digest. Meanwhile, Dylan was already handing the waiter his credit card.

God. This guy. As soon as he divulged a tiny bit about himself or his past, he shut me down.

"Don't shake it. Cover the nozzle with your mouth and inhale."

"Am I doing it right?"

"Take it in deeper. Wrap your lips around it."

I smacked his arm, laughing. "Enough with the double entendre."

"Look at you and your fancy French words."

I was laughing so hard and I hadn't even done the whip-it yet.

Dylan reversed out of his parking spot in front of the convenience store and pulled out onto the road while I tried to come to grips with how to do a whip-it. I angled the can into my mouth and covered the nozzle then sucked on it for a few seconds before releasing it. It made me lightheaded, a little woozy but I didn't love it. I tried it a few more times for good measure then shook the can and squirted whipped cream into my mouth.

"Mmm." I'd rather eat the whipped cream than get the nitrous oxide high. "Dessert."

"Fuck. You're making me hard." Leaving one hand on the wheel, Dylan adjusted himself in his jeans.

"Watching me eat whipped cream is making you hard?" I teased, squirting more whipped cream into my mouth. I grinned at him and leaned over the center console, armed with a can of Reddi-Wip. "Open up."

Angling his head toward me, one eye still on the road, he

opened his mouth and I filled it with whipped cream. Then he grabbed the can out of my hand and flung it into the backseat, guiding my hand down so I could feel what I'd done to him.

Feeling bold and adventurous, I unbuttoned his jeans and slid down the zipper. He tried to push my hand away. "I want to touch you," I insisted.

"What did I say?" he reminded me. This guy was so stubborn, I knew he wouldn't back down from what he'd said.

"Are you saying that you'd rather wait..." My hand wrapped around him through his briefs. I'd never touched him before but now I could feel how thick and hard he was and I wanted more of him. "That you'd rather deny yourself?"

He captured my hand in his and moved it away. "Are you saying *you'd* rather deny yourself?" he countered.

I licked my lips, feeling the inexplicable urge to taste him. To feel him inside me. To have all of him, any way I could get it. I wanted it. Wanted him. And he wouldn't let me have him unless it was all or nothing. Ollie had always been so careful with me. He'd treated me like I was made of glass. Fragile. Breakable. A part of me must have known that it wasn't enough for him, that he'd wanted more of me. Yet he'd never pushed me too hard. And now I understood why. He was scared of losing me. Whereas Dylan was the opposite. He pushed me to the limits because that was how he lived. Like he had nothing to lose.

It made me feel daring. Teetering on the edge of that rock cliff, on the verge of free falling into the unknown. That was how it always felt with Dylan.

Unclipping my seatbelt, I got on my knees and leaned across the center console.

"What are you doing, Starlet?"

"Giving you a blowjob."

"Say it. Say the words."

I took a deep breath and shoved my inhibitions aside. It was easier in the dark, the only light coming from his dash so he couldn't see my cheeks flaming. "I want to wrap my lips around your cock."

Dylan groaned, this low guttural sound that went straight to my core, and pushed down the waistband of his briefs. His dick sprang free, and I stared at it as if I'd never seen a penis in my life. Okay, I was not the most experienced girl around. But Dylan's was thick and long and hard, pointing straight up and it just looked so damn big to me. Was it bigger than average? Oh God, why was I thinking about the size of his dick? Probably because it was about to be inside my mouth. And maybe other places.

The stars tattooed on his abs were aligned but this time I didn't feel the urge to laugh. Not even a little bit.

My hand wrapped around the base and I squeezed, feeling it twitch and grow harder in my hand as I guided the tip to my mouth and wrapped my lips around it. I had no idea what the hell I was doing. I gave it a few licks.

"It's not a fucking popsicle," he growled. "If you're going to do this, you do it my way."

"What does that mean?"

I soon found out. His hand tangled in my hair and he held the back of my head, guiding me to where he wanted me.

"Suck hard," he commanded.

I tried to take in as much of him as I could. I'd never been into giving blow jobs before, and the times I'd tried, I ended up chickening out and giving a hand job. But hearing Dylan's ragged breathing and the words that came out of his dirty mouth like a growl had me so turned on, I was squeezing my thighs together to ease the delicious ache as I sucked him hard, my cheeks hollowed. And even though I had no idea what I was doing, it didn't seem to matter.

It made me feel powerful to know that he was coming undone because of me, thrusting into my mouth so hard and so deep I could feel him at the back of my throat. I gagged a little but found my rhythm as we barreled down the freeway, Blackbear's "Girls Like U" blasting from the speakers.

"I'm going to come," he warned.

"Mmm hmm," I hummed, the vibration pushing him over the edge.

"Fuuck," he said as spurts of warm, salty liquid came into my mouth. I felt the car swerve a little until he righted it because, of course, the first time I gave someone a blowjob I'd do it in a speeding car while they were driving.

I ran my tongue over the slit, catching the last drop before I released him and sat back on my heels, licking my lips. He glanced over at me before he returned his attention to the road and tucked himself back in his jeans, zipping them up but leaving the button undone.

"Not bad for someone who doesn't give blowjobs."

"Not bad?" I asked, brows raised in indignation.

"Pretty fucking amazing." I smirked. "Take off your jeans."

"Why?" I looked out the windshield and confirmed that we were still on the freeway.

"Just do it."

I hesitated a moment then sat the right way around in my seat and undid my jeans, convinced that if he asked me to jump off the Golden Gate, I'd do it. I kicked off my black Vans and lifted my butt off the seat to push them down. Wriggling out of my jeans, I tossed them on the floor, leaving me in pale pink cotton boy shorts. I was wearing a black lacy bra under my off-the-shoulder black sweater.

"Touch yourself."

"Touch myself?" I asked stupidly.

"Mmm hmm."

I'd never done anything like this before. Not in front of someone. But the ache between my thighs was so delicious it was almost painful, and the thought of making myself come while he watched excited me. So I fastened my seatbelt, planted my bare feet on the dash and slouched down in my seat, slipping my hand inside my panties. I was already so wet, my clit so swollen and throbbing, it wouldn't take much at all to make myself come.

"Fuck your fingers," he said.

I slipped two fingers inside and slid them in and out, my breath coming out in little pants, my thumb rubbing the tight bundle of nerves.

"That's it. Slower. Yes, just like that," he rasped. His hand moved on top of mine and increased the pressure of my own, forcing me to go in deeper. "Let me see you come undone."

My thighs quivered and my walls contracted around my fingers, my vision blurring as the orgasm crashed over me like a wave, building in intensity until it rocked my body. I collapsed against my seat, my feet hitting the floor and slowly I returned to the here and now. My cheeks heated when the realization that I'd just masturbated in front of Dylan sunk in. He, however, had no qualms whatsoever.

"You're so fucking beautiful. Let me taste you."

I guided my fingers to his mouth and his lips wrapped around them, sucking on my fingers like they were his favorite treat.

Grabbing the back of my neck, he yanked me toward him, crushing his mouth to mine and shoving his tongue inside. The taste of me mingled with the taste of him as our tongues tangled and danced with no rhythm and the clashing of teeth. My seatbelt flew back in the holder with the flick of his hand and he dragged me into his lap, the steering wheel digging into my backside, my fingernails scraping his skull. There was nothing sweet about this kiss. It was hungry and primal and urgent and I could feel him growing hard again, his erection pressing against my thigh.

When he pulled away, I was panting for more, giddy and

half delirious, ready to promise him anything he asked. His hooded eyes roamed my face, and his lips tilted up on one side in that sexy, half-smile, like he'd read my mind.

Coming to my senses, I glanced out the window. We were parked in his driveway and I hadn't even noticed. This was happening. I was under no illusions. Tonight we were going to cross the line. Obliterate it.

"You want me to drive you home?" he asked, giving me a chance to back out as his lips brushed the side of my neck and his calloused palm slid under my sweater, making it impossible to think straight.

I didn't even hesitate, not for a single second. "No."

"Thank fuck. Because tonight I'm going to ruin you for every other guy."

That sounded like a promise.

"You're gonna get dirty for me, Starlet," he said, his voice husky. It was a statement, not a question.

Lord help me. I was hell-bound and about to become the dirtiest girl in town. There was no doubt in my mind that he would ruin me, and I had nobody to blame except myself. I was going to be an active participant in my own demise.

19

DYLAN

We were barely through the door when I grabbed her waist and pushed her up against the closed door. I grabbed her hands and held them above her head, pinning them to the wood. Pressed up against her, I dragged my tongue down the shell of her ear, down her neck, and alternated between sucking and biting. She was squirming, trying to get closer to my cock, but I wasn't giving in so easy.

I needed her craving me, wanting me more than she'd ever wanted anything. I needed her *begging*. Preferably on her knees, hands folded in prayer. I released her arms and lifted her sweater over her head. Her breasts spilled out over the cups of her black lacy bra and I needed to taste them.

Jesus, she was perfect. I didn't even bother unclasping her bra—I pulled it down and sucked and teased her nipple, its rosy peak growing harder. Alternating between the right and left breast, she tugged my hair and chanted, "more, more."

That's right, I'd give her more than she'd ever had before.

My tongue and hands ran down her stomach as I squeezed her ass and she whimpered. I'd never get enough of that sound. On my knees now, I undid her pants and pulled them down, revealing the pale pink cotton boy shorts. It was so Scarlett, mixing the sweet and innocent with the forbidden. I found it sexy as hell that she didn't care if I would prefer lace or silk. But they had to go. I slid them down her legs and licked and sucked her pussy. It was dripping, so fucking wet it would take me an hour to lick it clean.

"What do you want, Starlet?"

"You," she said, panting, her short nails digging into my shoulders, her hips rocking, trying to fuck my face. Not happening. The next time I let her come, I'd be buried so deep inside her my dick would have its own zip code. "I want you."

"Try again." I pressed my calloused thumb against her swollen clit and she moaned, the sound going straight to my rock-hard cock and making it swell impossibly harder, straining against the zipper of my jeans. I knew that if I pressed hard enough, she'd explode and I didn't want that. It was a miracle I hadn't fucked her yet. "What do you want?"

"I want you to..." I teased her clit, just enough to get her whimpering, not enough to give her an orgasm then dragged my fingers through her wet lips, and pressed one finger against her other hole, circling it.

"Oh God," she moaned as I got to my feet and glided my tongue around her nipple and between the valley of her breasts.

My hand wrapped around her throat, testing her reaction. "Harder," she said, eyes at half-mast.

"Tell me what you want." I squeezed harder before I withdrew my hand.

"I want you to fuck me," she said, her eyes glazed over with lust, her voice low and seductive.

"That'll do." I kissed her hard before I lifted her off the ground, her legs encircling my waist, her mouth crushed to mine as I carried her up the stairs to my bedroom.

Unceremoniously, I threw her on my bed and felt around in

my bedside table drawer for the condoms I kept in there. She scooted back on the mattress, her eyes on me as her bra straps slid down her arms. I tossed half a dozen foil packets onto the bed and her eyes widened, a small gasp escaping her lips. I chuckled and stripped naked, her eyes still on me, her pretty pink tongue darting out to lick those plump lips that had been wrapped around my cock on the drive from Santa Ana. I'd nearly wrecked the fucking car but it would have been worth it.

"Get on your hands and knees for me," I said, rolling a condom over my erection while she stared at it like she'd never seen one before.

She hesitated a moment, debating, and I got the feeling that I'd been right. Missionary was the extent of her sexual experience. That was about to change.

Starlet wasn't always so compliant, she pushed back, she challenged me, but not this time. She wanted this. She got onto her hands and knees, her ass in the air and looked over her shoulder at me. My palm smacked the flesh of her ass cheek and she gasped as I spread her cheeks with my hands, dipped my head and bit one cheek and then the other, rimming her other hole with my finger. She pressed back against it, moaning loudly, desperate for more. I straddled her thighs, fisting my length, and guided my tip to her entrance. In one thrust, I was buried to the hilt and fuck, I had found my heaven. She was tight as a fist, her pussy so wet and warm and perfect I wanted to live inside it forever.

I stilled, giving her a moment to adjust before I started to move.

"Ohh... ohh..." she moaned, her arms giving out and her chest collapsing against the mattress, one side of her face pressed against my charcoal gray sheets. I fisted her hair and yanked her up off the mattress, and she looked over her shoulder at me. Leaning forward, I kissed her hard and deep, my hand reaching underneath her to rub her clit. She exploded instantly.

"Oh my God. Dylan," she screamed, her tight walls clenching me, her whole body convulsing. My balls tightened and the sound of her harsh breathing and the feel of her trembling body threw me into an orgasm that temporarily blinded me. Not one of my best performances. How many minutes had I lasted? Not enough to retain my cock's dignity, that was for damn sure. But I didn't even care.

After I disposed of the condom, we just lay on the bed together, her head on my chest, my arm wrapped around her and I felt this strange sense of peace come over me. We were quiet for a few long moments, no sound except for our breathing, and I realized that being with her made me happy.

"I'm going to hell for this," Scarlett said as I smoked a post-coital cigarette, her head in my lap, my dick getting hard for her again.

A fallen angel. Call me Lucifer. "Good. I could use the company."

I fucked her two more times and she fell asleep with her body draped over mine. Limbs tangled, her cheek pressed against my beating heart, my hand wrapped around her thigh. That was how we slept, our bodies fused together like star-crossed lovers.

And that was when I knew I was well and truly fucked.

When I woke up a few hours later, the sun was just starting to rise, fingers of pale yellow sunlight dancing across Scarlett's golden skin. Careful not to wake her, I peeled her body off mine and pulled the covers over her.

Grabbing my phone from the bedside table, I cursed under my breath when I saw the missed calls and the voicemail from my mother. My phone had been on silent. I took it into the bathroom with me. Might as well see what my crazy mother wanted. After I took a piss and washed my hands I listened to her voicemail, and then I listened to it again before calling her back, a sick feeling in the pit of my stomach.

My call went to voicemail. I tried her again. And again. But she never picked up.

Fuck.

My premonitions hadn't been about Remy. They had been about my mother.

I pulled on my jeans that I'd left on the floor and grabbed a clean shirt from my dresser.

"Hey," came Scarlett's sleep-groggy voice from behind me. I sat on the edge of the bed to put on my high-tops, my mind focused on the logistics of getting to Vegas as quickly as possible. She wrapped her arms around me from behind and rested her chin on my shoulder. "What are you doing up so early?"

I removed her hands and stood up, gathering her clothes from the floor and tossing them in her general direction. "Get dressed. I'll drop you off," I said brusquely.

She sat back on her heels and looked out the window. It was barely light outside. "Okay. Are we still going surfing?"

"Change of plan."

Her brows drew together in confusion. "Oh. But—"

"For fuck's sake. I don't have time to debate this. I've got shit to do. Get dressed." I stalked out of the room, feeling like shit for snapping at her when she'd done absolutely nothing wrong, but fear and dread had rendered me incapable of exchanging pleasantries.

We were silent on the ride to her apartment. She was chewing on her bottom lip, upset or hurt or both, but I couldn't think of a damn thing to say to make it better. So I settled for my default mode. I said absolutely nothing.

"Was this a mistake?" she asked when I stopped in front of

her apartment. "I mean, yeah, I know it was, but do you feel like—"

"Something's come up," I said, cutting her off. Right now, I didn't have a fucking clue how I felt about anything, and I didn't have the mental capacity to talk about feelings and shit. "I need to go."

"Yeah, okay, I see how it is. God. I really am so stupid." Before I could say another word, not that I had a ready response because my mind was elsewhere, she was out of the car and slamming the door.

No sooner was it closed, I hit the accelerator and tore off down the street, leaving Scarlett and Costa del Rey in my rearview.

20

DYLAN

I decided to drive to Vegas. The way I drove, I could get there in under four hours. I'd have my car and wouldn't have to deal with flights, rental cars or taxis.

Music blasting, I drove on autopilot, shattering the speed limit even though a part of me knew I was already too late. The problem with having hundreds of miles of road stretched out ahead of you and nothing to do but drive was that it gave you too much time to think. An onslaught of shitty memories assaulted me, things I'd tried hard to forget pushed to the forefront of my mind.

The time I was twelve and my mother's douchebag boyfriend tried to rape Remy. When I'd burst into Remy's locked bedroom, baseball bat in hand, Russell's pants were down around his knees and he was on top of my sister, his meaty palm clamped over her mouth to keep her quiet, the piece of shit. I was still small and no match for a two-hundred-pound asshole, but I had always been a fighter so that hadn't deterred me. Rage and adrenaline had fueled me, blocked the pain when he punched and kicked me. I kept bashing him with a baseball bat, fury rendering me deaf and blind and half-crazed. I would have kept going and left him for dead if Remy hadn't stopped me.

My mother had finally turned up, late to the party as usual, and found us hiding behind the dumpsters. She told us to get in the car and then she just drove and drove, straight through the night and all the next day. Across the heartland and the flyover states until we reached the desert. That was how we wound up living in a trailer park in Vegas.

I remember sleeping on a lumpy sofa, one eye open, ever vigilant over the men my mother brought home. Sometimes I used to fall asleep on the floor right outside Remy's bedroom door, so they'd have to get through me before getting to my sister.

Remy was beautiful, men noticed her, and I vowed never to let anything happen to her again. Not on my watch. One night while we were living in Vegas, my mother came home with a fucked-up face and broken ribs. I nearly cried myself to sleep when I found out that some asshole had knocked her around. But instead giving in to crying, I'd gotten drunk on my mom's beer and punched the wall until the skin over my knuckles ripped and shredded.

My view on Vegas? It was the place where hopes and dreams went to die. Where else would you find pawn shops and strip clubs next door to wedding chapels? That right there said it all. This town set you up to fail.

So the last place I wanted to be right now was Sin Fucking City.

My mother's apartment was in downtown Vegas, about a ten-minute drive from the strip. Her apartment complex was one of those places that promised an oasis but didn't deliver. Two three-story faded yellow buildings faced an empty swimming pool surrounded by brown palm trees swaying in the desert wind, the sunshine highlighting the shabbiness. It was exactly the kind of place my mother would choose to live. You could give the woman millions of dollars and tell her she could live anywhere, sky's the limit, and she would end up in a trashy trailer park or a derelict house on the wrong side of town.

She had never believed she deserved better and she had passed that belief on to her kids. Why strive for something good when the world was just going to kick you back down where you belonged?

After banging on her front door and getting no answer, I used my key and let myself into her apartment. Technically, the apartment was mine. The lease was in my name. I paid the rent. I paid the utilities. I took care of her the only way I knew how. By throwing money at her.

The air inside her apartment was stale and smelled like cigarettes from an overflowing ashtray filled with red lipstick-stained filters on the scarred coffee table. An ugly as shit brown plaid sofa with stains on the cushions sagged against the beige wall. It looked a lot like the one I'd slept on in my teens. Dust motes floated in the air, the sun filtering through the vertical blinds in the living room, and I took it all in, trying to process the mundane, everyday existence of my mother before I ventured farther into her apartment.

I scrubbed my hand over my face and stopped in the hallway, trying to breathe. My chest was tight, and my stomach was churning. "Mom. Get your ass out of bed."

My voice echoed in the quiet apartment. Not a sound came from the other side of her closed bedroom door. And I just stood in the hallway with those dingy beige walls closing in on me and I waited. For nothing.

My footsteps were slow and measured, my leather high tops squeaking on the linoleum as I got closer and closer to the door, the dread increasing with every step I took. I wrapped my hand around the doorknob and turned it. Pushing the door open, I stepped inside my mother's bedroom and nearly gagged on the scent of her cheap perfume. I fucking hated that perfume she wore. It was sweet and cloying and smelled like cheap chemicals. Her bedroom was empty.

She might not be here. She might have gone out.

That's what I was hoping when I stopped outside her closed bathroom door. Same drill. Deep breaths. Inhale. Exhale. I wiped the sweat off my forehead with the back of my arm. The collar of my black Henley was choking me.

Fucking hell. I opened the door and stood in the hallway, my feet rooted to the spot as I tried to process the scene in front of me. At first, I was too shocked to register what I was seeing.

A sea of red.

So much fucking red.

Her dress. The blood on the white tiles. The bathwater. Her lipstick.

She was wearing a dress in the bathtub. Lips painted red. Nails to match. Her skin was ghostly pale, stark against her jet-black hair.

And the blood... it was everywhere.

Bile burned the back of my throat. I leaned over the toilet and vomited until there was nothing left in my stomach.

As I straightened up, wiping my mouth with the back of my hand, my eye caught on her phone. Lying in a pool of blood that had dripped from her wrist. Next to an empty bottle of Jack Daniels.

Without stopping to think, I scooped her up in my arms and carried my dead mother down the hallway and to her bedroom. I didn't know why I didn't leave her in that bathtub. I left a trail of red water from the bathroom to the bedroom and laid her down on top of her dusty rose bedspread. It was the cheap silky kind, like her dress that clung to her gaunt frame.

Mascara tears trailed down her cheeks and I returned to the bathroom and grabbed two cheap, thin towels, lathering one up with soap and water. I scrubbed her face clean, erasing every trace of makeup like it was my sole mission in life to peel back the layers of artifice and reveal her naked skin.

Why had she put on all that makeup? Like she'd put time and effort into her appearance before she slit her wrists. Vertically, not horizontally.

She knew I'd be the one to find her. She fucking *knew* it would be me.

When I was a little kid, I thought my mother was the most beautiful woman in the world. She taught me to dance. Slow dancing of all things. I used to lead her around the kitchen or the backyard of whatever place we lived in. Her hand in mine, my arm around her waist like I was a man and not a little kid, and we were two people from another century. I'd spin her out and reel her back in, embarrassed but secretly proud that I was so good at slow-dancing. It used to put a smile on her face. It brought her joy and that had made me feel like a fucking king.

Rae St. Clair used to be pretty before all the hard living caught up to her. She used to have dreams. I didn't know what happened to them. Or to her. Life, I guess.

Sliding my phone out of my pocket, I replayed the voicemail she'd left at two in the morning when I'd neglected to answer, and I stood in the bedroom with my dead mother, bloody bathwater dripping onto the floor, leaving a puddle at my feet as I forced myself to listen to every word again.

"Wayne left me, baby. He promised he'd stay. I really thought he would be different. I wish you'd pick up the phone. I want a chance to tell you things I should have said before. I'm just so tired, baby. So weary, you know? I know I screwed up. I know I wasn't a good mother, but I wanted to be, I really did. They all tried to talk me into giving up my babies, but I wouldn't, so I ran away from those hypocrites and I never looked back. They called me the devil. Well, let me tell you, that Baptist minister was no saint, was he?

"I love you so much. You were my first love and I guess

you'll be my last. Hope you always remember that. Even though you're all grown up now, you'll always be my baby boy. It wasn't all bad. We had some good times too, didn't we? And look how far you've come. And your sister, well, I guess I was jealous of her--I still am. My own daughter. Imagine that. She was the beauty. Turned all the boys' heads. When she got to be a teenager, men didn't notice me anymore like they used to. They all wanted Remy, didn't they? And I never wanted to believe that about Russell... I'm sorry. I just didn't."

She was crying, her words garbled by tears, and I heard the sound of running water in the background. She was pouring a bath, the bath that she was going to die in. "Truth is that I always loved you the most. And I guess that's a terrible thing for a mother to admit. Your sister got so high and mighty, thinking she was better than me. And you... you always chose her over me. I guess I just wanted you all to myself. I hope you can forgive me someday. Goodbye, baby."

Forgive her?

Son of a bitch!

I hurled my phone across the room. The mirror above her dresser shattered, a kaleidoscope of cracks distorting the image of the woman lying on the bed.

"No!" I roared, driving my fist into the drywall. "You don't get to do this to us. You don't fucking get to do this."

I kept punching the wall, the skin over my knuckles busting, blood dripping onto the parquet floor. The plaster cracked, the wall riddled with holes and still it wasn't enough. I wanted to tear down the world and set it on fire.

My chest heaved as I swept my arm across the dresser, sending makeup and perfume bottles flying. I tore up her room, upending furniture, the cheap wood splintering as it crashed against the wall, and when there was nothing left to destroy, I sagged against the wall, and slid down it, my ass hitting the floor. Dropping my head in my hands, I sat on my mother's bedroom floor, amidst the wreckage, the weight of her love a burden that squeezed all the oxygen out of my lungs. I rubbed the blank space over my heart to ease the ache, but it didn't help.

You call that love? What you did, what you have always *done to me, is not love.*

Her love was sick and twisted. Every single shitty, soul-destroying thing that had happened to me and Remy growing up was because of *her.* Our own mother. The person who was supposed to protect us from the big bad world when we were too young to do it for ourselves had brought trouble to our doorstep and robbed us of a childhood.

Now she'd taken the easy way out and once again, she'd left me to clean up her fucking mess.

I lit a cigarette, clamping it between the fingers of my fucked-up hand—the cuts raw and bloody—and took a drag, filling my lungs with nicotine and tar. After I smoked the cigarette and ground it out on the floor like the classy bastard that I was, I retrieved my phone. The screen was cracked but it still worked.

My thumb hovered over the green call button. There was the only person I wanted right now. I just wanted to hear her sweet voice. No lies, no empty promises, no cunning or manipulation. Honest and true and brave.

Instead of calling Scarlett, I dialed 9-1-1.

After the police arrived and I answered all their invasive questions, and after my mother's body was removed, I cleaned up the mess.

Then I went in search of Wayne Briggs.

He spent the night in the ER. I spent the night in the drunk tank. Not the first time I'd spent a night in jail. But it would be the very last time I'd ever fight for my mother.

21

SCARLETT

"Are you going to answer that?" Nic asked, shoving a handful of parmesan popcorn into her mouth. We were binge-watching *Riverdale,* like I needed more drama in my life, but now my eyes were glued to my phone screen.

Why was he calling me at midnight?

Four days. It had been four days since he'd dumped me outside my apartment and taken off like he couldn't get away from last night's mistake fast enough.

Being with him had been wrong on so many levels, yet so right in the ways it shouldn't have been. Sure, the sex had been great. Had left me wanting more. But it was the moments between and the moments after that had consumed my thoughts over the past few days.

His kisses. Soft and sweet. Hungry. Teasing. Playful. His hands and mouth caressing my skin like he wanted to memorize every inch of it.

If it had just been sex, it would have been easier to forget. And I think that's what made Dylan so dangerous. Rough, to the point of being almost painful one minute, gentle and tender the next. He was the perfect storm. Wild. Unpredictable.

Impossible to tame or control. A thing of beauty that could wreak havoc. Destroy you if you got too close.

And I always got too close to the storm.

But my heart couldn't handle another rejection.

"I have no interest in talking to him," I said when my phone stopped ringing. This time Nic didn't try to defend him.

My phone started ringing again, and once again I didn't answer. He called three more times before Nic grabbed my phone. "If you don't answer, I will. Just see what he wants so we can get back to our show."

I snatched the phone out of her hand and I answered. "What do you want?"

"Need you to pick me up," Dylan said, his words slurring. I strained to hear him over the sound of Guns N Roses' "Welcome To The Jungle" blaring in the background. "Need a ride to the hospital."

"Why are you out getting drunk?"

"Come and get me, Starlet."

"I don't even have a car. Call a taxi."

I cut the call and chewed on my thumbnail. Why should I feel guilty? I shouldn't.

"What did he want?" Nic asked.

"A ride to the hospital. He's drunk."

"Asshole."

"Exactly."

"But he did nurse you back to health," she added, our eyes drawn to the phone in my hand that had started ringing again.

I tried to think about this rationally, like a sane person who didn't feel the sting of rejection. His sister was having a baby. He wanted to be there and was obviously too drunk to drive. He was calling me for help.

Why me? It made zero sense to call a person who didn't even own a freaking car. He should have called Cruz.

But I couldn't take the incessant calls anymore, so I caved, and I answered the phone.

"Where are you?" I snapped, not even attempting to hide my annoyance. New song in the background. Still loud. Def Leppard?

"He's at the Last Stand, darlin'."

My brows drew together. I didn't recognize the voice. "Um, who's this?"

"Name's Cal Whitaker. Your boy's in a bad way. I think he could use a friend."

"He's not my boy and we're not really friends." Now I was just being petty.

Cal chuckled. "Whatever you say. Think you can come and get him? His car's here but he's in no shape to drive and neither am I."

"Do you need a ride somewhere?" I thought to ask.

"No, darlin'. Just come and get him."

"I'll be there as soon as I can."

After I hung up, I looked at Nic.

She sighed. "Let me get some clothes on."

We scrambled off the sofa and got dressed in record time. Minutes later, we were headed to The Last Stand with Nic cracking last stand jokes while I chewed on my thumbnail.

When Nic pulled up outside the bar, we both stared out the window. Dylan was leaning against the brick wall, a lit cigarette clamped between his lips, the neon sign above his head bathing him in blue. The smoke from his cigarette curled into the air, forming a smokescreen over his face. Dressed in black, dark hair messy and disheveled, with his tattoos and his cigarette, he looked like he belonged on an album cover.

"He looks really shitfaced," Nic said. "Do you need me to drive you guys?"

"No, thanks. His car's here. I've got this."

"I'll just wait here to make sure you're okay."

I reached across the center console and hugged her. "Love you. Thanks for being the best friend ever."

She laughed and swatted me away. "Get out of here. Your boy needs help."

And man, did he ever. I walked toward Dylan and stopped in front of him as he exhaled smoke from the corner of his mouth, his bloodshot blue-grays trying to bring me into focus. Dark circles rimmed his eyes and he had stubble on his jaw like he hadn't shaved since I'd last seen him.

My heart stuttered when I saw the sorrow and pain etched on his face, a bruise on his cheekbone like he'd been in a fight. He took another drag of his cigarette then tossed it to the ground and let it burn. I crushed it under my boot and focused on him again.

"Are you okay?" I reached for his hand, not to hold it, but to inspect the damage. Even though my touch was gentle, he winced. His knuckles had scabbed over, and his hand looked swollen. "What happened?"

"Doesn't matter." He lightly brushed the backs of his knuckles over my cheekbone. "Sweet, sweet Scarlett."

I pulled away from his touch and took a deep breath, trying to steel myself against the tenderness in his voice and the sadness in his eyes. When he said he'd ruin me for other guys, he hadn't been joking.

"We should go."

Wordlessly, he handed me his keys and pushed off from the wall then stumbled across the parking lot to his car. He was so drunk, it took him three tries and a lot of muttered curses to click the seatbelt into the holder.

The drive to the hospital was quiet. He was passed out in the passenger seat while I navigated his big-ass SUV, sneaking furtive glances at him while he slept. When I pulled into the hospital parking deck and cut the engine, I released my seatbelt and turned in my seat, watching him for a few minutes until his eyelids fluttered open. He sat up, running both hands through his hair and looked around him in confusion.

"We're at the hospital. Remy's having her baby," I reminded him. He shoved the door open and tumbled out of the car, grabbing hold of the door before his knees hit the concrete.

"Fucking hell," he said, forcefully slamming the door shut like it had wronged him.

"She's gonna be okay," he said as we waited for the elevator after having confirmed that the birthing center was on the fifth floor. "She has to be okay. Can't fucking lose her." The words were ripped from his throat like it was painful to say them and for a brief moment, I got a glimpse of the boy, not the man. The achingly beautiful boy with messy dark hair and a vulnerability that made me want to wrap my arms around him and soothe his troubled soul.

How could he make me want to throat punch him one minute and cry for him in the next? It was his superpower. It was how he got under my skin, into my heart, and into my head.

"You're not going to lose her, Dylan. She's going to be fine. You're going to be an uncle soon. Everything is going to be okay," I assured him as the elevator doors opened and we waited for a few people to get off before we stepped inside. We rode to the fifth floor in silence and followed the signs for the Patient Check-In desk. The fifth floor was decorated in blond wood and celery green with brushstroke paintings on the walls. It was calming and serene, the space open and airy, and looked more like a hotel than a hospital.

My plan was to leave Dylan in the waiting area while I checked at the desk for news. If the nurses got one whiff of his whiskey fumes, they might pass out or send him home. A few people cast curious glances at Dylan as he swaggered over to a seating area. His shin crashed into the coffee table and he cursed and kicked it. Once. Twice. Three times. Then he sent an upholstered chair flying. It crashed on its side, the sturdy wood frame still intact, thank God.

What was wrong with him? I righted the chair and gritted my teeth as he plopped down in a seat and massaged his temples with his tattooed fingers.

An older woman, her purse resting on her lap, ankles crossed, scowled at his obvious drunken state.

"You should be ashamed of yourself, showing up here like that," she hissed, narrowing her eyes at him. She was wearing a lavender twinset and pearls, her graying brown hair swept into a smooth chignon.

Dylan barked out a laugh and gave her the middle finger. "That's how much your opinion matters to me."

Oh my God.

Her jaw dropped. "I should have you removed from this waiting area."

"Go fuck yourself," Dylan said, his eyes closing as he leaned his head back against the wall like he needed it to support him.

The woman stood up in a huff and cast another dirty look at him before she scurried away toward the Patient Check-In Desk. "Wait," I called after her. I deserted Dylan and chased after the lady, catching up to her before she reached the desk. "Please. He's just... he's not usually like this. He's—"

"An abusive drunk." She pursed her lips and wrapped her arms around her purse which she held against her chest as if she needed the protection.

"He's not abusive." Okay, well, he had just verbally abused her, but he wasn't an abusive drunk in the sense that she was implying. "Please. Just..." I looked over my shoulder. Dylan was asleep, his head lolling to the side, the picture of innocence. Or as innocent as a tattooed bad boy dressed in black from head to toe could look. "He won't cause any more trouble."

Knowing I couldn't make that kind of guarantee, she gave

me a skeptical look. "Take it from me, honey." She patted my arm. "Boys like that will only break your heart."

Having delivered that sage advice, she returned to the waiting area but moved to a seat on the opposite side of the room. Crisis averted, I let out a breath of relief and checked at the desk. There was no news of the Wilder baby yet, so I returned to my seat next to Dylan and scrolled through my phone for a while. Feeling his eyes on me, I turned my head to look at him. Under the hospital lights, he looked even worse. Like he hadn't slept in days.

"What happened to you, Dylan?"

He ignored my question and pulled my hand into his lap, his much larger calloused hand engulfing my smaller one and I stared at our clasped hands, our interlaced fingers, and tried to make sense of this. But I couldn't.

Boys like that will only break your heart.

How right she was.

I needed some air and some space, and he needed to sober up quick. What would Shane and Remy think about him turning up drunk like this? Coffee. I needed to get him some coffee. He'd still be drunk but at least the caffeine might make him more awake when he heard the news.

Decision made, I stood up. "I'll go and get you some coffee."

"You gonna leave me, Starlet?"

"I'll be back soon."

"Everyone leaves," he mumbled. His eyes closed again, and I watched him for a few seconds, trying to figure out what was going on with him, but I had no idea what went on in that big brain of his. He was an enigma. A jigsaw puzzle with missing pieces. A bad boy who was going to trample all over my heart if I let him get close again. From now on, I needed to keep him at arms-length. No sex. No kisses. No intimate moments on rooftops or in speeding cars or anywhere else.

I took a deep breath and walked away in search of coffee.

22

SCARLETT

"I'll come back to pick you up in the morning," I said when I pulled into Dylan's driveway. Shane and Remy had a boy. But we didn't get to meet him. Not in the state Dylan was in.

"Stay," he said.

One word. A command. He hadn't even remembered calling me for a ride to the hospital. Zero recollection of it. So no, I wasn't going to stay at his house and submit myself to more torture. I'd done my part by helping him out and that was as far as I could go.

"I'm going home. I'm tired. You're tired. I don't have any clothes at your house—"

He leaned over the center console, cut the engine and pocketed the keys. "You're not fucking going anywhere."

That's what he thought. I slammed out of the car, ordered a taxi and walked to the end of the driveway to wait for it. Was I being dramatic? Maybe. But while I'd gone to get coffee, another ugly thought had reared its head. What if Dylan had lied? What if he wasn't really over Sienna like he'd claimed? What if the news of her engagement had sent him spiraling down? Maybe that was why he'd taken off for days and had gotten falling down drunk tonight. Or maybe this was the way he operated. Hit and run.

There were too many maybes and not enough answers and I was too tired to think about it.

A few minutes later, the taxi arrived, and I tugged the door open. A hand wrapped around my arm pulling me back, then he stepped forward and closed the car door. "Don't leave."

"I need to go home, Dylan. Just let me go." I was weary of this battle.

He wrapped his arms around me from behind and buried his face in the crook of my neck. "I don't want to be alone. Stay. Please," he added, and it almost sounded like he was begging me to stay.

Dylan never begged. Never said please. But tonight he'd done both. And I remembered what Nic had said about Dylan nursing me back to health. She told me he'd been so amazing, checking my temperature throughout the night, wiping my forehead with a cool washcloth, and worrying about me.

Could I be the bigger person and do the same for him?

"Are you coming or not?" the taxi driver asked impatiently.

Clearly, I was a glutton for punishment. Someone must have dropped me on my head when I was a baby because I shook my head no when I should have nodded yes. "Sorry about that."

The driver huffed and pulled away, leaving me with Dylan who took my hand and led me back to his house. It had been a long night and I felt weary and confused as I followed him up the stairs to the second floor.

In his bedroom, he opened a dresser drawer and gestured with his hand. "T-shirts are in there. Take what you want."

I hovered in the doorway until he disappeared into the master bathroom, leaving the door open. A few seconds later, I heard the shower running so I grabbed a soft gray T-shirt from the drawer and wandered down the hallway to the last bedroom on the left. Dressed in his T-shirt that hit mid-thigh and smelled like fabric softener and not like him, thank God, I rubbed toothpaste over my teeth with my finger and gargled with mouthwash I found in the cabinet.

Crawling into bed, I covered myself with the downy white comforter and rolled onto my side. The moonlight streamed through the French doors, casting the room in shadows.

Oh, Romeo, why did you have to crawl into my bedroom window all those years ago? I was never supposed to fall for you.

I heard the bedroom door open, and closed my eyes, feigning sleep.

Seconds later, his minty breath skated over my face, the scent of his shower gel masking the stench of whiskey. I kept my eyes closed and my breathing even waiting for him to leave.

But I should have known better than to think he'd give up that easily.

The covers slid down my body and he lifted me up and carried me in his arms like a bride, over the threshold and down the dark hallway, his stride surprisingly steady for someone who was so drunk.

"What are you doing?" I struggled to break free of his hold, but he just held on tighter. "Put me down."

"Thought you were asleep."

"I was until you woke me up."

He snorted, not buying my lie for a minute, and tossed me on his bed. I scrambled to get off it, but his hand clasped my ankle and he dragged me back and pulled my body against his.

We were spooning. Dylan was spooning.

"Are we... cuddling?" I got a grunt in reply. I could feel his erection pressing against my backside. "What are you doing?"

"You're safe, Mother Teresa. I'm not going to fuck you tonight," the charmer said, sliding his hand under my T-shirt and splaying it across my stomach. I looked over my shoulder at his face. His eyes were closed.

Seconds later, he was snoring softly. His chest rose and fell, his breathing even, and I knew he was asleep. I stared into the darkness, my body curled into the curve of his, and I fought to stay awake. I knew that if I closed my eyes, and allowed myself to relax, I'd sleep like a baby in his arms.

But I needed to leave. My fragile heart demanded it.

23

DYLAN

The next morning, I arrived at the hospital with flowers and a gold-foil box of candy. As if a hundred-dollar bouquet and a dozen hand-dipped chocolate covered strawberries would make up for a damn thing.

My memories of the night before were hazy. I hadn't remembered calling Scarlett, but I did remember that she drove me to the hospital. I remembered when Shane came in to the waiting room and told me it was a boy. And I remembered begging... fucking *begging*... Scarlett to stay with me. It was humiliating how much I'd needed her. When I woke up this morning after a fitful sleep, I was still exhausted, and Scarlett was gone.

Now, in the harsh light of day, with the mother of all hangovers, I was going to meet my new nephew. I checked the text Shane had sent with Remy's room number. 503. The baby's name was Kai James Wilder, a healthy boy born at 1:42 AM, weighing 7 pounds, 8 ounces. Remy was okay. Mother and baby were doing well, he'd assured me.

When I entered Remy's room, she looked over at the doorway, her face lit up with a smile. My sister had always been beautiful, but today she was stunning. She was happy. She had her own little family now.

The sun shone through the tall arched windows of her suite that overlooked the hospital campus, a green park with benches and a playground, not a single cloud marring her joy. And I knew I couldn't tell her about our mother today. I didn't know when the right time would be but it sure as hell wasn't now.

"Dylan. You're here." She looked down at the baby in her arms and fuck, he was so tiny, a little blue hat covering his head, his body wrapped in a white cotton blanket like a baby burrito. "Can you believe this?"

I couldn't. It was amazing.

I handed the flowers and chocolates to Shane to deal with. He scowled at me, and I didn't think it had anything to do with the gifts I'd just foisted on him. But I knew he wouldn't have said anything to Remy about the state I was in last night. He wouldn't have wanted to upset her. And finding out that her brother had turned up at the hospital too drunk to string a coherent sentence together might have upset her.

"I would have brought you a celebratory cigar or a blunt, but you don't smoke," I told Shane.

"It's the thought that counts."

"Do you want to hold him?" Remy asked with a soft smile.

I nodded and moved closer to the hospital bed.

"What happened to your face?" she asked, her voice tinged with worry.

"Just sparring at the gym," I said, the lie ready on my tongue. Thankfully, she bought it and didn't question me further.

"Well, next time tell them to stay away from your pretty face."

I snorted. "Cover up your tits, would you?"

"Like you've never seen boobs before," she scoffed. I didn't need to see my sister's and they were practically hanging out of the bra she wore under a black robe. "He might be small but I'm starting to feel like the Dairy Queen. Here. Take him."

I had no idea how to hold a baby, but I leaned down, and she transferred him into my arms and adjusted her robe for modesty's sake. "Just make sure you support his head. Other than that, just love him," she said as I straightened up, the baby in my arms.

Shouldn't be hard. I already loved the shit out of this little guy. Unconditionally.

Shane pulled up an armchair next to his and I took a seat, making sure to support the baby's head as I settled in and studied my new nephew's face.

Let's face it, on the whole, babies were funny-looking. But this baby was fucking perfect. Beautiful. I was in awe of his tiny fingers and his pink pursed lips. The thin veins underneath his closed eyelids.

So fragile. So needy. So trusting.

"How are you feeling?" I finally thought to ask Remy.

"Tired and overwhelmed but I'm good." She smiled at Shane who looked a little worse for the wear. If anything, Remy looked more well-rested than he did. "You should go home and get some rest," she told him, squeezing his hand.

"I'm not going anywhere. Stop trying to get rid of me."

"Never. I'm keeping you forever."

"You doing okay?" Shane asked me. His voice sounded casual but the look on his face told me a different story.

I grunted and shrugged one shoulder. The beauty of being me was that nobody really expected me to converse like a normal person would.

"He's overwhelmed by his new uncle responsibilities," Remy teased.

"That must be it." Shane eyed me skeptically.

"Are you sure you're okay though?" Remy asked. "About Sienna's engagement?"

Sienna's engagement? I'd completely forgotten about it. In the greater scheme of things, it barely warranted a second thought. The news had not been that shocking. "We're over, Rem. Have been for a long time."

"Okay," she said slowly. "I just thought... I mean, it would be understandable if you're upset."

"I'm fine with it." My tone was harsher than I'd intended. "It's all good."

I looked down at Kai's face just as his eyes opened. They were a shade of murky blue like they hadn't decided what color they would be yet. His face scrunched up and turned an alarming shade of beet red, his tiny body going rigid in my arms before it relaxed again.

"Oh shit," I said, with a laugh, welcoming the distraction.

"Literally." Shane took his son from my arms and waltzed him over to a changing table with a smile on his face like he couldn't imagine anything more exciting than changing his kid's dirty diaper. It was a two-man job. He and Remy were laughing as they tried to figure out the best way to clean up the baby and get him into a clean diaper without getting peed in the face.

"Hey, hey, hey," Travis said, entering the room with his brother Ryan, both of whom were bearing gifts. They were big on fist bumps, and I stood up from my chair to exchange greetings. "We're here to meet the future world champion."

"With a dad like Shane, the kid will be catching air in no time," Ryan said.

"Let's give him until he's three or four," Shane said.

"Hello baby mama. Looking gorgeous as always," Travis said, planting a kiss on Remy's cheek and handing her a stuffed seal. "Reminded me of those seals Shane spotted a million years ago in J-Bay."

Shane snorted. "Those were sharks."

"That was the first time we met," Remy said with a smile.

"Best day of my life," Shane said

Time to go. I interrupted their trip down memory lane long enough to say my goodbyes. "I need to get to work. Call me if you need anything," I told Remy.

"Okay. I'll see you soon. I'll let you know when we're home."

As I walked down the hallway, the sound of their laughter trailed after me. Despite being a nice hospital, it still smelled like a hospital. Babies were born. People got sick. They died. A reminder of our mortality.

I couldn't stop picturing all that blood on the white tiles. My mother's lifeless body. Her ghoulish face.

Sweat beaded my forehead, and I tried to breathe but it felt like the air was trapped in my lungs.

The hallway hadn't seemed so long and narrow when I'd arrived.

I was really sweating now. I could smell last night's whiskey seeping from my pores. The fuck was wrong with me? It felt like the walls were closing in.

I punched the elevator button. Once. Twice. Three times. Where was the fucking elevator?

The doors opened, and I made a move to get in, but the arrow pointed up not down. Scarlett stepped off the other elevator, also going up, and stopped in front of me. She looked beautiful, her long blonde hair loose and wavy, falling around her shoulders, her baby blues clear and bright. I was tempted to bury my face in her hair and just breathe her in. Forget the world.

But since completely losing it in front of Scarlett was not on my list of fun things to do, I punched the elevator button again. My eyes darted around, looking for the stairs. Where was the exit?

"In a hurry?" she asked.

"Need to get to a meeting." Lies. I wiped my forehead with the back of my arm. It must be a hundred degrees in this hospital.

She was talking, and I tried to tune in, but I'd obviously missed whatever she'd said because she sighed. "What's that?" I asked.

"I was just..." She stopped and shook her head. "What happened to you last night, Dylan?"

"Got drunk," was my brilliant response.

"Are you okay?" she asked, her brows pulling together as she studied my face.

No, I was not fucking okay. I was so far from okay, I didn't have a word for it. "It's all good."

"Okay. You know what?" She looked around then lowered her voice. "Let's just chalk it up as a mistake. I think it's for the best that we don't see each other anymore."

A mistake? I'd made plenty of mistakes, but Scarlett was not one of them. Unfortunately, those words didn't come out of my mouth because I couldn't form a coherent sentence to save my fucking life.

Little black dots were floating in front of my eyes and I was two seconds from passing out. I planted my hand on the wall to keep me upright and loosened the collar of my shirt. Pretty sure I was dying.

"Okay." She backed away. "Well... guess I'll see you around then."

She hesitated, waiting for me to say something. When I didn't, her face fell in disappointment. Then she spun around and walked away, and I had no choice but to let her go because I was too busy losing my shit.

The elevator doors slid open, fucking finally, and I got the hell out of there.

When I got inside my car, I rolled down the windows and had a full-blown meltdown. A freight train was racing through my head and my heart was beating so fast I thought I was having a heart attack.

It took me twenty minutes to pull myself together.

I'd been through a lot of shit in my life and nothing like this had ever happened to me before. It made me feel weak which made me angry for not being able to keep it together.

By the time I got to my office, it was eleven in the morning and I was so fucking exhausted I felt like I'd just finished a triathlon.

Work helped, always had, so I threw myself into it and blocked out all the noise in my head. It would come as a surprise to absolutely nobody that Cruz handled the client-side of the business, while I focused on software development.

I'd always excelled at two things—math and coding. Two disciplines that required zero people skills. Straightforward. Logical. Numbers didn't dick you around or fuck with your heart. It was my safe place where I retreated when the world got too much.

Simon Woods was still playing his pathetic games, trying to throw his weight around and blocking my plans at every turn. After I'd hired the new construction crew, things had been moving along. Then everything ground to a halt when the planning commission filed a petition, claiming that I didn't have the proper permits to open a surf hostel. Total bullshit.

For shits and giggles, I hacked into his email account. Interesting what you can learn from people's emails.

Oh, and would you look at that? Simon Woods was not, in fact, intending to turn The Surf Lodge into a boutique hotel. Turns out, I was a cog in his wheel. The only thing preventing him from knocking everything down and building a luxury beachfront hotel and an esplanade with fancy shops. Woods had the mayor in his back pocket as well as the members of the old boys' club who were on the council and the planning commission.

On a lark, I'd once applied for membership to the Bellavista Country Club. Not because I golfed or wanted to hang out with any of the founding families of Costa del Rey but just to see what would happen. Shocker. My application was denied.

I was no stranger to getting my hands dirty, and even though I hated to stoop to Simon Woods' level, The Surf Lodge was important to me. So was Costa del Rey. If Simon Woods went through with his plans, it would completely change the landscape of the town I loved. Small family-run businesses and surf shops would get pushed out to make way for Woods' grandiose redevelopment plans.

Luckily, this was California and you couldn't swing a Prada bag without hitting droves of activists, hippies, and environmentalists. The good citizens of Orange County had a right to know what was going on in their own backyard.

Oops. Look at that. The information got leaked. Now I just had to sit back and wait.

It didn't take long to get people petitioning. Within days, half the town jumped on the bandwagon. God Bless America. Looks like the mayor was in a bit of a pickle.

A few days after the shit hit the proverbial fan, Simon Woods barged into my office. His brown hair was graying at the temples but other than that, he looked like the same asshole I'd met ten years ago. A rich bastard with an air of entitlement in an expensive suit, looking down his nose at me.

"To what do I owe this dubious honor?"

"I know you were behind this."

He had no proof. I wasn't a rookie. I'd been hacking into accounts since high school and I'd always been careful. No need to tangle with the US government. Which was one of the reasons I didn't do it anymore. Last time I did it, I dug up dirt on John Hart to help Remy and Shane get him off their backs. Not that they ever needed to know about that. Much better to let Remy think she'd taken care of it on her own.

"Behind what? You'll have to be more specific."

"Don't play dumb. You leaked that information."

"Careful," I warned. "You have no proof to back up your accusation. I might be a worthless punk but even in my world, that's called slander."

He pointed his finger at me. "You might think you've won the battle, but I'm going to show you what it takes to win the war."

"You do that. In the meantime, I'll be fucking Cecily," I said, referring to his PA who he also happened to be fucking. Another thing I learned from his emails. He really should be more careful not to leave a paper trail of his indiscretions. "I'll leave her begging for more."

"You son of a bitch."

At least he'd gotten that right. I was the son of a bitch. A bastard too.

"I'm going to take you down," he said with a satisfied smirk like he had this in the bag. He brushed imaginary lint off his tailored suit jacket as he rose to his feet and checked the fifty-thousand-dollar Swiss timepiece on his wrist. "It won't take long," he said as if he planned to get this done and dusted over his lunch break. "You're not even a worthy adversary."

"It would be a mistake to underestimate me." I stood up and slapped my palms flat on my desk. "Now I suggest you get the hell out of my office before I call security, and have you removed from the premises."

He strode out of my office and left the door wide open. Which was not an open invitation for every Tom, Dick, and Melanie to encroach on my space but that's exactly what happened.

"Close the door on your way out," I told Melanie after she dropped off a stack of paperwork that needed to be signed.

As much as I would love to celebrate, revel in the thrill of victory, take satisfaction in knowing I'd won this battle, I couldn't. He knew the right people, had all the right connections. Had the majority of decision-makers in his back pocket. And me? It was still painfully obvious that I was the kid from the hood made good. Wouldn't get me anywhere in this town.

But I'd never been one to bow out gracefully or accept defeat. I'd go down fighting, just like I always had. Fuck him and his pedigree and his country club membership.

I spun around in my swivel chair and stared at the ocean, trying to find the peace that always eluded me.

To torture myself, I scrolled through my phone, reading all the sweet, funny messages Scarlett used to send. Then I opened her website and stared at her photos for a few minutes. Like a pathetic loser, I stalked her Instagram before I shut it down, cursing myself for wondering how she was, what she was doing, if she was okay.

Reality check. Her father was my sworn enemy. Her sister was my ex-girlfriend who had done enough damage to make me swear off relationships for all eternity. And Scarlett was the girl I'd been fucking when I let my mother's call go to voicemail.

"I think it's for the best if we don't see each other anymore."

No doubt about it. It was in her best interest to stay away from me. I was the kind of trouble she didn't need. But Scarlett wasn't just a random fuck, and she wasn't so easy to forget.

I just needed a little more time. Then I'd try to win her back and we'd go back to doing whatever we'd been doing before I'd gotten derailed by my mother's suicide.

My mother's suicide. Fuck me. The pen in my hand snapped in two.

24

DYLAN

Three and a half weeks had come and gone since Kai was born, and I still hadn't broken the news to Remy. Motherhood was overwhelming, and her emotions were all over the place, so every time I stopped by to visit Kai I found another excuse to keep it to myself. I wanted to spare her. I wanted to protect her and give her this time to be happy, but I didn't know how much she'd appreciate being left in the dark. If it were the other way around, I'd be pissed that she kept it from me.

Time to rip off the Band-Aid.

Shane answered the front door, masking his surprise that I'd turned up after Kai's bedtime, and ushered me inside. Remy was curled up on the sofa wearing sweats and an oversized hoodie that I suspected was Shane's. She looked happy and sleepy, a soft smile on her face just for me, and I fucking hated to do this to her.

"Hey. You just missed Kai. We were about to watch a movie. Do you want to join us?"

"I need to talk to you. You and Shane," I added, because he was always banging on about how we're family and I needed to start trusting him.

Shane took a seat on the sofa next to Remy and wrapped his arm around her shoulders as if he already suspected that she'd need his support. I sat on a chair across from them and tried to find the right words. Not my strong suit.

"What's wrong?" Remy prompted, her brows furrowed.

I raked my hand through my hair. "It's Mom."

"Oh my God, why didn't I realize that?" She smacked the sofa arm. "She *always* upsets you. Did you talk to her? What's she done now?"

I cleared my throat. There was no easy way to break this to her, so I just came out with it, and fed her a half-truth. "She OD'd."

"Fuck," Shane muttered.

Remy stared at me in disbelief. I waited for the words to sink in. I waited for her to call me out as a liar, as if she'd somehow know that I was withholding the truth and that our mother's death had been far more gruesome than downing a bottle of pills and drifting off to sleep.

My mother haunted me now. The slashed wrists. The blood. The red dress she'd bought for fucking Wayne. I'd never be able to erase that vision from my head, but I'd be damned if I'd let my sister carry that same burden.

The less Remy knew, the better.

"What do you mean?" Remy shook her head, trying to come to grips with this. "Mom doesn't do drugs. I mean, she never used to... OD'd on what?"

"Pills." The lie came easily. I didn't feel an ounce of guilt for cushioning the truth with a lie.

"When did this happen?"

"A month ago." I winced at the expression on her face and cursed myself for waiting this long.

"A month ago? But... what? Before Kai was born?"

"A few days before."

"Dylan," she whispered, her eyes filling with tears as it finally hit home. "Mom is dead?"

I nodded.

"Did she... leave a note?"

A voicemail Remy would never hear. I'd deleted it. I shook my head no. The lies were piling up, but I'd been prepared for these questions.

"Maybe it was an accident," she mused.

"Yeah." I fed the lie, grateful she had jumped to that conclusion.

There was so much Remy didn't know about our mother's life, and I'd wrestled with how much to tell her. I understood why Remy wanted our mother out of her life, and I'd honored that wish. Right up until the bloody end.

Was it wrong to keep that voicemail from my twin? There was no judge and jury, only my conscience that told me it was the right thing to do. How could it benefit Remy to know that our mother was jealous of her own daughter? It wouldn't.

"Where was she living?"

"Vegas." I'd considered lying about that too, but chances were good that she would never call to check up on my story. Why would she doubt me? "I went out there to take care of everything, so you don't have to worry about any of that."

"You went by yourself? And you didn't tell me?"

"I didn't want to upset you."

"So you went. All by yourself? Did you tell anyone else?"

"No. I wouldn't tell anyone before you."

She was quiet for a few seconds, mulling over the information. Shane still had his arm around Remy, quietly supportive, giving her time to process everything. "But you shouldn't have had to do that on your own, Dylan. I'm your family. Shane's your family. You and me, Dylan. We always had each other's backs. We promised we'd always be there for each other. Remember?"

"I had your back, Remy. I didn't want you upset. Not when you were about to have a baby any day." I looked to Shane, a silent plea to back me up here. *Family, dude, remember?*

"He's right," Shane said, taking my cue. "There was nothing you could have done."

Remy turned her head, her eyes meeting Shane's. "It didn't happen yesterday, Shane. It's been *a month*."

"I was trying to save you from having to deal with it. I didn't want Mom to fuck up something that was supposed to be a happy time for you, Rem." Why couldn't she wrap her head around that?

"You're missing the point. Don't you get it? God, Dylan, why are you such a bonehead?" Her face crumpled, and she burst into tears.

Shane pulled her into his arms, his hand holding the back of her head, the other one stroking her hair. Sobs racked her body, and she was crying so hard I was starting to worry. I could see by the look of concern on Shane's face that he was, too. He kept stroking her hair and telling her everything was okay, but he looked as helpless as I felt. It felt like I sat there a lifetime listening to her cry until she finally pulled herself together and the tears subsided.

For want of something better to do, I grabbed a roll of toilet paper from the downstairs bathroom and handed it to her.

She stared at it for a second then started laughing as she took it from me and I returned to my seat. "Oh my God. That is so you. We have Kleenex on the kitchen counter."

"Does the same job."

She unwound a few strips of toilet paper, wiped her eyes, and blew her nose while Shane and I watched her closely trying to figure out where her head was at. I'd only seen Remy cry that hard twice in my life. Both times for Shane. She hadn't shed a tear after that asshole almost raped her. She hadn't shed a single tear when we were abandoned at the truck stop. Or any of the other times Mom had left us behind. So, I hadn't expected her to break down like that because of our mother.

"It kills me that you felt you had to do that on your own, Dylan." Her eyes filled with tears again and she wiped them away, and only then did it dawn on me. She wasn't crying for Mom. She was crying for me. "I'm so angry at her for making you feel like it was your job to protect her. I'm so angry that you never got a childhood. I look at Kai and I just think... I'd never want my baby to go through everything you did."

"It wasn't just me, Rem. You went through it too. You had it worse than I did." Like this was a stupid contest and we were competing over who had it worse.

"I didn't. She... you were the one she always dragged into her shit. You were the one she always turned to. I remember how you used to bring her home from the bar when she was drunk. And I used to stand outside her door and listen. You were so good with her. You used to always tell her to sleep it off, that things would look better tomorrow. And then when she left us, you thought it was your responsibility to pay our rent and our bills. It was never your burden to carry alone but you always did. You were so stubborn. I had you to look after me, but you didn't have anyone, Dylan. You were so alone."

"Don't dredge up the past. It's ancient history." I was a hypocrite for saying that. I'd spent the past few weeks doing nothing *but* dredging up the past. And what I'd concluded was that it was better off staying buried.

"Just... please. I need you to know how much I love you for everything you did. I need you to know that you're not alone, Dylan. I'll always be here for you, okay? *Always.*"

I couldn't look at her. I couldn't even swallow past the lump in my throat. And it took me a good few minutes of silence before I was able to speak. Clearing my throat, I asked, "Are you okay?"

"About Mom?"

I nodded.

"I have Shane. I have Kai. I have you. So I know I'm going to be fine. But I could have been there for you, Dylan."

"It's done. It's over. I'm good. Let's move on."

"You're not good, Dylan. I just wish... I wish you could find what I have. I want you to be happy. Find someone special. Get married. Have a family."

"I'm not like you, Rem. I never wanted those things." That wasn't entirely true. I liked the idea of all that but in reality, I didn't see it happening for me.

She gave me a sad smile that I couldn't bear to look at. It was time for me to go. I'd delivered my news, having edited out the parts she didn't need to hear, and Shane would look after her from here. Just like he had been doing for years.

The following night Shane paid me a visit. "This feels familiar. Like we've been here before," he said, sliding down against the glass fence to sit next to me on my manicured lawn. The last time Shane and I sat here together was nearly two years ago, the night Sienna and I called it quits for good.

This was my favorite spot to sit, under the stars with a view of the hills and the canyon and a sliver of sea in the distance. When I bought this house, it was this view that made me appreciate how far I'd come. Like I was sitting on top of the world. Still looking down the bottom of the bottle though. Proof that I was still the same fucked-up guy I'd always been.

The only thing that had changed was that my booze was more expensive, and my view was better.

I took another swig of whiskey, feeling the burn as it slid down my throat. The alcohol made all the edges blur, the lights from the houses in the hills a hazy glow.

"Did Remy send you?" I asked.

"She's worried about you, but I came on my own."

I offered him the bottle, but he declined so I took another fortifying drink.

"Do you want to talk about it?"

Since when had I *ever* wanted to talk about *anything*? "Nothing to talk about."

He side-eyed me. "Then I'll just sit here for a while. Stargazing." That lasted for all of twenty seconds. "You should call Scarlett."

"Whatever happened to stargazing?"

"Change of plan."

"Why would I call Scarlett?" I couldn't help asking.

"Because she cares about you." I had no idea how he knew that or why he would even think it. "And I think you care about her too."

"Playing matchmaker now?"

He snorted. "Not sure it'd be a smart move to push you two together. I was thinking you could use a friend."

A *friend*. That dirty f word again.

"Why did you call her to drive you to the hospital the night Kai was born? Why did you talk us into selling her designs in the shop? Why did you talk me into hiring her as a surfboard designer when I wasn't even looking for one? What was all that about?"

"So many fucking questions. You're making my head spin."

"That's the whiskey. When's the last time you've been sober?"

When I was thirteen. "I didn't invite you over here."

"When are you going to get it through your thick skull that I give a shit about you? There's more to it, isn't there? What really happened?"

Instead of answering his questions, I drank more whiskey. Then I lit a blunt and smoked it, hoping he'd take the hint and leave. You couldn't get blood from a stone. But that didn't stop him from trying.

"Who found her? Who found your mother?"

"I'm two seconds from kicking you out of my fucking house."

He nodded as if he had it all figured out. "That's what I thought."

After that, he sat next to me in silence for a while, stargazing or navel-gazing or whatever the hell Zen people did, before he finally stood to go. "Come surfing with me tomorrow."

"Don't you have a wife and kid to take care of?"

"That's why I surf. You're no help to anyone if you don't take care of yourself. I learned that the hard way. Whatever you're going through, it helps to let people in. The right people. The ones who care about you. I know you always act like you don't need anyone, but you fucking do."

With that little gem, he left me to my peace and quiet. I didn't tell him this, or anything else of any value, but he was starting to sound more and more like his dad. And as much as I would love to be more like Shane, more like Jimmy, I wasn't built that way.

You and me, baby, we're two of a kind.

That's what my mother told me. Had always told me. And as much as I didn't want to believe it, I was starting to think it was true.

Time to end this pity party for one. Time to move on and let go of the past. I'd worked too hard to get this far. It would be too easy to lose myself at the bottom of a bottle and I couldn't allow that to happen.

I wrapped my hand around the neck of the whiskey bottle and took a swing at the fence. And then another. And another. The bottle smashed, the glass shattering and I left the jagged pieces on the lawn, the whiskey soaking into the lawn as I walked away.

Stripping off my clothes, I dove into my heated pool. The blood from the cuts on my hand clouded the water and I swam, and I swam, and I swam.

I tried to forget the first woman I had ever loved. My mother. The tragically lost, careless, manipulative bitch who could sometimes be loving and kind and funny and so full of life it was contagious. But my good memories of her were so distant, so long ago, that I sometimes wondered if they'd all been nothing but a dream.

What kind of idiot would mourn the loss of someone who had always let him down, who had fed him lies and empty promises, who had rarely shown up to be a mother? The same idiot who had gotten into countless fights, defending his mother's honor. Despite her failings and her disregard for anyone other than herself, *I* was that idiot.

By the time I finished swimming my last lap, I was ready to let go and move on.

All I wanted now was that little fucking ray of sunshine.

I wanted her to put the broken pieces of me back together. To revive something inside of me that had died a long time ago.

In other words, I wanted the impossible.

25

SCARLETT

S ienna's engagement had given my mother a new lease on life, and I'd been coerced into attending the engagement party. Everything had to be perfect. Including me. Things like this mattered to her, and I didn't want to ruin anything for her or Sienna. So I had promised to be on my best behavior. Which meant that I'd barely said three words.

Sienna and Chase stayed close to each other's side throughout the night. He had an entitled look about him that always made me feel like he thought he was better than everyone. Like my father. They even had the same Ivy League haircut. Short and tapered with a side part. He wore a dark suit and a pressed white shirt. Sienna wore a liquid gold dress and a smile.

"You look beautiful, Scar," Sienna had said when I arrived, pulling me into a hug. I had waited for the guilt to come but somewhere along the way, guilt had taken a backseat to heartache.

Even though I knew I shouldn't, I missed Dylan and I still thought about him all the time. Judging by the radio silence, he didn't give me a passing thought. It shouldn't hurt but it did.

"Thank you. You look beautiful too." She did. Sienna was undeniably beautiful. We were both blonde and blue-eyed but that was where the similarities ended. She was tall and willowy, her features classically beautiful, with an air of elegance that I'd never have.

"Mom was worried you'd turn up looking like a hobo." Sienna laughed.

"That's why she sent me feathers and red-soled shoes."

"They're so you."

"Sure they are."

I'd never in a million years pick out this ensemble—a short black strapless concoction of tulle and feathers with black and white jacquard Louboutin's. This little outfit cost as much as a used car. I was mentally calculating how much I could get for it on eBay when my mother grabbed my arm.

"Where's your father gone?" she asked, her voice hushed as if she didn't want her guests to catch on that she'd lost her husband.

"I don't know." I was busy avoiding him. So far, so good.

"Go find him," she said under her breath, smoothing a hand over her blonde hair, freshly highlighted for the occasion. "He's been gone for half an hour."

"I'm sure he'll turn up soon. Like a bad penny."

"Scarlett." She squeezed my hand, her eyes pleading. "Please."

"Fine."

"Thank you. And you went a little heavy on the eyeliner, honey. Stop in the downstairs bathroom and fix that." She patted my arm before she swanned away to entertain her guests. It never ceased to amaze me how my mother could be hypercritical one minute and completely dismissive the next. I couldn't remember the last time she asked me how I was doing, and actually listened to my answer.

When would I get it through my head that she really didn't care?

I weaved through the people milling about, in search of my father. When I didn't find him in the living room or dining room, I made a beeline for the library. That's where he conducted business during these social gatherings. For my father, every party was a networking opportunity. No doubt he was plotting world domination.

The library door was slightly ajar, and I stopped outside it as my father's voice reached my ears. "See to it that you shut this down. We haven't come this far only to lose to that little shit."

"It's not only St. Clair you're up against," another male voice said. The mayor? "A lot of people are opposed to your plans."

That little shit. One of my father's many pet names for Dylan. I'd heard about my father's plans. It was the talk of the town, so it wasn't a secret. I felt bad for Dylan though. I knew how important The Surf Lodge was to him.

"Who put you in office, Hank?"

"The voters."

"Bullshit. I put you in office. And don't you forget it. You work for me. The council... the planning commission... they work for me. Find me the weakest links and I'll take care of the rest."

I bet he would.

I backed away from the door and hid under the oak staircase, my back pressed against the damask-papered wall as the mayor and another man walked out of my father's library and headed in the opposite direction from where I stood.

Coast clear, I plastered on a smile and walked into the library. It was all dark wood, leather, and Oriental rugs with a Medieval-looking tapestry above the polished mahogany bar.

My father was pouring himself a scotch from a crystal

decanter and looked over at the doorway, brows raised in question.

"Hey Dad." Smile still firmly in place. "Mom's looking for you."

Scotch in hand, he came around from the back of the bar and stopped in front of me. As much as I tried to put on a brave face, my father still intimidated me. "Have you been eavesdropping again, Scarlett?"

If he'd wanted to conduct business behind closed doors, he should have made certain the door was closed.

"I just came to find you. And I didn't want to interrupt." I should have left it at that. Played dumb like I hadn't heard a single word of his conversation. "Why are you going after him? Can't you just let him have this? It's really important to him."

My father's eyes narrowed. "Why are you defending that punk?"

Once again, I'd gone too far but as usual, I couldn't stop myself. "I work for his sister, so I know why he wants The Surf Lodge. He just wants to do something good for the town."

"Something good for the town," he said with a harsh laugh. "I know what this town needs. And as for Dylan St. Clair, he'll get what's coming to him."

"But why? What's he ever done to you?"

"He's a worthless little shit who tried and failed to drag your sister down to his level. As far as I'm concerned, he can crawl back into that gutter he came from."

I opened my mouth to protest. He wasn't a worthless little shit.

"Go back to the party, Scarlett. And try not to stir up any drama."

I shut my mouth and walked out of the library.

It wasn't my place to defend my sister's ex-boyfriend to my father.

"What is this?" I asked the server, my hand shielding my mouth which was full of something that was not, in fact, chocolate mousse in a mini pie crust like I'd assumed.

"Chicken liver mousse," he said before moving on to his next victim, silver tray balanced on the palm of his hand.

"No wonder it tastes like ass," I said under my breath.

Trying to be as subtle as possible, I spit the chicken liver mousse into my cocktail napkin, crumpled it up, and hid the evidence next to a Ming vase filled with gold-dipped roses. Behind me, I heard a deep masculine laugh.

"Not a fan of eating ass?"

I mentally face-palmed myself and turned around to put a face to the voice. The guy had a devil-may-care look about him. Brown hair tousled to perfection, a wicked grin, and a gleam in his eye like he'd found a kindred spirit.

"You heard that?" I asked, trying to suppress my smile.

"Your secret's safe with me." He clinked his champagne flute against mine. "I'm Logan, Chase's brother."

"Oh right. I'm Scarlett, Sienna's—"

"Younger sister. I know." He loosened the collar of his white dress shirt, his eyes darting around the room like he was looking for an escape hatch. I knew the feeling. "Do you want to get some fresh air?"

"I'd love to."

We weaved through the shiny, plastic people milling about sipping champagne and cocktails in their designer dresses and suits, smiles firmly in place. I'd never enjoyed these types of social gatherings. It all just seemed so fake and so, so dull. The laughter and small talk so contrived it made me want to scream. We passed two couples discussing yachts and another group talking about the best place to buy a second vacation home. Gag me.

Logan set his empty champagne glass on the mahogany sideboard as we passed through the dining room and we side-stepped members of the catering crew who had taken over the kitchen. Emerging from the French doors onto the back patio, I filled my lungs with cool night air. This was the first time I'd breathed properly since I arrived at this party.

"Do you have it too?" Logan asked, studying my face. He was handsome. Almost *too* handsome.

"Have what?" I fished the raspberry garnish out of my champagne and popped it into my mouth to rid it of the taste of chicken liver. Blech.

"Younger sibling syndrome. It's a thing, you know. Prevalent in dysfunctional, rich families."

I laughed. "I guess so. I have that and other things. I'm the family rebel," I said with a sigh. "But I'm trying to be on my best behavior tonight."

"You're doing an admirable job." There was amusement in his voice, but it didn't sound like he was mocking me. It felt like we were on the same team.

"I know the feeling. I'm the black sheep of the family." He smiled, his teeth so white in the moonlight, and I found myself wanting to know more about him and his family dynamics.

"Do you and Chase get along?"

"For the most part," he said, and I sensed that he was holding back the same way I did whenever I talked about my relationship with Sienna. "He loves your sister. They're good for each other."

"In what way are they good for each other?" I asked, my curiosity piqued. I'd only seen Chase and Sienna together a few times, and it was always at family occasions, so it was hard to tell what they were truly like as a couple.

"Chase needs to lighten up. He has an unfortunate tendency to act like he has a stick up his ass." That made me laugh. "It's getting better now that he's with your sister. And Sienna..."

He hesitated, not sure if he should go on.

"And Sienna?" I prompted, encouraging him to finish his train of thought.

"I just get the feeling that she needed someone reliable. Someone she can depend on. Chase is that guy. He's always been the more responsible one. Truthfully, he's a good guy."

"Dependable and reliable."

"Exactly."

I mulled over Logan's words. I guess I could understand why Sienna would be drawn to that kind of security after having been with Dylan. Chase was the safer bet. I wondered how difficult it would be to seek shelter with someone who was reliable and dependable after surviving the storm that was Dylan.

"Do you have a boyfriend?" Logan asked, holding up his hands. "I'm not hitting on you. Just curious."

"Um, well... no, I don't."

"You don't sound too sure."

This was one of those times I needed to keep my mouth shut. Confiding in my sister's future brother-in-law didn't seem like a smart move. "I don't have a boyfriend. Do you have anyone special?"

"I have a lot of someone specials," he said with a crooked grin. It didn't surprise me that he was a player. He was the whole package. Rich, handsome, charming. Not my type but he was fun to hang out with.

I told him about my designs. He told me he lived in LA—Venice Beach—and we talked about his recent backpacking trip around South America.

Logan's phone pinged with a message and he checked it before pocketing his phone. "What do you say we get out of here?"

"Yes," I said a little too enthusiastically, making Logan laugh. "Did you drive? Do you think I could bum a ride?"

He nodded. "I drove, and my chariot awaits." He held out his arm and I looped mine in his.

"You're a lifesaver."

"And you're just the excuse I needed."

"Let's go," I said, hurrying us through the house, in a rush to get out of there. My father's voice brought us to a halt in the great room.

"I'd like to make a toast," my father said, commanding the attention of everyone in the room. His arm was wrapped around my mother and she was beaming, so thrilled to have his attention even though it was just for show. He was putting on airs and graces for their guests. "To Sienna and Chase and their upcoming marriage. Margot and I are delighted to welcome Chase into our family. He's become like the son we never had. I think I speak for both families when I say that I couldn't imagine a better union. Chase and Sienna share the same core values and life goals, and I anticipate a bright future for both of them."

My father's little speech earned him a splattering of applause and everyone lifted their glasses to drink to Sienna and Chase. Sienna hugged Dad and he held her at arm's length, his smile brimming with pride and joy. "I'm so proud of you. For all that you've achieved. And for being the best daughter I could ever ask for."

With great restraint, I resisted the eye roll. He was laying it on thick tonight. Sienna was lapping it up, her smile dazzling, her eyes glossy with unshed tears. I guess it must be intoxicating to earn my father's praise and admiration. Why else would my mother and sister be vying for it? Why else would they try so hard to please him?

I'd spent so many years convincing myself that his opinion of me didn't matter that I'd almost started to believe it. But on nights like this, when he heaped praise on my sister, I felt like the world's biggest loser.

Logan slung an arm around my shoulders, tucking me close to his side like he was protecting me. Though I appreciated the gesture, I quirked my brows at him in question.

He grinned and leaned in close, his voice low. "Nobody puts Baby in the corner."

I burst out laughing at the *Dirty Dancing* reference. Inadvertently, my laughter drew my father's attention. His brows rose in surprise, and he looked from me to Logan who kept me tucked into his side as we crossed the room and stopped in front of my parents.

"I've offered to drive your daughter home." His smile was polite, unlike the genuine one he'd given me earlier.

"And I said yes," I said with a big smile like I'd just accepted his marriage proposal.

"Oh. Well, that's lovely," my mom said, clapping her hands together, her smile mega-watt. "Isn't that lovely, Simon?"

My father's eyes narrowed, trying to figure out what game I was playing. He hated that he couldn't control me. What more could he take from me? His money? His love? His approval? I'd lost them all a long time ago. "Indeed. Thank you for taking care of her," he told Logan.

"My pleasure."

We said our goodbyes. Air kisses all around. My parents drifted away to mingle with their guests and the front door beckoned but first I needed to say goodbye to my sister. She was talking to our cousin Phoebe.

"Thank God you came to your senses," Phoebe said. "I was worried there for a minute. I mean, can you imagine him at tonight's party?"

"Not really," Sienna said, forcing a smile that I knew was fake.

"Slumming it with the trailer trash was not a good look for

you," Phoebe said with a laugh, taking a sip of pink champagne that matched her dress.

For someone who was absent from this party, Dylan got a lot of press.

Never far from her side, Chase swooped in and wrapped his arm around Sienna and I took that opportunity to say my goodbyes.

"You're leaving already?" she asked, disappointed.

I nodded. "I have to get up early for work. But I had a great time."

Sienna rolled her eyes. "You're a shitty liar. But we'll make plans soon. You can come to LA and we'll hang out. We could double-date," she joked, giving Logan a little slug on the arm that told me they were close enough to tease each other. "Although I'm pretty sure Scarlett isn't the kind of girl your parents have in mind for you. She'd rock the boat too much."

"My kind of girl." Logan gave my shoulder a little squeeze. "Let's run away together."

I winked at him. "Just give me the date and the time and I'll be there."

"Don't say something like that to Scarlett," Sienna said. "She'd do it in a heartbeat.".

"At least Scarlett has a job," Chase said. "Logan spends his nights clubbing and his days sleeping it off."

"And it's time to go," Logan said. "Always good to see you, bro."

After suffering the little digs, Logan and I got out of there as quickly as possible and stopped next to a gunmetal gray Tesla parked at the end of the cul de sac. "Slumming it tonight," I joked when he opened the scissor door for me.

"Left the Maserati at home."

"Next time."

26

DYLAN

While I'd been sitting on the hood of my car waiting, I'd had plenty of time to think this through. I hadn't called or texted to let her know I'd be here. Something like this had to be done face to face.

And tonight, I was planning to tell her everything. I'd just lay it all on the line.

I wanted her to know that I liked her. I *more* than liked her. Over the past month, I'd missed her more than I would have thought possible.

And it wasn't just the sex I missed. It was her. Her face, her smile, her laughter, her unfiltered mouth, her honesty.

Right or wrong, I wanted Scarlett in my life and I was feeling pretty damn good about my decision.

Headlights illuminated the darkness and I watched from my spot across the street and a few houses down as the car stopped under a streetlight in front of Scarlett's building. I tossed my cigarette on the ground and crushed it under the sole of my boot, my eyes on the Tesla. The driver's door opened, a man stepped out, and I took it all in—the expensive tailored suit, his height and build and stupid-ass hair, like he'd styled it for a GQ photo shoot.

Rich. Handsome. Entitled.

This scene was giving me flashbacks. Been there, done that, got the fucking T-shirt. Last time this happened, his name was Chase Fucking Carruthers. The jury was still out on whether Sienna cheated on him or on me. In the end, it didn't matter. She chose him.

Everyone, including Scarlett, seemed to think that Sienna and Chase hooked up at her cousin Phoebe's wedding. *After* we broke up for the last and final time. That's not the way it happened. Sienna met Chase at Phoebe's New Year's Eve party eight months before that wedding. I hadn't been invited to the party or the wedding.

Now, I watched as Prince Charming opened the scissor door and held out his hand. I saw red when Scarlett emerged from the car in a little black designer dress, six-inch stilettos, and a dazzling smile. For him. Not me.

She hadn't seen me skulking in the shadows like a fucking stalker.

Her laughter, sweet and melodious, reached my ears and hit me like a sucker punch in the gut. They were standing close. Too fucking close for my comfort. He said something, his voice too low for me to hear and she nodded, smiling up at him like he was the answer to all her prayers.

Before he could get his goodnight kiss or lure her into bed, I stalked toward them.

Scarlett's eyes widened when she saw me and she quickly averted her head, focusing on the GQ model standing in front of her. "Thanks for everything," she told the douchebag.

What exactly did *everything* mean?

"Anytime." His eyes ping-ponged from me to Scarlett, waiting for an introduction or an explanation for the guy glowering at him. When none was forthcoming, he said something in Scarlett's ear. She nodded, and he kissed her on the cheek and squeezed her shoulder.

With a final glance at me, he climbed into the driver's seat. Scarlett waited until his taillights disappeared before she turned around to face me.

"Who was that?" I asked, voice deceptively casual. No need to jump to conclusions.

"A friend."

"A friend. Huh. Are you fucking this *friend*?"

"I don't see how that's any of your business," she said breezily, sauntering past me in her fuck-me stilettos. I shouldn't be noticing her legs or the sway of her hips or the way her dress hugged all her curves but I was. Because she'd worn that fucking dress for a Tesla-driving GQ model douchebag. Not for me. For *him*. She was mine, all fucking mine, and I wanted her back.

"*You're* my business," I growled, stalking after her.

"Oh my God." She spun around to face me, hands on her hips, blue eyes flashing with anger. If anything, she looked even more beautiful when she was angry. My eyes dropped to her heaving chest. Sick bastard that I was, it made me hard.

"You're unbelievable. I haven't seen you in a month. *You left me.* So you don't get to show up here and question me or act like anything I do is your business." She got right in my face, taunting me. "I can *fuck* whoever I want."

Her words hit me like a slap on the face followed by a swift kick to the nuts. I staggered back a step. Looks like baby sister was armed for battle. Two could play this game.

My eyes raked over her in a slow, leisurely descent, taking in the little black designer dress and heels before returning to her face. She didn't look like herself tonight with that smoky eye makeup and perfect hair.

"You know what's funny?" I wrapped a loose curl around my fingers. She lifted her brows, waiting for my next words. "I thought you were different. I thought you and Sienna were night and day. But I was wrong. Because here you are with your shiny new boyfriend and your designer clothes."

I released her hair, ignoring the flash of hurt in her eyes, and hooked my finger in the strap of her dress, sliding it up and down, feeling the shiver go through her. "I bet Daddy will give you back the keys to the kingdom now that you've fallen into line. Are you letting him choose your boyfriends now, too?"

"You have no idea what you're talking about," she gritted out, shoving my hand away and turning to go. I gripped her waist and pulled her against me, her back flush with my chest, my arm locking her in place.

"I liked the old Scarlett better." Moving her hair aside, my teeth grazed her neck, soft but bruising, her scent heady and delicious, like her. But destroying good things was my specialty so I delivered the final blow. "This just looks like a desperate attempt to follow in your big sister's footsteps. But guess what? You've fallen short, baby sister."

Tears welled in her eyes and she swallowed hard, forcing them back as she turned to face me. "You know what's funny? Really funny? I've always defended you, Dylan. *Always.*" Her voice quavered on the words, but pride forced her to look me straight in the eye when she dished up my just desserts. "I never believed that you were an asshole. I never *wanted* to believe it. But I was wrong to give you the benefit of the doubt. You *are* an asshole. Congratulations. Just when I thought I couldn't feel shittier about myself, you proved me wrong."

She walked away from me, her back ramrod straight, her blonde hair glowing in the moonlight and it was safe to say this night had not gone to plan.

It was also possible that I'd fucked up.

Why would she have felt shitty about herself?

As I stood on the street and watched her leave, it slowly sunk in. The realization that I was repeating old mistakes.

Someone hurts you, you retaliate and hit them where you knew it hurt most.

Scarlett wasn't Sienna. Scarlett had never betrayed me. Had never cheated on me. Had never made empty promises or told me lies. She had never done *anything* to deserve the way I'd treated her.

And I had this sinking feeling that if I let her go now, I'd lose something precious to me.

"Scarlett." I strode after her and climbed the stairs to her apartment, stopping outside her front door. "Wait."

The door slammed in my face and I heard the locks click into place with a ring of finality. I pressed my forehead against the wood and banged my head against it a few times.

Asshole.

27

SCARLETT

I uploaded my new design photos to my website. While they were loading, I gathered my hair into a messy bun and secured it with a pencil.

Should it be taking this long? I stared at the laptop screen and drummed my fingers on the surface of the glossy white desk, resisting the urge to dive into the gold foil box of hand-dipped chocolate covered fruit. Orange slices and cherries. My favorites. I grabbed the box and tossed it in the trash can under Remy's desk. Then I stared at the box for a few seconds before retrieving it and setting it back on the desk. No sense in wasting perfectly good chocolates. I'd give them to Ryan. His girlfriend liked chocolate.

My phone vibrated on the desk and I glanced at the screen.

With a sigh, I answered, surprised she'd waited three days to call me. "Hey Mom."

"Hello sweetie," she sing-songed. Someone was in a good mood. While my mother recapped the highlights of Saturday night's engagement party, I typed up the description for my Voodoo Surf collection. "So, did you make any plans to see Logan again?"

I rolled my eyes. "No. He just gave me a ride home. That's it."

"Hmm. Well, you could make an effort. He comes from a very good family. They own a big pharmaceutical company." She'd only mentioned that a hundred times since Sienna and Chase had gotten together. "They said we're always welcome to use any of their vacation homes. I thought it would be nice if we all went away together. With Chase and Logan, of course."

Of course. One big happy family. I'd rather stab myself in the eyeball with a red-hot poker than go on a family holiday.

I spun around in the swivel chair and stared out Remy's office window at the salmon pink façade of the electric bike shop. Jewel-toned flowers cascaded from the hanging baskets and the sun peeked out from behind a wispy cloud, bathing the alley in sunlight.

"I'm pretty busy with work so..."

"Don't be ridiculous. It's not like you have a real job. I'll arrange everything and send you the dates."

"Mom, the last time we went on a family vacation, it was a disaster. I'd really rather not put myself through that again. And I'm not going to go away with Logan or do anything else with him for that matter, so you can stop matchmaking. It's not happening."

"Well, that's what your sister said before we fixed her up with Chase."

My gaze swung to the framed surfing photos of Shane. Give me Zen, dude, I could use it right about now.

"I'm not Sienna," I said through my clenched jaw, still feeling the blow from Dylan's words. I'd never really seen Dylan's cruel side before, but I should have known he'd be capable of hurting me more than anyone ever could. I'd provoked him, had incited his jealousy, and he'd retaliated.

"And I'm sorry to disappoint you, I will *never* be Sienna. For better or worse, I make my own choices and the size of someone's bank account doesn't impress me. Not to mention that this is not the eighteenth century so arranged marriages are not really a thing anymore."

My mother sighed loudly. "Why must you always be so difficult?"

"I need to get back to work," I lied. I was on my lunch break, but she was messing with my vibe which was already less than chilled thanks to the asshole who had crushed my heart. *Again.* "Goodbye Mom."

I cut the call and slumped in my seat, internally screaming.

"I know you're not Sienna," came a low, husky voice behind me. "You're not a disappointment. Not even fucking close." I squeezed my eyes shut, trying to block out the hurt his words had caused, and heard the door close behind him.

I spun my chair around to face Dylan but didn't lift my eyes to look at him. "What are you doing here?"

He set a Starbucks cup on the desk next to my laptop within easy reach of my right hand. I ignored the peace offering.

"I might have fucked up the other night."

Might have?

He rubbed the back of his neck. "I didn't mean what I said. You looked beautiful."

I let out a harsh laugh and stared at the laptop screen. The words danced in front of my eyes but didn't register.

"I don't like seeing you with someone else," he said, still trying to explain his behavior.

"You made that pretty clear." I gestured to the door, shooing him away. "You can go now."

"I had no right to question you."

This was starting to feel like a good grovel. I hadn't thought him capable of that. But we were irrevocably broken and no amount of groveling or chocolates or coffee was going to fix us.

He came around to my side of the desk and sat on the edge of it, one booted foot planted on the floor, his eyes intently studying my face while mine studiously avoided him. Bad enough that his scent invaded my senses, I didn't need a visual reminder of the guy I'd vowed to keep at arms-length.

"Please leave."

"Starlet, look at me," he said softly, and it was that softness in his voice, his words like a plea, that drew my eyes to him and had me taking my first good look at him since he'd walked in the door. Big mistake.

Scruff on his jaw, his hair all messy and disheveled, in ripped black jeans, combat boots, and a black Pearl Jam T-shirt that said: don't give up.

I remember that T-shirt. I remember that he used to love Pearl Jam. When I was fourteen, he told me "Black" was his favorite song. I listened to it on repeat for an entire summer. Pathetic, I know. Just like me.

Why did he have to look so sexy today? How unfair that I still found him irresistible.

And here we were again. Close enough to touch, close enough to breathe the same air, close enough to study the tattoos on his veiny forearms. And just like always, my pulse was racing, and my heart was jackhammering in my chest.

Then I reminded myself of the things he had done and the words he had said, and my need for self-preservation kicked in.

Shielding myself with invisible armor, I scooted my chair back until it hit the wall. As far away from him as the small office allowed. I needed space and breathing room and I needed answers which was the only reason I hadn't already walked away.

"What do you want from me? Why did you show up on Saturday night?"

"I missed you," he said simply.

"Right. You missed me." I laughed hollowly. "It was just sex. You got what you wanted, and you dumped my ass. So what was that? A booty call?"

"You thought it was just about sex?" He sounded so incredulous I would have laughed if not for the fact that I didn't find any of this even remotely funny.

"How should I know? You don't talk. You just show up and act like a Neanderthal and say hateful things. Or you call me when you're drunk and then don't even remember calling. You said you don't play games, but this entire thing has felt like one big stupid game. And guess what? I'm done playing your game."

Dylan scowled. "It was never a game."

"You're right. Games are fun, and this wasn't. Your words hurt me. And you... you hurt me, okay?" I wrapped my arms around myself for protection, all my truths spilling from my lips. I'd never been very good at keeping things inside.

"I tried to tell myself it was just sex, that it didn't mean anything. I tried to tell myself that it was for the best. You and I were never meant to be together. But none of that made up for you just leaving and never explaining why or..." I averted my face. I always said too much. Made myself too vulnerable. It was my tragic flaw.

I wore my heart on my sleeve. A giant target for his poison arrow. And he always hit the bullseye.

"You weren't a mistake. I fucked up."

"Why did you lash out like that if you didn't mean it?"

"It's what I do."

I shook my head, not ready to let him off the hook so easily. "That's not an excuse."

He exhaled loudly.

"Give me an honest answer or leave," I said firmly, pointing to the door.

"Seeing you with a guy like that, dressed like that... it re-opened an old wound." His face was more open and vulnerable than I'd ever seen it, his words honest. But they hurt me nonetheless because I knew that this was all about Sienna.

I should have known. Hadn't he compared me to her and I'd fallen short?

"He's not my boyfriend. He just gave me a ride home from Sienna's engagement party. But you lied to me, didn't you? You're not over her."

That was the only logical explanation for his behavior. I stood up from my chair and skirted past him. Since he didn't seem inclined to leave, I would.

"I didn't fucking lie to you," he gritted out.

I ignored his words because he'd given me no other explanation. "I'm not Sienna. And I'm not your consolation prize."

My hand was on the doorknob ready to leave when his words stopped me.

"I know that." His voice grew closer, but I kept my back to him, waiting to hear what else he had to say. "She fucked with my head, and I'm over her, but I still bear the scars. We were bad for each other. I know I fucked up. Give me another chance to get it right."

Slowly, I spun around to face him. He bit his bottom lip, his stormy eyes so hopeful it made my heart ache. More than anything, I wanted to give him another chance but I couldn't. "It hurt so much when you left me like that. It hurt more than it should have because we hadn't even been together that long."

"I feel like I've known you forever."

I took a shaky breath. His honesty was so disarming. "What happened to you? Why did you leave like that?"

"My mother died. Committed suicide." I sucked in a breath. Oh, my God. "She called me that night I was with you, but I missed her call. And I spent the last month thinking that if I'd answered her call, maybe I could have stopped her."

I could hear the guilt in his voice, and the grief, as if he actually believed that his mother's death had been his fault. Sucking in a huge gulp of air, I tried to come up with something, anything, I could say to make his pain stop. There was nothing.

"I'm sorry. I'm so sorry, Dylan."

"Don't be," he said gruffly. "She was a shitty excuse for a mother."

"But you loved her." It was a guess. He'd never really talked about his mother.

He lifted one shoulder in a shrug, his eyes not meeting mine. "In my own fucked-up way, yeah, guess so."

Not knowing what to do but needing to do something, I wrapped my arms around him, tentative at first. When he didn't pull away, I held him tighter and his arms came around me.

I held onto him like I never wanted to let him go. This beautiful broken boy who could be so cruel. The only boy I'd ever loved.

The events of the past month ran through my head. The way he'd hurried me out of his house that morning then dropped me off. The night he'd gotten so drunk and begged me to stay because he didn't want to be alone. But I'd left him and now I wondered if everything would have been different if only I'd stayed.

Everyone leaves.

And I did too.

I knew something was wrong when I saw him by the elevators that morning, but I'd been so frustrated by his lack of communication. And he'd never said a word about what he was going through.

"I could have been there for you, if you'd have let me," I said, tears springing to my eyes unbidden when I remembered the pain etched on his face the night I'd picked him up outside The Last Stand. "It wasn't your fault, Dylan. Your mother's death wasn't your fault."

He buried his face in my hair for a few seconds before he released me and took a step back, scrubbing his hand over his face. Sometimes, like that night at the hospital and right now, I got a glimpse of the boy that he must have been. And something about seeing this tough guy looking so vulnerable made my heart ache.

"Why didn't you tell me? Why didn't you say something?"

"I needed to tell Remy first. I only told her a couple days before I came to see you."

It was Remy's mother too. I'd been so wrapped up in my own drama that I'd forgotten that. I hadn't seen Remy since I stopped by to visit Kai last week, so she hadn't known yet. And I guess it wasn't the kind of thing Shane would go around telling people.

"But why?" I asked, confused as to why he would keep it from his own twin.

He looked annoyed like he'd been questioned before, most likely by Remy. "She just had a baby. I didn't want to fuck that up for her."

He was trying to give her that time to be happy, I guess. But why did everything have to be so complicated with him?

"Are you okay?" I asked.

"It's all good." I gave him a skeptical look. He cradled my face in his hands and tipped it up, his eyes searching mine. "Are you okay?"

A lump formed in my throat from those words. It was such a simple question, the kind of thing people asked each other all the time without really wanting an answer. But when Dylan asked, it sounded like it really meant something. Like the answer mattered.

I nodded a little. "I'm okay."

He kissed me softly. His tongue swept over my lips and I parted them, letting him in, my arms wrapping around his neck as he deepened the kiss. I got caught up in the taste of him. His heady scent. The feel of his hands on my body.

It was too easy to get lost in this kiss. To get lost in him again. I pulled away and took a step back.

He ran his hand through his hair and raised a brow in question, his unspoken words asking what's wrong.

"What are we doing? What are we, Dylan? You say it's not *just* sex, you say we're not *just* friends, so what are we?"

He sighed in exasperation and carved his hand through his hair. "You wanna slap a label on it?"

"No. I want an answer."

"I don't know what we are. But I know that I want you. And I don't want anyone else to have you."

To me, that sounded a lot like a relationship. But with all the obstacles in our way, how could that even be possible? "You're still my sister's ex-boyfriend," I pointed out.

"I can't change history and that's all we are. History."

But she was still my sister and always would be. "My dad's out to get you," I admitted. "I overheard him on Saturday night."

"Don't worry about him. That has nothing to do with us. We'll figure it out," he said, sounding so confident. He checked his Omega Speedmaster for the time. "I need to get to a meeting. Wish me luck."

"Why? Who's the meeting with?"

"The planning commission, the council, the mayor. Pretty sure daddy dearest will be there," he said calmly, like none of this fazed him.

My eyes widened and then I started laughing.

His thick brows drew together. "What's so funny?"

"You." I looked at his ripped jeans and combat boots. On closer inspection, they looked like the ones he used to wear, the leather cracked and worn, the laces undone. He looked like trouble and I loved it. But not exactly what you'd wear to a council meeting.

"Are you trying to make a statement with this outfit?" I asked, laughing again.

He winked at me. "Once an asshole, always an asshole."

"Good luck. I believe in you, Dylan St. Clair."

His eyes softened, the cocky expression disappearing as his eyes roamed my face searching for the truth in my words. "I don't deserve it. But those words... they're fucking everything."

My eyes filled with tears. I was such a cry baby. But I knew how much those words meant to him.

He left me with a 'see you later' and a soft kiss on my forehead that was sweeter than the chocolates he'd sent.

After the door closed behind him, I plopped down on the swivel chair and took a sip of the Starbucks he'd brought me. Caramel macchiato. He remembered. I lifted the lid off the box of chocolates and popped a cherry into my mouth, moaning softly when the tart and sweet juices exploded, blending perfectly with the milky chocolate.

Food porn right there.

I was licking the chocolate off my fingers when there was a knock on the door and Shane entered the office.

Shane. My boss. I'd just been making out with his brother-in-law in his wife's office.

My face heated. It felt like it was on fire. "Hey. How's it going?" I flashed him a smile, trying to cover my embarrassment and offered him a chocolate which he declined.

"I need you out front. I have a board for you to paint."

"Oh. Yeah. Sorry." I'd lost all track of time. I shut down my laptop and slid it into my messenger bag as I stood up. "I was just—"

"Hanging out with my brother-in-law." He ran his hand through his hair and sighed. I got the feeling I wasn't fooling him. He saw more than he was letting on.

"We were just talking," I said, rounding the desk to join him.

Shane rubbed his hand over his jaw and studied my face. I tried to school my features, scared of what he might see.

Too much, judging by the next words out of his mouth. "I'm in no position to judge. I fell in love with a sixteen-year-old when I was twenty-one. So I'll just ask you one thing. If you walked away right now, could you move on and forget all about him?"

My first instinct was to lie. Pretend that I was unaffected by Dylan. But I was pretty sure my face gave me away and he'd see right through my lie, so I shook my head. "No, it's already too late for that," I said quietly. "It's hopeless though."

Shane gave me a little smile and squeezed my shoulder. "Never. There's always hope."

I took some comfort in his words. Shane and Remy had beaten impossible odds and their love was still holding strong. But Dylan and I weren't Shane and Remy. I didn't know what we were.

Two wrongs that make a bigger wrong. *Then why does it feel so right*?

"Dylan told me about his mom. Is Remy okay?" I asked, following Shane to the front of the shop.

"She's okay. She's more worried about Dylan."

"Why? I mean, obviously, I know why he'd be upset... why they'd both be upset. It's a horrible thing. But why is she more worried about Dylan?"

Shane thought about it for a moment before he answered, trying to decide how much he should tell me. "She worries because he holds everything inside. They went through a lot of shit growing up and their mother..." He shook his head and I got the feeling that Shane had not been a big fan. "That woman was a piece of work. But Dylan always felt like it was his responsibility to look after her. Protect her. Provide for her. Pretty sure he did it up until the day she died."

"It should have been the other way around."

"In an ideal world, every kid would have loving parents." He gave me a soft smile and I thought, not for the first time, that

Kai was the luckiest little boy in the world to have two awesome parents who loved him unconditionally.

We weren't all so lucky. But maybe that was the goal in life. Despite your upbringing and circumstances, you just had to rise above and try to become the best person you could be.

28

SCARLETT

I pointed to the liquor store a few doors down as Dylan slid his card out of his wallet, his phone wedged between his ear and shoulder.

His brows drew together. "Cruz. Hang on." He jerked his chin at me, his way of asking for an explanation.

"I'll meet you in the wine store." I gave him a quick kiss and a smile and waved over my shoulder, leaving him to get cash from the ATM and finish his call with Cruz. From the little I'd overheard, they were having problems at work. They'd just lost one of their biggest clients.

I rubbed my hands over my bare arms covered in goose-bumps. Summer had come early. It was the end of April and for the past week, the temperatures had hovered in the high eighties during the day. But I should have grabbed my hoodie from the car. It cooled off in the evenings and now the air felt chilly, made worse by my flushed skin from all the sun I'd caught today.

My phone pinged, and I slid it out of my shorts pocket, checking the screen.

Nic: Since you're ordering Vietnamese, you want to pair it with a Riesling. I'll text you the info.

I shook my head, laughing, and lifted my eyes from my phone, promptly ramming into a brick wall. I took a few steps back. "Oh God, I'm sorry. I need to watch where I'm going."

"S'alright. You can run into me anytime, beautiful." The guy grinned, his dark eyes roaming down my body, over my tank top and cut-off jean shorts, and down my bare legs before they returned to my chest, not my eyes. I hated that.

I folded my arms and sidestepped him.

"Hey, hey, hey." He grabbed my arm. "Where you going? Me and my buddy are heading down to the beach with some brews." I looked over at the guy he was with. They both looked like gym rats, beefed up and brawny with corded muscles and shaved heads. "Come party with us."

I shook my head. "No, thanks. I'm good."

"Bring a friend," the other guy said as if I hadn't just shot them down.

"She's with me." Dylan slung an arm around my shoulders, tucking me close to his side.

The guy held up his hands. "My bad. Just inviting her to a beach party."

"She's not interested," Dylan said tersely.

Dylan ushered me into the brightly lit wine and liquor store, his arm still around my shoulders. I looked up at his face. His jaw was clenched. "Was he hassling you?" he asked.

I shook my head. He studied my face for a moment and I gave him a smile. "No. It was fine. I accidentally bumped into him."

"That guy's an asshole."

"Do you know him?"

"We used to go to the same gym."

"If you ask me, he pumps too much iron. He's too bulked up."

"Not your type, huh?"

"Nope." I squeezed his bicep and gave him a flirty wink. "I like my men lean and mean."

His brows raised. "Your men? What's all this talk about men?" He nuzzled my neck. "You've only got one man."

"And he's more than enough."

He grinned and gave me a little smack on the butt, his good mood restored. The past month had been like a dream. Everything had been so good that I was starting to question if this was really my life.

"What are we looking for?" he asked.

We stopped in front of the white wine selection and I slid my phone out of my pocket, checking the text from Nic. I showed him the screen and he read the text then we moved down the aisle to the imported wines, scanning the bottles on the racks, looking for the one Nic had recommended. She was turning into a wine snob.

Two weeks ago, Cruz had whisked her off to Napa or a weekend getaway. The poor guy didn't even like wine but he'd do anything to make Nic happy, so it was a weekend of wine tasting for him. He told me he'd spit most of it in the bucket which made me laugh.

Dylan plucked out a bottle of Riesling from the rack and studied the label then held it up to me for closer inspection. "Is this the one?"

"I think so." I double-checked Nic's text and confirmed he'd gotten it right. "Yeah, that's the one."

Then I checked the price and my eyes widened. "Put it back. That's way too expensive for a bottle of wine."

Instead of putting it back, Dylan grabbed two more and carried all three bottles to the counter and set them down.

"Dylan. Seriously. She's ridiculous. Put it back." I tried to grab the bottles, but he swatted my hand away.

"Stop being a pain in the ass."

"But, I can't afford that."

He scowled. "You need to stop worrying about money. I'm buying it so get over yourself."

"Dylan. That's ninety bucks for three bottles of wine. That's ridiculous."

"Which part of stop did you not understand?" He looked at the man behind the counter. "Ring them up before she puts them back. I need to grab some beer."

"Sure thing."

I sighed loudly while Dylan went off to get his beer and leaned my hip against the counter, texting Nic to let her know that she was fired as my sommelier. Cheap domestic wine was just fine for me. Not like I was a wine connoisseur. I wouldn't even appreciate this overpriced wine.

"Just so you know, I'm not with you for your money," I told Dylan when he returned with a measly six-pack of IPA which cost nothing in comparison to my ridiculously overpriced wine from the Alsace.

"You're with me for the sex," he said, his voice low but loud enough for the man behind the counter to overhear it.

The man coughed. I blushed. Dylan chuckled.

I smacked his arm on our way out the door. "Stop embarrassing me."

"Stop fighting me on money. What good is money if I can't spend it on you?"

Dylan was generous, but thankfully, he wasn't one of those guys who flashed his money around. He only bought what he needed and wasn't really into luxury items or fancy toys. And I never got the feeling there were strings attached when he spent money on me. So I guess it shouldn't really be an issue.

But still. That wine was way too expensive.

Male voices drew my attention to the parking lot across the street and I stopped next to Dylan's car before climbing in. It took me a few seconds to comprehend what I was seeing.

The parking lot was dark except for the beam of light from the headlights of a pickup truck. I recognized the two guys who I'd run into outside the liquor store and I recognized Corbin.

"You motherfuckers!" Corbin screamed, lashing out blindly. His face was bloody, long brown hair matted to his head, and his eyes were wild. I raised my hands to my mouth, watching in horror as the guy punched Corbin, bringing him to his knees.

Dylan tossed me his car keys. "Stay in the car."

"What are you doing?"

He didn't hang around to answer. It was pretty obvious what he was doing. He sprinted across the street to the parking lot just as one of the guys kicked Corbin who was on the asphalt, curled into a fetal position.

Dylan ripped the guy away from Corbin, spun him around and planted his fist in the guy's face. Before he even knew what hit him, Dylan delivered two more punches and my feet carried me closer, my heart beating in my throat.

The other guy got Dylan in a headlock and I winced when the douchebag from the gym punched Dylan in the face. These guys were looking for a fight and they'd found one. Dylan wasn't backing down and now it was two against one.

It took me a few seconds of watching the fists flying, and flinching at the sickening sound of bone and muscle before I came to my senses.

I reached into my pocket, my shaky hands fumbling to grip my phone, my eyes trained on the fight in the parking lot.

Stomach churning, I called 9-1-1 and chewed on my thumbnail.

Dylan was fierce. I'd seen him fight before, of course, but it had been years ago.

"...what is your emergency?"

"There's a fight. In the parking lot across from El Camino Wine & Liquor. Please hurry." I finished my call with the dispatcher then went in search of someone who could help until the cops arrived.

"How about those brews down at the beach, beautiful."

I whirled around and came face to face with the douchebag from Dylan's gym.

"Get away from me. You make me sick."

He moved closer, his eyes drifting to my chest. "Is that right? Your nipples are telling a different story. They look excited to see me."

"Fuck you."

I turned to go, Dylan's car keys clasped in the palm of my hand. The guy grabbed my arm to stop me. I heard a loud roar, and the guy's hand released me. I turned and backed away, slamming into the back of Dylan's G-Wagen as he and the douchebag hit the asphalt. Dylan had him pinned to the ground, his face contorted with anger as he drove his fist into the guy's face.

The wail of sirens cut through the air, thank God, and I sagged against the back of the car, my legs too shaky to hold me up.

The pickup truck skidded to a stop and the douchebag's friend yelled out the open window. "Get the fuck up, man. We need to get out of here."

Dylan laughed and got to his feet, knowing they were too late. The blue and red lights flashed across his face and I flew to him, my arms wrapping around his waist, my face buried in his chest.

"You okay?" he asked, wrapping his arms around me and holding me close.

I nodded against his chest then lifted my eyes to his face. He wiped his bloody nose with the back of his hand and I took his face in my hands to inspect the damage. "Are you okay?"

Running his tongue over his busted lip, he did that half-smirk, half-smile thing he did. "Feels like old times."

"Don't worry about it," he said, pulling my hand away from his face. I'd been tending his cuts and bruises, cleaning off the blood with a washcloth and treating his cuts with antibiotic ointment because, of course, he'd refused medical treatment when the ambulance and paramedics had shown up.

"Tough guy, huh?" I rinsed the bloody washcloth in the sink and wrung it out then washed my hands and dried them on a kitchen towel.

"I can take a punch. Been doing it all my life." He disappeared into the laundry room with the washcloth and returned when I was taking two plates out of the cupboard for our dinner that was on the way.

"So, how do you know Corbin?" he asked, pouring a glass of the overpriced wine and setting it in front of me on the island.

It made my heart hurt that those assholes had picked on Corbin. The story they'd told the cops was that Corbin had tried to mug them and it had been self-defense. Which was ridiculous.

"Just from walking to work. He sleeps behind the dry cleaners in the alley. A few months ago, I started dropping off food for him on my way to work. We talked a couple times." I took a sip of the wine and had to admit it was pretty good. "He did two tours in Afghanistan. I don't know what happened to him but whatever it was it messed up his head. He used to have a wife and a little girl, he told me. I don't know what happened to them though."

Dylan took a swig of his beer, eying me. "Where did you come from, Mother Teresa? How did you turn out so good?"

I laughed a little. "You know I'm not good."

"You are. In the ways that count."

"You just jumped right in, no questions asked."

"Not because I'm good. I love a fight. Can't get enough of them."

I smiled. "Well, good thing there's always something to fight about then. For your sake."

"I'll always fight for you. *Always*."

Those words just about killed me. I was so crazy about this guy and here he was, pledging to always fight for me. I chose to hear his words differently, that not only would he fight for me physically, but he'd fight to keep me. At last, that was what I hoped.

Conscious of his busted lip, I kissed him softly. It had only been a month since that day he showed up in Remy's office, but it felt like our relationship had been taken to the next level. It felt real and good and I knew that I loved him. And that I was in love with him.

The doorbell rang, and our food arrived before I could open my mouth and spill any true love confessions. Being Dylan, he'd ordered almost everything on the menu. The black granite island was covered in a sea of takeout containers, the spicy, garlicky aroma making my mouth water. I didn't know why I'd bothered with plates.

We used our chopsticks and ate right out of the containers, passing them back and forth until I was so stuffed I couldn't eat another bite. And then we stumbled upstairs, buzzed on wine and beer, lost our clothes and tumbled into bed.

"Every asshole in your life has let you down," Dylan said, pinning my wrists to the mattress, his dark hair falling over his forehead, his face hovering only inches above mine. My legs cinched his waist, trying to pull him closer, wanting to feel him deeper inside me. I rocked my hips, needing more. He tortured me by gliding out until only the tip was inside me.

He dipped his head and flicked his tongue over my pebbled nipple then tugged it between his teeth before he did the same to the other one. Torture. Pure torture. My back arched off the mattress. "Dylan. I need more," I gritted out.

He ignored my plea.

"I don't want to be just another asshole," he said, pushing my wrists into the mattress when I tried to break free of his hold and take control of this frustrating situation.

"You're not. You're in your own league. You're *my* asshole."

That made him laugh. Hard. So hard it split his lip again.

"Your face is a mess."

"Your face is beautiful," he said, voice husky, eyes stormy as he thrust inside me, finally giving me what I wanted. I stopped short of singing Hallelujah when he lifted me off the mattress, my breasts pressed against his bare, sweaty chest, my thighs squeezing his and he was buried to the hilt.

I kissed his jaw and his black eye and his bloody lip and razor-sharp, bruised cheekbone and when I came, I screamed his name.

"We're a beautiful mess," I said.

And I didn't want to give him up for anything or anyone.

29

DYLAN

Scarlet was wearing a tiny white bikini and a sheen of sweat. I reached for a cold beer from the ice bucket on the pool's edge, my reward for swimming fifty laps, or a hundred, I'd lost count, and took a long pull as I watched her working. Her brow was furrowed in concentration, her plump bottom lip caught between her teeth as the paint marker in her hand moved across the rail of my new surfboard. She was painting a giant wave, undeterred by the blazing sun beating down on her sun-kissed skin.

For the past two months, we'd been spending most of our free time and most of our nights together. Fucking, talking, laughing, falling in love. I had no idea how the hell the love part had happened, but it had.

Scarlett was good at love. She was good at loving my fucked-up self.

She called me out on my shit and did it in a way that forced me to own up rather than retreat.

Meanwhile, I was still at war with her father. The whole fiasco with The Surf Lodge was still being dragged out. Except now he was attacking my business. We'd lost two of our biggest clients. He was forcing my hand, and it was time to shut him down. I would take the war to him, the war he had started that I'd never wanted, and I would fucking end it.

But today was a Saturday and it was Memorial Day weekend so the war could wait.

"You look hot," I told Scarlett.

"Thank you," she sassed.

"Hot and soon to be wet."

I levered myself out of the pool and stalked toward her. Her eyes widened. "No! You wouldn't dare."

Didn't she know me yet? Marker still in hand, she scooted back and stood up, making a dash for the house.

"I need to finish—"

I caught her around the waist, spun her around and tossed her over my shoulder in a fireman's carry. Her small fists pounded my back and she tried to struggle out of my hold. It was laughable.

"Let me down, you Neanderthal," she shrieked, laughing.

"You need a spanking?" I smacked her ass and she squirmed in my arms, gasping for air between her laughter.

Unceremoniously, I tossed her into the deep end and dove in after her. She came up spluttering and pushed the hair off her face, lunging for me, her hands grabbing my shoulders, nails digging in. "You—"

I dunked her before she got another word out. When her head emerged, she narrowed her eyes on me. "You're an ass."

I laughed. "Like a donkey?"

"Like a jackass."

"You love it."

"I do not love being manhandled," she said primly. Little liar.

"You love it when this man handles you."

She wrapped her arms around my neck and her legs around my waist. "Only when you handle me with care."

"Have you seen my back lately?" I asked, lifting my brows.

She winced. "I might have gotten carried away. Good thing I don't have long nails."

"I love the pain you give." My mouth latched on to her neck and I sucked on it. She tilted it to the side for better access and I marked her skin before she came to her senses and realized what I was doing.

"Are you giving me hickeys?"

"I'm marking you. *Mine.* Just like this pussy." I slid my hand between her thighs. "All mine."

"But are you mine?"

"Nobody else gets to touch me. Only you."

"That's not what I mean."

I kissed her on the lips and she swam away from me and got out of the pool then proceeded to torture me by drying off every inch of her skin with a beach towel. I watched her saunter over to a lounge chair before I got out of the water and carried my bucket of beer over to where she was sitting. Easy access. To the beer. And her.

Setting the bucket on the teak side table littered with all her Sharpies and paint markers that were all over the house, I sat on a lounger and reached for her waist, pulling her down on top of me, with her back against my chest. She rested the back of her head on my shoulder and let out a little sigh of contentment as my hands skimmed over her sun-warmed body. I kissed her neck just below her ear and felt the shiver go through her.

Scooping an ice cube out of the bucket, I trailed it down her chest and over her taut stomach, squeezing her nipple between the fingers of my other hand. "Mmm. That feels good," she said.

"If you like that, you're going to love this." I hooked my hands under her knees and lifted, nudging her thighs apart so she was spread wide open. She rewarded me by grinding her ass against my erection while my hand ventured lower and slipped inside the waistband of her bikini bottoms.

I teased her clit with the ice cube, testing to see if she liked it. She arched her back and let out a little yelp.

"More?"

"More," she breathed.

I slid the ice cube inside her warm pussy and she gasped. "Oh, my God."

I pushed it in deeper with my fingers, my thumb rubbing her swollen clit in a circular motion. Her head fell back against my shoulder and she fucked my hand, grinding against it to chase her release.

I abruptly pulled my hand away. She needed to be tortured a bit longer.

"Stand up," I commanded.

When it came to sex, she did exactly what she was told. *Usually.* Starlet was adventurous, up for anything, always ready to experiment and push her own limits. I spun her around and pulled her closer to me. Reaching for another ice cube, I put it in my mouth and gripped it between my teeth.

Hearing her breath hitch, I started at the column of her neck and slowly trailed the ice cube down, down, down. Running it over her nipples, between her breasts, barely covered by two white triangles. Water droplets trickled down her skin, goosebumps raising the blonde hairs on her arms. Lower and lower I went, wanting her to suffer through the sweetest torture until I was buried deep inside her, giving her an orgasm that would make her scream so loud the whole fucking neighborhood would hear it.

The ice cube melted from the heat of her skin, so I used my ice-cooled tongue to lick off the drops of water.

Hands, tongue, teeth all over her until I landed right between her legs. I slid her bikini bottoms to the side and my tongue delved inside her pussy, the one I'd claimed as mine.

She tasted like sin and the sweetest temptation, and I devoured it, feasted on it like I'd been starving, and this was my favorite meal.

I knew she was close, but I didn't want her to come until I was balls deep inside her. I stood up, grabbed her face in my hands and drove my tongue inside her warm, sweet mouth. Lifting her up, she wrapped her legs around my waist and her arms around my neck and sucked on it, leaving her own mark on my skin as I carried her across the Moroccan tiles. We'd both be bruised purple tomorrow. I chuckled under my breath at the thought of it. I hadn't sported a love bite since I was fifteen or sixteen and had wised up enough to warn girls that they didn't get to touch me unless I said so.

"You're going to pay for this," I growled.

"Are you going to punish me?" she asked breathlessly.

"Mmm hmm." Her back slammed against the rough stucco and I felt her smile against my lips before she sank her teeth into the bottom one.

"You've been calling the shots for too long," she murmured, sucking on my bottom lip to ease the sting. "It's my turn."

"What did you have in mind?" I asked as she unwrapped her legs and slid to the ground, giving my chest a shove. I stumbled back a step, my hand over my heart but it was just for show. She rolled her eyes.

"Drop your shorts, Romeo."

She sauntered over to the daybed on my Moroccan patio and plopped down on it, crooking her finger. I scrubbed my hand over my face to hide my laughter. She looked so adorable, actually believing that she was calling the shots, so I humored her. I dropped my shorts and stalked over to her, fisting my cock in my hand. "Where do you want it, baby? In your mouth? Or wait... you want me to fuck you up the ass, don't you?"

She ignored my questions and patted the seat next to her. "Sit."

I sat, releasing my cock and waited to see what she'd do next.

She pushed down her bikini bottoms, a wicked gleam in her eye as she lifted one leg over me, giving me a flash of pink before she seated herself in my lap.

Her warm hand circled my cock, her tongue darting out to lick her lips as she shifted forward, sliding my cock between her wet folds, cradling it in the closest thing to heaven I'd ever found. My hands landed on top of her thighs, gripping hard as she started rocking, her hands braced on my shoulders.

"Fuck, Starlet."

"That's the idea," she said, her voice sweet and sultry.

She lifted up, guiding my tip to her entrance before sinking down on me, fully seated. My hands flattened on her back, pulling her closer, kissing and biting her tits. Scarlett moaned, hands sliding through my hair to keep me close. I sucked on her collarbone, her shoulder, the sensitive spot beneath her ear, leaving my mark while she set the rhythm, a punishing pace that had her grinding against me, her head flung back and neck fully exposed.

"Dylan," she panted, her moans intensifying.

Time for me to take back the control. I flipped her onto her back, lifted her leg over my shoulder so I could go deeper and thrust into her.

"Oh my god, oh my god," she chanted. Sweat dripped off my forehead onto her heaving chest and her nails dug into my shoulders, her cries loud enough to be heard from the canyon. Fuck, yes.

No woman had ever felt this good.

No woman had ever felt this good.

Fuck. My balls tightened, and I wasn't going to last much longer. I pulled out and sat back, jerking myself hard and coming all over her stomach.

When my eyes met hers, she lowered her lashes but not

before I saw the flash of hurt. "I told you I'm on birth control. You don't trust me, do you?"

Something on my face must have told her that I didn't because she climbed off the daybed and turned her back to me, pulling up her bikini bottoms and grabbing a towel from the deck to clean herself off.

"I'm not Sienna," she said, like I needed a reminder.

She tossed the towel in my face and I watched her walk away and disappear inside the house before I pulled on my boardshorts and parked my ass on the daybed. Fuck. I scrubbed my hands over my face. This was the kind of shit I was bad at. What could I say?

Yeah, well, your sister assured me that she could be trusted but look how that turned out.

Somehow, I didn't think that would cut it.

I was the asshole who knocked up Sienna when we were seventeen. She told me she was on birth control, so we had nothing to worry about. The worst part? She'd never even told me she was pregnant. Hadn't even thought to consult me or ask what we should do about it, just like it didn't concern me and I had no say in the matter.

One day in August, I was cleaning their pool and her father confronted me.

"I had your mistake taken care of, you little shit. Do you really think I'd let my daughter bring your worthless bastard into this world?"

As if a human life was so disposable you could have it 'taken care of.' What had really pissed me off, on top of every-thing, was that I'd had to find out from him and not Sienna.

So yeah, that was the last time I'd ever had sex without a condom. Lesson learned the hard way. Not even birth control was enough to prevent accidental pregnancies. So I always wrapped it up.

But why would Scarlett think this was about Sienna? She'd

only been eleven at the time and the way her family operated, all cloak and dagger, I highly doubted anyone would have told her about it.

I needed a cigarette. But I got my ass off the lounger and went in search of Scarlett. I found her sitting on the kitchen counter, eating Cherry Garcia straight from the container. She jammed the spoon back into the carton and set it aside.

"Sometimes it's just hard, you know? Thinking about you with Sienna."

The big difference between her and Sienna? Scarlett didn't sulk or hold it all inside, letting it fester. She just came out with it, plain and simple, and stated the problem. And fuck if I didn't appreciate that because I was not a mind reader and I couldn't deal with passive-aggressive bullshit.

I stood between her legs and rubbed my hands over her thighs. There were a million things I could tell her that would make her see that she had nothing to worry about. But it didn't seem right to trash her sister or dish the dirt on our relationship. "How did you know?"

"I overheard my dad talking to you. I was in the kitchen getting a snack and the doors were open."

I tucked a lock of sun-bleached hair behind her ear. When her hair dried, it was a mess of crazy waves and I loved it that she never tried to tame them. Not only was she completely unlike Sienna personality-wise, they didn't even look alike. "I don't think about her when I'm with you. Or ever, really."

She nodded and chewed on her bottom lip. "It's just..."

"Just what?"

"I love you," she blurted out.

Her eyes widened and for a few seconds there was nothing but silence and the dull thud of my heart dropping to my stomach as her words hung in the air between us and I said absolutely nothing. Three little words but they packed a powerful punch.

I opened my mouth to speak, maybe to say the words, but we'd never know because the doorbell rang.

She hopped off the counter and turned her back to me, stowing the ice cream in the freezer, and I suspected she was trying to hide her face from me. It was easy to read. She wore her emotions and rarely hid behind a mask. "It's probably Cruz and Nic."

I groaned on my way to the door. "What are they doing here?"

"We invited them, remember?"

"No." I hadn't invited anyone. Must have been Little Miss Congeniality who excelled at socializing.

I answered the door to a smiling Nicola and a smug-looking Cruz. It was his usual expression these days, like he'd figured out the secrets of the universe and they all pointed to one person. Nicola. These two were so loved up it was nauseating. A few days ago, I'd caught him signing a text with the smiley face heart-eyes emoji. What self-respecting man uses a heart-eyes emoji?

I was convinced he'd grown a vagina.

"Did you fire up the grill?" Nic asked me.

"No."

She put her hands on her hips. Her hands were free to do that whereas Cruz was loaded down with about a hundred bags. "I texted you and told you to get the grill ready."

I snorted. Who did she think I was? Cruz? Which was exactly what I told her. She rolled her eyes and breezed past me, cursing me out for not following instructions while Cruz trotted behind her like a dutiful puppy dog, his eyes glued to her ass.

"She's got a whole menu planned. Do as she says, stay out of her way, and nobody will get hurt," he said.

"She's got you pussy whipped," I said, shaking my head.

"I need a cold beer," he said, unloading his bags onto the

kitchen island and helping himself to a beer from my refrigerator.

"And a set of balls."

He gave me the finger and took a long pull of beer. "Fuck, it's hot today."

Scarlett greeted Cruz with a hug and chatted for a few seconds, completely ignoring me, then sauntered out to the pool in her tiny bikini to join Nicola who was no doubt acquainting herself with my grill. I rubbed the blank space over my heart, thinking about her words and our unfinished business. But now that Cruz and Nic had crashed our party for two, there would be no further discussion of love or sex without condoms. Which was a relief.

I wasn't ready to say the words. Without actions to back them up, words were meaningless. I'd rather show her than tell her.

"Does she know you're planning to take down her father?" Cruz asked, cutting into my thoughts, his voice low so as not to be overheard. Not that anyone would hear us over the music blasting.

"You're not even supposed to know that."

"But I know you. Your back's against the wall. You'll come out fighting."

He wasn't wrong about that. Simon Woods was going down and yours truly was going to do the honors.

"He's so much like Jimmy, isn't he?" Remy said as I watched from my poolside lounge chair.

I'd normally scoff at that. Kai was only three months old. But I got what she was saying. Kai was one chilled-out little dude, and nothing made him happier than being in the water, kicking his chubby little legs, a gummy smile on his face.

Remy's phone alarm went off and I shut it off. Must be
feeding time. Sure enough, Remy propelled Kai to the side of
the pool and stopped in front of my lounge chair.

"Hey Dyl, can you take him? I need to get his bottle ready."
She had him on a strict schedule and had read every parenting
book on the market. I got it though. She wanted to make sure
Kai's life was structured and organized so he would know that
food and sleep and bath time were all taken care of, just a part
of his regular routine.

I got off my chair and crouched at the side of the pool,
ready to accept my nephew from his mother's arms. Kai was
slippery wet, and it made me nervous as shit that I'd drop him.
I stood up with him in my arms and carried him over to the
chaise lounge. Remy dug around in her giant bag of baby tricks
and handed me a diaper and a onesie. I got him out of his wet
trunks and swim diaper and into the dry diaper and clothes
without a hitch and lifted him into my arms again.

"You're an old pro now," Remy said and flashed me one of
her big-ass smiles. I knew what was coming next. Sure enough,
her camera was aimed at me and Kai and she was snapping
photos like a madwoman.

"Enough with the fucking photos already. Your kid's starving. He's going for my nipple."

Remy laughed but I wasn't lying. Kai was rooting around,
his gums latching onto his hand and that spurred her into
action. "Be right back."

When she disappeared inside, I nuzzled the top of his head
with my nose. "Hey little buddy. You're a lucky little dude, you
know that? Your parents love the shit out of you. I kind of like
you too," I said with a chuckle.

I kept him snuggled against my chest and kicked back in my
chair, giving him my finger. He latched on and sucked the shit
out of it. The kid wasn't stupid though. It didn't take him long to
figure out that my finger wasn't what he wanted or needed. By

the time Remy came back with a bottle, his cries had reached ear-splitting decibels and I was bouncing him up and down as we paced the pool deck.

Remy jammed the nipple in his mouth and like magic, the crying stopped.

"Do you want to feed him?" she asked, smoothing her hand over the blond peach fuzz on the top of his head.

"If it'll help you out," I said, like it was some great hardship. She smirked as I took the bottle from her and repositioned Kai, so he was in the crook of my arm and we were back on the lounge chair under the shade of an umbrella, so he wouldn't get sunburn.

"I feel like I never see you anymore," Remy said, lounging on the chair next to mine, out of the shade of the umbrella so she could soak up some afternoon sun. She was wearing a black bikini, and you'd never know she'd given birth two months ago. If anything, she was too thin.

"I see you all the time. Are you eating?" I asked.

"I eat like a horse. It's the breastfeeding. I pumped enough for today because I know how weird you get when I whip out my boobs. Breastfeeding is supposed to shrink your uterus--"

"Yeah, okay. Spare me the fucking details."

She laughed. "What I meant is that it's been a while since we've talked, just the two of us." Oh hell no, here we go. Question time. She didn't pull any punches either. "So what's the deal with you and Scarlett?"

"I don't kiss and tell."

She sighed loudly. "Yeah, I know. You never even talked about Sienna. But this... it's different. I care about Scarlett. I don't want to see her get hurt. You do know that Sienna will hate her for this when she finds out, right? She's going to lose her sister over this so if you're not serious about her—"

"You think I'm just playing her?"

"No. I just... you know that all I've ever wanted was for you to be happy. Do you love Scarlett?"

If I hadn't told Scarlett yet, I sure as hell wasn't going to tell my sister.

We'd been spending all our free time together. Fucking, talking, laughing, hanging out. I liked being with her and I missed her when she wasn't around. This morning, we'd gone for a sunrise surf before she went to work, and we'd most likely see each other later tonight. So yeah, guess you could call this a relationship.

But love? That was all kinds of complicated and I was bad at shit like that. As proven by my first and last disastrous relationship. It had not all been Sienna's fault. Not by a long shot. But we'd practically destroyed each other and getting over Sienna, the *idea* of Sienna, hadn't happened overnight. Plenty of booze, plenty of weed, random hookups, and too many long hours in the office. It had been a slow, painful recovery. Who the hell wanted to put themselves through that again?

"Dylan, seriously. Sienna is going to find out eventually. If you're not serious about her—"

"I wouldn't have gotten involved with her if I didn't care about her." Subject closed as far as I was concerned.

I pried the bottle out of Kai's mouth—he was sucking on air now—and the nipple released with a pop. Setting the bottle on the table, I put him over my shoulder and lightly thumped his back until he let out a satisfying burp and dribbled some warm milk on my shoulder.

"Can I just say one more thing?" Remy asked. Kai had drifted off to sleep and we were just chillin' on a sunny May day. Or trying to.

We both knew the question was rhetorical. Remy wasn't waiting for my permission to speak. She'd say whatever she wanted whether I liked it or not. So I kept my eyes closed, my hand rubbing Kai's back as he slept on my chest.

Don't grow up, kid, I told Kai, imparting my wisdom tele-
pathically in hopes he got the message. It's a big, bad world out
there. Stay young and innocent. Don't take that first sip of beer
or try drugs. Fucking ever. Don't fall in love with the wrong girl.
And whatever you do, don't take after your big bad Uncle
Dylan. No fistfights or asshole behavior for you.

It's a slippery slope, little dude. If you run into any trouble,
call me. I'll take care of your dirty work.

Remy was talking. I realized this as I was startled awake by
the sound of her voice. "What's that?"

My arms were empty, and for a second I panicked until I
saw that Remy had put Kai in his car seat, her big-ass bag of
baby tricks packed and ready to go. "I need to go. I have some
errands to run."

"You can leave him here if you want."

"Thanks. But I'll take him with me."

She had never let anyone except Shane look after Kai. A bit
extreme, if you asked me. "Careful there. You're turning into a
helicopter parent."

"I don't care. I'm not letting him out of my sight until he
goes to school and I'm forced to be separated from him. I don't
want to miss a thing, Dylan. Not a single thing."

Couldn't fault her for that. She wanted to be a good mother,
unlike our own. It surprised me that she'd never mentioned our
mother since the night I delivered the news, but I guess she had
Shane to bounce shit off of which was fine by me. I'd rather not
talk about it anyway. I stood up and grabbed the car seat by the
handle. These things were surprisingly heavy and awkward as
shit to carry.

"I've got him. Get your Mary Poppins bag."

She laughed and slung the bag over her shoulder, collecting
his swimming trunks that were drying on the lounge chair. It
was ridiculous how much shit one baby needed. I walked her
out to her Range Rover and clipped Kai's seat into the frame,

making sure it was secure and he was safely belted in before I closed the door and circled the hood. Remy rolled down her window and called me over.

"Yeah?"

"What are you doing for our birthday? Do you want to celebrate it together?"

Our birthday was the fifth of June, and I'd be celebrating it with Starlet. "Can't. I'm taking Scarlett to Cabo for a long weekend."

Her brows raised in surprise. Yeah, I know. We were going on a weekend getaway. Shit was getting serious.

"Wow. Okay." Remy tilted her head, studying my face a little too closely, a smile spreading across her face. "She makes you happy, doesn't she?"

"Guess so." Scarlett made me happy. And even though I hadn't said the words, hadn't really wanted this to happen, somewhere along the way I'd fallen in love with her.

"At the risk of sounding like a bitch, Sienna never deserved you. But Scarlett does."

On that note, Remy reversed out of my driveway and took off down the street with her precious cargo.

Question was, did I deserve Scarlett?

SCARLETT

Dylan handed me a fruity rum cocktail and tipped his chin in thanks as the bartender handed him a rum and soda with lime.

I clinked my glass against his and smiled. "Happy Birthday, Dylan."

We drank to that and Dylan pulled me into a rum-drunk kiss under a blazing sun, the sky so blue it hurt your eyes to look at it. From the swim-up bar in the infinity pool, we had a view of the crystal sea. We were staying in a private spa villa at a luxury resort in Cabo that cost as much as my month's rent per night. I should be happy. On top of the world. I was with the man I loved and even though I thought he loved me too, he'd never said the words whereas I had let it slip twice.

It was Dylan's twenty-seventh birthday, and I just wanted to live in the moment and enjoy the day without thinking about those three little words or the fact that we had no future together.

"Move in with me," he said a little while later when we were poolside, lying side by side on lounge chairs, his hand skimming over my thigh.

I laughed to cover my shock. Where had that come from? Most likely, he was joking. "I can't move in with you."

He was silent for a beat and I thought he'd just drop the subject. "You spend most of your time at my house anyway. Half your shit's over at my place."

I rolled onto my side and studied his face. His eyes were shielded by Wayfarers but his expression told me he was dead serious about this. "How many of those rum cocktails have you had?"

He scowled. "I'm not drunk."

"I still have my own apartment. Nic and I signed a lease."

"When's it up?" he persisted.

"November."

"I'll buy you out of it."

"Um, no. I can't let you do that."

"Why the fuck not?"

There were so many reasons, I wouldn't even know where to begin. We'd spent months sneaking around. We were a badly kept secret and it was a miracle that nobody in my family had found out about us. But I couldn't keep living like this. I was as bad as my father with his mistress, but the difference was that the guilt was starting to eat away at me and my conscience was troubled.

"Why do you want me to move in?" I asked, picking up the conversation again on our way back to the villa. I was sun-drowsy and a little bit buzzed from the rum cocktails.

"I'll show you why."

I padded across the smooth dark wood floor, knowing exactly what he intended to show me. We stripped naked and fell onto the bed diagonally, the sheets so crisp and white, the ceiling fans cooling my skin, a sea breeze floating through the open doors. It was the golden hour, the light softer and warmer, magical, making this feel almost dreamlike.

His hands, lips, tongue caressed every inch of my body,

leaving chills in their wake on my sun-kissed skin, sending ripples of heat between my quivering thighs. Damp heat circled my nipple then he tugged it between his teeth, pinching my other nipple between his fingers. I thrust my hips, seeking the friction as his hard length glided through my slick heat, teasing me with the promise of more.

"You're so wet for me," he said, his lips ghosting down my neck, his voice low and husky. "Fucking drenched."

"I want you inside me," I gritted out as he continued his gentle assault on my body, teasing and coaxing, withholding the one thing I wanted most. It was a familiar theme. Him making me wait until I was so desperate, he had me begging for more. Dylan liked to have that control.

"I love the way your sweet little pussy clenches my cock."

I whimpered, my core clenching just at the mention of it. I *ached* for him. Nobody could turn me on like Dylan could. He didn't even have to touch me to make me wet for him.

"Love the sounds you make when I pound into you."

Oh God. I whimpered again.

Arms braced on either side of me, he hovered above me, his muscles flexing and bunching. I reached up with both of my hands and cradled his face, pulling his mouth to mine. We moaned into our kiss, and I inhaled his exhales, filling my lungs with his every breath, my hands gliding to the back of his head, fingers tugging on the ends of his hair.

Until finally, *finally*, he guided his tip to my entrance and he was inside me in one quick thrust. My legs clamped around his back, his hips gyrating, grinding and circling, not giving me a chance to adjust to this fullness.

"Do you need more incentive?" he asked, and I'd forgotten the reason for his question.

"I need more of everything," I panted. *More of you. All of you.*

He was kissing me again, his hands strong and gentle,

stroking me. And I was nothing but my body. This sweet exquisite torture with no barriers between us.

"Fuck. You feel so good." A groan escaped my lips when he slid out, leaving me empty. Bereft. "Tell me who owns this fucking pussy." He pinched my clit between his fingers and I let out a yelp of pleasure mingled with pain.

My fingernails dug into his back, scraping the skin, my breathing labored.

"Say it," he commanded.

"You do," I gritted out as he drove back into me.

"Nobody else gets to fuck you." *Thrust.* "This pussy is mine." *Thrust. "Mine."*

Then he stilled and he looked down at me, his blue-gray eyes locked on mine, and something in his expression had me furrowing my brows in concern. I placed my palm on his cheekbone, wanting to soothe his troubled mind. "What's wrong?"

"Fuck, Starlet. What have you done to me?" he asked, his voice raw, anguished like it was painful to say the words.

I didn't answer. It was the same thing he'd done to me. Ruined me for all others.

I watched his face and it felt like this was the first time he had ever let me see him, *really* see him. His naked vulnerability, so real and raw and beautiful. It felt more intimate than any of the other times. It was heady, so intoxicating it was almost too much.

This wasn't fucking. He was making love to me. His eyes never left my face, and I took the weight of his body, welcomed it, as our fingers entwined, our hands clasped on either side of my head while he glided in and out, his pace unhurried like he wanted to make this last forever.

Nothing, *nothing*, could hurt as much as it did when Dylan made love to me. And it was in that moment that the thought of losing him became almost unbearable. A physical ache that squeezed my heart and stole the breath from my lungs. I would

---

have cried if he hadn't been watching me so intently, like he could read my every emotion.

Our climax wasn't fast, it wasn't pounded into me, rather coaxed and drawn out, my body unfurling like a flower reaching for the sun. A slow climb to uncharted territory. It felt like he was deeper inside me than ever before, our bodies fused to the point that I didn't know where he left off and I began. My thighs clenched tighter around his hips, my clit rubbing against him as our bodies soared into shared orgasms that left us breathless and clinging tightly to each other. Like we might fall off that imaginary cliff if we let go.

His forehead dropped to mine, our chests heaving as we struggled to regain our breath, and for a few long moments we stayed like that, not talking, not moving, just breathing the same air with him still inside me.

Afterward, he rolled off me and we lay side by side, staring at the ceiling, his tattooed hand wrapped around my thigh, his thumb making lazy circles on my skin. It felt like the point of no return. An all or nothing moment. I wanted all of him. Nothing less would satisfy me. And that revelation was as exhilarating as it was frightening.

Like free falling off that rock cliff with no safety net to catch you. I was all in, but was he?

Love was only for the brave. It made you more vulnerable than anything ever could. When you gave someone your heart, you also gave them the power to destroy you. Here, take my heart and don't trample all over it was what you were saying by uttering those three little words. And maybe that was why he'd never said them. Down deep, he was just as scared as the rest of us mere mortals.

I rolled onto my side and propped my head on my hand, peering down at his face, my hand over his beating heart. He was just staring at the ceiling fan, lost in thought. I wanted all his thoughts and all his words and all his memories. I wanted all of him, every broken piece and jagged edge and twisted truth. "Why did you leave this space blank?"

He didn't say a word. His stormy blue-grays studied my face, and there was so much intensity in his gaze that I had no idea what he was thinking. He was silent for so long that I gave up waiting for an answer. I withdrew my hand and flopped back on the bed, staring at the ceiling fan. Mixed up, confused, and hopelessly in love with someone who couldn't say the words. Was I the only one who felt this way? Maybe I'd been fooling myself all along. Why had he asked me to move in?

My head turned when he grabbed a Sharpie from the bedside table and guided my hand to his chest, placing my palm flat against it. Tipping down his chin, he traced my hand onto his skin in blue marker then lifted my hand to his lips and kissed the inside of my wrist before he released it. I watched the marker move over his skin as he wrote a word in block letters inside the hand: HER.

It almost filled up the blank space. *Almost.* Unshed tears swam in my eyes, distorting the image.

"Dylan," I whispered, brushing away the tears. He was mine, and I was his.

He smiled like he hadn't just stolen another piece of my heart. "Yeah, babe?"

I shook my head. "I don't know. I just..." I swallowed, trying to find the words but there were only three words and I'd already overused them. So, I just kissed him, a long, lingering kiss that would turn into something more if I didn't stop it now. This was an emotional overload. I was two seconds away from bursting into tears, and I didn't know how to handle it. So I pulled away and stood up. "I'm going to take a shower and get ready for dinner."

I could feel his eyes on my back as I walked away. Before I stepped inside the bathroom, I looked over my shoulder and my eyes met his. He was lying on his side, his head propped in his hand, heart beating under the Sharpie tattoo, an expression on his face that I couldn't decipher.

"What are you thinking about?"

I expected him to make a sexual comment or not even bother to answer. But he rarely did or said what I expected. "I was thinking that this is the best birthday I've ever had. Nobody has ever loved me the way you do. Don't let me ruin this. Don't let me ruin us."

And I died. I was so choked up I couldn't speak. Couldn't move. Couldn't even breathe.

This was what Dylan did. This was why he owned me. Body, heart, soul. I couldn't take my eyes off him. His naked body was a masterpiece. A work of art, from the tattoos inked on his sun-bronzed skin, so dark against the white sheets, to the chiseled muscles, he was lean and lithe and so masculine.

But how could I promise him that? I couldn't.

He was busy on his phone now, dark brows drawn together, scrolling through texts or emails, not even looking at me. "Go take your shower, Starlet," he said, his eyes still on his phone screen.

After I showered, I slipped into a short cotton dress. It was simple, off-the-shoulder, the color of the clear blue sea on our doorstep. Dylan stood behind me and I watched him in the mirror. He brushed my hair off my shoulder and placed a kiss on it, the stubble on his jaw lightly scraping across my skin sent shivers up and down my spine. It didn't matter how many times he kissed me, touched me, devoured me, he still made my knees weak. This couldn't be good. Why did I have to feel so much of everything?

He left the bathroom door open and I watched him step under the rain shower.

Before I had a chance to fully appreciate the view, my phone rang, dragging my attention away from Dylan's naked body. It was my mom, and while I was tempted to ignore her call and let it go to voicemail, after what had happened to Dylan, I closed the bathroom door and answered the call, taking my phone outside to the terrace with a sea view.

"Hey Mom. Are you okay?"

"Hello darling. Are you at home?"

I watched the pink and tangerine sky as the sun dipped lower into the sea. This wasn't home. It was the place where I came to lose my heart. "Um, no, I'm—"

"Just a minute. Your father's home. Simon," she called. "Have you eaten dinner yet?"

I sighed as my mother conducted a conversation with my father before she came back on the line a few seconds later. "He's been working too hard. He comes home exhausted."

"I'll bet," I muttered, not bothering to point out that today was Saturday.

"Good news. Your father was able to pull a few strings at the club. So the date is set for the last Saturday in October. It's a lovely time of year to get married."

"They're getting married at Bellavista? But I thought Sienna wanted to get married in—"

"It's perfect," my mother said. "Your father has already paid the deposit. So we need to get moving. Two weeks from today we have a busy day planned. We'll start with brunch on the verandah at the club at eleven so we can sample the menu and choose a cake. Followed by dress shopping. I'd prefer to do it the other way around, but we'll have to limit our intake so we're not bloated..."

I paced the terrace. I couldn't do this. How could I be my sister's maid of honor? I couldn't. The very idea was giving me heart palpitations. The wedding wasn't supposed to be until next spring but now it was only a little over four months away.

Which made my need to tell Sienna more imminent. "Mom, I have to work that Saturday, I can't—"

"Don't be ridiculous. This is your sister's wedding. Besides, it's not like you have a real job. Ask for the day off."

"Mom, I—"

"Have you seen my watch?" Dylan called from inside. I turned as he appeared on the terrace in a white linen button-down cuffed to his elbows—*white*—and shorts. He looked delicious, good enough to eat. I held my finger to my lips, pleading with my eyes for him to keep his mouth shut. His brows rose in question and I mouthed. *My mom.* I thought that would have him running for the hills, but he plopped down on the daybed as if he didn't want to miss a word of this conversation.

"Who's that?" my mom asked. "Who are you with?"

I turned my back to Dylan so I wouldn't have to see his face when I betrayed him. "It's, um… it's nobody." I squeezed my eyes shut. Dylan was not 'nobody.' "I need to go. I'll call you tomorrow." I cut the call and winced as I turned around to face Dylan.

"Am I your dirty little secret, Starlet?"

"No. Yes. But I don't want you to be. I need to tell Sienna. I can't keep doing this."

"You want me to tell her?"

"What? No. You'd do that?"

He shrugged one shoulder. "Why not?" His eyes narrowed on me. "We're in this together, right?"

"Right. And I swear on my life that I'm going to tell her. But it has to come from me. I'm seeing her in two weeks so I'll tell her then." The thought of it made me feel sick to my stomach. I took a few deep breaths, trying to keep the nausea at bay. Oh my god, I was going to be sick.

"You okay?"

I mustered a smile and nodded. He wasn't fooled.

"Hey. It's going to be okay," he assured me, sounding more confident than I felt.

I nodded again, wanting to believe him but I knew in my heart it wasn't true. It wouldn't be okay. But it was his birthday and tonight we were celebrating and I didn't want to think of how Sienna would react to the news that I was in love with her ex-boyfriend. "I need to get ready for dinner."

"You look ready."

"I need to do my makeup."

"You don't need that shit."

"I want to make an effort. We're going out in public."

"Let me do it."

I laughed at the ridiculousness of that, but he was dead serious. "Do you know how? Have you ever done it before?"

"If you don't like it, you can wash your face."

"Okay," I said, perplexed but intrigued as I walked my makeup bag over to him and handed him his Omega Speedmaster that I'd found in my bag. He patted the coffee table in front of him and I sat on it, my legs between his spread ones while he studied my face like he was a cosmetician at a makeup counter.

"Close your eyes," he commanded, a smug look on his face like he had this all figured out.

I did as he said and heard him rooting around in my makeup bag. This whole thing was so ridiculous, I couldn't stop laughing. "What are you doing?"

"Shh. No peeking."

No peeking. Well, that had me doubling over with laughter. I laughed so hard my stomach hurt. Dylan said 'peeking.' That was hilarious.

"You done yet?" he asked, exasperated.

I nodded and took a deep breath. "What's in your hand?"

"My secret weapon," he said, keeping his fist closed. "Now close your eyes."

Seconds later, my eyes were closed, I wasn't peeking, and I smelled the cherry scent and his minty breath inches from my lips as the tube of Chapstick glided over them. Then he cupped my chin and his lips captured mine in a slow, dirty kiss that wiped my lips clean and had him smacking his.

"Mmm. So fucking sweet. All done," he murmured.

My eyes flew open. "All done? Chapstick isn't makeup."

He leaned back on the daybed, fingers laced behind his head, his tongue slowly gliding over his bottom lip. "It's perfect. I like to see your face. You're beautiful," he said, his voice low and husky, and what I heard instead was, *I love you.*

Forever the optimist. Forever the believer in Dylan St. Clair. And two weeks from facing the firing squad. Lord, help me.

Dylan

I lit a blunt, using the flame from one of the twenty-seven candles in glass holders that covered every surface of our room, compliments of my little fucking ray of sunshine, and watched her through a haze of smoke. She was lying on the Egyptian cotton sheets, her skin bronzed by the sun, her blonde hair framing her beautiful face, naked except for the secret smile she wore.

I wasn't sure what had possessed me but tonight at dinner, over margaritas and Mexican food under the moon and stars, I'd told her more about myself than I'd ever told anyone. I had talked about my mother, I'd told her the truck stop story and about the places we'd lived and how sometimes there hadn't been enough food so me and Remy used to dumpster dive. I told her about all the fights I'd gotten into and I told her that my mother had always told me and Remy that she loved us but never backed it up with actions. The words had become meaningless, and I thought she understood what I was trying to tell her. Why I found it so hard to say three simple words that tripped off her tongue with ease.

Leaning over her, I moved my mouth over hers, covering it. Her lips parted and I shotgunned the smoke into her mouth. Pulling back, I studied her face as I took another drag. She was beautiful. She made me ache for her. Crave her like a drug. I wanted to climb inside her skin and live there.

I had nightmares now. I'd wake up covered in sweat, my heart pounding, gasping for breath. It made me angry that my mother wouldn't leave me alone, not even in death. But Scarlett... she was always there with her soothing touch, her sweet voice telling me it was just a dream, her arms wrapped around me, holding on so tight like she alone could protect me. I hated it. It made me feel weak and pathetic and needy.

"I love you, Dylan," she said now, not expecting to hear it in return.

"Show me." Sex. My go-to when all else failed. I put out the blunt and knelt over her.

Snuffing out a candle, I dipped my finger in the melted wax.

"What are you doing?" Her eyes widened as I held the candle over her.

"Trust me?" I asked. It was a test, and she knew it. I was always testing Scarlett and she always passed because she was good and honest and true in all the ways that mattered most. She wore her heart on her sleeve and unlike me, she never harbored a grudge.

Her eyes locked on mine and I waited for her answer. She placed her palm on the handprint I'd tattooed with a Sharpie over my heart, and she nodded, her eyes and voice unwavering. "Yes."

I love you. I'm in love with you. I fucking love you.

But I didn't say the words. They remained locked inside me.
I tipped the candle. Warm wax dripped onto her bare stomach. She gasped, her back arching off the mattress as I poured wax over her tits, circling her pebbled rosy nipples.

"Oh God," she moaned, writhing below me, her eyes closing, her lips parting as melted wax dribbled over her silky soft skin while I knelt over her, worshipping without touching her.

Had I ever even loved Sienna? It felt like a distant memory, but I don't remember ever feeling like this with anyone, including Sienna. Maybe this was how it felt when you found the right person. You could just be yourself, in all your fucked-up glory, and the other person accepted you as you were.

With Scarlett, I felt like I was enough. I'd never had that before. I'd never had someone believe in me the way she did.

"What are we, Dylan?" she asked now, like she often did.

"We're everything, Starlet. Every-fucking-thing."

Her smile told me that I'd finally gotten it right. What she didn't know was that I had no intention of letting her tell Sienna on her own. We were in this together, and I'd never been one to shirk my responsibilities, so I would be right by her fucking side when she told Sienna about us. I already knew it was going to be a shit show. I knew that Sienna wouldn't take it well. But she'd just have to get over it.

No way in hell was I giving Scarlett up. She was mine, and I was hers, and it was just that fucking simple.

31

SCARLETT

"I can't believe he's four months old already," I told Remy, tickling Kai's belly. He kicked his legs and gave me a gummy smile. I wiped the drool off his chin with a cloth then smoothed my hand over the blond hair on his head.

"I can't believe it either. He's getting so big. He keeps outgrowing all his clothes."

"That's what babies do. They grow up, don't they?" I cooed, holding out my finger for him to grasp.

"I want him to stay a baby forever," Remy said wistfully.

I gave her a little smile and sat back on my heels, my gaze drifting to the glass doors as Shane and Dylan came out of the house, their dishwashing duty fulfilled. Sunday barbecues at Shane and Remy's had become a weekly thing now. They were both cool with me and Dylan being together. For the most part. Although Remy did advise me to tell Sienna before she found out another way. Which I planned to do next Saturday when she came to Costa del Rey.

Something like this couldn't be done over the phone. It had to be done face to face. I was dreading it but even if Dylan and I broke up tomorrow which I really hoped we didn't, it was still wrong to keep this from Sienna.

Regardless of the consequences, I wanted my relationship with Dylan to be out in the open. My biggest fear was that my parents would see us together and report back to Sienna. So, I needed to get it all out there before that happened.

Remy checked her phone for the time and stood up. "It's bath time for Kai." Remy had him on a strict schedule and bath time was our cue to say goodnight to him.

Dylan swooped Kai up into his arms and nuzzled his neck. "Hey little buddy. See you soon."

I watched him holding his nephew and stood up, brushing the grass off my shorts. I rubbed Kai's back and gave him a kiss on his chubby cheek before Dylan handed him to Remy.

"Ready?" he asked me, spinning his key chain around his finger.

I nodded, jamming my feet into my flip-flops, my hand slipping into his as we said our goodbyes.

The sun was setting but it wasn't dark yet when we drove away from Shane and Remy's house, so I slunk low in my seat, my bare feet planted on the dash.

A warm breeze floated through the open windows, bringing with it the scent of Dylan and the sea. He reached for my hand and clasped it in his. I lifted it to my lips and kissed his scarred knuckles then lowered our hands to my lap and traced my finger over the tattoos on his hand. The skull. The rose. His tattooed fingers.

I couldn't remember the last time I'd been this happy.

"Do you need ice cream?" he asked, glancing over at me before his eyes returned to the road.

"Maybe. Are we binge-watching Netflix tonight?" We were cool like that.

"None of that *Riverdale* bullshit though."

"Secretly, you love it," I teased. He didn't.

He parked in front of the convenience store, and I hopped out of the car and met him by the glass entrance doors. We cruised the aisles, stocking up on junk food and microwave popcorn and stopped in front of the freezer section. I debated over the ice cream flavors, my brow furrowed like I was trying to come up with a solution for global warming.

"Need some help, Starlet?" He wrapped his arm around my middle and kissed the side of my neck. I leaned my back against his chest, playing eeny, meeny, miny, moe with the ice cream flavors.

I tapped my chin with my index finger. "I can't decide between Caramel Choo Choo and Chubby Hubby."

He snickered at the names, reached inside the refrigerator and grabbed both tubs of ice cream. He handed them to me then grabbed two more random flavors for good measure and strode to the counter.

"This is excessive. I don't need all of these," I said, taking two of the tubs off the counter to return to the freezer.

"Ring up all four," he told the guy, taking the ice cream out of my hand and setting it back on the counter with an exasperated sigh. None of this was unusual behavior for us. I was always trying to be more frugal, Dylan was always insisting that more is better. We'd grown accustomed to these little tussles.

"Fine. You win," I said like I was doing him a huge favor.

He just laughed and shook his head, putting his credit card back in his wallet and tucking it in his back pocket. Dylan grabbed the bags and slung an arm around my shoulder, pulling me in for a kiss before we pushed through the glass doors of the air-conditioned store and into the muggy evening.

"Fuck," Dylan said under his breath, his arm falling from my shoulders and dropping to his side.

I looked up at his face first then followed his gaze and I froze. Not a sound came out of my mouth. My feet were rooted to the spot. I couldn't move. Couldn't speak.

I was barely breathing.

Dylan recovered first and stowed our bags in the back of his car then closed the hatch and returned to my side, jerking his chin at Sienna. "What are you doing here?"

That was his first question? What are you doing here?

I stared at my sister's tear-stained face, her eyes red and puffy as if she'd been crying for hours. She was standing right in front of us and her BMW was parked at the gas pumps.

"What am *I* doing here? I came to see my sister and I find..." She exhaled a shuddering breath and shook her head. "I can't believe this."

She was in shock. That made two of us.

I cleared my throat, forcing myself to speak. "I'm sorry, Sienna. I was going to..."

She ignored me, her gaze focused on Dylan. "My sister? Of all the girls you could have gone for, you went for my sister? Do you hate me that much, Dylan?"

He carved his hand through his hair and let out a breath. "I don't hate you."

"Are you trying to get revenge? Is that what this is?"

"No." He rubbed the back of his neck. "That's not what this is."

"Then tell me what this is. I came back here to see Scarlett because I needed someone to talk to who might understand. Instead, I find my sister and my ex-boyfriend... oh my God. I can't..." She shook her head. "How could you do this to me?"

I didn't know if that question was directed at Dylan or me. Either way, we'd both done this to her. I took a few steps closer, searching for the words, any words that would help this situation. But there were none.

"I'm so sorry, Sienna," I said, trying again. "I was going to tell you next weekend. I never meant to—"

Her gaze swung to me. "You never meant to what? My God,

Scar. Dylan wasn't just some guy I hooked up with. I *loved* him. And you knew that."

"I know," I said, my voice barely louder than a whisper. "I'm sorry."

She shook her head, and I knew that all the I'm sorry's in the world weren't going to mean a thing. "How long? How long have you been hiding this from me?"

I stared at my indigo blue toenails, wishing the ground would swallow me up. "Since January."

"You were with him when you came to my engagement party?" she asked incredulously. I lifted my head, not bothering to explain that we hadn't been together then. It was irrelevant. "You've been with him all this time and you never said a word to me? You know what's funny. I was coming to see you because I thought we could talk. If anyone would understand, it would be you."

"Understand what?"

"I left Chase."

"What? But why?"

She shook her head. "I don't want to marry my father. I don't want to end up like my mother. And now my sister... betrayed me in the worst way. I thought you were the best one out of all of us. You broke away. Did your own thing. *With my ex-boyfriend*. My God. How stupid am I?" She laughed hollowly, tears streaming down her cheeks. "I'm so stupid."

"Sienna. You're not. This is all my fault and I don't know how to..."

"It was my fault," Dylan said, stepping up.

Sienna wiped her face and averted her head. "You know why I left Chase?" She focused her gaze on Dylan. He shook his head a little. "Because I don't love him the way I loved you. Because I've been trying to get over you for years, but I still haven't found a way to do that. I loved you, Dylan. So much it hurt. I loved you. *So. Much.*"

She was crying harder now. Instinctively, I moved closer and reached out to hug her. She held up her hands to ward me off and I took a step back.

"But nothing we ever said or did to each other has ever hurt me like this," she told Dylan.

Oh God.

She turned and stumbled across the parking lot to her car, her shoulders shaking from the tears she was crying.

"You can't let her leave like this," I told Dylan.

His eyes locked onto mine. "I'm not leaving you."

"Go to her," I said. I didn't know why I thought that she'd accept his help when she'd pushed me away, but I got the feeling that she'd rather talk to him, not me. "Please."

He scrubbed his hands over his face and then he nodded.

I stood in the parking lot and watched my boyfriend stride over to my sister. I watched him stand in front of her and cradle her face in his hands, lifting it up to his. I watched his lips move as he said something that made her close her eyes and clasp his wrists in her hands. I watched him brush her tears away with the pads of his thumbs. And I watched him pull her into his arms and hold her, his hand stroking her hair and his eyes closed while she cried on his shoulder and held onto him like she never wanted to let him go.

You belonged to her first.

I've never belonged to anyone.

It's almost funny, the lies we tell ourselves. The way I actually believed that he could ever be mine.

I forced myself to stop watching them.

Grabbing my bag from Dylan's car, I slung it over my shoulder and hazarded one more glance at Sienna and Dylan.

I didn't want to give him up for anyone or anything. But I had to.

Neither of them noticed when I walked away. Nobody heard the sound of my heart shattering. Nobody but me.

32

DYLAN

It had been nearly two years since I'd laid eyes on Sienna. She looked the same. Blonde beach waves, a golden tan, in one of her little designer skirt and tank top ensembles. She felt familiar. Like a song I used to know by heart but hadn't heard in a long time. She even smelled the same. Like citrus and flowers. My muscle memory kicked in and as her hot tears soaked into my T-shirt, my hand stroked her hair and my eyes closed. We'd been here before. With her crying on my shoulder. Too many fucking times.

When I'd imagined confronting Sienna about me and Scarlett, I'd conveniently forgotten there might be tears. I could deal with Sienna getting angry. Screaming at me. Calling me an asshole. But I'd always hated a woman's tears. I wanted to make it better. Fix it. Find a solution to the problem as if it was a math equation. But there was no solution. She was her, and I was me, and the sum of our parts had disaster written all over it. Always had. Always would. No amount of time or distance would ever change that.

I released her and took a step back, my eyes going to the

spot where I'd left Scarlett. She was gone, and I wanted to chase after her. Eat ice cream in front of the TV. Laugh, fuck, talk about stupid shit. Just be happy.

"Dylan." I turned my head to face Sienna. "Can we talk? I mean, *really* talk?"

Oh hell, no, here we go. I opened my mouth to tell her there was nothing left to say. I had a girlfriend to chase after.

"If nothing else, you owe me that much. I tried to call and text you so many times, but you never responded, and you never answered my calls."

I'd blocked her number, that's why. I rubbed the back of my neck and even though it was the last fucking thing I wanted to do, I nodded.

We bought a six-pack and a fresh pack of smokes—thanks to me, Sienna was a closet smoker—and we drove to the beach in separate cars. On the way there, I considered calling Scarlett to make sure she was okay. But it was a short drive and that would be a long conversation, so I decided against it. After I got this talk over with, I'd go to her apartment and we'd figure out a way to get through this. Together.

Sienna and I got to the beach in time to watch the sunset. It felt wrong, being here with her on a deserted strip of beach with the bluffs behind us and the ocean in front of us, and my ex-girlfriend sitting close enough that I could smell her floral shampoo and the scent of her skin. I drank my beer, my gaze on the horizon. As far as sunsets went, it was a beautiful one, my favorite time of day on the West Coast. Maybe I should have spoken first. Maybe I should have apologized. Maybe I should have said a lot of things. But I sat in silence and watched the seagulls circle and dive. I watched the waves build and crash against the shore, and I waited for her to speak.

I lit two cigarettes and handed one to Sienna, falling into an old habit without even thinking about it. It was my first cigarette in weeks. I'd been trying to kick the habit. Cigarettes not weed. So much for best intentions.

She laughed softly as she took the cigarette from my fingers. "I always thought that was so sexy when you did that."

"Did what?" I asked.

"Lit two cigarettes. One for me and one for you."

I took a deep drag, feeling the rush of the nicotine hit my bloodstream, and said nothing. We were no longer a couple and I didn't want to act like one. *No more lighting her cigarette, you stupid fuck.*

"Remember your seventeenth birthday? We got drunk on my dad's whiskey and high on your weed and rode down to the beach on your bike. I was on your handlebars and you rode with one hand on the handlebar, your arm wrapped around me, so I wouldn't fall off. And I remember thinking, I'd go to hell and back with this boy."

She took a drag of her cigarette, her eyes on the ocean, her blonde hair lifted in the soft breeze while she tripped down memory lane, my least favorite place to visit. "It was late at night and the moon was out and we were floating in the ocean. And you sang Pearl Jam's "Black." It was so sad and angry and beautiful. Like you."

I sucked on my cigarette, needing it to calm my nerves. I remembered that night so well. My mother had forgotten our birthday. Completely forgot about it. No cards, no gifts, no Happy Birthday, not a fucking mention of it. I remembered Sienna that night too. I remembered thinking that a girl like her would never end up with a thug like me. And I'd been right.

But now, instead of feeling like shit about it, I was grateful. Because I'd found something so much better. And I was already feeling antsy, wishing we could fast forward to the end of this conversation, so I could get the hell out of here. I'd even watch *Riverdale*, that's how fucking desperate I was for this to end.

"Where did we go wrong, Dylan?"

I wanted to laugh at that question. Nothing about us had ever been right. "We don't have that kind of time, princess." I took a swig of my beer and a drag of my cigarette. Whose idea was this, to bring beer and cigarettes like we were two old friends sitting around shooting the shit?

"Did you ever love me?"

I took another swig of beer, thinking about her question. It was cocked and loaded, and I wouldn't be surprised if the bullet exploded in my face. "There was a time I would have done anything for you. Anything you asked, I would have fucking done it. But you never..." I pinched the bridge of my nose. I didn't want to go down this road. I didn't want to be on this beach with her, reliving old wounds and bitter words and all the shit that went down in our eight-year on-again, off-again disaster of a relationship.

"I never what?" she prompted, her voice so sad that I couldn't even look at her because I knew what I'd see.

"You never believed in me," I said, my voice low, with a bitterness that surprised me. You would have thought I'd be over it by now. "You never had one single ounce of faith in me. You were so fucking scared of being poor. Of living like I did. You were always half in and half out. And every time your father gave you an ultimatum, every single fucking time he threatened that you'd lose your trust fund or whatever the hell he was using to keep you in line... you dumped my ass and ran scared. You made promises you never kept. Over and over again. Different day, same old shit. You wanna talk? Really talk? You had a fucking abortion and never even told me."

Yeah, that's right. Let's talk. That shut her up.

"Dylan..." Her voice quavered. My jaw clenched, and I took deep breaths through my nose. She was turning on the water-works again. This was what she did.

"You wanted to talk. Fucking talk. Or we'll go. Stop wasting my time. Stop fucking dragging me through all this shit all over again. You called me an asshole more times than I can count. But you made me fucking crazy, Sienna."

"I did it for you," she said quietly.

"*For me*?" I laughed harshly. "Didn't you fucking know me at all? I would have done anything it took to take care of you and the baby."

"I know that," she said, her voice raised. "And that's why I did it for you. God, Dylan. You were barely getting by. You were selling drugs and fighting to pay the rent and the bills for you and Remy because your piece of shit mother was never around. What was I supposed to do? Saddle you with more responsibility? It was my fault. I fucked up the birth control. I missed a few days and I should have told you, but I didn't. I was so scared you'd do something crazy like drop out of school. And you were so smart. I couldn't do that to you. Don't you see? I did it for you."

I swallowed hard, hearing the honesty in her voice, and I knew she was telling the truth. Yet all these years, she'd kept that to herself. And I realized it was because we never really talked. Not about the important shit. We just got mad and yelled at each other. Walked out in the middle of conversations.

"We were so young and so stupid, Dylan," she said, brushing away her tears and taking a shaky breath. "We were so bad at love. But I loved you. So much. And I tried. I tried so hard to be the girl you needed but I didn't know how. I was scared. You're right. But it wasn't money I was worried about. It was us. I was scared that I'd give up everything for you and then you'd leave me and where would I be?"

"Why did you think I would leave you?"

She shook her head. "Because I knew that you never loved me the way I loved you. Your mom did such a number on your head. You never even believed me when I told you I loved you.

And I told you all the time. But you always threw it back in my face. You could never say the words in return. And it hurt. The more you held back, the harder I tried to be what you wanted. But the more I tried, the more I failed. It was like this vicious cycle and we kept going round and round and ending up back where we started. But I kept coming back for more. Because when it was good, nobody had ever made me feel the way you did. You were my drug. My crack. My addiction. And I'm so scared that I'll never love anyone the way I loved you." Her voice cracked on the words, and I didn't know what to say or do.

I had never been scared of her leaving me. I always knew she'd come back. I was the one who finally ended things. If it had been left up to her, we'd still be doing the same old tired song and dance.

"Dylan," she said softly.

"Yeah?" I answered as I ground out my cigarette in the sand.

"Can you... can you just hold me? I know we're over but... please. Just one more time."

I hesitated. The last thing I wanted was Sienna in my arms. "Sienna, I don't think . . ."

She ignored my words and moved closer, wrapping her arms around me. She buried her face in the crook of my neck, and placed her hand over my heart, and it was so wrong, but I was telling myself that it was okay. This girl was a part of my past, and we were awash with memories, nothing more. And maybe, like she'd said, I owed her this. Earlier, she had said she needed closure. And that's what this was. Time to close the book on the past and move on.

The first time I ever saw Sienna, we were sixteen. It was the first day of our junior year in high school and I walked into my fourth period English class. The only desk available was in the back row, right behind Sienna.

I ignored her for most of that school year. Had immediately pegged her as the queen bee. Rich, spoiled, beautiful, smart.

On her better days, she was funny and generous. She was also insecure and worried about every bite of food she put into her mouth. Her beach waves looked natural and carefree, but I knew it took her forty-five minutes, a shitload of styling products and three appliances to achieve. Same with her outfits. She used to spend a ridiculous amount of time deciding what to wear. Sienna pretended that people's opinion of her didn't matter but it wasn't true. Sienna used to dress for me. Chose silky lingerie with me in mind.

"*I'm so worried about losing you that sometimes I forget who I am without you.*"

She'd told me that once, years ago, when I was too young to analyze it or figure out what the hell it meant. But even then, I'd had a feeling that was a bad thing. That you should never lose yourself in the process of loving someone. If anything, love should make you a better version of yourself. That's how I felt with Scarlett—I'll always love her. She made me want to be a better man.

"Dylan." Her hands cradled my face and before I'd had a chance to process what was happening, her mouth captured mine. And just like that, I was kissing my ex-girlfriend on the beach under a sky that was getting dark.

Her arms wrapped around my neck and her tongue was in my mouth. It took me a second to come to my senses and push her away. "The fuck are you doing?" I stood up.

She smiled as she got to her feet. It wasn't a sweet smile. It was cunning. A glimpse of the other side of Sienna, the side of her I'd forgotten. The side that showed me she was more like her father than she realized. She ran her hand down my chest and I clasped her wrist and pushed it away as my eyes met Scarlett's over Sienna's shoulder. She was farther down the beach, and dusk had descended, but there was enough light to make out that it was definitely her. Besides, I'd know her anywhere.

Scarlett turned, and she ran, and I fucking hated myself.

I glared at Sienna, my jaw clenched. "You saw her," I gritted out. "You fucking knew she was there."

Sienna's eyes narrowed on me. "She stole my ex-boyfriend. My first love. And you know what's crazy? While we were sitting out here talking, I'd almost forgotten about that. Because it was just you and me again, and it felt so good to be next to you and to actually talk. And for a little while, I remembered how good things used to be. And I remembered the things I loved about you. But then I saw *her,* and it all came rushing back. If I can't have you, why should she?"

I brushed past her and strode away, so fucking pissed I couldn't see straight. "You don't know what love is, Sienna."

"You're an asshole, Dylan," she screamed, shoving my back. I spun around to face her, and she pummeled me with her fists, her chest heaving. I grabbed her wrists to stop her from using me as a human punching bag and pushed her away. She came at me again, screaming like a madwoman, and planted her fist in my face.

I rubbed my jaw as she cradled her hand and fell to her knees on the sand.

"The fuck are you doing?"

"How could you do this to me?" she cried, her hands covering her face, her shoulders shaking while I played monkey in the middle, caught between the past I wanted to run from and the future I wanted to run to. Sienna had made damn sure that her sister would pay for her sins, and so would I.

One fucking kiss.

"I didn't do anything to you," I seethed. "I fell in love with your sister."

"Why? What does she have that I don't?" Sienna asked, scrambling to her feet. "Why *her*?"

There were a million reasons why I loved Scarlett, but I wasn't about to share this information with Sienna.

"Because she's not you. She's everything you're not and I love her." I left her on the beach and I strode away.

"Good luck explaining why you were kissing your ex-girl-friend, asshole," she called after me.

Fuck. Fuck, fuck, fuck.

33

SCARLETT

I had it coming. I did. But I had no idea it would turn out like this. I'd expected a conversation. Angry words. Tears. Apologies. I could have withstood that. Could have taken everything she threw at me. But this. I hadn't seen it coming.

Why had I gone to the beach? Why? I thought it would help put things in perspective. Or, at the very least, I thought it would give me a bit of peace.

I took another sip of my margarita that I was drinking out of a mason jar and licked the salt off my lips. I was buzzed, well on my way to getting shit-faced. Hollowed out and empty from all the tears I'd shed. Personally, I would have gone straight for the tequila shots and not have bothered with the mixers. But the margaritas were good and the salt on the rim of the glass tasted like my tears, so I drank up, my legs draped over the side of the armchair, my eyes on the boring white ceiling.

My mind replayed the scene in front of the gas pumps. The way he'd pulled her into his arms and brushed away her tears. And the scene on the beach. I couldn't get the vision of that kiss out of my head.

He'd kissed her. He'd kissed Sienna.

My heart hurt so much. Physically ached. I didn't think this pain or that memory would ever go away. It was branded on my heart forever.

"We need to change the playlist. This is depressing," Nic said, her words slurring a bit. She was slouched down on the sofa, feet propped up on the coffee table, margarita in hand. "It's putting me in a weird funk."

Neither of us made a move to change the music. Instead, we suffered through John Mayer singing about slow dancing in a burning room. And I thought about dancing with Dylan. On the beach. In Mavericks. On the terrace in Cabo on his twenty-seventh birthday. I didn't even bother trying to stop the tears from falling.

"Maybe it wasn't what it looked like," Nic said. "I mean, maybe they weren't really kissing. You said you weren't that close to them so... it could have been an optical illusion... delusion? Or whatever the word is..." Her voice trailed off.

There was no point in having this conversation again. We'd already gone over it in detail. And there was nothing she could say or do to make it better. Even if I hadn't seen them all cozy on the beach, the fact remains that what we'd done was wrong. No amount of justifying it could make it right. A part of him still loved her, and I don't care how many times he denied it, I saw it with my own eyes.

I didn't want to be his second best. His consolation prize. He couldn't even tell me he loved me.

There was only one thing left to do. I needed to leave. It would be too hard to stay in this town. Everywhere I went, I'd take the risk of running into him. Everywhere I went, I'd be reminded of him. It would be too hard to see him, longing for him yet knowing that I couldn't be with him. All of my memories of Dylan, from the time I was eleven, were in Costa del Rey. And I think that's what made this so much more painful. I hadn't only lost my boyfriend tonight—I'd lost the life I so desperately wanted.

For ten years, Dylan had starred in all my dreams. He'd been my wish on every star. My knight in tarnished armor. My Romeo. For a little while, I had even deluded myself into believing that he was not only my past but that he'd be my future too.

My mind was made up. I needed to get away from here. Away from him. I grabbed my phone from the coffee table and scrolled through my emails, pulling up the one from the international volunteer organization that I'd contacted back in November.

"Nic?"

"Hmm?"

"Don't hate me, k?" I asked, typing out an email to let the organization know that I was ready and willing to go anywhere they needed me. The farther away the better.

"I could never hate you. What are you talking about, bitch? You're my bae."

"And you have Cruz. And your friends from work. That girl with the purple hair," I continued. "What's her name?"

Nic bolted upright, her drink spilling over the rim of her glass as she slammed it down on the coffee table. "No. No. Nuh uh. Don't you dare."

She lunged for my phone, but I pulled it away and hit send before she grabbed it from my hand.

"What have you done?" she asked, staring at my phone screen then at me. She opened her mouth to speak just as a knock sounded on the door. "If that's him, I'm going to kill him."

She flew to the door and flung it open so hard, it banged against the wall. I slunk lower in my seat and chugged the rest of my margarita, tuning out whatever Nic was saying to Dylan.

Not that I'd looked to confirm it was him, but I wasn't surprised he'd turned up here.

"I need to talk to her."

"No."

"Step aside, Nic, and fucking let me in."

"If you wanna get to her, you'll have to get through me."

"Just let him in," I said, feeling weary. "Might as well get this over with."

"Get this over with? The fuck does that mean?"

"It means we're over. We'll say our goodbyes and move on."

"We're not over. I love you. I'm in love with you. I fucking love you, Scarlett. Only you."

I'd waited so long to hear those words. It felt like I'd been waiting half my life for him to say that to me. But now that he had, all I wanted to do was cry.

I set my glass on the coffee table and walked out of the living room, down the hallway and into my bedroom. He trailed after me, closed the door behind him and turned on my table lamp.

I flopped down on my bed, not sure why I'd come to my bedroom. I just wanted to fall asleep and wake up and have this whole thing be a bad dream.

"Did you hear what I said? I love you."

"I heard you." I reached up a hand and ripped the fishing wire off the wall, dragging all my photos down with it. "You see all these photos? These are my memories. My happy memories." I drew my knees to my chest and wrapped my arms around them. "We've destroyed too much, Dylan. You asked me not to let you ruin this. Ruin us. But we're ruined. We were from the start. How could we have ever expected to make this right?"

He sat on the edge of my mattress and angled his body toward me. "We're right. You and me."

"I saw you with Sienna, Dylan. I saw you kissing her. I saw the way you looked at her. You're still in love with her."

He scrubbed his hand over his face. "I'm not in love with her. Whatever you think you saw..." He stopped and took a deep breath. "It wasn't what it looked like. I didn't kiss her. She kissed me."

I laughed incredulously. "Oh. Okay. Next you're going to tell me you didn't wrap your arms around her and wipe away her tears."

His jaw clenched. "I'm not in love—"

I held up my hand to stop him from continuing. "It doesn't matter. None of this matters. It doesn't change anything. If you kissed her or she kissed you. It happened. I was there. I saw it. But this... us... it's not just about that kiss on the beach. I can't be with you anymore. Seeing you with her tonight... it just made me realize how wrong this was."

"I can't fucking lose you."

"You already did," I said quietly, my voice resolute. "I love you, Dylan. I do. But we're over. So you need to leave."

"We'll find a way. I'll make it right. I'll do whatever the fuck it takes. I told you I would always fight for you. *Always.*"

All I'd ever wanted was him. Be careful what you wish for. Pushing him away was killing me. It was the hardest thing I'd ever done but I knew it was what I had to do. It was the right thing to do.

He reached for me, but I pulled away. If he touched me, if he held me or kissed me, all my defenses would crumble and fall. I couldn't allow that to happen. "Please, Dylan. Just go. I can't... please just go."

He carved his hand through his hair then he nodded and stood up. "We're not over, Starlet."

I turned my back to him and curled onto my side.

It was only after I heard the door close behind him that I let my tears fall.

Dylan didn't give up. Not that I'd expected him to. He was stubborn. It had been two weeks since the night everything fell apart. Two weeks of planning a future that didn't include him. Two weeks of crying myself to sleep every night. I missed him so much. And it only made matters worse that he showed up every single day. With Starbucks or ice cream or chocolate chip pancakes, depending on the day and the time.

This morning it was an iced caramel macchiato. I took a deep breath and squared my shoulders as if I was going into battle as I walked toward him. He handed me the Starbucks he'd brought, his fingertips brushing mine in the hand-off, and I felt those old familiar shivers run up and down my spine. The plastic cup was wet with condensation and the label on top read: Starlet.

"You need to stop showing up. You're making this so much harder."

"Good," he said, showing no signs of remorse for causing me mental anguish. Most days I just kept right on walking and didn't even talk to him. Undeterred, he just kept coming back day after day after agonizing day.

"Why are you all dressed up?" I couldn't help asking. He was wearing ripped jeans, a faded black T-shirt and his ancient combat boots with the laces undone. My fingers itched to run through his messy, disheveled hair. I fisted my hand, my nails digging into the palm. "Important meeting?"

He smiled, and it was beautiful, like a song or a poem that made your heart ache. "Just remember." Catching me off guard, he leaned in close and kissed the tip of my nose. My eyes closed for an instant and I inhaled his scent. Pure sex and pheromones and masculinity. "I love you."

I had no idea what that was all about but didn't even bother questioning it. He climbed into his G-Wagen and drove away, and I carried my iced coffee and my broken heart down the street, the sky overhead blue and cloudless, the sun on my face, and it seemed all wrong that the day was so beautiful. It should be gray and rainy to match my mood. On my walk to work, I called Sienna. I'd been calling her every day for the past two weeks and she never answered.

When I heard her voice on the end of the line, I stopped in my tracks. It took me a few seconds to recover and find the words.

"Hi. Sienna. Hi," I said again. "I was hoping we could talk—"

"I got all your voicemails," she said, her voice so flat and cold I barely recognized it. "You can stop calling now. You can stop apologizing. There's nothing you can say or do to make this better. It's done."

"I could come to LA," I said, stupidly trying to make this right even though she'd just said there was no way I could. "If we could just sit down and talk face to face—"

"I don't even want to *see* your face. The funny part is that you had everyone fooled." She laughed harshly. "Everyone thinks you're the honest one. The brave one. The least likely to stab someone in the back. But from where I'm sitting, you're a liar, a cheat, and a coward. What you did is unforgivable."

I sucked in a breath. I deserved this and more for what I'd done. But that didn't make it hurt any less.

"Stop calling me, Scar. There's nothing left to say." She cut the call and I squeezed my eyes shut.

Shane had been wrong. This was hopeless.

I tossed the iced coffee in the trash can and walked to work on leaden legs, my heart heavy, an ache in my chest that made it hard to breathe.

Remy looked over at the doorway as I entered the shop and clearly, my face told her everything she needed to know. She was across the shop, pulling me into a hug before I'd even made it three steps inside. And like a fool, I was crying again.

She didn't have to ask what was wrong. She already knew

that I fell in love with Dylan and that I was leaving next month. I'd miss her and Shane, I'd miss my job, and Nic and SoCal and a million other little things about my life here. But the thing I'd miss most was her brother.

Boys like that will only break your heart.

34

DYLAN

I couldn't fix all the shit that was broken or mend all the relationships that had been destroyed. But what kind of man would I be if I didn't at least try?

After delivering the iced coffee to Scarlett, I drove to LA to visit Daddy Dearest in his steel and glass office building in the Financial District. Pompous ass that he was, he thought I came to grovel. His daughter might be Mother Teresa, but I sure as hell wasn't. I came to finish the war *he'd* started. Armed with enough information to do serious damage to his reputation and his bank account, I knew that this time I would walk away the victor.

Whoever said that revenge wasn't sweet had never tasted it.

The beauty of my plan? He'd never tell anyone it was me who brought him down. His pride wouldn't allow him to admit that he'd been bested by a "worthless little shit."

"Those are my conditions," I concluded after I'd laid it all out for him. I slid the document across his polished mahogany desk, so it was right under his nose.

Read it and weep, motherfucker. I'd wait. I especially appreciated the way his face turned an alarming shade of beet red when he read the fine print.

"You're out of your goddamn mind if you think I'm going to sign this over to you."

I kicked back in my chair, used his desk as a footstool for my boot-clad feet, and laced my fingers behind my head. If not for the hermetically sealed windows, and the fire alarm on his ceiling, I'd smoke a celebratory blunt.

"Not to me. To Scarlett," I clarified, in case he'd missed her name written in bolded letters. "The way I look at it, you have two choices. I turn over all the information I have on you. If you're lucky, you'll get a reduced sentence in a white-collar prison. I hear it's a lot like that country club of yours." I laughed, knowing that was bullshit. There was no such thing as a country club prison. "Or you sign this over to your daughter." I tossed a pen at him that I'd stolen from the receptionist before I'd barged into his office.

"You little shit." Yeah, that was getting old. He needed a new line. "I guess you think you'll get my daughter to marry you, so you can get your hands on it."

"This is probably a concept you'd never understand. But your daughter... neither of your daughters are merger and acquisition deals. They're fucking people. You don't own them. You don't get to barter their love for money. You're the piece of shit for treating them the way you do. And I wouldn't take a single penny of your money if I was homeless and dumpster diving for my next meal. Been there. Done that. And guess what? I survived. That's the difference between you and me, Simon. You wouldn't have lasted a day in my world whereas I could survive a fucking Armageddon."

"Get out of my office, you little cockroach." Points for originality. "You've wasted enough of my time. You don't have anything on me."

"That's where you're wrong. I dug deep and unearthed a

few skeletons. Or should I say shell corporations." I sat back and let him chew on that for a minute. His face paled and beads of sweat gathered on his forehead, that's how fucking scared he was. I lapped this shit up. Sat back and fucking reveled in it.

"I'm sure your investors would love to hear about all the money you skimmed off the top. You got greedy. Dipped your fingers into too many pies." I tsked and shook my head like I was disappointed in him.

Ironically, Simon ran a dirty business while mine was squeaky clean. I played by the rules, made sure not to piss off the IRS, and every single penny was accounted for. I didn't rob my clients blind, didn't so much as write off a coffee on my expense account. The skeletons rattling around in my closet were personal, not business-related, and the only thing he could hit me with that would hurt had already been done to me.

As I suspected, Simon Woods signed on the dotted line. "If you mess with me or my business or the people I care about again... if you so much as breathe one bad word about me, I'll turn over every single piece of evidence I have against you and you will lose everything. That's a promise."

"This is blackmail."

"This is me giving you a chance to do the right fucking thing." That was a lie. If he did the right thing, he'd own up to his investors. But they were multi-million- dollar corporations, not personal investors, and eventually he'd get caught with his hand in the cookie jar. That was his problem, not mine.

I slapped a Post-It note on top of the page. "Write Scarlett a nice note. Tell her you love her and that you're fucking proud of her for being who she is."

He clenched his jaw and wrote a note that was a bit frostier than what I'd had in mind, but she probably wouldn't have believed it if he'd sprinkled it with unicorn dust and rainbows. Good enough.

"I hear Nicaragua is the place to be," I said, giving him a helpful tip before I strode out of his office, leaving the door wide open.

On the way out, I stopped in Cecily's office. Nice set-up for a PA. She was blonde and blue-eyed and bore an uncanny resemblance to his eldest daughter. No wonder Sienna had daddy issues. "How's it going?"

"Um... fine?" Her hand wrapped around the phone on her desk. She was two seconds away from calling security and having my ass hauled out of here. "Can I help you with something?"

"I need an envelope." I held up the papers in my hand as proof that I came in peace. Sort of.

"Okay." Good old Cecily was efficient. She produced said envelope and slid it across her desk, withdrawing her hand quickly as if she was afraid I'd bite it off. "Thanks. And top tip. Fucking your married boss is not a good career move. You can do better."

Her jaw dropped. I was laughing as I swaggered out of her office.

On the drive back from LA, I sucked it up and called Shaggy Doo. I'd gotten the number off Scarlett's phone and since I was going down this road, might as well go all the way. No sense in half-assing this shit.

"This is Dylan St. Clair."

He huffed out a laugh that did not sound merry. "What do you want?"

His surly tone nearly had me ending the call but if I were in his shoes, I would have acted a hell of a lot worse, so I forged on. "I want you to call Scarlett. She could use a friend."

"You broke her heart, didn't you?" he accused.

"If it makes you feel any better, she broke mine." And when

the words were out, I realized just how true that was. It hurt like a motherfucker. I needed to get her back. My life was emptier without her. Not even scoring a victory over Simon Woods could fill the heart-shaped hole she had left. I missed her. Had been missing her for a long time. Maybe for longer than I realized. Because even when she was a teen and far too young for me and off-limits, I had felt something for her that I never should have.

A part of me had always been missing Scarlett. Maybe that's why I'd gotten her a job working for Shane. And it was why I'd pursued her, knowing it was wrong, yet it had felt so right.

"She didn't mean to, but it happened anyway," I said, giving him more information than he deserved.

He was silent for a moment. "Well, damn. Didn't see that coming."

That's life. You don't always see it coming. And then it hits you like a fucking freight train. "If you ever cared about her at all, give her a call and be a fucking friend."

I stopped short of adding, *Just* a friend. Pretty sure that went without saying.

"Why are you doing this?" he asked, suspicious.

I thought about Scarlett's wall of photos, all her happy memories. Ollie was in most of them. The other guys from the band were in a lot of them too. And Nic. At one time, they'd all been close. They'd had the kind of friendship I'd never had when I was growing up and in high school. I'd never let anyone get that close. Cruz was my only real friend and we hadn't met until college. Scarlett's friends were important to her, and she was important to me. I'd stop at nothing to get her everything her heart desired, even if it meant apologizing to Shaggy Doo who didn't entirely deserve it, if you asked me.

"She misses you and I fucked up that friendship for her." *Suck it up, Dylan.* I cleared my throat, the words getting stuck. "Sorry about that," I said grudgingly.

Not exactly a grovel but it was pretty damn close.

"You really do love her," he said, sounding amazed.

"Looks that way. Call her. Be a friend." I cut the call. No need for small talk or a friendly chat with Shaggy Doo. That would be pushing it. I'd extended the olive branch and it was up to him what he decided to do about it. Guess we'd see whether or not he was a true friend.

My final stop was the Woods' residence. This should be fun. I had never once walked through the front door of their Tudor McMansion. It had approximately one hundred rooms and looked like it belonged in the Black Forest, not in the heart of SoCal. But it was fake. A new-build mock Tudor meant to look like something it wasn't. Since Margot Woods had never worked a day in her life, I knew she'd either be home or at the nail salon or at the club, drinking Chardonnay and gossiping with her so-called friends.

I pressed the doorbell and heard the chimes playing inside. It sounded like a funeral dirge. The door opened and the smile on Margot's face slid off when she saw who was standing on her doorstep.

"What do you want?" she hissed, her eyes narrowed on me. "Haven't you caused enough trouble?"

I wasn't done yet, so no, apparently not. I brushed past her and her jaw dropped. It took her a moment to recover. By the time she did, I was already prowling through the house, checking out the hideous décor. Being rich didn't equate to having good taste, that was for damn sure.

"What do you think you're doing?" she asked, bustling after me. "I'm going to call the police and report you for breaking and entering."

Not the brightest spark, was she? "I didn't break in. You answered the door," I pointed out as I stalked through the living room and stopped in the dining room. An ornately carved table sat in the middle, big enough to seat eighteen, by the looks of it.

Just for fun, I pulled out the chair at the head of the table. It weighed at least twenty pounds, also ornately carved with a red velvet upholstered seat that I parked my ass in.

"Is this where you have your family dinners?" I asked conversationally.

She was so bewildered that she nodded. "Yes. Why?"

I surveyed the room. The glass-fronted dark wood cabinet that held shelves of what I was sure was fine bone china, crystal glasses, tureens and shit I didn't even have a name for. My eyes raised to the crystal chandelier hanging from the forest green ceiling and finally to the coat of arms and gilt-framed paintings of horses and landscapes on the green and gold papered walls. Sitting in this room that smelled like furniture polish and the souls of dead ancestors, I was beginning to understand why Sienna had never invited me for a family dinner. Not only would I have embarrassed her by not knowing which fork to use, I would have felt like I was suffocating. Wasn't hard to see why Scarlett had wanted to break away and distance herself from all this pretentious bullshit.

I rose from the table and continued my house tour with Margot trotting after me, wringing her bejeweled hands.

"What is the meaning of this?" she asked as I poked my head into what I assumed was the library, judging by the book-cases filled with leather-bound books that nobody in this house had probably ever read. I ran my hand over the mahogany bar and scanned the bottles of top shelf liquor. Then I stalked down the labyrinth of hallways until I came to the enormous kitchen with its oak cupboards and marble countertops. I ended my tour outside on the limestone patio overlooking the Woods' swimming pool. The pool I used to clean the summer I was seventeen when I thought this house was grand and beautiful and beyond anything I'd ever imagined in my wildest dreams.

Funny how time changes your perception of everything. The

pool looked smaller to me now, the water not as crystal blue, the grass not as green. If I wanted to, I could buy this house or one just like it. I didn't want to. But I *could*. As I stood under the blazing sun, the air scented with orange blossoms from the potted trees on the patio, a scent I remembered so well, I realized that I'd come a long way. Once upon a time, I didn't think I was good enough for Sienna. I thought that because these people had money, they were better than me and that I really was the worthless piece of shit Simon had always accused me of being.

Choosing Sienna had been my way of giving him the middle finger. We'd been with each other for all the wrong reasons. Whereas with Scarlett, I'd chosen her because I actually liked her. She was the best thing that had ever happened to me. And I loved her for who she was as a person, not for what she represented. Scarlett had opened my eyes, had made me see my life so much more clearly. Where I'd come from had nothing to do with who I was today.

Still an asshole, always would be, but an asshole who was in love with a girl and wanted to give her the fucking world. If only she would see that we were always meant to be.

I turned my head at the sound of Margot Woods' voice and suspected she'd been talking for a while. "What's that?"

"I said that you need to get out of my house right now or I will call the cops," she repeated, her voice rising a few octaves, the shrill sound cutting through the peace and calm of this June day.

"I'm leaving. I got all the answers I need."

She huffed, her heels clicking behind me as I strode to the front door. When I was on the other side of it, I turned, putting my hand on the wood to stop her from slamming it in my face. "I remember why I came."

Her lips pursed, and her head tilted, curious despite herself. Sienna looked more like her mother than Scarlett did. Same nose. Same bone structure. But Sienna's face was more expressive, her eyes not as dull and vacant.

"Your daughters love you. And from where I'm sitting, they're the only good thing in your life. Start acting like a fucking mother before you lose them too."

Her eyes flared but it was hard to tell if she was angry or not. Her face gave nothing away. It was so Botoxed, nipped and tucked, it looked like a mask she wore rather than actual human skin. It was sad as fuck. Vacant and empty, like her life. Who got all dressed up in designer clothes, hair and makeup and nails perfect, only to sit around—*alone*—in this mausoleum she called a house?

"Who are you to tell me anything?" Her eyes roamed down my outfit and she sniffed in disapproval, her nose in the air. "You're still a no-good punk. What did my daughters ever see in you? The very idea of you makes me sick."

I removed my hand from her door and it slammed in my face just as I'd suspected it would.

"Still causing trouble?" a man asked, hedge clippers in his hand, a smile on his face, more weathered than the last time I'd seen it, but the smile was the same. This man always had a smile and a kind word for everyone. Quite a gift, one I was starting to appreciate more and more.

"Hey Pedro." I shook the hand he extended, his warm palm calloused and dry from all his years of working outdoors. "You good?"

"Yes, sir. Everything is good in my world. I have a new granddaughter now." He pulled up a photo on his phone, pride and joy in his eyes as he showed it to me. "That makes three grandbabies for me. Two boys, one girl."

"Good for you."

"Family is everything." He glanced at the front door then shook his head and sighed. "Too bad some people don't know that money can't buy happiness." He glanced at my G-Wagen. "You finish the college?"

"Yeah, I did."

"No more cleaning the pools for you, huh?"

"Nope."

"I'm proud of you, Dylan." He nodded, smile still firmly in place, his teeth so white against his suntanned skin. "You did good." And with that, he got back to his gardening duties and I drove away, laughing to myself. Pedro barely knew me, yet he'd sounded genuinely proud.

I drove through town, past all the boutiques and restaurants and surf shops on the main street and past the pier and The Surf Lodge, its weathered wood getting a fresh coat of paint, and I wondered if Jimmy would be proud of me or if he would have hated that I'd stooped to conquer, that I'd played dirty to get what I wanted. I'd never know the answer to that but for all of Jimmy's Zen and sage advice, he'd been a fighter too. And I thought he would have been cool with it, knowing that the cause was a good one. It was what I chose to believe, anyway.

I didn't know what more I could do to show Scarlett that I loved her, that I would do whatever it took to make her happy.

Come back to me. Come back.

But she didn't come back.

She fucking left my ass.

35
_____

SCARLETT

F<i>our Months Later, Hanoi</i>

These past few months had been eye opening. I had somehow managed to mend my heart just a tiny bit—although the stitches holding the seams together were crooked and there were times the pain took my breath away. The children I'd met and worked with have helped take my mind off of Dylan, even for just a short while. I learned that even with a broken heart, I'd been able to give a little of what's left of it to these kids who had nothing. Sometimes you had to work through the pain and I tried—so hard. All I could hope for was that the work I'd done and the love and care I'd shown them would help them realize that they were worth something.

The future was unclear, and I wasn't sure when I would find my new normal, but I had learned a lot about myself. I wasn't my father's daughter. Money meant nothing if you didn't have love. Showing you care and giving a piece of yourself to someone in need was priceless. It also helped me realize what Dylan must have gone through when he was younger. When you came from nothing, you felt like you were worth nothing and seeing these kids who barely had enough food to eat, who oftentimes had no one to take care of them, made my heart ache for what he went through.

After what had happened with Sienna, I knew that my choices destroyed her. I didn't know that she'd ever forgive me, but all I could do was try my hardest to prove to her that I never meant to hurt her.

I stopped walking, and all the noise from the motorbikes zipping past and the voices and laughter from the sidewalk tables outside the noodle shop and the raucous cheers from the bar next door, quieted. The pedestrians crowding the sidewalk and the streets clogged with mid-afternoon traffic ceased to exist.

I felt him. He was here. In this crazy, beautiful city of Hanoi with its French colonial architecture and smiling, friendly people and the Vietnamese street food I couldn't get enough of. Made evident by the pho, spring rolls, and dumplings Oscar and I had just stuffed our faces with.

I looked across the street at the yellow façade of the small, slightly shabby, cheap hostel where I'd been staying for the past three months, and there he was. I saw him through the glass doors, his back turned to me. But I'd know him anywhere.

It was him. My mind wasn't playing tricks on me. I felt him. The hairs on my arms stood on end and all the air was sucked out of my lungs.

"Keep walking." I grabbed Oscar's arm and dragged him down the street, turning my back to our hostel. Over the past three months, Oscar and I had bonded over our hopeless love lives, 80s movies, and debatable fashion sense. Today he was sporting a sarong with a tank top I'd designed and a man bun.

"What is wrong with you, girl? I need a siesta."

"It's... we can't go in there." I wasn't thinking clearly. I released his arm and tried to breathe. "Actually, you can go in there. But I can't."

"Does this have anything to do with a hot, tattooed guy?" Oscar said slowly, his eyes widening as he watched something —or *someone*—over my shoulder. "Oh my God," he said in a stage whisper. "It's him."

I should have never shown Dylan's picture to Oscar. Now he was gawking. I squeezed my eyes shut and tried to rein in my racing pulse. When I opened my eyes, Dylan was standing right in front of me, his eyes roaming my face and body while I did the same to him. He looked the same. Dark hair messy and disheveled. Scruff on his jaw. In a plain white T-shirt and faded denim. My eyes stopped at the Old Skool Vans on his feet then returned to his face. It was so strange to see him here. Out of our normal environment.

"Why are you here?" I asked.

"Why the hell do you think I'm here?" He scowled, his gaze drifting to the narrow tree-lined street I lived on--no wider than the alley I used to walk to work on--as approximately one thousand motorbikes flew past. Every time you crossed a street in Hanoi, you took your life in your hands and prayed for the best. There was no such thing as traffic rules or stopping for pedestrians. It was survival of the fittest out there. I bet this was Dylan's personal hell. Too loud, too many people, too crowded. "I'm here for you."

"Dylan... I told you..."

He wrapped his hands around my upper arms. His warm, calloused palms on my bare skin, his nearness, the scent and heat of his body, made me dizzy. "Tell me you don't love me, Starlet.

"Starlet. Swoon," Oscar said, reminding me that he was still here, watching this play out like a bad 80s romcom. He put his hand over his heart and patted it a few times. "This is so romantic." I glared at him. "What? I'm just all up in my feels." He held up his hands. "Fine. I can take a hint."

Oscar darted across the street, dodging the oncoming traffic and my eyes returned to Dylan. Now it was just the two of us in our own little bubble on a busy street in a foreign city so far from home. How did we end up here? Standing on a sidewalk in front of a Vietnamese mini-mart in the middle of Hanoi?

For a few long moments, we just stared at each other.

Dylan's penetrating gaze was focused solely on me. "Tell me," he repeated. "If you can look me in the eye and tell me you don't love me, I'll leave."

I looked him in the eye and opened my mouth, but no words came out. I cleared my throat. Words. I needed words. He smirked. "That's what I thought."

"This has nothing to do with not loving you." I pulled away and took a few steps back, putting distance between us, my hands rubbing my upper arms where his hands had just been.

Dylan crossed his arms over his broad chest. Oh God, he looked so good. I wanted to throw myself in his arms and never let him go.

"Nothing short of you not loving me is going to keep me away."

Dylan grabbed my arm and strode across the street, his body shielding me from oncoming traffic, not the least bit concerned about the motorbikes that were forced to go around him. He led me through the glass doors of the hostel, and across the black and white tiled lobby that smelled like bleach. He stopped in front of the elevator and punched the button, the traitorous doors opening immediately. Ushering me inside, he pressed the button for the fourth floor. How did he know my room number? "Dylan... we can't..."

"Don't tell me what we can't do. I traveled halfway across the world for you. And I'm not fucking going anywhere until we talk this through."

"I'm not having sex with you." As soon as the words were out, I wanted to punch myself. Filters, Scarlett. What the hell. I was just putting ideas into his head.

Dylan snorted. "We'll see about that, Mother Teresa. I've been living like a fucking monk."

"Oh. So... you haven't hooked up with anyone?" I asked as the elevator doors opened and he stepped out, taking a right as if he knew exactly where he was going.

Wrong way, Romeo.

He checked the room numbers and figured out his mistake quickly, doubling back and passing me. I stared at his back. He stopped outside the room I shared with Georgia who was also a volunteer and looked over his shoulder at me. "You planning to open it, or do I need to kick it in?"

With a sigh, I met him outside the door and unlocked it before the Neanderthal made good on his promise. Wouldn't put it past him.

"In answer to your question, no. There's been nobody. You?"

I shook my head. "No."

"Thank fuck." He scrubbed his hand over his face and yawned. "I'm too jetlagged to beat the shit out of anyone today."

A laugh burst out of me. "You're ridiculous."

He kicked off his Vans and flopped down on my bed with the comforter I'd brought from home, his head on my pillow, and patted the space next to him. There was barely enough room for two on that bed and he took up most of the space. I shook my head no.

"Get over yourself. Lie down next to me." He folded his arms over his chest. "I won't even touch you."

As if I had no control over my own body, my feet carried me to the bed. I stepped out of my flip flops and lay down next to him, rolling onto my side, my head propped on my hand. He rolled onto his side to face me, and we were close. Too close. I could see the silver flecks in his black-rimmed irises.

"So you worked with kids?" he asked, as if he didn't already know that. As if he hadn't donated boxes and boxes of supplies to the childcare center. He'd sent them anonymously. Even though there was no return address, I knew they were from him. No one else would have done something like that.

I smiled, thinking about the kids. My volunteer assignment had been for twelve weeks and yesterday was my last day. Tomorrow I was leaving Hanoi to go traveling with Oscar and Georgia. I had a feeling he knew that my time here was up. "Yeah. I worked at a childcare center. The kids were great. We did a lot of art projects."

"And your designs?"

"Still working on them." I was starting to make money from them, but I suspected he already knew all of this. Cruz or Remy probably kept him updated. "Why are you here?" I asked again.

"I love you, Starlet. I'm no good without you. Come back to me. Or I'll stay here. Whatever you fucking want."

"I can't."

"Why the fuck not? We love each other. We belong together. You can't tell me we don't."

"Nothing has changed. You're still my sister's ex-boyfriend. What we did was wrong." Dylan had tried to make it right. I knew that. A few weeks after I got here, Ollie had called me and told me about his conversation with Dylan. Since then, we'd been texting and I was happy to have my friend back but like so many other things, it would never be the same. That wasn't Dylan's fault though.

"You say wrong and I say right. What I had with Sienna was bad love. It was toxic. Nothing like what I have with you. I can't fix what happened, but the damage has already been done. Us not being together won't change a damn thing."

He was keeping his promise. Not touching me. But he didn't have to lay a single hand on me to make me feel him. Just being this close to him, I was hyper aware of his scent and his body and the way his eyes darkened when he looked at me. I felt like he'd stripped me bare. I felt like I was more naked than I'd ever been with him. I should have looked away, but I couldn't.

"Do you miss me the way I miss you? Do you dream about me at night? Do you crave me? Do you want me so badly that it's physically painful? Do you, Starlet?" he asked, voice low and husky, going straight to my core. The air around us was charged, my body trembling with want and need. "Tell me."

"Yes," I whispered, my eyes filling with tears.

"I never thought I'd find someone like you. And now that I have, I can't let you go." He took my hand in his and guided it to his beating heart. "You're here. In my heart. Under my skin. In my fucking head. And I can't get you out. What's more, I don't want to. Tell me you love me."

His eyes bored into mine, waiting for me to say the words. "I love you. But—"

He placed his finger over my lips. "No buts. There are no buts in love. You're either in or you're out. You're not my second choice. You're not a consolation prize. You're everything I never knew I needed. You're my number fucking one. You *own* me. And I'm not leaving here without you."

"Do I have a choice?" I asked. The question was more for me than for him. When it came to Dylan, my heart didn't stand a chance. I had never had a choice, it had always been him.

"Here are your choices. Choose me. Or choose me."

Who was I fooling? No amount of time or distance would ever change the way I felt about him. I could run to the ends of the earth and it still wouldn't make a difference. He'd always be there, in my heart, in my head, under my skin. "I choose you."

"Good. Because I'm going to fuck you so hard, all of Hanoi will hear you screaming my name," the charmer said.

I laughed and then he sat up and whipped off his T-shirt and the laughter died on my lips.

The space over his heart wasn't blank anymore.

EPILOGUE

Scarlett

One Year Later

"Are you on your way home yet?" Nic asks as I drive along the coast with the top up and my windows rolled down. Dylan gave me the Mini Cooper convertible for my twenty-second birthday. It's cream with camel leather interior and I love it.

"Dylan threatened to come over and physically drag me out of the shop if I didn't leave in two point five seconds." He's still impatient. Still likes to call the shots and boss me around. Not that I always listen but tonight I did. Three months ago, I opened my own design studio, right next door to The Surf Lodge. I've been working long hours, and Dylan has been so busy with work that lately, it feels like we haven't spent much time together. "So yeah, I'm on my way home."

I smile just thinking about home, a beachfront Spanish style house that sits on a bluff and overlooks the Pacific Ocean. Even though it was love at first sight, I argued that it was too expensive. Dylan said you can't put a price tag on happiness. It was his dream house so he bought it and we've been living in it for the past year.

"Wait. Why do you ask?"

"Oh. No reason," Nic says. "Gotta run. Call me tomorrow."

O-kay. She cuts the call like she's suddenly in a rush and my music comes back on. It's a perfect October night, the air still warm, and a big orange moon in the sky. The past year has been a whirlwind and it feels like I've barely stopped to take a breath. Except for my relationship with Sienna, which seems to be damaged beyond repair, but not for my lack of trying, life has been good.

One of the biggest surprises of the past year was when my mother finally asked my father for a divorce. He and Cecily are expecting a baby at Christmastime. Good luck to her. I don't speak to him. There's nothing to say. As for my mother, she's become active on the town council now, and she's finding her voice.

For too many years, my father had oppressed her, and made her feel worthless.

When she left him, she moved out of the house, claiming that she'd always hated it and moved into a beach condo. Over the past year, my mother has gotten to see a different side of Dylan and while I wouldn't say they're close, they've called a truce. She doesn't call him a punk anymore and he tries his best to bite his tongue and be cordial when he sees her.

The house is dark when I pull into the driveway. Weird. Dylan usually has all the lights blazing. I park in the garage next to his G-Wagen, grab my bag from the passenger seat, and walk inside the house.

"Dylan?" I call out as I move through the rooms. I've injected color into his monochrome design and decorated the house in a modern vintage style. Midnight blue, jungle green, dashes of blush pink and brushed gold. Like my website. My aesthetic. He was happy to let me have free rein.

The scent of garlic and tomato sauce wafts from the kitchen but he's not in there. Not that he actually cooks. But he's good at ordering takeout.

I stop in the living room, my eyes going to the open glass doors where he's standing, waiting for me by a table set for two on the terrace. There must be a hundred candles dotted around the terrace and the infinity pool, the flames dancing in the sea breeze, shedding light into the darkness. And there he is, looking like every fantasy I've ever had. He still makes my knees weak. Still takes my breath away.

"What's going on?" I ask. He's wearing a plain white tee and faded jeans. "Did you cook?"

He shrugs one shoulder. "Yeah. Got the recipe from Nic." He carves a hand through his hair and lifts one of the silver domes like this is a restaurant and he's the maitre d'. Where did he even get those silver covers? I stare at the food on the plate. It's my favorite. Chicken Milanese with a side of spaghetti. It looks perfect. Amazing. "Not promising it's any good."

It will be good. Dylan doesn't half-ass anything. He replaces the lid to keep it from getting cold and I'm confused as to what's happening.

"Are we, um... eating? I mean... what's the occasion?"

"You are. You're the occasion, Starlet." He takes my face in his hands and I stare at his gorgeous face. His pouty lips and chiseled jaw and sharp cheekbones.

"Are you happy?" He's serious, I know it from his tone and his expression, but I'm shocked that he still feels the need to ask.

"I'm so happy. Because I have you." I have a million other good things too but he's the most important one.

"I never want you to regret choosing me."

"I never will," I say with complete certainty. "I will always choose you. Again and again and again."

"Thank God you said that. Otherwise, this could be awkward as fuck."

Before I can process what's happening, he's dropped to one knee. Dylan St. Clair is on one knee in front of me. He's holding a small velvet box and I'm dying.

Dying.

"Dylan, what—"

"Shh. Let me talk." I nod, just now realizing that an acoustic version of "Wicked Games", a female cover, is piping over the surround sound. He's planned all of this. For me. And even as he starts talking, I can't fully concentrate on the words because I'm so overwhelmed by it all.

"I love you, Starlet. There's nothing in this world I wouldn't do to make you happy. I would move heaven and earth for you. I know there will be times when I'll fuck up. I'm still an asshole sometimes. Doubt that will ever change. But I can promise you that I will always be loyal and honest and true to you. I will always fight for you. You're my first *true* love. Until you came along, all I'd ever seen of love was the bad shit. You showed me what real love looks like. And I want to spend the rest of my life with you. Only you. Always and forever."

My hand covers my mouth, the lump in my throat so big I can't speak.

"Fucking say something."

"Oh. Well... you didn't ask me a question."

"Fuck. Shit." He clears his throat like he's gearing up for something monumental. Because he is. It's huge. "Will you marry me, Starlet?"

I can't help it, I'm laughing and crying at the same time and all I can manage is a nod.

"That's a yes?"

I nod again. "Yes."

Dylan exhales loudly like he's been holding his breath this whole time. I drop to my knees in front of him and practically knock him over when I throw my arms around him.

"Let me put the goddamn ring on it," he says, but he's laughing too and I'm covering his face in kisses. He pulls me to my feet and takes my hand in his, slipping a ring on my third finger. It's a pink diamond. So perfect and so beautiful that I can't stop the tears from falling.

He brushes my tears away with his thumbs before his mouth captures mine. I kiss him through my tears and my laughter and the kaleidoscope of butterflies that have invaded my stomach while his hands roam my body and my clothes magically disappear. Moments later I find myself naked in the hot tub, straddling him. Funny how that keeps happening. We've christened every surface of this house and I don't think I'll ever get enough of him.

I have a feeling our dinner is going to get cold, but neither of us cares. We have the flames of a hundred candles, a big orange moon and we have each other.

"What are we, Dylan?" I ask as I sink down on him, my arms wrapped around his neck.

"We're everything, Starlet. Every fucking thing. We're life."

Five Years Later

I'm crouched on the sidewalk in front of my design studio, writing on the chalkboard sign when two girls in their late teens, early twenties saunter past in tiny bikinis, bottles of Fiji water in hand. They stop walking and turn to face the beach.

"He's hot," the blonde says to her friend, sliding her sunglasses down her nose.

"Mmm hmm," the brunette agrees.

I ignore them, don't even turn my head to look in the direction of the beach across the street. I don't need to check out hot guys. I'm married to the hottest guy in SoCal. He's hotter than the surfer dudes on the beach or the lifeguards that the teen girls are always gawking at. He's five-alarm fire hot and heat flushes my face just thinking about how hot last night was. Despite being married with two kids and being crazy busy, I'm willing to forfeit sleep for sex with Dylan. I never thought I'd like being blindfolded with my hands tied to the headboard but if you never try it, you never know. And I'm willing to try anything once.

"Totally a DILF," the blonde says.

That has me whipping my head around to check out who they're talking about. Now I'm on my feet, hand on my forehead shielding my eyes as I search for the DILF.

My husband. Shirtless and barefoot in nothing but a pair of black board shorts slung low on his narrow hips, his ink and his abs and his deliciousness on display. He has a bag over one shoulder, and a girl in each of his arms, biceps flexing and bulging as he carries them across the beach and sets them down, along with the bag.

I watch him toss a few towels on the sand and he and the girls unpack all the plastic toys, dragging them down to the water's edge. Now I'm staring, just like the girls next to me to see what he'll do next. Everly and Isla are laughing, trying to jump on his back as he crouches down and fills a bucket with sand.

They're building sand castles. Oh, my heart. There is my world, right there. On the beach under a bright blue sky and a blazing sun. My everyday crush, the three loves of my life sharing smiles and laughter.

"Let's help him build a castle," the brunette says.

My jaw drops and my hands go to my hips as I watch the

two bikini-clad girls saunter across the beach toward *my* husband. Even after all these years it still makes me feel stabby when girls hit on Dylan.

Yo, bitches, he's mine. Back off.

"Spying on your husband again?" Frankie teases as she joins me on the sidewalk. Cruz's sister and I have gotten close. Like her brother, she has a head for numbers and takes care of all my accounting and paperwork.

I cross my arms as I watch them trying to strike up a conversation with the DILF under the guise of *helping* to build a sand castle. But I force myself to relax. Dylan is loyal to the core. He only has eyes for his two little girls right now.

"Looks like you have nothing to worry about," Frankie says with a smile that I return before she goes back inside and my gaze returns to Dylan and our girls.

Isla is a miniature version of Remy, their resemblance so strong it's uncanny. Everly looks more like me, her blonde waves messy and tangled. Their skin always looks sun-kissed, their eyes so blue they rival the bluest skies. To see them together, you'd never know they were twins. To see them now, so strong and healthy, you'd never know that they came into the world weighing less than two pounds each, their entrance dramatic and terrifying but also miraculous.

If I had ever had a doubt when I was younger, I don't have a single one now. I know that Dylan would walk through the pits of hell for me and I would do the same for him. When his baby girls were born, he never left that hospital. He was by my side through all the long days and nights spent in the NICU. He was my pillar of strength.

The boy who climbed into my bedroom window all those years ago became the man I can't live without.

Our names are inked over his heart. Scarlett. Everly. Isla. They are my heart, and he gives us life.

I watch the girls dart to the water's edge only to get scooped up in Dylan's arms. They're shrieking with laughter as he throws one over each shoulder in a fireman's carry and jogs across the beach, headed straight toward me. To think I get that DILF every single day and night. How lucky am I?

I cross the street and meet them on the beach path as he sets Everly and Isla on their feet.

"Mommy, we're building a castle," Everly says, her blue eyes wide, her hand pointing at the sand castle they were building before they'd gotten sidetracked.

"I can see that."

"Now we're hungry," Isla says.

Everly nods enthusiastically and rubs her tummy. "Really, really hungry."

"Starving for somethin' sweet. Like Daddy."

"I'll bet," I mutter.

Dylan chuckles and pulls me into a kiss.

"I saw you had a couple admirers."

He gives me a crooked grin. "Jealous?"

"Pfft. Why would I be jealous? I have my very own DILF."

His grin stretches wider and he leans in close, his voice low in my ear. "You want me to throw you over my knee and give you a spanking? You can call me Daddy."

I snort laugh and shove him away. Bet he'd love that.

"Daddy. We want ice cream."

"Ice cream, ice cream, ice cream," they chant knowing damn well their daddy will get them anything their hearts desire. They have him wrapped around their cute little fingers.

"Only one scoop this time."

"With sprinkles." They fold their hands in prayer and Dylan's nodding his head in agreement. I snicker. He shoots me a look.

"Sucker."

"You want ice cream, Starlet?"

"Do I get two scoops?"

He winks. "And extra sprinkles."

"You drive a hard bargain." I smile. "I love you."

"Love you more."

Dylan

The sun is starting to sink into the sky and I pull Starlet into my lap, burying my face in the crook of her neck and breathing her in. She smells like honey and vanilla and suntan lotion. She smells like home. She turns her face to mine and my mouth captures hers, my tongue sweeping into her mouth. She tastes like sunshine and the freshly squeezed lemonade she drank earlier. She tastes like the good kind of love.

I never thought a guy like me would ever find this kind of happiness. My girls are my world. They're everything that's good and true and I'm fucking amazed every single day that this is my life.

Never in my wildest dreams had I imagined that I'd go from having nothing to having everything. Because of her. The girl who believed in me even when I didn't deserve it. I like to think that her love has made me a better man. I like to think that I've come a long way from the place where I started.

I am hers, and she is mine, and we are everything.

THE END

Have you read Shane and Remy's story yet? You can find Wilder Love here: mybook.to/WilderLove

ALSO BY EMERY ROSE

ACKNOWLEDGMENTS

As always, a huge thank you to my family for always supporting me through the ups and downs and all the crazy. Love you so much!!!

A huge thank you to Jennifer and Monica. This story would not be what it is without you. Thank you for loving Dylan and Scarlett as much as I do. Thank you for your time, your thoughts, your encouragement, and your attention to detail.

Ellie, thank you for the editing and for being so chill about my deadlines. I appreciate it more than I can say.

Najla, thank you for creating another gorgeous cover. You are such a joy to work with, thank you.

Jen Mirabelli and Wildfire Marketing Solutions, thank you for the promo and marketing.

Bloggers! Thank you so much for taking the time to read and review and share. I appreciate you and everything you do for the indie community.

Rambling Roses, thank you so much for all your support and comments and book discussions. It's my favorite place on the Internet. Love you all! Special shout out to Emily for all the "research", weekly posts, and creative hashtags. And to Carol for your friendship, for the music, and for lifting my spirits when self-doubt takes over.

And last but certainly not least, a huge thank you to the readers. I couldn't do this without you and I'm so grateful to each and every one of you for reading my words.

If you enjoyed reading Dylan and Scarlett's story, please consider taking a few seconds to leave a short review. They mean so much to indie authors.

Thank you so very much.

Emery Rose xoxo

ABOUT THE AUTHOR

Emery Rose has been known to indulge in good red wine, strong coffee, and a healthy dose of sarcasm.

When she's not writing, you can find her binge-watching Netflix, trotting the globe in search of sunshine, or immersed in a good book. A former New Yorker, she currently lives in London with her two beautiful daughters and one grumpy but lovable Border Terrier.

Stay in touch!
    Facebook
    Facebook Group
    Instagram
    Twitter